Stunned with shock, I went under completely. When I recovered the power to move, and my head broke the surface, I realized in horror that something dark swam in the pool beside me. Before I could strike out and escape, hands clasped around my ankles. In an instant I was pulled to the bottom of the pool. With all my strength I tried to break free and swim, but the awful weight crept up my legs and wrapped around them like chains, once more pulling me down.

There was no air left in my lungs. They were bursting. At the last instant, my legs were released and I kicked myself desperately to the surface, to gulp air. Immediately my feet were grasped again, and I barely had time to hold my breath as I went under, pulled to the bottom, my ankles pinned in that steely grip.

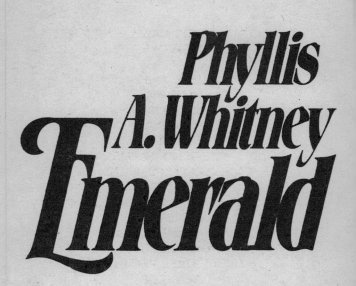

Phyllis A. Whitney
Emerald

FAWCETT CREST • NEW YORK

A Fawcett Crest Book
Published by Ballantine Books
Copyright © 1982, 1983 by Phyllis A. Whitney

Library of Congress Catalog Card Number: 82-45369

ISBN 0-449-20099-X

This edition published by arrangement with Doubleday & Company, Inc.

Manufactured in the United States of America

First Ballantine Books Edition: December 1983

FOREWORD

Palm Springs was most hospitable to me, and a number of people helped in my background search. I want to thank Henry Weiss of the Palm Springs Public Library, and his wife Jacqulyn. Carol Morton helped in a number of ways, and introduced me to the Eldorado Country Club. My old friends from Chicago days, William and Maureen Daly McGivern, were generous with their time and assistance.

Here at home, my thanks go to Roland West, who loaned me all those wonderful books about Hollywood; and to Annette and Charles Bassett, who allowed me to "borrow" their cat.

Finally, I am grateful to my daughter and her husband, Georgia and Ed Pearson, for driving me patiently wherever I wanted to go.

ONE

How bleak and empty the California desert seemed to my unaccustomed eyes. My rented car cut straight through, leaving the mountains of the coast behind. Even desert growth was the color of sand, and all the mountains that pulled in the distant edges of space were a bare, rocky umber. A somehow ominous landscape, reflecting my own fear and anxiety. It was natural to see danger behind every rock and drift of sand—it would be there in reality soon enough.

I'd always expected to love the desert on sight. I'd read enough about it, and in one of the foster homes where I'd stayed as a child, there'd been a woman—Helen Johnson—who had grown up in the Southwest. She'd filled my fanciful head with pictures and lore of the desert, so that I'd always been eager to see it for myself. But not under these circumstances. Not when endless stretches of sand gave me a threatening sense of exposure to eyes that might already be seeking me out.

As I glanced at my small son, dozing in the car seat beside

1

me, he stirred, whimpered, found a more comfortable position, and slept again. The bruise on his cheek was still cruelly visible, and rage burned in me all over again. A cleansing rage that I welcomed. For far too long anger had been futile and self-destructive. Now I would use it to save my son, to save myself. Perhaps even to save my own life. I had no illusions about the man who would hunt me, and I knew that my "accidental" death would free him to take Keith.

At least this new, steady anger would sustain and nourish me, give me real purpose for the first time in my life. What had happened during this last year—and longer—was unforgivable. Some things *are* unforgivable, and I must never forget that again. For too long I'd felt hopelessly trapped. To make any move seemed more dangerous than sitting still. When his father had struck Keith so brutally, I'd been suddenly freed to act, and I must never become trapped again.

Yet Keith mustn't know how deeply I raged. He'd suffered enough, and my anger would only frighten him more. He must be protected from further hurt with every ounce of strength I could manage.

I owed nothing to Owen Barclay but my fury. He was no longer my husband, and he'd forfeited any right he might have to his son. Nevertheless, he would be relentless in his effort to find us and take Keith away from me, no matter where we went. That certain knowledge lodged in me like a knife, and I could never twist fully away from the fear and the pain.

Outside our car the desert continued to stream past like a tawny sea, its ripples warming in the light of late afternoon. Ahead of us lay the green oasis of Palm Springs, surrounded by desert and mountains, shielded from the outer world—offering sanctuary, just as it must have done to early settlers, not all that long ago.

I didn't think it would occur to Owen immediately that we'd flee to Palm Springs. I'd never told him much about my relationship to Monica Arlen, even though she was my only living relative. From the first he'd put down as starry-eyed adulation my affection for the great-aunt I'd really known only through her letters. The fact that she had been a famous movie star in the thirties and forties made no impression on Owen. Since he had connections everywhere, movie stars were a dime a dozen in his world, bought and sold like everyone else. Once he'd dismissed Monica as someone he couldn't use at the moment, we never spoke of her again. So how could he possibly understand her curious influence on my life? Monica herself couldn't be expected to understand that. I'd kept our correspondence, such as it was, from Owen, as I'd learned to keep so many other things that were basic to my life.

Eventually, of course, he would think of her as a possible haven for Keith and me—or his spies would ferret this out—but by the time he located us, we should be safely out of reach in Monica Arlen's fortress of a house high above Palm Springs. Out of reach, for a time at least. Time was what I must play for—time to think, time to recover my own sanity and give Keith the love and the quiet that he needed to become once more a normal little boy.

We'd left a cool November behind us in New York, but here the air conditioner hummed softly as I drove. Yesterday we'd flown to San Francisco, picked up a car, and started south, staying overnight at a motel along the way. By taking a roundabout route to Southern California, we might be able to delay pursuit a little longer.

On the phone yesterday morning, when I'd called from New York, Linda Trevor, Monica's secretary-companion, had given me specific instructions. We were to go straight to a hotel on Palm Canyon Drive, where she would make a reservation for us. By the time we arrived in Palm Springs, Linda would have prepared my great-aunt for our sudden appearance in her house. Linda, however, wanted to "brief" me first, so we must wait for her at the hotel. "Brief" was the very word she'd used, and it made me uneasy.

I'd never known my grandmother on my mother's side—Monica's sister. All of the family was dead now, except Monica and me. I'd lost my parents in a car crash when I was seven, and I'd grown up in a series of foster homes. My mother had always kept in touch with her aunt, Monica Arlen, and when Mother died someone wrote to Monica to let her know. That was when my great-aunt started to write to me, and her letters had become the one bright and glamorous light glowing at the end of a very gray tunnel. Much of the time they were the only happy events I had to hold on to. Sometimes small gifts accompanied her letters, and these I treasured. She never came to see me, or invited me to visit her, yet this never seemed especially strange to me. I took it for granted that her life existed on a different plane from mine, and I didn't expect someone who was practically a national goddess to concern herself with a mortal like me.

As I grew up, I watched her old movies whenever I got a chance—especially the award-winning *Mirage*—and I identified with every role she'd played. I read everything about her I could find in old library files. Once a great deal had been printed about her, though little had been published lately.

I even read about the city to which she'd retired out in the desert—Palm Springs. That was a further way in which I came to know about the desert, and grew to love it in my imagination. As a little girl, Monica had lived on a ranch—like Mrs. Johnson—so I longed to push away city buildings and look into distances of sand. I even grew a not very healthy cactus because it was a desert plant.

Of course I had the foolish, and secret dream of someday presenting myself to Aunt Monica, but I knew that I must first achieve something in my life worthy of *her*. Mostly I existed in a wonderful world inside my own head, and kept reality from intruding whenever I could.

When a seventh-grade teacher told me that I wrote rather well, I began to drive myself. I *had* to accomplish something spectacular and be forever rid of all that was boring and stupid—and without love. Even though the dream of meeting Monica Arlen faded a little as I grew older, the drive to achieve remained and sustained me through that series of foster homes until I was eighteen.

By the time Owen Barclay strode into my life, I was blindly ready for him. Not all that happened between us was entirely his fault.

Aunt Monica never realized that she was my idol, nor did she take any but the most casual interest in me. After all, I existed for her only in rather shy letters and the few snapshots I'd sent her from time to time. While for *me* she was there on movie and television screens—practically flesh and blood!—to watch in all those marvelous pictures she'd made with her constant co-star, Saxon Scott. He too had played a role as the hero of my young dreams—handsome, exciting—not like ordinary men. And *I* was Monica in all those wonderful love scenes they played together.

What fantasies I'd built around the two of them during those growing-up years! Though my letters must have been awkward and self-conscious, she occasionally wrote to me in return. Always notes on pale azure paper, scrawled forcefully in ink the color of blue iris. She never had much to say, but I'd kept every word she'd written me. In my imagination she could never be less than perfection.

With age, when she began to have trouble with an arthritic wrist, she'd dictated, and her communications were typed by her private secretaries. Some years ago, while I was still in college, Linda Trevor had started to work for her, and had become a more personal contact for me with my aunt. I knew very well that Monica had merely been kind to a young relative who meant little to her, but I never faltered in my adoration. And when she suddenly and unexpectedly offered the money to send me to college, my hero-worship grew stronger than ever. It had been thanks to Monica Arlen that I was able to do something a little special, and thereafter my letters must have grown more open and loving.

During the last few years I'd heard from her only at Christmastime. She always sent the same card—never decorated with conventional holly or mistletoe—but with her own special iris symbol that she'd affected in her Hollywood days. The card was expensively engraved, with a few words scribbled in her strong, almost illegible handwriting.

By the time I finished college I was corresponding regularly with Linda Trevor, and we had become good friends because of our mutual admiration for the woman who had once been so great a star. Linda belonged to that curious species—the fan. I was a fan too, but I was also *related*.

During the last few years I'd come to know a little more

about Linda Trevor. She was forty-two and had never married, though she'd become engaged recently to a man named Wally Davis. He was a few years younger than she was, and that was about all I knew of him. In spite of our friendly correspondence, we'd both held to a certain reticence in personal matters. Linda said little about Wally, and I wrote nothing about Owen. Mostly I told her about my burgeoning career as a writer of articles and interviews—something I'd continued successfully even during my marriage. And of course I told her about my feeling toward Monica Arlen, which continued strong. After all, she was my only living ancestor: Only a foster child can know the need for any sort of ancestor.

Though even there I couldn't be wholly frank, because my secret affection for Aunt Monica couldn't be told in full. While her home might offer me refuge now, I'd chosen her for another reason as well. All my life I'd dreamed of meeting her, and had never quite dared to suggest it. I understood that she'd become a recluse, saw absolutely no one under ordinary circumstances, and would probably never invite me to Palm Springs. Now, because my need was so urgent, I must see her. And even in my present fear I felt a sense of anticipation about our first meeting—the rather tremulous anticipation that I might have felt as a very young girl. When it came to Monica, I hadn't entirely grown up.

I'd phoned Linda yesterday in desperation, and had tried to explain a little. She knew of my divorce, but now I had to tell her more. Owen had forced his way into my apartment in the dangerous, violent way that was characteristic of him, and had struck Keith viciously when my son tried to protect me. I'd suffered such attacks before—once to the extent of being put in a hospital, but this physical cruelty to Keith was new. Usually Owen reserved more subtle and demeaning torments for his son. Immediate flight had been the only answer.

Linda had been warmly sympathetic on the phone, but nevertheless a little cautious. She said, ''Monica is in a difficult mood right now. Carol—there's been some trouble here. So I won't tell her yet that you're coming. Just come, and I'll see that you get into the house. I know it will be all right, once you're here, and she'll be glad to see you when things quiet down.''

This hadn't sounded reassuring, but I had no other choice. My own need and growing fear drove me. The moment Owen knew we were gone, he would never stop searching until he found us. So we had to take refuge in a place where we could be safe for a time from anything he might try. The law couldn't protect us until he acted—and by then it would be too late.

In the past, Linda had written often about Smoke Tree House, which was Monica's own creation. It existed on the side of a mountain behind chain link fences, with a private, guarded road leading up from town. Monica Arlen, like many wealthy and famous people, had sought safety and seclusion, building her haven in Palm Springs long before her sudden and dramatic retirement so many years ago. Now it seemed not only the one spot where Keith and I could be safe, but also a place where we could recover from all that had happened in the past dreadful years. I would find the quiet in which to plan calmly what I must do now. First of all, I must draw Keith out of his fearful retreat from life, and give him new interests and friends. Equally important to both of us, I must begin once more to earn my own living.

I was stronger now, and a great deal wiser than I'd been more than six years ago when I'd worked in Manhattan for the magazine *Five Boroughs*. I had been a staff writer, doing interviews, tracking down special stories from the Bronx to Staten Island, under my own byline of Carol Hamilton. The editor had seen in me not only a certain freshness when it came to putting words on paper, but a human touch as well. Not hard to accomplish, since I'd always escaped by imagining myself in other people's more colorful lives. My stories seemed to work, both for readers and for those I interviewed. Some fairly famous people had made startling revelations to me—which I'd managed to handle diplomatically on paper.

On that morning when Owen Barclay had stormed into the *Five Boroughs* office, nearly everyone was out for lunch. I had a deadline and was still at my typewriter. Since I was the only moving object in sight, he vented his rage on me.

Who did we think we were, he roared—putting out a rotten feature like that? Filled with wild untruths and thoroughly slanderous besides! How could we possibly imagine that he wouldn't sue?

I had stared at him in something like terror. I hadn't written the piece, and I was hardly in charge, except for being the only person around. At twenty-two I'd never had to face so much overwhelming energy, such sheer, angry power. I knew who he was, of course. I'd read the article and thought secretly that he must be quite a fascinating man. He belonged to that glamorous world I'd longed to be part of ever since I'd watched my first Arlen-Scott movie. He seemed to have accomplished everything in his fifty-three years. He'd made several fortunes in the stock market, was chairman of the board here, president of a company there. To say nothing of his rumored connections with gambling and the underworld. Later I was to regret that I'd chosen to ignore the seriousness of that network. "Barclay" wasn't even his real name, which had been Middle-European and unpronounceable. He'd readily admitted that he'd selected Barclay because it had the ring of Harvard, at the very least—which amused him, since he was entirely self-educated.

I'd thought him remarkably handsome, with his striking curly gray hair, dark eyebrows, and full, sensual mouth. As I looked up from my desk, he seemed enormously tall and broad in the shoulders, emanating strength and power. Vitality! A dangerous, exciting man—like Saxon Scott, whom I'd so adored in all those movies. He was dressed immaculately in a conservative gray business suit that had a Brooks Brothers look. The dignity of his adopted name, and the way he dressed were, however, the only proper and conservative things about him, as I was to discover.

It occurred to me that such a man would usually send his lawyers and not trouble to appear in person without warning or appointment. The very fact that he chose to make this attack on his own and alone seemed to indicate an unbridled and explosive temper.

As the ferocity of the attack went on, I suddenly stopped being scared and began to get angry myself. He had no right to pick on *me*. Though I couldn't think what to say to him, I began to bristle. My wordless indignation finally got his attention, and he stopped in the middle of his diatribe and looked at me—really looked.

"Hey!" he said. "You're not even dry behind the ears. What are you doing in a dump like this?"

Chairman of *what* board would talk like that? But then, his lack of college degrees, the absence of polish, had all been touched on in the article, as well as his marriages and divorces—some of them rather messy. He prided himself on being a thoroughly rough diamond, and shone all the more brightly in conventional settings. He shone with an extra brilliance in my own lusterless world.

Somehow I pulled myself together and attempted an answer. "I'm a writer. I work here. I didn't write that article about you, though I wish I had. It's a good piece and it made you seem very—very human."

His dark eyes became slightly less intense and he began to laugh. Not the polite, subdued laughter that was considered proper in sophisticated circles, but an uninhibited roar of sound. I found him as completely alarming and fascinating as a predatory tiger.

"Come along," he said when he could catch his breath again. "I'm taking you to lunch. I want to hear more about how human I am. Nobody's pinned that on me for a long time."

"I can't," I told him, trying to sound firm. "I have to finish this interview. I'm late getting it in, as it is."

Without the slightest hesitation he leaned over and ripped the page from my typewriter and dropped it in a wastebasket.

"Nobody tells me *no*. Come along."

That was his first outrage and my first warning. But what else could I do when a tidal wave swept me off my feet—what else but go along paddling? Besides, hadn't I heard Saxon Scott say those very words once in a movie?

If he was a novelty to me and a glimpse of another world, so was I a novelty for him. Even as I paddled, I tried to swim against the wave. In those beginning months of our relationship, he actually enjoyed this, and I was tremendously flattered and

9

excited by his attentions. He told me frankly that he preferred blondes to brunettes—as though I were a sort of commodity that could be ordered in sizes and colors—but that he rather liked my dark brown hair, and he was always mussing it with a careless hand. I refused to listen to my own faint stirring of resentment at his appropriation of my person. No one had ever cared enough to appropriate me until now, and when he called me "Carol" in a way that caressed my name, I was lost in an agony of love. What I thought was love. The young have very little equipment for good judgment in that area, and a great deal of heedless emotion to expend.

I learned a lot about what *wasn't* love in the first years of my marriage. When Owen took off his velvet gloves, the fists were steel. I learned quickly that there were outside matters that I must close my eyes to—the world of politics, gambling, business affairs—all a little shady, if examined too carefully, so that it became safer not to look. Sometimes strange men came and went in our apartment without explanation, and there were often bodyguards around. I wasn't without blame, but I had to close my eyes or live in perpetual terror. While he told me nothing, I sensed quickly that Owen Barclay sailed very close to the edge of the law in some of his dealings, and I'd better not learn how close, if I valued my peace of mind. . In any case, by that time I was pregnant and trapped.

Owen didn't know. He'd been away for a month—I wasn't sure where—leaving me alone in New York. I hadn't reached the point where I'd give anything to be alone, and I was eager for his return. I knew he would be excited about my pregnancy. He'd had three children by other wives—all daughters, in whom he took no interest. He wanted a son. So when he came home late one night and closeted himself in a room I'd been forbidden to enter, I couldn't wait. I burst in to tell him the wonderful news.

There was a man in the room whose picture I'd seen in the papers—a man wanted by the law. Owen had ordered me angrily from the room, but he hadn't let it go at that. Later, when his visitor left, there was an explosion of rage. I'd been slapped before, but this was a beating. In fact, he hurt me so badly that he finally took me to the hospital himself, telling

them that I'd fallen down a flight of stairs. I was too frightened and sick to contradict him, and more than anything else,
worried about my baby.

The next day when Owen came to see me—he could often
be contrite after the fact—I told him between swollen lips that
I was going to have a child, and that what he'd done might
have lost it for us. Owen broke down and cried—an amazing,
disturbing man, who still fascinated me, even while he
frightened. There was no Keith then to make the difference.
Only the beginning of Keith.

For a year after Keith's birth my husband was almost a
changed man. Not until the baby began to walk and talk did I
see the direction Owen meant to take with his son. Keith must
grow up strong and tough and hard. Never mind if he hurt
others. Sympathy with another viewpoint was a weakness.
There was only one viewpoint allowed—Owen's. From the
first, Keith was not to be permitted a childhood—as Owen
had never been permitted one of his own.

The way Keith began to look even before the divorce had
broken my heart. Owen hated cringing, yet he knew very well
how to make a small boy cringe. No one realized better than I
how smilingly cruel Owen could be—I'd suffered that myself—
and the time came when I knew I must get Keith away. The
divorce had been ugly, with Owen using every possible trick
to defeat me and gain custody of Keith. It was my good
fortune to have an uncorruptible judge, to whom Owen revealed himself more than he knew. The decision was in my
favor.

A few months ago Owen had managed to snatch Keith
outside his school. He'd hidden him from me and from the
world for sixty-five days. I'd counted every one of them in
my own blood!

From the first, Keith had been a symbol to Owen—never a
real boy. He was Owen Barclay's *Only Son*—and therefore
priceless beyond measure. He must be turned into exactly
what his father wanted him to be—a replica of himself. I'd
had six years of marriage in which to discover to my horror
just what that self was like and I would not have it for Keith.
Kidnapping his own son had been a way in which Owen

could punish me—with a total disregard for the harm he was doing to the boy.

On this occasion, I was once more lucky. I hired detectives, and since it was hard for Owen to be inconspicuous, Keith was found and returned to me. But I knew very well that next time Owen would never make the same mistakes. Next time might be for good.

By the time I got Keith back he had stopped being a joyous, bubbling child who never stopped talking, and had slipped into a grave, silent state—a child who jumped nervously at nothing, and who had grown suddenly older than his years. It wouldn't be easy to turn him again into the happy little boy he had a right to be. Certainly, this could never be accomplished while the threat of his father hung over his life.

There had been no close friends to whom I could turn in New York, since Owen had been suspicious of my few younger friends, and had insulted them when they came to our home. I hadn't minded this a great deal in the beginning, being wholly preoccupied with *him*. And too ready to accept judgments that I came to realize later were terribly wrong. So, when I needed such friends, I found they'd drifted away, and I had no one but myself to blame. There were only cool acquaintances and casual business relationships left.

Beside me in the car, Keith was awake now, and questioning. "Mom? Will he take me away from you?"

"No!" I said. "I promise you that's not going to happen. He can't come after us. He doesn't know where we've gone, and he won't even know right away that we've left." I wasn't sure how true this might be, but I had to offer reassurance, and then make certain it was justified by keeping him safe.

"He always knows," Keith said flatly with a terrible wisdom that had come to him too young.

This last encounter, when his father had struck him, had shown him the danger. He *knew* the threat. He had heard the words that still burned in my memory: "I'll see you in hell, my *dear* Carol, before I'll let you keep my son." There had been murder in Owen at that moment, and only the arrival of someone who had heard him shouting and come to the door had checked his violence. He'd stormed out in a fury.

Now that we'd fled, this need to destroy me would rise in him more strongly than ever.

The rage that I mustn't show was like a festering inside me. I carried physical wounds of my own from that last explosion, though Owen had taken care they wouldn't show on my face. These hurts were less than the pain I felt for my son. I glanced at him sitting still and tense beside me, and was once more glad that he didn't resemble Owen. Looking at my son was like looking into a mirror. He had gray eyes like mine, and brown hair that we both wore across our foreheads in a drift of sidelong bangs. Keith's five years hadn't yet determined the shape of his nose, but his mouth was as wide in proportion as mine. We both had what people called "a generous smile." Lately neither of us had done much smiling.

When we'd left New York I'd begun a game to distract Keith, and I offered it to him now. "This is an exciting adventure, darling. We've never been to Palm Springs before, and we've never had a chance to meet a real movie star."

Keith had met a number of famous television and theater personalities close to Owen, and he wasn't especially impressed, but it was the best I could do. I only hoped that Monica Arlen wouldn't mind having a small boy thrust suddenly into her household, along with a great-niece whom she didn't really know at all. But she *had* sent me through college, so that was something to build on. Wasn't it?

.As we neared what had been a tiny oasis in the desert, overlooked by the Spaniards and known only to the Indians, I tried to put Owen from my mind and think ahead.

Our car was rounding the base of Mt. San Jacinto—the great peak that stood as a barrier between Palm Springs and the mountains along the Pacific.

"We're nearly there, darling," I told Keith, and he sat up more alertly.

Anticipation and hope quickened in me. When I reached out to squeeze Keith's hand, he must have sensed the lifting of my spirits, because he squeezed back, though he still wore the grave expression that had become habitual, and broke my heart.

More than anything else in the coming days, I wanted to see my son happy and laughing again. To that end I must give all my efforts—which meant keeping us both out of Owen's hands.

TWO

KEITH AND I STOOD ON THE GALLERY OUTSIDE OUR HOTEL ROOM and stared in astonishment at Mt. San Jacinto. Its rocky base started only a few blocks away and the precipitous rise of that bare brown mountain was awesome. Its peak touched the western sky, rising nearly eleven thousand feet, almost straight up.

There were higher mountains on the American continent, but this was the steepest escarpment, and it gave the oasis setting of Palm Springs much of its dramatic force. No matter where you turned, the mountain was there at the end of every street that ran west. The surrounding desert and the rest of the San Jacinto range bowed to its dominance. To some extent it held the elements back when storms surged out of the Pacific, and its shadow cast an early twilight over Palm Springs.

"Are we going up there?" Keith whispered, as though the stern brown mass were a giant to be placated.

"Not all the way," I said. "There seems to be only one house that we can see, so that must be Aunt Monica's."

15

Smoke Tree House had been built, not so much on, as into a high rocky shoulder. It looked rather like a Spanish hacienda, with its white walls and red-tiled roofs—a wide, two-story structure that stretched along the narrow ledge. From where we stood, the house seemed close above the town, yet it must be as secure as Linda had claimed. A low stone wall edged the steep drop from the front terrace, and its balconies and arched windows would command a tremendous view. Steep above the house, and set back as the mountain's contour was followed, terraced gardens flourished, filled with tropical vegetation that topped the roof. All this seemed to be shut in with chain link fences, and occupied no great acreage. The most had been made of every inch of available space. I noted the high gardens with special interest. If we had to stay for weeks, perhaps even months, these would offer a place where Keith might play outdoors safely.

On the lower level, and to the right of the house, a long, narrow road slanted to the base of the mountain. I knew that a steel gate guarded the road at the lower end, though it was hidden from our view by a grove of palm trees. A complex electrical alarm system further protected the house itself. Yes, this would be the right place for us—a fortress indeed. I felt impatient to be up there and safe at last. If I hadn't turned my car in, I might have ventured up on my own.

"Shouldn't that lady be coming soon?" Keith demanded, tiring of the view.

I nodded toward the street, where a car had pulled into the curb. "Perhaps that's Linda Trevor now."

I'd phoned Linda as soon as we reached our room, and eager as I was for us to be friends, I had been relieved to hear a welcoming warmth in her greeting. Nevertheless, I'd sensed that she held something back, and I wondered if Monica was still too upset to be told about our coming. Linda would be down to see us in an hour, she said, and took my room number before she hung up. However anxious I was, my questions would have to wait until she was here.

In the East I'd have called this place a rather luxurious motel, but I knew that word had long been banned in Palm Springs, which had only "hotels." No high rises were al-

EMERALD

lowed and only a tower or two stood above the low level of
the roofs. Happily, no neon signs were permitted, and holding their shaggy heads above all else were hundreds of
Washingtonia filifera palm trees, which belonged to this region and gave a special character to the streets. It was a town
unlike any other I'd visited—utterly clean and orderly and
well kept in itself, yet with the harsher reality of mountain
and desert pressing in all around. It was easy to see why
Hollywood's most glittering stars had always come here to
play and rest, and why so many had built fabulous homes in
the area. Yet in its perfection, its very isolation from a crasser
Los Angeles, the place had a certain unreality. The real world
could easily cease to exist in a town like this.

Down on the street the woman was getting out of her car,
and she stood looking up at us, her beige pants and green
pullover blending with sand and palm colors. I recognized
Linda from snapshots she'd sent. She waved enthusiastically
and came running up the outside stairs to our stretch of
gallery.

Linda Trevor's dark hair was short and fluffy, her brown
eyes huge, with quite spectacular lashes, yet at first glance
the face she turned toward us so eagerly seemed plain. Only
as they flashed into excitement did her features seem to light
in an illusion of prettiness.

From her letters I knew that she had grown up in the desert
and had once gone the Hollywood route, playing bit parts
when she was younger. Lacking any special talent, she'd
wound up working in secretarial posts at the studios. Of
course Monica Arlen had been long gone from Hollywood by
the time Linda arrived, but eventually someone had suggested
her to Monica and Linda had come to Palm Springs to work
for the woman she'd admired for so long.

Now that she stood beside us, I saw how small she was—
not nearly as tall as my own five-five, though she made up
for any lack of size by being constantly, enthusiastically, in
motion—her hands, her eyes, even her feet, as she whirled
into our big room. Not until later did I understand that this air
of constant motion that took over when she was anxious and
excited wasn't particularly characteristic of Linda Trevor.

17

Clearly, she was uncomfortable about our being here, and my
hope of rescue dropped a notch or two.

"I'm glad you've come," she said, not convincing me,
and touched Keith on the shoulder with a light pat. Then she
went to look out the far side of the room, where glass doors
opened on a private balcony overlooking the inevitable swimming pool. Here endless sunbathers, who seemed to have
nothing else in the world to do, were a permanent decoration
around the pool. This was November in Palm Springs!

"You seem comfortable here." Linda turned back and
dropped into one of the two big chairs.

Her slightly explosive movements, her obvious uneasiness,
were making me more uncertain by the moment. I sat down
opposite her.

"You still haven't told Monica, have you?" I asked.

Keith came to lean against me, watching Linda solemnly,
as though he saw right through to something that frightened
him.

She shook her head and her brown hair bounced above her
ears. "Carol, of course I'd have told her if she'd been feeling
better. She's still upset and cross, and it's better to wait for
the right moment. She's really very generous and kind."

Linda's eyes were bright with sincerity, but I felt not at all
reassured. I'd hurled us here—into Monica's arms, so to
speak—and I was beginning to realize that they might not
open to receive us. So much for all my secret fantasies!

"What are we to do?" I asked.

Linda caught the desperation in my voice. "It will be all
right, Carol. Really it will. It's just that we'd better smuggle
you in at first and tell her later."

My heart dropped to my toes. Being "smuggled" in seemed
especially humiliating. Alarming, too, that it should be thought
necessary.

"I don't know . . ." I began. "How can we go into her
house if we're unwelcome?"

"Nonsense!" Linda spoke with a little too much assurance,
her fingers lacing and unlacing—more evidence of a tension
she was now trying to hide. "Of course you'll come up to the

house the first thing tomorrow morning. Even if I haven't told her.''

"How will you keep her from seeing us arrive?"

"That won't be hard. She has her own apartment at the southern end of the house because she dotes on the sun. But when she goes into one of these retreats, she pulls the draperies across the windows, turns on the stereo, and lives in a cave. She won't hear the car come up the mountain. She doesn't even realize I'm away now. Ralph can call for you around nine, and he'll drive you up.''

"Who is Ralph?"

"Ralph Reese.'' Linda flung up her hands expressively and made a derisive face. "He's part of the present trouble. I'd like to see him out altogether, and he'd like to be rid of me. He's not my favorite character, but he's useful to Monica. I suppose you'd call him a chauffeur-gardener-handyman. He doubles as guard and escort as well. Not that she goes out very often, and then only under those big hats she wears, and behind dark glasses. Though I doubt that anyone would recognize her anymore. I guess you'd say Ralph is a necessary evil at the moment.''

This sounded worse and worse. "Won't he tell her about us?"

"I've twisted his arm," Linda said dryly. "I found out ages ago that it's a good idea to have something on Ralph at all times. Useful.''

Her words left me feeling even more desolate. I'd just fled from a world of intrigue and arm-twisting, and here I seemed to be confronted with it again.

"Never mind," Linda said. "Ralph doesn't matter. If it wasn't him, it would be someone else. Monica has to have a man around to amuse and flatter her. He'll keep still for a while—though only because he's a little afraid of me.''

Even though she smiled as she spoke the words, I could guess that she might make Ralph nervous. She was certainly making me nervous, and I drew my fingers across my cheek in an absent gesture.

Linda stared. "You look like her, you know! Oh, not your features, exactly, but the way you lift your head. And the way you stroked your cheek just now—that's a Monica Arlen gesture!''

"From watching her pictures, I suppose. Dreaming about her, and copying her, when I was very young," I said ruefully.

"You'd better be careful," Linda warned. "She won't like mimicking."

"I have to be myself. If I resemble her, I have a right to, you know."

"Of course. I didn't mean . . ." She broke off unhappily.

Keith had grown bored with our talk and he went to stand on the balcony overlooking the swimming pool.

Linda lowered her voice. "That's a dreadful bruise on your son's cheek. How are you handling this?"

"I'm trying to call it an adventure, make it a game."

"He'll be safe up the mountain. You both will. You can't imagine how careful she is. You get that way after the Hollywood fishbowl."

"She doesn't miss all that?"

"It was a long time ago. Though she's a very deep lady, and I don't always know what she's thinking. Look—I need to get back before I'm missed. Even though she's shut herself in, she can want me at any time, and she doesn't like me to disappear without letting her know. We'll meet in the morning, Carol, when you come up to the house."

"All right," I said hesitantly, and went with her to the door. What other choice did I have?

Out on the gallery that ran past the rooms, Linda paused. "You'll want dinner and there's a good restaurant connected with the hotel. It's down there to your right. If you go early you won't need a reservation."

For a moment she looked off at the massive rise of the mountain, as though she might say something more, then shrugged and went toward the outside stairs, moving with less bounce than when she'd come up.

Linda Trevor, I thought, might be a very deep lady too, and she quite clearly had concerns on her mind. But I could take this only one step at a time.

I tried to tell myself there was no danger in our staying

overnight at this hotel, but I'd known Owen Barclay long enough to be aware of the means he could summon to his service when the need arose. Power and money could accomplish almost anything. My only hope for the time being was to get beyond the guarded gate of Smoke Tree House, and under Monica Arlen's protection. For now I would simply have to wait until the hours passed and tomorrow morning came. Only then could I breathe a little easier. For a time at least.

Keith had come to the rail beside me and was watching Linda get into her car. "She hops around a lot, doesn't she?" he commented.

I could only agree. Linda Trevor had always seemed much calmer in her letters.

We went inside and changed for dinner. I shook out a dress of saffron tie silk, put it on, and brushed my hair. It was nearly six o'clock and the restaurant should be open. Out of his jeans, Keith looked handsome in gray pants and blue blazer, and he'd combed his own hair.

Outside, we followed the lower level past tropical plantings, where steps led to great double doors of carved wood, brass-studded. For just a second I hesitated uncomfortably—and recognized the cause. For the last six years I'd never stepped into a good restaurant without Owen's commanding presence at my side. A conditioning I'd be happy to overcome.

Then, as I paused, I noticed the name of the restaurant arching above the doors and I forgot everything else. In bold black letters the sign read: SAXON'S.

Was this why Linda had hesitated, and then decided to let me find out for myself? A little of my depression lifted as I took Keith's hand and we went through the doors together. If there was a "Saxon's," then the owner of that name must still be alive, perhaps even living here in Palm Springs. So very close to Monica Arlen—when they'd broken off in hot anger all those years before?

An excitement came alive in me. There might even be a story here. And I must think of articles and writing them as soon as possible. How fascinating if I could actually meet and talk to Saxon Scott!

We entered a large, pleasant room with sand-colored walls. Tables were still empty at this hour, and I stood looking around. Tall screens of Spanish leather stood in each corner, and high ceiling beams had been painted a light beige like the ceiling between, making the room seem bright and airy. Tablecloths were avocado green, with yellow napkins perked at every setting, and ladder-backed chairs with leather seats carried out the Spanish-Mexican effect.

The headwaiter came toward us courteously, but with no great enthusiasm for two such early and modest-looking diners.

"I haven't a reservation," I told him.

He considered the tables as though every one was occupied, and decided to put us out of sight. "May I suggest the Mirage Room?" he said. "It won't fill up until later."

We followed as he led the way. The Mirage Room! I urged Keith ahead of me, and in the doorway I stopped to stare. I had been here so many times before. I knew this intimate room in its every detail. I recognized the red-checked tablecloths, the stubby candles in glasses, the single anemone in a bud vase on each table. Even the bentwood chairs were familiar. The entire room had been re-created from that immortal scene in Monica's and Saxon's most famous movie.

The headwaiter had pulled out a chair at a corner table and was waiting expectantly. Keith ran across the room and I followed more slowly, still looking. On the walls hung framed and autographed photographs of Monica Arlen and Saxon Scott, both smiling in the stunning beauty of their youth. On either side of the central portraits were framed stills from *Mirage,* one of them a restaurant scene—a duplicate of the room in which I stood. The movie had been made just after the war, and was more bittersweet, less saccharine, than the earlier ones.

"I've seen the movie," I told the waiter as we sat down. "Does Mr. Scott own this place?"

He looked slightly bored as he pointed to the legend on the back of the menu, which would tell me about the restaurant and this room. It was all there—it was true.

When I'd ordered for us, and the waiter had gone, Keith glowered at me. "I look funny, don't I? Everybody stares."

"They just feel sorry that you got hurt," I told him gently. "Let's go look at the pictures."

It was something to do. In the past Keith had never been one to keep still for five minutes. His bright mind had examined everything, and his chatter had lightened my life. But in the last months he'd become disturbingly quiet, and his very silences pained me.

I tried to talk about the pictures as we followed them down the room in scenes I remembered very well. I told him about the one when Saxon, a very clever thief in the film, had entered by the balcony of Monica's bedroom, to find her in the act of taking too many sleeping pills. He'd sat beside her bed and talked to her about the joy of being alive, no matter what. One of his best scenes ever. Her response had been touching, moving—that of a lost lady who needed to be given the will to live. *Mirage* had taken a more serious turn than earlier pictures, and had seemed to promise even more for the future. Arlen and Scott had received nominations for Oscars for their roles in the film, though neither had won, and a great to-do had been made by the press when neither showed up at the Oscar ceremony.

As we moved from photo to photo, I found myself lost in the past. Even though Monica Arlen's marvelous old Warner Brothers pictures—witty and a little wry, always entertaining— had been made before I was born, they were a part of my growing up. I could remember times when I'd sneaked downstairs late at night, wherever I was living, to watch Monica Arlen and Saxon Scott as they'd shone again so brilliantly on the late shows across the television screens of America— miraculously restored to the great days of their youth. When I was older, I'd saved my allowance (when I had one) so I could visit any theater that might be playing one of their old films. I could always watch them over and over, and I still knew some of their lines by heart. Indeed, I'd played a few of Monica's roles in front of my own mirror, even while I laughed at myself.

In the late thirties and early forties, those two had been called, "golden," "stunning," and of course, "forever romantic." Monica's faintly tilted eyes and breathless, parted lips had become almost a cliché from long imitation. Imitation too often became caricature, but no one had ever done Monica Arlen as well as Arlen herself. She had symbolized so much of glamour and romance in those days of screen heroines and heroes—of STARS.

On a few occasions that made me practically ecstatic, someone who knew of my relationship to Monica (I hardly kept it secret!) would say there was a resemblance between us—just as Linda had done. But though I searched, I could never find it in my own face. My eyes had no exotic tilt, and my nose was just a nose.

One of the things I'd always watched for and loved in Monica's pictures was her own special signature. On screen and off, she was given to carrying a silken iris done in beautiful shades of blue. There had been scenes in her pictures when she'd gestured with it to graceful effect. Of course she repeatedly denied any imitation of Gloria Swanson's famous red carnation, though one wondered. The iris (she had them especially made by hand) became her symbol, in real life even more than on a screen. Once I'd stood for half an hour before a mirror with an iris stalk in my hands, trying— not very successfully—to achieve her gestures.

I had been fortunate in a way. The families I'd lived with were kind enough, though they thought me a strange child, and probably found me hard to love—except for Mrs. Johnson, who told me desert stories. I'd loved her, and I think she loved me. But foster parents often moved away, or changed for other reasons. She'd written to me for a little while, but it had hurt too much to write back. I just couldn't. Mostly the people I lived with weren't especially imaginative—which wasn't their fault. So how could they cope with a girl who lived too much inside her own head?

As for Saxon Scott on those screens—how could I ever forget that slightly satyr-like expression he so often wore when he looked at a woman? Or the startling emphasis of white plumes set prematurely in dark hair at either temple, or the dashing mustache he'd borrowed from Ronald Colman, before either Gable or Flynn had made such mustaches famous?

Since Monica had so obviously loved him, I must love him too.

What a pair they'd been! Legendary. Blessed by the gods of the cinema. Once I'd found a stack of old fan magazines in a secondhand bookstore, and I'd bought them all, to pore endlessly over their sepia pages. They'd been filled with stories of that great and boundless love, that exciting romance between Arlen and Scott—chattily depicted in the vernacular of the day. A love that must have been as passionate off-screen as on, so that when their lips met in the carefully timed kisses the Hays Office allowed, the screen fairly sizzled and audiences knew they were seeing the real thing.

How convincingly they'd wept and laughed and fenced with each other through all those comedy-dramas, where actors spoke dialogue ordinary people only wished they could emulate. And writers must have knocked themselves out to achieve. How they'd fought as well, and as passionately, sometimes in public, so that restaurant bric-a-brac flew and they'd ended up laughing in each other's arms—all of which was duly reported in the gossip columns and on the radio, to the delight of millions of fans.

Until that last picture, *Mirage*. The picture this little dining room belonged to. Their unforgettable best, all the critics had said. A four-handkerchief job, if there ever was one, but something that had touched millions of hearts, and still reached lonely watchers at night and brought tears to the eyes. All the more moving because of the legend itself. The dissolution of a screen love that had seemed to promise so much more than it could ever fulfill, had made an entire country sad. In the end, it prophesied that nothing could last. Not beauty, not youth, not any "forever" love.

Sometimes, as I'd read about all this, I'd ached a little for the suffering of that fabulous woman—of my own blood! —whom I'd never been able to meet.

The breakup between Arlen and Scott had come about when Monica walked out at the end of the picture and said flatly that she would never act again. One of the things aficionados still watched for in *Mirage* was the lack of any luster in her performance during those scenes that had been retakes. As though her heart had already died, and when she was called back to redo those scenes, she could summon no more make-believe to get her through. Seeing that picture again and again, as I had, I'd thought there had seemed a hint of fear in those shadowed scenes; something almost terrified that had haunted her famous slantèd eyes when she looked at Saxon. There was no denying that his own performance grew stony in just those few retakes. As though something had gone out of him as well, and could never be rekindled. Nevertheless, I'd wondered if this would really have been noticeable except for hindsight.

When Monica Arlen walked out for the last time, she had closed her magnificent home, Cadenza, in Beverly Hills, and had retreated to her fortress of a house above Palm Springs. There she had been safe from the intrusion of public and press—or anything else she might have feared. *Mirage* marked the end of her acting life. All this had happened some thirty-six years ago, and I'd read that she and Saxon had never met again after that.

Saxon had gone on in pictures without her for a time, but in the end he'd had to accept the fact that they'd made such a splendid combination that the public wanted to see them together, and *only* together. Each had been trapped by the legend. Playing with another woman, he'd never seemed himself—not the old Saxon Scott. In those last pictures he'd made without Monica, it hadn't been the same. No electricity had been generated. The legend had been too powerful to overcome. So Saxon too had faded from the public eye, and I hadn't even known whether he was alive, let alone here in Palm Springs.

In my letters to Linda, I'd asked about Saxon once, but she'd never replied, and I could only suppose that there were certain subjects she'd been told not to discuss with me.

The years of the Second World War had brought all the beautiful film fantasies to an end, and the screen had turned to a harsher, more realistic world, and gradually to a different sort of fantasy. Only night audiences still watched the dreams become real again on that smaller screen in the privacy of their own homes. Arlen and Scott were not forgotten, but the legend was different now—more nostalgic, and for the young, sometimes funny.

There had, of course, been endless speculation at the time of Monica's retirement. I'd heard about that. But much of it was gossip and so embroidered that it was hard to know what was imaginary, or what had actually happened. One thing was strongly rumored—that Saxon himself had broken with Monica before the end of the picture, and that she had been devastated, so distraught that she could never continue her career without him.

At about the same time, Monica had lost her secretary and companion—Peggy Smith, who had died a suicide. After that tragedy, Monica's affairs had fallen into disarray for a time, and gossip said her grief for two terrible losses, her lover and her friend, had made her inconsolable.

When her co-star had married a year or so after the breakup with Monica, the story had hit the headlines, as had Saxon's divorce a few years later. After that there had been only silence.

Now in the Mirage Room, I moved on to a photograph that showed Monica's graceful hands, my attention caught by the famous ring she was wearing. There had been so many accounts of this gift Saxon had made to Monica when they started work on *Mirage* that I was familiar with it. Monica had hated diamonds, and this was a large square emerald— the color of an oasis in the desert, she'd said. I recalled that the ring was the work of a woman whose hobby had been creating imaginative jewelry from precious gems. When Saxon had asked her to create something unique for Monica, she had etched an intaglio design into the fine stone—a delicate iris, Monica Arlen's symbol. Traced forever in the deep green of the great emerald, it would also become legendary.

From the time when Saxon put the ring on Monica's finger and they'd embraced each other, as they always did at the start of work on a picture, she'd never taken it off . . . or so the story went. Fan magazines and gossip columnists had chattered on avidly. I wondered if Monica still had the emerald, or if she wore it anymore. She must remember those old days constantly, but how much of the past did she regret? If she'd married him, he would have been her third husband, and with two failures behind her, perhaps she'd hesitated too long.

For a while, studying the photographs, I'd been carried into another world, escaping briefly into the make-believe that had always entranced me. Keith, however, grew tired of my dreaming, and when he saw that the waiter had brought salads to our table, he nudged me. As I turned to follow him, I glanced into the outer dining room and again stopped to stare.

A man had paused to speak to a couple just seated at one of the tables, and I'd have recognized him anywhere. His thick hair was completely white now—no more contrasting plumes at the temples. Indeed, so white that it was almost blond, and the mustache was gone. He seemed heavier than I remembered, though still athletic-looking and trim. He wore a white dinner jacket that emphasized a great tan, and though he was well into his seventh decade, Saxon Scott looked amazingly fit and handsome, and a good deal younger than his years. I wondered if Monica had managed as well.

I suppressed a ridiculous urge to introduce myself as Monica Arlen's great-niece. I wasn't a teenage fan any longer, however, and that would be a highly inappropriate intrusion. Just the same, as I took my place at the table with Keith, I wondered again about a possible interview with Saxon Scott. Next to interviewing Monica herself—which she would probably never permit—an article about Saxon would be my next choice. Perhaps I could find a way, once I settled down to working again. I didn't want to exploit Monica or Saxon in any way, yet I had to earn a living now, somehow.

Unexpectedly, Keith smiled at me. "You look nice," he said. "Your eyes are all sparkly."

His words reminded me how much I had been showing my cruel anxieties. For Keith's sake as well as my own, I must try to get control of myself and make sound and realistic plans. Our flight from Owen was nearing its end, and perhaps when we reached Smoke Tree House we'd be reasonably safe for a while. Or so I tried to convince myself. Certainly I must climb out of a gloom and anxiety that was affecting Keith as well.

Through the rest of the meal I made an effort to be cheerful, and it was good to see my son respond, and even laugh a little at my nonsense. I too was to blame for his grave withdrawal. My initial mistake in marrying Owen had been disastrous in every respect but one: it had given me this son to cherish and defend. I must help him to find his own strengths, but I mustn't place on him unfair burdens that were really mine to carry.

Back in our room, sleep seemed far away, and now the photos in the restaurant haunted me. My restless dreams were filled with Monica Arlen—whom I would meet for the very first time tomorrow.

THREE

IN THE MORNING WE BREAKFASTED IN OUR ROOM AND WERE READY when Ralph Reese came knocking on the door. He was a large young man, muscular and sandy-blond, with rather staring blue eyes that examined me warily. As though I might be a threat to him in some way. Perhaps as Monica's only relative? Nevertheless, his smile had an air of self-satisfaction, indicating that he had total confidence in its effect on me. He was probably twenty-five—more than forty years younger than Monica Arlen.

"Our bags are ready," I said when we'd exchanged good mornings.

He picked them up as though they weighed nothing. "Hi, kid," he said to Keith. "How about you helping me with this one?"

I could almost like him for giving Keith a useful task by handing him a flight bag, and we all went down to the impressive old white Rolls-Royce he said belonged to Miss Arlen.

We drove through streets that seemed bright and clean to eyes accustomed to New York litter. Palm trees grew everywhere, their high green fronds rustling in the breeze, and dead stalks hanging down to make thick brown collars beneath. Ralph pointed out to Keith a man on a ladder, "shaving" a palm tree to get rid of dead branches. The shops we passed were smart and expensive, displaying famous names and obviously catering to a wealthy clientele. The town had a washed green look to it, thanks to the ever-present water supply, so that brown grass was not the pattern here, as it sometimes was in Southern California.

We turned past a golf course at the base of the mountain, and came to the high steel gates that guarded Monica's private road. These were operated electrically by a guard in the small gatehouse. We drove through and started up inside the chain link fence. Below us, Palm Springs spread out in neatly ordered squares, a relief map in green and white and red and tan.

Keith was growing excited now, and even ready to chatter. It was to Ralph's credit that he tried to keep up with my son's questions. The road was narrow, so that passing another car would have been impossible, and I presumed there was some sort of signal used at the gatehouse when a car was going up or down.

At the top another gate, this one of ornamental wrought iron, stood open, and here there was no guard. We drove through to park at one end of the brick-paved terrace in front of a long garage. The latter had been built into the mountain near the far end, and held the car that Linda Trevor had driven last night, as well as a smaller sports car. Ralph's, perhaps?

The red-tiled roofs of the house and white walls spilling over with purple-red bougainvillea blazed in the morning light. Straight up behind it rose the dark mountain peak, and the air was already warming in the sun. Air that smelled clean and fresh and slightly toasted.

Linda came to one of several arched doors that opened from house to terrace, and promptly whisked us inside. I hated the feeling that we must be taken quickly out of sight, but for now at least, I could do nothing about this.

The end room nearest the road was obviously a drawing room—not a large room, but grand in a threadbare way. The ceiling was high, with dark beams and white plastered walls. Rugs from old Persia covered the floor, and the furnishings were fine traditional pieces, the upholstery—exquisite in its day—now faded and worn. Rose silk brocade on chairs and sofa, a cabinet with tortoiseshell inlays, a Waterford chandelier—all were formal, and made no bow to California except for brownish-red tiles that showed beneath the rugs.

Very little must have changed in this room since Monica Arlen had furnished it many years ago. Space in a house built into the very side of Mt. San Jacinto must be limited, but the room's formal dignity gave it an air of importance.

At the rear, a narrow hallway led to a staircase of dark wood running straight up to the floor above. A far cry from Monica's Beverly Hills home. I'd seen pictures of Cadenza's famous winding black marble staircase, and I wondered if she still owned that house.

"I'll show you to your room, so you can settle in," Linda said. "Ralph, will you bring up the bags, please?"

Keith clung determinedly to his flight bag as we followed Linda upstairs. A narrow upper hall with tall windows along one side edged the mountain for the entire width of the house. At the far end a heavy carved door partitioned off what was undoubtedly Monica's apartment.

The bedroom into which Linda showed us occupied prize corner space, and had its own upper balcony commanding the tremendous sweep of view. Keith ran at once to look out, and I followed him. As Ralph set down the bags and stood waiting in the room behind, Linda came out to stand beside us.

"It's beautiful, isn't it?" she said. "Sometimes when people first come here, they hate to see brown sand and brown mountains all around. But you'll find nothing is really bare and dead. There are even plants that cling to what looks like sheer rock. You should hear my brother Jason go on about the desert. It may look dead to you at first, but it's really *alive*."

From time to time in her letters, Linda had mentioned her younger brother, who was a naturalist, and she'd always written of him with admiration and affection.

Keith, quickly bored with the view, returned to the room to talk to Ralph, and I was glad of a chance with Linda alone.

Before I could put my question about Monica, however, she forestalled me as she gestured toward a cluster of rectangular buildings directly below us.

"That's the Desert Museum down there—where Jason has worked as assistant science curator. Right now he's acting as a free-lance consultant and doing various odd jobs, so he's on his own time. There are reasons why he needs to be free." She hesitated as though she might add something, and then went on. "I've invited him to lunch today, so you'll meet him soon. I suppose I'm prejudiced, but I think he's the wisest person I know. He may even be able to help with some useful ideas about your problem, Carol. That's why I've asked him to come."

I must have looked surprised, but she gave me the quick, warm smile that could so change her face.

"Don't worry—he understands why you're here. I had to tell him. He always sees through me when I lie. And besides, I thought he might help. Not that he approves of us up here. He hates my working for Monica Arlen, and I'm afraid he'll never understand how you and I feel about her."

I wished she hadn't spoken so frankly to her brother about my personal problems. Didn't she understand that I must keep my presence here quiet for as long as possible?

"Why doesn't he want you to work for Monica?" I asked.

She heard the coolness in my voice and touched my arm lightly. "It will be all right, Carol. You'll see, once you meet him. It's just that he thinks movies and all that goes with them—stars and notoriety, all that fantasy and escape—don't have much place in today's world. None of that is real to him. Not nearly as real as his desert. Though sometimes"— she sounded unexpectedly wistful—"sometimes I like the make-believe world better than the real one. It's much more satisfying."

As a narcotic could be satisfying? I wondered. It was a

disturbing thing for her to say, though who could understand better than I?

She became suddenly brisk and down-to-earth, so that I had again the sense of a very capable woman. "I'll leave you to unpack now. If there's anything you want, I'll be right downstairs in my office. Come down when you're ready and I'll show you the house. Carol—I hope you'll be happy here."

"I hope we'll be safe," I said. "Linda, you still haven't told Monica that I'm here? Hasn't anyone told her?"

She turned in the balcony doorway. "We have to move slowly. This morning she seemed less jangled and nervous than she did last night. So I'll talk to her soon. Perhaps right away. I promise."

"Yes—please do that," I said.

For these moments I'd almost forgotten Ralph, who still stood in the room beside our bags, watching with that staring blue gaze, obviously listening to every word, even while he talked to Keith. It seemed surprising that Linda would speak so openly before him, and again it perturbed me that she seemed to have so little respect for either Monica's privacy or my own. I wondered what it was she held over Ralph that made her so confident and careless.

When she hurried off, as though to avoid further questions, Ralph followed her, with a quick backward glance for me that was clearly sly.

When they'd gone, I stood at the door to the rear hall, looking out through the opposite glass at the sheer brown rock of the mountain rising scarcely an arm's length away. At any other time, I might have felt shut in by that formidable barrier, but now it offered safety. Surely no one could get in from that side. I could see the stretch of garden on the higher level, visible through a chain link fence, and I would explore it later for reassurance.

Linda's words had darkened both my hope and the morning. Even this first step of reaching Smoke Tree House in my flight from Owen hadn't lessened my real anxiety. Until Monica knew we were here, and said we could stay, this was not even a temporary refuge. Keith and I were utterly vulnerable unless Monica offered her protection. To the very end, Owen would be merciless.

Linda's prevarication seemed especially discouraging. She was putting this off because she was afraid of the result of telling Monica we were here.

I turned back to the pleasant room, finding a momentary relief in its soothing blue and sand colors. In contrast to the formality downstairs, this room seemed plain, easy, comfortable. Probably it had been refurnished by someone other than Monica Arlen, since her tastes, as reflected in the drawing room, had been formed in a more opulent age, when stars were expected to live like stars.

"Do you want to help unpack?" I asked Keith.

He paid no attention, his eyes fixed on the open door to the hall. "Look, Mom," he said.

A regal Siamese cat had stepped haughtily into the room. She was purely bred, with velvety sable boots and black markings against smoky brown fur. Her eyes were a deeper blue than Ralph's, the sound of her mewing imperious and demanding, though I couldn't tell what it was she demanded. We were to learn that her name was Annabella and that she knew very well that she could talk.

"Be careful," I warned Keith. "Sometimes Siamese cats aren't friendly with strangers."

I wasted my breath. Keith and the cat were already friends. Watching them, a sick remembrance returned to me of a scene with Owen in New York two years ago. I'd brought home a kitten for Keith, without knowing that Owen abhorred cats. We had been sitting outdoors on our high terrace above Sutton Place, and when Owen joined us, Keith had run innocently to him with the tiny kitten, and placed it on his father's knees. In one swoop of revulsion, Owen had thrown the little thing violently over the parapet to die on the pavement far below. There had been no more pets for Keith. My son's suffering over the incident had been almost more than I could bear, and I still felt nauseated when I thought of that time.

So now I could be especially happy watching Keith with the cat. Then, as a still greater bonus, two fluffy white

Persian cats followed the Siamese to the doorway. Their triangular faces were wide-eyed and angelic—far more innocent than that of their leader. Clearly they knew their places as court maidens to the queen, and they had nothing to say. They merely sat in the doorway, listening and watching. Keith was in heaven at this largesse of cats, but when he moved to pet a white one, the Siamese made a slight, menacing gesture with one paw. The royal prerogative was clear.

As soon as I'd hung up the hurried collection of clothes I'd brought along, we went downstairs, forming an entourage as the cats escorted us, her majesty in the lead.

No one was in sight in the beautiful little drawing room at the foot of the stairs, but other doors opened into a series of connecting rooms that ran along the terrace and opened on to it. First came Linda's office, where she sat at her desk; then a dining room with a long oval table, and beyond that the open door to a kitchen, where a blond woman busied herself at a stove. Unless doors were closed, one end of the house was visible from the other.

Linda turned in her chair and smiled when she saw Keith and the cats. "I see you've made friends with Annabella. Which means that Seraphim and Cherubim—Monica's names, of course—will welcome you too. Monica dotes on cats. We used to have six of them, heaven help us! I'm glad they're down to three. They have a tendency to take us all over. At least Annabella does."

The Siamese sat down and regarded us intently, muttering to herself.

Linda waved a shooing hand. "Look, your highness, how about going someplace else for now? When you talk all the time, the rest of us can't get in a word."

The cat rose disdainfully and strolled to the terrace door, the two Persians following her.

Linda let them out on the terrace. "Sometimes Annabella gives me the creeps. I don't know whether she thinks she's a person, or Monica thinks *she* is a cat." Her words seemed only half joking.

Keith followed them outside, and Linda waved me into a

chair. "Sit down, Carol. We need to talk." She still looked grave, but not especially downcast. I was relieved to find her much less excitable than she'd seemed yesterday, and glad that she'd stopped evading me.

Her office was furnished in rattan, with green chintz cushions. Bookcases stood along one wall, and a glance at titles showed that many were about the movies and the golden age of Hollywood.

"If you've already told her, you must have done it pretty quickly," I said.

"It didn't take long. I told her, and she threw a hairbrush at me. I only had time to state that you'd come with your little boy to visit your adored aunt, and that we had to keep you for a little while. She said, 'I don't want to see her. Send her away at once.' So I told her that wasn't possible right now, and she threw the hairbrush. I left her alone to think it over."

I closed my eyes for a moment against bright sunlight that flooded in from the terrace. "What are we to do now?"

Linda produced her flash of a smile. "Nothing. She can only give orders. She really depends on me. So you'll stay. Eventually I'll get her to listen to why you're here, and she'll come around. If there's one thing that still gets through to her, it's the plight of a woman who's been mistreated by a man. It's too bad that awful bruise isn't on *your* face instead of Keith's."

I didn't tell her I had bruises of my own, even if they didn't show. Bruises I could never forget, or tell anyone about. Though Linda's bluntness might be uncomfortable, at least I liked the fact that she didn't pussyfoot. She wasn't what I'd expected from her letters, but then, I probably wasn't what she'd expected either.

"What do you think your ex-husband will do?" she asked.

It was difficult to explain Owen, to reveal my very private life, and impossible to speak of my own blindness and lack of judgment that had led to tragedy. Whatever wisdom I'd gained, I'd earned the hard way through humiliation so deep I could never talk about it. So how was I to speak frankly now to this woman who was more of a stranger to me than she'd seemed in her letters? I made an effort.

"He'll use his own people, and I suppose he'll hire detectives. We won't be hard to find."

"Then relax," Linda said. "No one can get through our gates. I've given special orders to the guards. And it would be pointless to try to come down the mountain on this side. You'd need ropes and crampons. At night we lock the upper gate to the road as well, and you know the house itself is fully protected by the most sophisticated alarm system we could put in. I told you it was a fortress, Carol, and it really is."

I felt somewhat relieved, yet at the same time increasingly concerned. "What is it *she* is afraid of?"

Linda shrugged. "Who knows? Security is *the* word out here. It's not only crime our celebrities are disturbed about. They don't want to be bothered by all the people who come to gape. To intrude. You'd be surprised at the lengths to which a few foolish ones will go. Of course there've always been tours wherever movie people live, so their houses can be stared at. Goodness knows why. Bob Hope was smart. He's built that huge spaceship of his on top of a hill, where it can only be seen from a distance. You can view Smoke Tree House from all over Palm Springs too, but nobody can get *up* here. Monica arranged for total security right from the beginning, and the new electronics have helped. She's always been more frightened than most."

I remembered that fleeting look on Monica's face in those retake scenes in *Mirage*, remembered feeling that something had frightened her, even then.

"Saxon Scott expressed himself very well in an interview a long time ago," Linda added. "He said that all an actor ever owes his public is the best performance he can give. I agree! Even though I'm one of the few lucky fans who came to know them both personally." She stood up. "Let's call Keith in now, and I'll show you the rest of the house. He may feel confused at first, but there are lots of places he can explore safely. We'll try to make it interesting for him."

I went through the terrace doors to find Keith playing catch with Ralph Reese. Whatever his unpleasanter traits, Ralph seemed to like small boys, and Keith clearly liked him. He wasn't the friend I'd have chosen, but for now he would have to do.

Annabella was not enjoying the ball game. She sat on the wall, her black velvet tail twitching slightly as she made sarcastic remarks. Her angelic companions remained in silent attendance on either side, ears pointed as they listened attentively to their queen. They moved their heads in unison with the tossed ball, even as they listened. A movement Annabella scorned to follow.

Out here on the terrace, bougainvillea spilled abundantly over balconies, and decorative plantings had been set about in great earthen pots. In one grew a lemon tree hung with ripening globes—a splash of sunny yellow—while red geraniums thrived in a planter. Even a few potted palms grew in this limited space.

The view was endlessly fascinating, with the low buildings of Palm Springs spread out in divided squares trimmed neatly with palm trees, the desert and all the Coachella Valley beyond, reaching to the brown mountains on the horizon. I'd already studied maps and knew that Palm Canyon Drive ran along the base of Mt. San Jacinto, turning into Highway 111 at the city limits, and then following the range through the little neighboring cities. South of Palm Springs came Cathedral City, then Rancho Mirage, Palm Desert, Indian Wells, and on through Indio—all their boundaries touching, so that it must be difficult to tell where one ended and the next began.

"We're going to look around the house," I told Keith. "Want to come along?"

He turned first to the Siamese and they exchanged a few secret remarks. Annabella, satisfied to let him go, walked along the wall, sweeping the expanse of the valley with her cool blue gaze.

Linda spoke to Ralph. "I think you'd better go up to Miss Arlen. She may not be feeling very well."

The young man cocked an eyebrow, made a slightly mocking salute, and disappeared toward the far end of the house.

Beyond the garage area there appeared to be a second, private terrace, exclusively Monica's. Chairs invited, though no one sat in them. Linda said that the room behind was Monica's private living room, but that she seldom used it, preferring her upstairs apartment.

"He'll get her quiet," Linda said as Ralph went off. "In his way he's useful. Now we'll just have to wait and see what turn she takes next."

Again these seemed ominous and discouraging words. So much for my fantasy of finding someone of my own blood, to whom I could become close. So much for all those years when I'd ached for family of my own, and set Aunt Monica in that empty place in my heart. Well, I was a big girl now, and I had Keith to fill my life.

At least my son seemed more cheerful since his game with Ralph, and I could be thankful for that as the three of us went into the house to explore.

The blond woman I'd noticed earlier turned from her stove with a pleasant greeting as Linda introduced us. There was no gray in her smoothly combed hair, and her face was plump and lineless. Yet in spite of her smile, her light blue eyes were watchful. Everyone at Smoke Tree House seemed to watch everyone else, I thought with that continuing sense of unease.

"Helsa Carlson has been with Miss Arlen many more years than I have," Linda explained. "We couldn't get along without her. Helsa, this is Carol . . ." Linda hesitated, and then to my relief said, "Miss Carol Hamilton, Miss Arlen's great-niece. You remember, I've spoken about her over the years."

Helsa bowed courteously, watchfully, and said she was pleased to meet me. I had the feeling that she'd had no idea I was coming.

We went up a second flight of stairs and Linda pointed out bedrooms as we followed the upper level. When we'd returned downstairs, Linda spoke to Keith.

"We'll go outside now. I want to show you our own secret garden."

We went out a door into the forbidding rise of the mountain

that made a constant rock barrier behind the house. On the higher ledge above us, palm trees flourished behind the chain link fence, and slab steps pointed upward to a narrow entrance into the garden above.

"I'm going up there!" Keith cried.

Linda put a hand on my arm as I moved to stop him. "Let him go. There's no way he can get off Monica's property, and there's not even a place where he can fall off the mountain."

With Keith out of hearing, I voiced the question that had been troubling me. "Something's very wrong, isn't it? Something you haven't told me."

The bright smile Linda had produced several times faded, and she ran a nervous hand through fluffy brown hair. "Monica Arlen was my greatest idol when I came to work for her. Of course I was full of the way she used to be on the screen, and I'd read so much about her in magazines. I'm trying to preserve some of that, Carol. But she's a bitter woman now, consumed by old resentments, and I'm afraid it's getting worse. Sometimes I think she'll die of her own corrosive emotions if she can't be turned around. Maybe it's already too late. Or maybe you can do something to help. That's one of the reasons I wanted you to come."

Her apparent sincerity touched me for the first time. "Tell me what you mean."

She hesitated, considering. "Monica had a phone call from Saxon Scott a few days ago. It upset her badly, though she wouldn't tell me why he called. That's when she went into this latest 'retreat' of hers."

"Has Mr. Scott kept in touch with her over the years?"

"Never—as far as I know. That's why his call was especially strange. I'm worried because I don't know what's up."

"You said you knew Saxon Scott—can't you ask him?"

Caution altered her expression. "Yes, I know him," she said shortly, and started up the granite steps leading to the garden above.

My momentary relief faded. As soon as it was possible, I must see Monica Arlen myself—and alone. I didn't know

41

what was going on, but the sooner I found out the better. Perhaps—and this was a new thought—I might even have some responsibility here.

Moving with a new determination, I climbed the stone steps and followed Linda through the narrow entrance into a glorious tropical garden.

Four

A STRETCH OF MOUNTAIN LEDGE HAD BEEN FILLED IN WITH SOIL, SO that fig and orange and plum trees thrived in this place of morning sunlight. A paloverde had been transplanted here, and in the central spot grew the little smoke tree that gave the house its name.

"Smoke trees usually grow in sandy washes in the desert," Linda said, "but this one has done well up here."

Following a natural ledge, the garden wound along the hillside, overlooking the red-tiled roofs of the house, its character changing from the cultivated to something wild and untended.

Keith ran ahead through a small latticework pavilion, also tiled in red. Its benches offered shelter from summer heat, and its open sides looked out over what we could see of Palm Springs beyond the roof of the house. A California gazebo. Farther along, we came upon a swimming pool that followed the mountain's contour in its curving form. A strip of tiles offered comfort for sunbathers, and there were deck chairs, empty now. In morning sunlight the water shone blue.

"She used to come up here to swim every morning," Linda said, "but lately she's stopped. She's lost interest in everything." Linda moved to one of the chairs and stretched out. "This is a good place to talk—away from the house. Keith, why don't you look around for a bit?"

"Okay. When can I go swimming, Mom?"

"Later," I said. "And not ever alone. Remember that."

Owen had seen to it that his son learned to swim at one of his own private clubs, and we often flew to St. Thomas to stay with a friend of Owen's, so Keith loved the water. I was grateful for those past luxuries now, since at least he could get some safe exercise that would be unavailable if we were hidden away in an apartment. Perhaps Keith's naturally adventurous spirit would return in these surroundings. If only I could remove the threat he feared so deeply and terribly.

As he ran off to explore, I too stretched out in one of the deck chairs and closed my eyes, wishing I could block out anxiety as easily as I could relax my body in the sun. I'd taken to jumping as nervously as Keith at every shadow, and every unknown corner seemed to hide an enemy.

"How will you live?" Linda asked, direct as always. "Do you have any money of your own? Will you keep on writing your Carol Hamilton pieces?"

"I must," I said. "I'll need to do a lot more with my writing now. I do have some savings, but I must earn an income as quickly as possible."

When I was first married, I'd been afraid that Owen might want me to give up writing. I hadn't realized then just how much he valued success. He never read my articles, but when they appeared in *Vogue*, or *Town and Country*, and other good magazines, he added my triumphs to his own. He enjoyed possessions that gave him class, did him honor, and since he didn't care what I did with "pin money," I put those modest payments away in my own account. He was amused that I kept my maiden name as a writer, Carol Hamilton, and simply took care to make it known where it counted, that I belonged to him.

During these last years I'd made it my specialty to write about the famous and successful—the very people who had always attracted my admiration and envy—and I'd developed a talent for coaxing them to talk to me. The fact that I was genuinely interested, that I really cared, got me past a good many guards. While I wanted to reveal the unexpected truth about those I interviewed, I tried to do it sympathetically. The hatchet, or the sneaky undercut, was never for me. Which was one of the reasons people were willing to talk to me. Now that my name was becoming known, good assignments came my way, and I would have to make that work for me in earnest now.

First, however, and before anything else, I must draw Keith back into a life where he could trust again, and feel love around him without threat.

"I suppose you'll go on writing interviews and articles about leading personalities?" Linda went on.

I opened my eyes and looked at her searchingly. She'd taken dark glasses from a pocket of her jeans, and I couldn't read her expression.

"That's probably what I do best, though I'm willing to write about anything that strikes me as interesting. Last night in the restaurant I even thought of introducing myself to Saxon Scott. Why didn't you tell me there was a Saxon's?"

Linda's mouth quirked, but I was not sure that her expression was mischievous. "I wanted you to be surprised."

"Perhaps he'd be a good person for me to start with, since I already know a lot about him. Do you suppose he'd be willing to talk to me?"

"Why not? I can get you an introduction, if you like."

"Mentioning that I'm related to Monica?"

"Naturally. He's a fascinating man, and kind as well, unless you step on his toes. Of course Monica will give you a whole other view of him."

I had to challenge her. "In all the time we've been corresponding, you've never once mentioned Saxon Scott. And when I've asked questions, you haven't answered. Why not?"

The dark glasses hid not only her eyes, but a good part of her face, and she turned her head away from me. "I don't know . . . divided loyalties, perhaps."

That was enigmatic, but I sensed that it was useless to follow up right now. The very turning of her head rejected my question, and I tried another tack.

"Do you know the story of their breakup?"

"Not all of it. That's one of the things Monica will never talk about. I've always wondered what would happen if they should come together again."

Her voice had softened, taking on a dreamy quality, and I sensed something gentler beneath the front Linda chose to show the world.

"I suspect you're basically a romantic," I said. "I've always been one too. Until lately. The idea of a meeting between those two is almost irresistible, isn't it?"

The softness vanished as she sat up and swung her feet to the tiles. "Not when I'm in my right mind! That's the sort of fantasy that only happens in old movies. Monica's feelings are fragile just now, and I don't want to see her badly hurt. But there's no reason why you shouldn't talk to Saxon Scott, if you want to."

"He hasn't given an interview in years. Still, I'd like to follow through, if you think he'd see me."

"Maybe nobody's asked him lately. Monica's always seemed the mysterious one—a better story. Especially since Saxon hasn't hidden himself away as she has. Her disappearing act increased her publicity value, you know. Though of course you'll be on tricky ground if you go after him. I mean, if Monica knew you were talking to him, there'd be no way to keep you here. She'd explode all over the place. Something happened all those years ago for which she's never forgiven him. And I think he feels the same way about her. It's the deep dark secret at the bottom of their whole estrangement. That's why it's so odd that he should phone her now. Maybe it's wiser if you stay out of it for a while as far as Saxon's concerned. Though I'll fix it up, if you want me to."

"I'll think about it," I said.

Linda Trevor was a little like the desert. She drifted and changed subtly under my very eyes. Or perhaps it was just that her true goals hadn't as yet become clear, and her

seeming turns and twists were really taking her in one direction—
if only I could discover what that direction was.

Suddenly everything seemed too quiet on the sunny moun-
tainside and my brief sense of relaxation disappeared. "I
wonder what Keith's doing?" I said, and left my chair.

"Go and look. You might as well reassure yourself. I'll
stay here."

Knowing he couldn't wander far, I hadn't noticed the
direction he'd taken. When I walked on beyond the pool, I
discovered another small garden growing lushly, unrestrained.
Wherever water and soil met, plants thrived in this oasis.
Water, it seemed, was less a problem than elsewhere in
California, tumbling down canyons, bubbling from the ground,
even piped clear up here.

"Keith?" I called. Birds twittered, and from the shade of a
sprawling, gray-trunked fig tree a quiet figure looked at me.
For an instant I was startled. Then I realized that the un-
clothed lady was sculpted in stone—a young, lithe figure,
nearly life size, with a real robin perched on one cool shoulder.
In some ways the work was crude, unfinished, but an impression of life had been brought into the stone. Or was it an
extension of life? That extra dimension that is art? Whoever
had created this figure had more than ordinary talent.

"I beg your pardon," I murmured, and retreated, almost
falling over the stone fawn that rested at the statue's feet.

What a strange whimsy in this hidden place, where few
must ever come. Twisted vines that crept around stone and the
stains from years of weathering told me that everything here
was old and neglected. In this unlikely spot, with the mountain itself in opposition, Monica had built her retreat long
ago. A place to which she could escape when Hollywood
became too much for her? A place that had now become her
entire world. A marble bench rested under the fig tree, and I
could imagine her coming here to sit quietly in the company
of the stone maiden. To meditate? To grieve for what she'd
lost?

More than ever, I wanted to meet her, come to know her.
Not just as she'd been in the past, but as she was now.

I still hadn't found Keith, and I returned to Linda resting beside the pool.

"He must have gone the other way," I said, and went back through the red-tiled summer house and into the more ordered garden, where some effort had been made to restrain tropical vegetation. Another of Ralph's duties, I supposed, since Linda had mentioned "gardener" among his functions.

Keith was here, and so was Annabella. He and the Siamese cat were playing a game with dry palm fronds. Seraphim and Cherubim watched sleepily from a spot of shade, and once more relief swept through me at the peaceful scene. How long would it last, this intense anxiety about my son? There must be an end to fear somewhere, and a truly safe life for us.

I turned to view Monica's house from this upper level, looking down on its tiled roof and rear gallery. That was when I saw her. She stood on her own balcony, a little way below me, looking up the mountain's steep rise to the garden above. She must have been watching Keith, but now she turned her full attention on me, and the shock of what I saw was devastating.

I had always spun my own fantasies about Arlen and Scott. Theirs was Romance as it should be. When I was very young, I thought it was what *I* wanted from life. Once, foolishly, I'd even imagined the impressive and overpowering Owen Barclay in Saxon Scott's dashing role. Those bright visions helped me as a child and a young woman, when everything else had been drab and lifeless. That this magical being—Monica Arlen—was related to me, had been something to cherish in all my daydreams. Even married to Owen, I'd clung to the dream, unwilling to let reality tarnish it.

Now, in a single moment, the enchantment vanished. Those passing years that had treated Saxon Scott kindly had destroyed Monica Arlen. Materialized before my eyes was a wraith, a revenant, gowned severely in gray. A ghostly presence that seemed unreal, unearthly. I could only stare in shock and dismay.

Time had carved her to the bone, melting away soft contours, not wrinkling so much as stretching taut. Her slender nose with its delicate nostrils, her marvelous high cheekbones, could never be disguised, but the beautiful slanted eyes that had seemed so exotic on a screen had sunk into dark hollows. The once soft chin that had given her face a genuine gentleness—what was known in those days as a feminine look—was a grim line now, etched in bone and sharpened by age. Her shoulders had rounded, and the hands that grasped the railing before her, emerging from beneath a fringed shawl, were no longer beautiful. Nor did she wear on her finger the famous intaglio emerald ring, as I'd imagined her doing. Even her hair had coarsened, neither its original blond nor the chestnut shade she'd sometimes adopted, but a dull gray without shine—a color that did nothing to flatter, though she still wore it in the exaggerated pageboy style that had been fashionable in her movie days.

She had been staring at me as intently as I stared at her. Now, abruptly, pointedly, she turned her back and disappeared into the house. Before I could speak, or manage a greeting, she had dismissed and rejected me. In an instant she had ceased to be a ghost and became a presence that refused to have anything to do with me. That rejected me outright. So much for foolish dreams! This was the end of the picture—an all too modern ending. I must leave the theater forever and go out into the cold where no such brightness as I'd seen in Monica Arlen would ever comfort me again.

Keith stared after her in disbelief. "Was *that* Aunt Monica?"

I shrugged in an effort to recover, and sat down on a rock near Keith. I didn't want him to guess my shock and disappointment. "People get older. We couldn't expect her to be like the pictures I have of her when she was young." But I *had* expected, however foolishly.

"I'm scared of her," Keith said.

"You needn't be." I tried to sound reassuring. Keith must never guess how badly the brief, silent exchange had shaken me, and I tried to sound reasonable as I went on. "No one likes getting old. Especially someone who was beautiful when she was young."

"She doesn't want us here."

That was obvious, but I tried again for his sake. "Perhaps not, darling. But Linda thinks she'll change her mind."

His father had seen to it that Keith was never allowed those silver dreams that had nourished me for so long, and he believed none of this. The cat was more interesting to him, and much more real. He was becoming too fearful of human relationships, which, after all, had so often failed him.

For a few moments longer the back of the house offered an emptiness in which nothing moved, and I sat very still on my rock, too stunned for any activity. Only Annabella's need for "conversation" broke the mountain's silence. I was still trying to absorb my shock when a man burst suddenly through a lower door of the house and came running up to the garden level, shouting Linda's name. He was a stocky, slightly balding little man with a healthy tan and an excitable manner. To my New York accustomed eyes, his clothes seemed blindingly colorful—a firehouse-red shirt overhanging plaid pants of no accepted tartan.

When he saw Keith, the cats, and me, he stopped to regard us in surprise. "Oops! I was looking for Linda. I'm Wally Davis."

I remembered Linda's friend, her fiancé, whom she'd mentioned occasionally in her letters.

"Linda's over by the pool," I said. "I'm Carol Hamilton, and this is my son, Keith. Monica Arlen is my great-aunt."

Wally Davis had a plump, rather expressive face, and it changed from astonishment to recognition of my name. "Oh— you're the writer from New York? Linda didn't tell me you were coming."

"I didn't know myself."

He lowered his voice and nodded toward the balcony. "How is *she* taking it? Your coming here, I mean?"

"Not very well, I'm afraid. Linda wants me to be patient."

"Mm." He continued to stare at me with the searching air of a man who considers how to use this new piece of a puzzle. He paid little attention to Keith, and ignored Annabella's insistent comments.

"Well, come along," he directed. "I have something exciting to tell Linda, and maybe you're part of it now too."

Without waiting for me to precede him, he dashed ahead toward the pool, moving with remarkable alacrity for so rotund a man. It would have been hard to guess his age, because he had the sort of face that was unlikely to fade into wrinkles, though I knew from Linda's letters that he was thirty-nine—a little younger than she was.

"You can stay and play with Annabella, if you like," I told Keith, and followed Wally Davis toward the pool.

He was already bouncing around Linda's chair when I got there, and I thought unflatteringly of a colorful beach ball. She'd taken off her dark glasses, and her enormous brown eyes with their extraordinary lashes watched him with an amusement that was not entirely affectionate.

"Do calm down, Wally. I can't make head or tail of what you're saying. Have you met Carol?"

He waved me aside. "Yes, yes! You're just not listening! There's going to be a benefit at the Annenberg Theater in the museum. To honor some of the older stars who first came here from Hollywood. You know—the real thing."

"That should be a good fund raiser," Linda said dryly, "though not exactly original."

"Oh, it will be! Everybody's thrilled about my contribution. I've suggested that they make it an Arlen-Scott affair and show *Mirage*. That El Mirador scene in the picture gives it a tie-in with Palm Springs. Then if we can get Monica and Saxon to come out on the stage together and receive an award—that will be the whole show. A first! After all these years, together again!"

"You're a lunatic." Linda's tone was still not entirely fond. "You know perfectly well that Monica never leaves this house unless she's in disguise. And she hates Saxon. She'd never set foot on the same stage with him. Nor would he with her. Don't be a fool."

"Ah-hah!" Wally sounded triumphant. "That's where you're wrong. I've already talked to Saxon and he's agreed. *If* we can get Monica to appear."

Linda shook her head. "It's not remotely possible. I'm even surprised that *he* would agree. And I know damned well how upset she'd be if I even suggested it. Or breathed it!"

I was sure she was right. The woman I'd just seen would

prefer to hide forever from a world that remembered only her beauty.

Wally was still circling Linda's chair, but now he stopped before me. "Maybe *you* can manage it?"

"With Aunt Monica?" I shook my head as vigorously as Linda. "She hasn't even met me. She's made it quite clear she doesn't want anything to do with me. And she's told Linda that we must leave. I saw her just now, and she pointedly turned her back on me and went inside before I could say a word. I hardly think I'd have any influence."

The small-boy delight went out of Wally Davis, but his determination never wavered. "Then we'll have to dream up something else. This is too good a chance to pass by. Never—not once since I've worked for Saxon, has he agreed to meet Monica. I've always said it would be top publicity, and he's always refused."

"You work for Mr. Scott?" I asked in surprise.

Linda explained before he could answer. "Wally is an entrepreneur of the old school. PR is his racket. He'd have thrived in early Hollywood. He keeps an eye on Saxon's affairs, and he lives and breathes publicity."

"But not for Sax," Wally said. "He won't allow me full rein. Though I've done a bit for his restaurant. The Mirage Room was my idea. He's always wanted to play it cool, stay in the background—until now. We could pack a theater ten times the size of the Annenberg if we could get those two together in public. Do you know how many times they've both been invited to present awards at the Oscar ceremonies?"

Linda changed the subject abruptly. "Never mind all that dream stuff. Is there any word yet about Al Brampton?"

"Does *she* know?" Wally glanced at me.

"I haven't told her yet, but I might as well. It's very bad news, Carol. I didn't want to worry you any more than you were already worried, but you have to know. Al Brampton has managed Monica's business investments for years, and we'd all trusted him."

"Not me!" Wally broke in. "And no, there's nothing new on the whole fiasco."

"Al skipped the country just a month ago," Linda said,

52

"and he took most of Monica's fortune with him. He must have been preparing this for a long time. Now she has hardly anything left. But it needn't affect you immediately, Carol. She may have to unload this place, and certainly her house in Beverly Hills. I don't know how good she'll be at tightening her belt."

"She could start making appearances again," Wally put in. "Give lectures or readings or something. She could name her own price."

I felt a sudden pity for the wraith I'd seen on the balcony. The idea of even one "appearance" seemed remote. No one would want to see *this* Monica Arlen. A sadness for her came over me, as well as new alarm for myself and Keith. Where else could we go? Where could we turn?

"It's a wonderful plan, Wally," Linda assured him more kindly. "But you'd better forget about asking her, even if Saxon is willing to appear."

He jutted out his chin stubbornly, and I suspected that he wasn't always cheerful and good-natured. There was a hint of bulldog here, and a suggestion that if he could reach the end he wanted, any means might do.

"Well, okay for now," he said. "I've got to get going. Do bring it up with Monica anyway."

"Can't you stay for lunch?" Linda asked. "Jason will be here too."

"All the more reason not to stay." Wally rolled his eyes at me. "Linda's brother doesn't consider me the best possible match for his sister." He dropped a quick kiss on Linda's cheek, gave me a casual wave of his hand, and rushed away, leaving the air behind in furious motion.

I was still staring after him when Linda spoke in the same dry tone I'd heard before. "I expect my main appeal for Wally is my connection with Monica Arlen."

"You don't sound very much in love."

"Who's talking about love? Marriage isn't always dependent on love. We're useful to each other, and I suppose we even complement each other. Neither of us is the type for a great and glorious romance, and anyway, marriage is a long way off, if ever. I met him through Saxon."

I returned to the question that had puzzled me earlier. "From your letters I never guessed that you knew Saxon Scott."

A slight, unexpected flush brightened Linda's cheeks, and I considered her reaction thoughtfully. One blushed for shame, embarrassment, guilt. Perhaps all three?

"Exactly what are you up to?" I asked bluntly.

"Nothing you need worry about, Carol." Her slightly cynical air of mockery fell away, and once more she reminded me of changing desert sands. "Anyway, I'd never do anything to hurt Monica. She has to come first with me. There's no one else to look after her. I just couldn't explain to you about Saxon in a letter, and frankly I don't want to explain now. Can you just leave it alone—take me on trust?"

I wasn't sure how far I could take her on trust, but I would have to try. Without Linda, and with Monica's obvious rejection, I was lost until I could find another place to hide, a place where we could heal our wounds and build a new life.

"If you want it that way," I said. "You know how grateful I am to you, and I don't want to make any more difficulties. I've caused enough trouble, judging by the way Aunt Monica looked at me just now."

Linda stretched and stood up. "I'd better go and see if she's all right. We're having an early lunch—eleven-thirty—since that's when Jason is free. I'm anxious to have you meet him."

I couldn't think about her brother now. "About this Brampton—the manager who's skipped—" I began.

"Not now, please, Carol. We're still trying to put the pieces together. Of course I had to tell Monica, and she's upset about it, though she doesn't quite believe it yet. The telephone call from Saxon is what really shocked her. If she would just tell me . . ." She left the thought unfinished.

"I'll collect Keith and we'll get ready for lunch," I said, moving toward the house.

A cloud crossed the sun and in the momentary shade I saw that the little smoke tree really bore out its name. Its thin, rather hairy foliage drifted like a haze of smoke, and in a strong wind I could imagine that it would blow like smoke.

When I called Keith, he left Annabella reluctantly. At least I was glad he'd made a friend.

As we went down the stone steps at the back, Ralph Reese came into view.

"She wants you," he told Linda. "She's in a real frenzy."

"I was just going up," Linda said. "Run along, Carol. We'll meet for drinks before lunch."

She went off and Ralph followed us into the house, his good-looking face marred by an expression of perpetual malice.

"I'm sorry if my coming has upset my aunt," I told him.

"Oh, she won't be upset for long. She'll recover as soon as you're gone."

He turned to give Keith a more friendly grin and disappeared toward the kitchen. I learned later that he ate all his meals with Monica, carrying up her trays and serving her, then sitting down to offer the only company she chose to tolerate just now. Though I disliked him, I could see that he sang for his supper in his own way.

While Keith, always independent, got into clean jeans and a pullover sweater, I took a small folder from my suitcase and sat on the edge of the bed to look through it. I needed some touch with my own realities before I dressed and went downstairs. Again and again, these few pictures had brought me a thread of comfort when my life had begun to seem intolerable.

There were two or three old snapshots of the parents I could barely recall. They weren't nearly so real to me as Monica had become. I stared at a favorite small photo of Monica, and tried to find something reassuring in her remembered face. But this was a face that no longer existed. It was as if Monica too had died—long ago—and as I studied the picture, foolish tears of loss came into my eyes. How terrible the change in her—and how young, how untouched by life was the lovely face in the print.

"Hey, Mom, you getting ready?" Keith prodded me.

There was no more comfort for me in old pictures. I put the folder away and got dressed. I hadn't much choice in the few things I'd brought, but my white linen skirt and a violet silk blouse would do. I changed my loafers for white sandals, and was as ready as I could be to face whatever else this disturbing day held for me. By this time I had no confidence in Linda's assurance that she would persuade Aunt Monica to let us stay for a while. Especially not with financial ruin facing her. And of course now *I* had to accept that all those letters I'd written to my famous aunt had never been addressed to anyone real, but only to someone who existed entirely in my imagination.

Keith had gone to stand on the front balcony of our room and was staring out over the low rooftops of Palm Springs. He had returned to one of the long silences that so troubled me.

"What are you thinking about?" I asked.

He turned, his small face devoid of expression. "About *him.*"

Not "my father"—"him." That was what Owen had done to his son. During the time when he'd taken Keith, Owen had even told him that I was dead and he should forget me. That fear too haunted his dreams and his silences, and sometimes made him cling to me.

Once more I tried to reassure him. "We're safe here, darling."

"Not if *she* won't let us stay."

"Linda thinks Aunt Monica will come around. So let's not worry. Linda's brother Jason, who works for the Desert Museum, is coming to lunch. That should be fun."

I wasn't sure it would be, since Linda had said her brother disapproved of her working for Monica, but it was the best I could offer. We sat on the balcony, waiting until it was time to go downstairs. Keith came to lean against me, and I held him close. There had been times when he could hardly bear to let me out of his sight.

Before long, a battered Dodge station wagon came up the one-way private road from town, and we watched as Jason Trevor parked beside Linda's car and got out. Then we went inside and down to the small formal drawing room. Linda hadn't appeared as yet, and I supposed she must be having a difficult time with Monica.

Her brother came in from bright sunlight to join us. "Hello," he said. "I'm Jason Trevor, Linda's brother."

I held out my hand and introduced Keith and myself.

He shook my hand rather coolly, and then took the hand my son thrust at him almost belligerently. Keith had begun to show a distrust of any man, so that it had been a relief when he'd accepted Ralph so readily. Owen, who could dispense with the idea of good manners for himself when he chose, had nevertheless insisted that his son be well taught—on however superficial a level. So Keith was going through the proper motions, even though suspicion was clearly uppermost.

"Hi," Jason said, accepting his hand, but not the challenge. "I was thinking about you this morning. I'm taking some kids on a field trip soon, and perhaps you'd like to come along. We'll have a great time, and even learn a few things about desert animals. Do you like animals?"

I spoke too hastily. "We're not able to go out anywhere at all just now."

Keith's face had brightened, but now he looked stoic again. Fun wasn't something he expected of life and I changed my course quickly, knowing I couldn't let my own fears, however real, do this to him.

"Keith's always been interested in animals," I said. "Perhaps we can manage a visit to the museum before long."

"That will be fine," Jason said smoothly, and went to sit in one of the damask chairs.

"Let me show you something I found in the desert a few days ago," he said to Keith, and took a small package from his pocket.

I watched, finding that Linda's brother resembled her very little. He was tall and his brown hair had been sun-bleached until it was almost blond. Its thickness encroached on his forehead as though combing didn't particularly interest him. His features were strong, well defined, and on the rugged side. A Palm Springs tan was startlingly dark in contrast to his hair, and vertical concentration lines centered his forehead between brown eyes that had a tendency to squint. As though he'd looked too long into a burning landscape.

If he noticed the bruise on Keith's face, he gave no sign as he showed him the small white skull of a desert creature—a kangaroo rat. Keith was immediately fascinated, and as they talked Jason Trevor continued to ignore me to the point where I began to feel invisible. From his first greeting I'd sensed his hostility toward me, and I resented its unfairness. My connection with Monica hardly justified his dislike of me.

When Linda joined us, she was still shaking from what must have been a thoroughly unpleasant scene. She threw herself onto the sofa beside me and reached gratefully for a glass as Helsa offered a tray.

"I need this! Try it, Carol. It's fruit and rum and a few other touches—something Monica Arlen invented a long time ago." As Helsa went off, Linda spoke to Keith. "Would you like to help get lunch on the table?"

Keith followed Helsa willingly, always glad of action. The moment he'd gone, Linda burst into words.

"I've told Monica everything about why you're here. I've never seen her quite like this. I really didn't think your coming would throw her so badly. I had to promise to send you away as soon as possible. That was the only way to get her quiet. But don't worry—I'm not going to do anything of the sort." She thrust out her chin, looking as stubborn as Wally. "We'll wait her out."

I sipped my cool drink and said nothing. Desolation flowed through me in a tide I could no longer swim against.

Linda continued, speaking now to Jason. "I've told Carol that you know why she's here. Maybe you'll have some ideas that will help. It's not as though she can't earn her own living—and very well, given a little time. She's a good writer and there are always loads of fascinating people to write about in Palm Springs."

This hardly mattered if we weren't allowed to stay at Smoke Tree House. Monica's rejection—first when I'd seen her on the balcony, and now through Linda—left me despairing. Hurt went as deep as the fear. So much had been lost so quickly, and the fact that some of this was due to my own rosy illusions didn't help. The ground had been cut from under me.

If Linda's brother had anything useful to offer, he kept it to himself, and in spite of my devastation, I was aware of his continuing critical reserve. How I wished that Linda hadn't arranged this uncomfortable meeting in the first place.

Helsa announced that lunch was served, and I tried to get myself in hand. Not for anything did I want Jason Trevor to guess what I was feeling. I had to meet his hostility with indifference and a pretense of poise, no matter how much I resented it.

The dining room was pleasant, with its long polished table, old silver, crystal, and woven place mats in an Indian design. It seemed agreeably cool, thanks to the tiled floor and a minimum of draperies, which gave it a feeling of air and space.

Not until we began with plates of clear soup did Jason return to Linda's comment. "Do you write only about personalities, Mrs. Barclay?"

I didn't trouble to correct the name, but Linda did it for me, all too quickly. With an effort I tried to speak as though what we were saying really mattered.

"I write about whatever interests me and might interest readers," I told him abruptly.

"If you don't have to concentrate on individuals, you might like to write about the Desert Museum," he suggested. "Of course there have been a lot of articles published about it, but coming in with a fresh eye, you might find a new approach."

He spoke courteously enough, but I heard the edge of challenge in his words, and I knew I hadn't been mistaken. Linda's brother seemed determined to carry his antagonism toward Monica Arlen over to me. Though my relationship to her hardly seemed a good enough reason.

I tried to answer him evenly. "I've written about museums before. New York museums, Washington museums. What is special about this one?"

His smile lifted the sharp lines around his mouth and lessened the severity of his look. "You'll have to see for yourself. I suppose we feel it's unique. People come from all over the world to study what we offer."

He seemed to warm a little as he spoke, and I knew that his enthusiasm was genuine. This was what he cared about.

"What kind of museum is it, really?" I asked. "What's its focus?"

"It has several. Natural history, of course—that's my department. The physical elements of the area. Whatever lives and grows in the desert and nearby mountains, the forces that created it all. There's a section on Indian arts too, since quite a few Indians live here. There was a curious land arrangement made here a long time ago. Alternate sections of land were given to Indians off the reservations, and these are still held by local Indians, who lease the land to home-owners and businesses. The result's what's been called our checkerboard."

"The museum goes in for the visual and performing arts, too," Linda said. "Paintings and sculpture, music, dance, film—there's a lot going on during the season."

"When is your season?" I asked.

"The cooler months. In summer the museum closes down."

"If I'm here long enough, I'd like to see the museum," I said, wondering if I would still be here in Smoke Tree House by tomorrow.

"Of course you'll stay!" Linda said vehemently. "So don't talk as if you were leaving. This—this rejection of Monica's is temporary. You'll see."

It wasn't temporary that her wealth was gone, and with it perhaps this very house.

"Are we moving somewhere else?" Keith asked, and I heard the familiar tension in his voice.

"You're staying right here, honey," Linda assured him, and he relaxed enough to regard the salad bowl Helsa had brought him with normal small-boy suspicion.

Jason noticed. "We're great on avocados out here, so you'd better start being a Californian," he said cheerfully.

The rest of the luncheon passed smoothly enough, with our talk kept safely innocuous. Yet all through it I was aware of trouble that lay beneath the surface merely being postponed. The crises were still waiting to erupt, and Keith and I were strangers without a home.

Keith finished his lemon ice and Helsa's homemade cookies and asked to be excused. The plaintive Annabella was waiting for him on the terrace, with the white Persians in attendance, and he ran to join them.

When he'd gone, Jason put a direct question to me without beating around the bush. "Just so I get the legalities clear— are you free to take your son across the country without letting his father know?"

"I'm the custodial parent," I told him. "That was the court's decision, and since I waived any support from my husband, I can do as I please. No, Mr. Trevor, I haven't broken any laws."

"She's just run away from the most awful brutality!" Linda burst out. "You've seen Keith's face. His father did that."

I didn't want to go into any of this with a man I'd just met, who seemed to dislike me for no good reason. Yet I had to make my position clear.

"It's not the law I'm afraid of," I said. "It's Owen Barclay. I want Keith to have a chance to get over what's happened in this last terrible year. He must be able to grow up without being afraid all the time. Whether or not his father will allow that, I don't know."

"That's why I told her to come here," Linda said.

"What do you think your ex-husband will do?" Jason asked. It was the same question Linda had put to me, but coming from this man it seemed curt and too direct. Yet when I looked at him again, reluctantly, I saw for the first time the face of a sensitive, thoughtful man, who was regarding me with a good deal of doubt.

I tried to answer honestly. "Once he knows where we are, Owen will turn California upside down to get his son back. And that won't take him long to discover. Laws don't really matter to him."

"Most fathers value their children," Jason said quietly.

"Yes!" In spite of myself I sounded indignant and defensive, and I made an effort to lower my voice. "Especially a son. A son is a symbol! Of blood, of heritage, perhaps of immortality. Only I don't care about all that. I only care about *Keith*. He's a boy—a real live boy, not a symbol. And he's been badly wounded in a lot of ways. Some of them don't show on the surface."

I didn't know whether I'd convinced Jason Trevor or not, and I really didn't care. Before I could say anything else, there was a startling interruption.

A woman had appeared in the open doorway to the terrace.

With the light behind her, so that her face was in shadow, she looked as beautiful and enchanting as I remembered her from all those films I'd seen. Her hair was a reddish chestnut— the color of the wig she'd worn for *Mirage*—and it curled in gently just above her shoulders. Her pale gown caught the color of the smoke tree, with a slash of crimson ribbon at the waist, and it floated about her, lifting like mist as she moved. In one hand she held a delicate, long-stemmed blue iris made of silk, and on the other flashed the deep green of the famous intaglio ring—the emerald ring that Saxon Scott had given her all those years ago.

Monica Arlen had made up her mind, and she had stepped out of the past to join us.

FIVE

I HEARD LINDA GASP AND STOLE A LOOK AT HER. SHE SEEMED both dumbfounded and entranced. Jason revealed nothing at all in the guarded expression he'd assumed, while I was too stunned to move.

It was Monica Arlen who held the stage. She was perfectly aware of what sunlight would do to the illusion she was creating, and she kept it carefully behind her, letting it backlight her as she approached an empty chair at the table. Jason rose and seated her, behaving admirably, as though her appearance in the role she was playing was an everyday matter. She placed the slightly shabby silk iris on the table beside her empty place, and when Helsa appeared from the kitchen she nodded regally.

"Just coffee, please, Helsa."

Four words, yet the old, whispery magic of that voice was there, unmarred by age, untouched by time. She had made up her face delicately and with a skill she hadn't forgotten, so that it didn't seem a painted mask, but enhanced those famous cheekbones and brought out the sunken eyes that still slanted in their own exotic way. It was a masquerade—a mirage of her own, perhaps—but skillfully, beautifully carried off. I felt as though I'd been given a reprieve. Perhaps my old, exciting dreams needn't be discarded after all.

Ralph appeared suddenly from the terrace and stood behind her. Without turning her head, she seemed to know he was there.

"Go away," she told him. "I don't need a keeper."

He shrugged and went outside to talk to Keith. Monica continued as though there had been no interruption. She'd acknowledged Jason's presence with no more than a remote "Thank you."

"So you are Carol?" the lovely voice went on—quite ignoring the fact that she'd turned her back on me, wanted nothing to do with me until this very moment. I couldn't speak, and I only nodded.

"I remember all those lovely letters you used to write me," she continued. "I'm sorry I was such a poor correspondent. I've always preferred the spoken word. Linda tells me you're a professional writer now. You showed promise even when you were very young. Did she tell you I still have every one of those letters of yours?"

"It's true," Linda said. "They're all tied up in special boxes."

I felt a lump rising in my throat, tears in my eyes. She could still weave the old enchantment, play on the emotions, and I was a sentimental captive to her charm. Besides, listening to her, watching her, a little of my own despair was abating.

Helsa brought coffee, and set a small blue pot of honey at Monica's place. I watched, fascinated, as she stirred a scant teaspoon into her coffee with a patterned silver spoon. No one had found much to say since the Star had made her dramatic entrance. She didn't seem to notice or mind. Perhaps she expected us to be stunned. Now she went on conversationally.

"Linda told me about that awful man you married, and how badly he's treated you and your son. Men! You did the right thing in coming here to me. You must stay as long as you like, of course, and I'll help you in any way I can."

I managed a faint "Thank you." Whatever had caused this surprising reversal, I was grateful for it; grateful for the fact that she clearly meant to remain at Smoke Tree House herself, however unrealistic this might now appear.

"So you're a writer?" She was half musing to herself. "I admire writers, since I have none of that skill myself. We actors would never amount to anything if words weren't put into our mouths. Are you going to do some writing now?"

"Yes, Aunt Monica," I found myself answering like an obedient child. "I hope to get to work very soon."

She nodded, and the smooth chestnut hair in its pageboy cut moved gently, if a little stiffly, above her shoulders. "And what are you going to write about?"

"Perhaps I'll do a piece about the Desert Museum. Mr. Trevor has been telling me about it."

"Ah, yes—the museum. I watched it being built right down there below my terrace. Though oddly enough, all I've seen of it are the roofs. They've wanted me to come to functions down there, of course, but I've refused all invitations. Someday I must visit it quietly, when no one knows. There's something there I'd especially like to see. And I understand they've put in a perfect little theater."

"It is perfect," Linda said. "You'd love it."

I sensed that Linda had fallen captive too, and I wondered if she might take this opportunity to mention Wally Davis' bold scheme for bringing Arlen and Scott together again at the benefit. She said nothing, however.

"What else will you write about?" Monica looked at me directly.

I decided to be bold myself. "I'd like very much to do an interview with Saxon Scott, if it's possible."

I remembered that lift of her shoulders, the very tilt of her chin, as she bristled. The masquerade was nearly perfect, and I found myself wishing she might never have to face the light.

"Saxon? What nonsense! Ridiculous! He's a very dull man by this time, I'm sure. He goes in for restaurants and golf courses. He's forgotten what he once was. I have never forgotten—so why don't you write about *me?*"

I stared at her in astonishment. "Do you mean you'd really let me? Would you talk to me?"

"I might. Providing you were willing to tell the *truth.*"

"Carol, what a wonderful idea!" Linda sounded suddenly excited. "Though it would make too long an article. Perhaps you'd need to turn it into a book."

"Oh, of course a book," Monica said complacently. "I've kept all my papers and photographs, and Linda has catalogued everything faithfully. So much has never been published—all sorts of memorabilia saved. The truth has never really been told. I've refused interviews for so many years that this will be fresh for readers."

"You've never been forgotten. I'd be lucky to have the chance to write about you," I said, sounding breathless and young to my own ears. To write about Monica Arlen had seemed something beyond my reach. The very thought of going back into that dreamworld legitimately enchanted me.

Jason made a sound that barely escaped being derisive. "If you'll excuse me, I've got to get back to work. Thanks for lunch, Linda. Good-bye, Miss Arlen. And I'm glad to know you, Miss—uh—Hamilton."

He sounded more mocking than glad.

"I'd still like to see your museum when it's possible," I said, challenging his derision.

"I share it with Palm Springs." He sounded as dry as his sister sometimes did. "Come down at ten tomorrow morning and bring your son. Just ask for me."

I thanked him stiffly, and he bowed to Monica, who still seemed scarcely aware of him, lost in her own preoccupation with herself. When he'd gone out to his car, she picked up the iris and waved it gently by its long, wired stem.

"I wasn't sure I had this anymore. But the moment I found it, I knew what I would do. You should have seen your face, Linda dear. You've been thinking of me as an old woman, haven't you?"

"I've never thought of you as anything but Monica Arlen,"

Linda said loyally. "You've been pretending to be old ever since I came here. So I'm glad you've shed your make-believe."

She couldn't have said it better, and Monica's eyes, so deep-set now, yet still with that slightly exotic slant, glowed with satisfaction.

"We'll have a talk soon," she promised me. "Perhaps when you come back from the museum tomorrow we can begin."

I hoped she wouldn't change her mind. Every writer of short pieces thinks of someday writing a book. That had always seemed far ahead to me. Now the moment was here and I wanted desperately to take the ambitious step. It would test me, stretch me out, demand everything I could bring to the task. Failure would not only be humiliating, but it could also mean a loss of income because of time invested in something I might not be ready to handle. There could also be disappointment for Monica, if she chose me as her biographer and I failed. She must have turned down a good many writers and publishers in the past. But none of these potential difficulties could lessen the surge of excitement that went through me. I *wanted* to write about Monica Arlen more than anything I'd ever thought of doing, and *I* was the right one to do it. If such a biography succeeded, the income from it might be something I could share with her—and that was an intoxicating thought. To help the woman who had been my idol for so long would be wonderfully satisfying.

She was still waving the silken iris that had been her signature in the old days, holding it delicately by its stem, so that the blue petals moved back and forth in a gesture I'd first seen when she'd used it in a picture. My imagination leaped ahead.

"We could put your iris on the jacket," I said dreamily. "And on the inside cloth cover. Stamped in gold on azure blue cloth. Perhaps we could even use it as a symbol at the opening of each new chapter."

"What?" Monica had been lost in her own make-believe and came back to the present querulously, the role of her younger self slipping a little. "What are you talking about?"

Linda laughed. "Carol's already printing the book about you!"

"I know," I said. "But that's the way it is when a really wonderful idea comes along. I begin to see everything about it all at once—like a mosaic that's already putting itself together."

Monica's moving hands, the veins and brown spots made invisible by her quick gestures, further caught my imagination with their familiar enchanting grace. I hurried on, lost in my own fantasy.

"That emerald ring is part of the mosaic! I must write about that as well. May I see it, please?"

The ring hung loosely on her thin finger, and I could see why she wouldn't wear it much anymore. She slipped it off and gave it to me across the table. Sunlight still backlighted her and I couldn't see her face sharply, but the touch of her fingers felt cold on mine, and the ring was cold, too, as I took it. The great square emerald that fanciful writers had likened to an oasis in the desert glowed green in my hand as I turned it about. The setting had been imaginatively wrought, with tiny gold iris leaves instead of prongs, intricately twisted to hold the gem. The intaglio carving of the flower was tiny and simple in its execution, though quite perfectly an iris.

"What a search was made for that stone!" It was Monica who sounded dreamy now. "That's a Colombian emerald, you know. They're the finest in the world. Of course the emerald and the color green have always belonged to Venus—that's what Saxon said, and he thought it appropriate." Her voice hardened a little. "You can see how brilliant it is, with no trace of yellow or blue. An elegant, unique stone!"

"Your secretary, Peg Smith, carved it, didn't she?" Linda asked.

Sadly, Monica nodded. "She was my friend as well. A gifted artist, you know. The one person I could really trust. You can see that the one is a small masterpiece in itself. Usually such carving is done on lesser stones to hide a flaw or lack of clarity. But Peg herself found this perfect emerald, and it cost Saxon a pretty penny. How we flung money around in those days!

I was holding a bit of romantic history in my hand. Monica watched me, and after a moment she went on.

"I wore it on my right hand during the picture, but it was really an engagement ring. We were going to be married when we finished making *Mirage!*"

"How wonderful." Linda sounded rapt. "You never told me that. Saxon Scott and Monica Arlen!"

"I seem to remember reading something Louella Parsons wrote about the ring," I said.

"She made up most of that. We didn't tell anyone, except Peggy, of course, since she was part of the secret. I've never spoken about our breakup, but perhaps now—if Carol writes this book—the time has come to talk."

Linda and I exchanged a quick look and kept very still, waiting for revelations.

Monica was lost in the past. "Of course it wasn't any secret when we parted and our careers ended. I was miserable—thoroughly unhappy before that picture was finished, and Saxon was behaving horribly. So there wasn't any marriage, though he wouldn't take back his ring."

I watched her, absorbed in what she was saying, savoring this moment. When she'd rejected even the sight of me earlier, the shock had as much to do with the destruction of a myth I'd lived for, as with my worry about where we would go if Monica put us out. The darkening of a bright beacon that had pulled me through so many bad times was devastating. Now, even though age lay heavily upon her, she could still summon old illusion, and make us believe. I loved her for that. She was still my beacon, even though my feeling for her was tinged with sorrow.

Monica had never had a small mouth, and cameras always played up its full-lipped lusciousness and up-at-the-corners warmth. Which made it all the more sad to see how the years had pinched it, taken away that wide generosity of the lips. Now her smile was thin and melancholy.

"What a terrible loss when Peggy died!" she went on. "She was a gifted sculptor, though I'm afraid I kept her so busy with my affairs that she never had much time to develop her own talents. I'm sorry about that now. I still have a few pieces she did. Some of them are large-scale sculptures, but she liked to work in miniature too, with gold and gems. So when Saxon asked her to design a ring for our engagement, she found the emerald after months of searching. She did the incising herself with the iris in reverse relief, working in Paris with a man from Cartier's. She even made the setting and mounted the stone—everything.'' Monica broke off, touching the ring as I held it out to her. "So much talent lost, wasted, never brought fully to what it might have been. I was partly to blame. Why she had to die, I'll never understand.''

"It was suicide, of course,'' Linda reminded me. "She was found out in the desert, where she went to kill herself. She—''

"Let's not talk about that!'' Monica broke in. "It was all too terrible, too senseless.'' Abruptly, she repudiated the ring. "No—you keep it, Carol. It reminds me of too much I can't bear to think about. And my fingers are too thin for it now. You can't write about any of *this* in your book.''

I said nothing. I'd been told this before by those I was interviewing, and I always respected my subjects' wishes. But in Monica's case, these were the very things I would need to write about. Clearly I must be careful with my questions until she was ready to trust me, ready to talk.

In a sudden change of mood, Monica laughed, and the sound had a bitter echo, its musical quality harshened.

"I surprised you, didn't I?'' she challenged us. "Ralph thought I was crazy when I started downstairs looking like this. But what does he know? I had a feeling that I could still do *her*—that I wanted to do her—that Monica Arlen of a long time ago. And I succeeded, didn't I? In being my real self again?''

"You're marvelous,'' I told her warmly, and slipped the ring on the fourth finger of my right hand. "I'll be proud to wear this for a little while, but of course I'll give it back to you.''

Monica sighed and began, quite visibly, to fall apart before our eyes. The crumbling was from the inside out, as though the strength of spirit that had driven her until now had finally sapped her energy, leaving only a shell that she presented to the world. Her performance had been due not only to the trappings of wig and costume, but to something inner that was suddenly gone. Curiously, it was as if seeing me put on her emerald had subtly drained her own fading vitality.

Linda got up quickly. "I'll help you to your room, if you like."

Monica could still lift her chin and answer sharply. "No! Call Ralph. He can get me up the stairs. He's a stupid boy, but useful. And he can play the game when I want him to. He can pretend I'm really the old Monica Arlen, even though he's never even seen *Mirage*."

Her laughter had a faintly wicked sound as Ralph appeared at Linda's signal and helped Monica from the table. What a fascinating and complex woman she was. She would have been wonderful to write about even if she hadn't been a legend.

At the terrace door, she turned to speak to me again. "When you visit the Desert Museum tomorrow, you'll find a small piece of me there. Ask Linda's brother to show it to you."

Then she was gone, and I sat staring after her, entirely spellbound.

"Well!" Linda said, and I heard excitement in her voice. "She's always pulling these reversals. But I didn't dream she had *this* in her anymore. Your coming has made a big difference. Perhaps now the whole story will come out. And Saxon—" She broke off abruptly and the odd, almost guilty flush that I'd noticed before rose in her cheeks. I had never seen a mature woman who could blush so easily, and I wondered again what *her* secrets were.

"Why didn't you tell her what your friend Wally is planning?" I asked. "I mean about the benefit affair at the museum, with Monica and Saxon onstage together? This would have been a good moment to reach her."

The flush faded and Linda regarded me with amusement. "I didn't tell her because you're going to," she said.

Before I could protest, Keith came in from the terrace looking woebegone because he'd lost his playmate—Ralph.

71

"Mom, what shall I do now?" It was the familiar cry of childhood.

"Let's go upstairs and see what we can find," I said.

From the first, I'd known that it would be hard to keep an active little boy occupied without ever taking him out, and I wondered if I might do as Jason had suggested and bring him with me to the museum tomorrow. It was so close to the house. And surely Owen's thugs wouldn't be active in Palm Springs this soon.

As we went through Linda's office, the phone rang on her desk. She picked it up, and the sudden tension in her voice stopped me.

"No," she said. "There's no such person here. You must have the wrong number."

"Run upstairs," I told Keith. "I'll be there in a minute." Then I turned back to Linda.

"It was a man who asked for Mrs. Barclay," she said. "But Monica's telephone isn't listed. So how did he get this number?"

"Owen can always find out whatever he wants. What did the voice sound like?"

"Rough. Not at all cultured."

"He wouldn't call. Not the first time. He'd want to make sure first. And he has a good voice on the phone. He must already know where I am. Oh, Linda, what am I to do?"

"Take it easy. He can't climb in here on the telephone wire."

Once more I could glimpse what my life in the next months—years?—was likely to be, even while Smoke Tree House offered us a temporary haven. I would shy at shadows, jump at the sound of a telephone ringing, be constantly terrified for Keith's safety—if I allowed myself to live like that. I knew Owen well enough to realize that he would do everything he possibly could to frighten me, and would enjoy doing it. But I was no longer as weak, or as vulnerable, as he might think me. Somehow, I must find a way to win this battle. Win it on a permanent basis—for life.

Writing about Monica Arlen could be a big step in the direction of freedom. I might even be in a position to use publicity itself against Owen if I had to. The very fact that Monica had refused interviews for so long gave me a certain power. The public and press might even back up a woman who was fighting against tyranny, and fighting for her child. I might be able to threaten Owen back!

If I could do a good honest piece of writing, it might be lifesaving for us both. Monica needed money now, and I needed not only an income, but something I could throw myself into and work at with all my heart. A straw to the drowning! All the sources were here to draw from. Monica herself, of course, but there would also be a great many people alive who had touched her world in the old days. And I knew exactly where I should start.

"Linda," I said, "will you go ahead and get me that interview with Saxon Scott?"

SIX

THE NEXT MORNING, WHEN LINDA DROVE ME DOWN TO THE Desert Museum, I left Keith behind in spite of his protests. After that disturbing phone call, I couldn't risk taking him out. As it happened, I was very glad that I hadn't brought him with me.

Not far from the gatehouse at the end of Monica's private road, a blue Chevy was parked. I noticed uneasily that it started up as we turned toward the museum and followed us along the road past the golf course. This might not have meant anything, except that the blue car trailed us the short distance to the museum parking lot. When we left our car a man got out of the Chevy and stood watching us boldly. He wore dark gray slacks and a pullover that matched the car. I knew the type. One of Owen's "thugs."

When I told Linda, she said I was probably being paranoid, and Keith was perfectly safe on the mountain.

She led the way to the front entrance of the museum and stopped. "Just stand here for a minute and look."

A central fountain sent plumes into the air in continuous crystal motion, and there were sunken gardens below the walls on either hand. The low, wide building, with its outflung wings, echoed not only the colors of the desert, but the very texture of rock and sand as well. Its unexpected angles were the angles of the mountains around Palm Springs. Directly behind the museum rose the bare brown backdrop of Mt. San Jacinto, and the man-made buildings seemed to belong at its foot as though they'd grown there.

Huge, windowless wings faced with volcanic rock framed the entrance. Rock that with its eternal wearing qualities matched the subtle tones of the mountain—charcoal and black, tinged with burnt sienna and lavender and warm umbers. These were the real colors of the mountain, if one looked closely enough.

Everywhere the desert itself had been dramatized. In structured concrete walls that lined the sidewalk, the formalized ripples of sand dunes had been reproduced, and this play of light and shadow gave the eye variety and pleasure.

I knew now why Jason Trevor had warmed to such enthusiasm when he spoke of the uniqueness of this museum. Only here in Palm Springs could it exist so suitably; the architect had matched it perfectly to the place.

Double outside stone steps rose on either side of the fountain, offering wide access to the level of the main floor, ten feet above. When Linda started up the right-hand flight, I went with her. The overhang of the building had a coffered ceiling, while underfoot large quarry tiles of olive brown warmed the floor with their natural sheen.

At the top of the steps I stopped and looked down. The man from the blue Chevy stood on the sidewalk watching us. It didn't matter, I told myself—this was to be expected. It was exactly the sort of harassing Owen would try. But this hood of his couldn't really do anything. Linda had already alerted the guards whose business it was to keep strangers away from Monica. I mustn't panic or I would spoil every moment of my life here. There would always be someone following me now, and I must learn to accept it without falling apart.

Jason Trevor came to meet us at the door, and Linda patted my arm. Away from the house, she seemed freer this morning, easier to be with. Though she hadn't mentioned an appointment with Saxon as yet, and I hadn't pressed her further.

"Don't look so worried," she said. "Everything will work out. Jason, Carol really *is* going to write a book about Monica."

"Interesting," he said in a tone that indicated the contrary.

I resented the arrogance of his disapproval. "I find her an interesting subject. As much so as a museum. Though she isn't quite that yet."

He actually grinned at me. "You haven't seen this museum."

In the sharper light of morning his hair seemed more sun-streaked then ever, and his brown eyes with the concentration lines between them still regarded me warily. At least he had smiled.

"Where is Keith?" he asked.

"It was wiser not to bring him." I hesitated. "I do have a reason. Do you see that man down there on the sidewalk? He followed us here from Monica's gate."

"Do you want me to speak to him?" Jason asked.

"Not yet. It doesn't matter if he follows *me*. I just want you to notice him, in case anything comes up later."

Linda needed to get back to the house. "Call me when you're ready to come home," she said, and left us together.

Jason led the way into a great high-ceilinged central room. The museum's huge open expanses had the feeling of desert and sky. The coffered ceiling of the entry gave way to airy space, with skylights high along one side to make the adjustment from sunlight easier for the eyes.

Vast stretches of carpet suggested desert sands, and more walls of lava rock with its subtle shadings gave again the feeling that the outdoor environment of mountain and desert had been brought inside. Against one wall a huge abstract painting had been hung, its brilliant colors lending contrast to the desert hues.

In spite of my resistance to Jason, I reacted with a sense of awe. "It's stunning. Tremendously impressive."

He actually smiled again. "We'll break you in a little at a

time, so you can do us justice in your article. Let me show
you around. First, though—a view.''

We walked toward a gallery of paintings on the left, and
when he turned me to face the big central room, I saw why.
This was indeed a view!

I seemed to look across the great room, not as though I
gazed through a window, but as though I looked straight out
into the panorama of desert and mountain. It was *there*, and
the sweep of it was surely real, even to the effect of what
seemed to be sunlight flooding the wide scene from some
radiant, hidden source.

It was a diorama, of course, but I'd never seen one more
effectively presented.

''Yes!'' I said. ''That's it exactly. It matches everything I
remember.''

''What do you mean?''

I spoke half to myself, remembering. ''One of the foster
homes I stayed in when I was ten belonged to a woman—a
widow—who'd grown up on a ranch in the Southwest. Mrs.
Johnson told me endless stories about the desert, and about
her life as a child—riding horses and all the rest. I loved to
listen to her. I think she wanted to shut out the ugly neighbor-
hood where she lived and remember the sun again. She gave
me a feeling for the desert before I ever saw it.''

Jason was watching me curiously, and when he spoke his
tone had softened. ''Come along and I'll show you more,'' he
said.

We crossed the central room to the National Science wing.
Embraced by the diorama, it was again as if we stood in the
open, with the desert stretching away under a blue California
sky to bare mountains that rose in the distance. Nearby palm
trees were real, as was the nearest stretch of sand, so that the
demarcation between the real and the painted scene was
hardly to be detected. Little desert animals seemed ready to
dive into their holes, and the sense of far reaches was so
convincing that I began to feel soothed and calmed, as though
I really stood outdoors.

''It's strange,'' I said. ''When we drove through desert

country coming here, I didn't feel at home with it, as I'd expected to. It frightened me a little.''

"That's a natural reaction. Though with some people it never wears off. You either love the desert—or you hate it.''

"I'm going to love it.''

"Don't be sure too quickly. It's not a place for romantic notions. We leave all that to Palm Springs.''

"Tell me about this." I gestured toward the diorama.

"All right—I'll do my thing. This is the Coachella Valley— where we are—as it was before anything was built out here. It's still this way when you leave the towns behind. There's a lot of empty country—space—and I hope it stays that way. Man always has to pave and build and domesticate.''

I heard the same intensity, the same absorption in his voice that I'd heard in Linda's, and a curious notion struck me.

"You and your sister are alike in a lot of ways, aren't you—even though you're so different.''

He looked straight at me, and for the first time I saw the burning quality of his dark eyes. There were banked fires smoldering in Jason Trevor, well concealed most of the time, but hot and deep. And sometimes angry. I wondered why he should be angry with me, however polite on the surface. I'd felt this yesterday, and it was still there, even though his lighter manner disguised it.

"What do you mean by that?" he asked.

"Only that Linda lives in a make-believe world. And perhaps you do too. There's not necessarily anything wrong with that—I know I do it myself. I suppose it depends on the degree. We're all constantly imitating what's real. Interpreting, according to our own viewpoints.''

"With a few differences," he said coolly, moving on to the next room. "At least you and I go to the real thing for our inspiration. But that world up on the mountain—Monica Arlen's world—is dead. It's over and done with, and there's no point in trying to resurrect it. It always was artificial, even in its heyday.''

Part of what he said was right, of course, yet he missed something important, and I didn't know how to make it clear to him. Or even to myself. Magic is always hard to explain to someone who doesn't believe. My world and Jason's were very far apart.

"Right now," he went on, "I'd like to interest you in writing about this museum."

"I'd like to try," I said. "I don't entirely agree with what you say about Monica and that life she used to live, but that doesn't matter. I want to do some short pieces, even while I work on the book. Perhaps the museum will make a good place to start. Let me get an overview first. Then I'll come back again for more detail. Of course there will be people I must interview, questions I'll need to ask."

"Right. When you're ready. I'll help set up what I can for you." He sounded stiff again, as though he doubted my ability to cross from Monica's world into his. Perhaps I doubted it a little myself.

As we continued, I became more and more interested in the scope of the exhibits. There were displays of basketry and pottery from Indian artists, old and new. There were spacious galleries of paintings, and lovely outdoor sculpture gardens and courts, one of which was named for its donor, Frank Sinatra.

Now and then I made notes, mainly about things I wanted to visit again.

"Before you can really appreciate what we are trying to do, you need to get out into the desert itself," Jason said.

"I've already driven through it from the other side of Mount San Jacinto."

"That's not the same. Do you ride?"

"I've been on a horse a few times. Why?"

"That's the best way to see the desert. And the Indian canyons up the mountain too. Not in a car. Not even on foot, though I'm all for backpacking and hiking too."

"How would I go about this?"

In response to my direct question, he retreated suddenly, and when he didn't follow through I let it go. Though why he'd dropped the subject so abruptly, I didn't understand.

"Let's go downstairs," he suggested. "I want to show you the Annenberg Theater."

The broad stairway with its bright tangerine carpeting was

like a flash of sunset against the desert browns. One wall was again built of lava rock, with its subtle tones, while the opposite stair wall echoed ripples of sand in concrete. Overhead, as we made the landing turn down, a stunning chandelier seemed to shoot stars from its glowing heart in a burst of tiny, stemmed bulbs. On every hand the senses were stimulated, pleased, satisfied.

"We'll need to have the lights turned on in the theater," Jason said. "I'll find a guard."

When we stepped through to the rear of the small auditorium, however, we found that lights were already on, so that the area glowed with soft color. Again, browns and beiges echoed the desert, made even richer in contrast by curved rows of seats done in bright tangerine fabric. Enclosing the outer aisles, soft green draperies shut in the theater, suggesting the green of this oasis that was Palm Springs.

The jewel of the entire setting was of course the stage— small and intimate, framed in neutral colors that would allow the lighting to bring it to life.

Now the stage area too was lighted, and two men stood talking below its edge, one of them Linda's friend, Wally Davis, the other Saxon Scott.

"Let's go back," Jason said quickly. "We can come here another time."

I stopped him. "Please wait. If I do a book about Monica, Mr. Scott has to be part of it. I mustn't lose this chance to meet him."

Reluctantly, Jason followed me down the slanting aisle.

Wally saw us first and his manner grew even more enthusiastic. "Wonderful, Carol, do come and meet my boss. We were just talking about plans for the benefit."

Saxon turned and even though I'd glimpsed him at the restaurant, I couldn't help my young, thrilled reaction all over again. This man had been my first crush, and something in me hadn't forgotten. His pale hair seemed dazzling above a tanned, unlined face. Though heavier than the young man I remembered, he looked athletic and fit, as men were apt to in this outdoor community. The slight smile he gave me was polite and impersonal. He must long ago have learned to be wary with strangers.

"This is Carol Hamilton," Wally said. "And of course you know Jason."

I took the brown hand Saxon held out to me, not quite believing. He was still so much like that image on the screen that I felt as though his handclasp should have been less firm and real.

"You know, Sax," Wally said, "Carol is Monica Arlen's great-niece."

Saxon Scott really looked at me then. It was strange to know so well the expression he wore—because I'd already seen every nuance on the screen. He looked at me with a new, intense interest, and he didn't let go of my hand. I was aware of Jason stepping back from us a little, removing himself from something he clearly found distasteful. Snobbery, I thought, and ignored him

"You resemble Monica a little," Saxon said. "Perhaps around the eyes."

I was pleased, but had to shake my head. "Not really. My eyes don't have that exotic tilt—not like Monica Arlen's."

His sigh seemed genuine in its hint of regret. "No, of course they don't. I suppose I saw that flash of resemblance that comes at first glance. It's already gone. But you're almost her only relative, aren't you?"

"As far as I know."

"Carol is going to write Monica's biography," Wally put in. "A marvelous idea!"

So Linda must already have been on the phone to this balding little man who seemed aquiver with boundless energy. Yet apparently she had not yet phoned Saxon to make an appointment for me. I'd have preferred not to have my nebulous plans thrown so abruptly at Saxon Scott, but there was no quenching Wally's exuberance. He was a born salesman, though I was beginning to wonder exactly what it was he was selling.

"That's interesting," Saxon said. "How does Monica feel about it?"

"She seems to like the idea," I admitted.

81

"That's one Hollywood biography that ought to be written," Saxon said. *"If* you can tell the truth."

Strangely, those were the very words Monica had used, and I wondered how different their two truths might be.

"Of course you're essential to Monica's story. Would you be willing to talk to me?" I asked.

"I might. If, as I say, you're willing to tell the truth. I've thought I might someday write my own memoirs, but I'm probably too lazy. And there are problems. Old problems. Perhaps we can explore this a little."

"Every story has its own truth, Mr. Saxon. I'd like to know yours as well as Monica's."

Wally had remained silent long enough. "The most important thing right now will be to get Sax and Monica up on this stage together after we show *Mirage*. He and I were just talking over the possibilities."

I turned to Saxon. "Are you really willing to go through with this? Appear onstage with Monica?"

He didn't answer me directly. "I'll be surprised if *she* consents. From what Linda says, she never plays the old Monica Arlen anymore. The public role, that is."

"She did yesterday," I told him. "She came into the dining room looking as beautiful as I remember her on the screen. She's still a wonderful actress and I think she wanted to show me she could be something besides an old woman."

"Monica Arlen was always her best role. But playing it for you in private is quite different from getting up on a stage before an audience. Do you think she can face that after all this time?"

"I haven't any idea, but if *you* can face it, she should be able to."

False words, I thought, even as I spoke them. Monica had changed so much for the worse, while Saxon hadn't. Besides, as I was beginning to sense, he had probably always played himself on the screen. In so many small ways I knew and recognized in him now.

I'd moved my hand as I spoke, and suddenly Saxon caught and held it up so that the great emerald with its iris intaglio shone in the light. For an instant he looked angry, his mouth tightening so that the youthful expression vanished. Saxon Scott wasn't young, either, and he would remember old hurts.

"It's only a loan," I said quickly. "She'd never give this ring away."

He let my hand go, as though the sight of the emerald had somehow shaken him.

"Perhaps it's time," he said enigmatically. "I've waited too long."

Jason took a step in my direction and spoke under his breath. "We have company."

I looked toward the back of the theater and saw the man from the blue Chevy sitting in a rear seat watching us. Owen's man. A sense of outrage began to shake me.

"Oh, no!" I cried. "How dare he do this?"

Saxon was quickly intuitive. "Someone your husband has sent?"

If Linda hadn't told him, then Wally had.

"Yes," I said. "He followed us here from Monica's gate."

"I'll get rid of him." Saxon strode up the aisle and the man watched his approach uneasily.

I remembered that flow of dangerous power that Saxon had always been able to summon on a screen. Macho, long before the word became common criticism, and obviously convincing.

"You'd better get out and stop annoying this lady," he said, his voice ominously low. "The police chief in this town's a good friend of mine, and if you bother Miss Hamilton again I'll have a talk with him."

The man in the pullover slid out of the seat and after one slow, insolent look in my direction, walked out of the theater. I suspected his retreat was due more to Saxon's impressive physical presence than to any hints about a sheriff. Bullies could often be bullied. Though I felt little relief at his leaving. I wouldn't be rid of him that easily.

I hurried up the aisle. "Thank you, Mr. Scott."

Unexpectedly, he laughed. "So I can still pull it off," he said, and I heard self-mockery in the words.

"Will you really let me interview you?" I asked.

His famous smile had always held a hint of sadness in it. Perhaps it was that very vulnerability in so strong a man that had broken so many hearts. Or perhaps he was still performing?

"Let's set a date soon," he said. "Ask Linda to bring you to my house in Indian Wells. Perhaps I can suggest some others you should see as well. Alva and Nicos Leonidas would have a lot to tell you. Linda will know how to reach them."

"Who are they?"

For an instant his expression was almost mischievous. He'd looked like that sometimes when he teased Monica on the screen. Though now there seemed a faint edge of malice to the mischief.

"Nicos Leonidas was Monica's favorite cameraman. Though not always mine. Actors are a vain lot, and we don't much care for favoritism if it's directed toward someone else."

At least he could mock Saxon Scott, as I suspected Monica would never mock herself.

"And Alva?"

"She was the only woman at the studio in the old days who was a makeup expert. Perc Westmore did that job. But Alva always worked with Monica. She concocted colorings and special lipsticks that were just right for her. Alva could make Monica look her best under any lighting, and Monica was devoted to her. The panchromatics and other new films were coming out fast, and Alva always managed the right effect for magnification on a big screen. She even did her hair. Monica would never play a scene without Alva in her dressing room."

I wondered why he was going on at such length. Then he paused and the quizzical look returned.

"You might as well know before you see her that Alva and I were married for a time—after Monica left pictures."

I knew about the wife he'd been married to for a few years, and it would be a real break if I could talk to her as well. Especially since she'd worked so intimately with Monica.

"Do you suppose she'd see me?"

"I can ask her to. We're still friends in a wary sort of way. After she married Nicos, they bought a place in the mountains up near Idyllwild."

He took my hand again to look at the ring. Whatever Monica had once meant to him, I didn't think the feeling had ___ entirely. It was clear that the emerald brought back memories. But when he dropped my hand his look was suddenly guarded.

"You might tell Monica that you mean to talk to Alva and Nicos. Her reaction could be interesting."

With that puzzling remark, he walked out of the theater without another word. As dramatically arrogant as he'd ever been on a screen!

I must certainly search for the "truth" they'd both spoken of, and discover the reason behind the strange warring that seemed to exist in Saxon Scott. I wished I knew why he had made that mysterious phone call to Monica that Linda had mentioned, and which had seemed to upset her so badly.

Wally didn't mean to let Saxon get away. He rushed up the aisle after him, passed me with a casual, "See you," and disappeared.

I sat down in a nearby seat feeling as though a strong wind had rushed into my already stormy life and was sweeping me along.

Jason came slowly to the back of the theater. When I looked up into his grave, unsmiling face, I realized that his expression was unexpectedly sympathetic; perhaps less critical than before. During my exchange with Saxon, he must have been weighing something in his mind.

"Will you come out to my ranch tomorrow—Sunday?" he asked. "It might help you to get the feeling of the desert. Besides, there's space enough out there to think things through. Perhaps you need that. You could bring your son along with you."

Regretfully, I was already shaking my head. "I can't take him away from the house just now—it's too risky. And I mustn't leave him often."

"We can smuggle him out in my car and I'll make sure we aren't followed. The ranch will do him good. If you agree, I'll phone Mrs. Sanchez that you're coming, and tell her we'll want her best Mexican food. But not too hot, since you're greenhorns."

Suddenly I wanted to go to his ranch. We needed Monica's fortress, but it would be a relief if we could occasionally escape it safely. I knew how much Keith needed this.

"I'd like to come," I said. "Thank you."

He nodded, stiffly remote again, as though he might already be regretting his invitation. Jason Trevor was a difficult man to fathom, but perhaps all the more interesting because he wasn't easily read.

"I've an appointment now," he said. "Would you like to wander around on your own awhile?"

I hesitated, my concern for Keith surging up again. "I'd like to stay, but—"

"Then stay. You won't help your son by constant worry. You need to do something for yourself too, or you won't be much good for him."

Again his understanding surprised me. It seemed to cut almost unwillingly through the antagonism he held against me.

"I know you're right," I said.

"I'll pick you up early, before your shadow expects any action. Seven o'clock? We can have breakfast at the ranch, if you like."

"We'll look forward to it," I told him.

As we started toward the stairs that led up to the main floor, I remembered something.

"Yesterday Monica mentioned that there was a piece of her in this museum. Do you know what she meant?"

"I think so. There are several outdoor sculpture gardens. Sunken gardens below street level. You'll want to explore them anyhow, and you can look there. I'm not sure where the Arlen bust is, but you'll be able to find it. You can go outside through these doors near the theater if you like. Theater crowds enjoy the garden during intermissions. It's one of our attractions."

Always when he spoke of the museum, Jason's voice warmed with enthusiasm, and I knew that for him this Desert Museum was no antiquated collection, but something with a life of its own that enriched the present.

I thanked him again, and when he'd gone I went outdoors and wandered through the gardens for a long, peaceful time. Jason's words had helped me to put aside for a little while that dark menace that haunted me.

Outdoors huge pieces of sculpture were shown in the open, where they belonged, and I discovered great names—Calder, Henry Moore, Hans Arp, and others. For now, however, I gave them no more than a passing glance because I was seeking the piece that held special significance for me.

In one outdoor section, diagonally placed slabs of concrete that echoed the cantilevers of the building formed walks between fountains and flower beds and made bridges over pools. Tropical plantings grew against high walls reaching to street level above. Thrust out from the building were angled windows of glass, reflecting pools, and sky.

I found a stone bench where I could sit quietly, listening to birds and to the soothing play of water. In this enclosed, protected space I felt for a little while an illusory peace, and could let my tensions flow away.

I don't know how long I sat there. Even the changing play of light and shadow comforted my senses. After a time I came to life again, and that was when the awareness of someone watching me began to grow. It wasn't the inimical feeling that I'd had with Blue Chevy, but more like eyes fixed upon me in an impersonal but unwavering stare.

Not until I looked about searchingly did I see her. Monica Arlen! The bronze bust rested on its pedestal in shadows that made it almost invisible at this time of day. I left my bench and crossed a concrete slab over a pool, to stand before the remarkable likeness. A small plaque offered lettering, and I leaned over to read the words. The bust had been sculptured and cast in 1946, the year after the war had ended. The same year in which *Mirage* was made. The sculptor was Peggy Smith.

As Monica had said, she'd been an artist in her own right—perhaps with natural gifts that had never been fully developed. Peggy Smith hadn't sought fame for herself during those years, but had lived in the shadow of Monica's fame, willing to serve her to the neglect of her own very real talent.

There was so much I needed to understand about Monica and that time long past. I knew the clues would come, once I gave myself fully to the search. One bit of exploration always led to another, until a subject that seemed simple to start with developed a complexity that could lead in rewarding and unexpected directions. This time I would have the space of a book in which to develop whatever I wanted.

One of the aspects I must understand was how Monica Arlen had been able to inspire such personal loyalty as Peggy Smith had given her, and which was now being shown again by Linda Trevor. There were depths here that I hadn't begun to explore, and I was lucky to have Linda as a living source to help me grasp what eluded me. Right now, however, my attentions had to be divided. Always uppermost was the threat to Keith and the danger of what Owen might do next. A peaceful interlude in the museum gardens was a gift to be grateful for, but it couldn't last.

For a few moments longer I studied the bronze face. The sculptor had caught Monica's subtle smile exactly—that screen smile suggesting laughter about to break, yet hinting of sadness as well. An enchanting, heartbreaking smile—even more vulnerable than Saxon's. Peggy Smith had caught the exotic tilt of the eyes—that accident of birth which had given a striking appeal to Monica's face and made it so memorable, so different from the patterned face of other screen stars. And still did.

For now, I had been too long away from Keith, and I turned from that fixed, impersonal bronze gaze and walked back through museum corridors. I found a telephone, and Linda said she would come for me right away. When I went outside to wait, I was relieved to see no blue Chevy in sight.

On the drive up the mountain I told Linda that Jason had invited Keith and me to the ranch tomorrow, and she seemed oddly uneasy.

"Don't you think I should go?" I asked.

"Of course you must go." Although she spoke quickly, I had a feeling of something being held back.

"Have you changed your mind about my staying here?"

"Of course not!" Again the words came quickly, and I wished I needn't doubt her sincerity. If I lost Linda as an ally, nothing here would work, and sometimes she puzzled me.

"Is it anything Monica has said?" I asked. "You do sound doubtful."

Her mood changed abruptly. "I'm sorry. I wasn't even thinking about Monica. It's Jason—but never mind that now. Of course you must go out to the ranch."

Near the gatehouse the blue car had been parked in the shadow of a palm tree, with a man behind the wheel. I didn't look at him as we drove through, but all my tensions swept back. Owen would never be satisfied with merely watching. Sooner or later he would move, and I would never know what to expect until it happened.

When we reached the terrace before the house, I went inside, bracing myself for a stormy session with my son, who was undoubtedly going to be upset by my hours of absence.

Instead, I found Keith sitting on the tiles of the dining room floor, playing a board game and arguing happily with another small boy.

Helsa Carlson came in from the kitchen, smiling. "This is my grandson, Miss Hamilton. Jonah Fernandez. His family lives in Cathedral City, and sometimes I invite him here to visit me. He's going to stay for a few days this time."

Jonah Fernandez! What a wonderful name.

I thanked Helsa warmly for understanding Keith's need. She seemed a little less guarded with me than she'd been yesterday. Perhaps because Monica appeared to have accepted me?

Jonah was as fair as Keith was dark, revealing his Scandinavian heritage in hair and skin. His eyes were almost black, however, and a Spanish love of fun twinkled in them. The boys' heads nearly touched as they bent over their game, and for once Keith didn't jump up anxiously and run to me. He was completely preoccupied, and couldn't be bothered with grown-ups just then. I blessed Helsa.

When the phone rang in Linda's office, I found myself starting, as I'd done ever since that disturbing call yesterday. But when Linda had answered, she came to tell me that it was Monica calling from her apartment. I was to visit her right after lunch, and I could bring a notebook if I liked, but no camera or tape recorder.

Luckily, I felt more prepared after a morning in which I'd met Saxon Scott and seen Peggy Smith's remarkable bust of Monica Arlen in the Desert Museum.

So now my search into the past was to start in earnest, and it must somehow help me to endure and get through the present.

SEVEN

AT LUNCH I TOLD LINDA THAT SAXON SCOTT HAD AGREED TO talk to me.

"I thought you were going to call him for me," I said. "Why didn't you?"

Linda shook her head unhappily. "I kept putting it off. I suppose I feel guilty because Monica will hate your seeing him. Sometimes I almost wish you weren't going to do this book. I'm afraid of all the painful things it may open up for Monica."

This vacillation on Linda's part wasn't going to help. "I must go ahead with it. And of course I'll need to see a number of people who knew her. Especially Saxon Scott. She has to accept that."

"I know. You'd better make it clear to her. She's only thinking about her own role. I can sympathize, since it is her story, and it should be written the way she wants."

That would bear arguing, but I let it go. No one stood alone, and there was much more to anyone's life than a single, personal viewpoint. I not only *wanted* to write this book and make it really good, but I needed to do it for Keith's sake as well as my own. More and more it loomed in my mind as a means by which we could escape Owen, and perhaps even fight him.

After lunch I left Keith with his new friend, and Linda took me upstairs to Monica's carved and brass-trimmed door. A formidable door—perhaps symbolic of shutting out the world.

Before she raised the knocker, Linda gave me a last warning. "Monica still doesn't know about Wally's scheme for getting her onstage at the Annenberg Theater with Saxon, so it's up to you to persuade her."

"It's not up to me," I insisted, "but I'll do what I can if there's an opportunity."

"It would be so beautiful if we could get them together on that stage."

Linda sounded dreamy again, and listening to her I felt the answer—some of it—to her years of devotion might lie in this very dreamworld she could slip into at times. When Linda put aside her wry cynicism, she was still wholeheartedly a *fan*. That too was a phenomenon I must explore. The devotion, sometimes the fanaticism of fans had its own strange psychological twists. One had only to think of Valentino's death, and more recently the whole Elvis Presley convulsion. I'd been a fan myself, but never to that extent, and by now my own fantasies had worn a little thin, so I could take a more realistic view—at least some of the time.

When Monica called for us to come in, we stepped into an airy upper level room, open from the mountain at the rear to the view over the town at the front of the house. The sun had passed its zenith so that a softer light than that of full morning glowed outside the stretch of eastern balcony.

The room was pleasant and comfortable, with no particular effort at "decoration." It looked like a room that had grown into itself over the years. The sofa, with its plump cushions, was beige, and so were two of the chairs. Only yellow and green cushions here and there lent color. Between round Moroccan rugs, the parquet floor gleamed in contrasting woods, and eggshell bookcases carried out the sense of light, as did walls and ceiling. There were a few pictures, framed originals, surprisingly modern, including a Roy Lichtenstein of an aviator. These seemed to indicate that Monica kept up to some extent with what was going on in the world. Strangely, there was not a single photograph from the Hollywood years. Because all that time was lost to her and had become too painful to recall, ending as it had?

This afternoon she had chosen to play Monica Arlen again, gowning herself in a flowing white silk caftan, caught in at the waist by a braided gold cord. Again, her makeup had been carefully applied, though today she wore no chestnut wig. Her natural gray hair was worn in the old-fashioned pageboy style of her pictures—now being revived as smart and modern. Daylight was far from kind to her, and nothing could hide the marks of age when she was seen close up. Yet all this became unimportant because of the inner illusion she could create of a far younger, more beautiful woman—that woman I had seen so often on a screen. She had the confidence, the air, to carry it off, so that the make-believe never seemed pitiful.

Beside her, the royal Siamese lay curled on a green cushion, her blue eyes surveying Linda and me as suppliants before a throne. Her two attendant angels, with the plural names, Seraphim and Cherubim, played background chorus to Annabella's center stage. Both cat and mistress knew their own importance.

On the balcony outside, Ralph Reese sat smoking as he stared idly over the town. He didn't trouble to look around as Linda and I came into the room.

With her own familiar grace, Monica rose to greet me, her hands outstretched and all her lovely charm in evidence. Her movements were exactly as I remembered—and *she* remembered—making no concession to debilitating age.

Watching her, I knew again that an honest and revealing biography of Monica Arlen was going to be difficult to do. In the beginning she would play exactly the role she chose, and no other. She would tell me what she wanted me to know, and nothing else. The problem would be to get past the actress to whatever real woman might exist. The "real" woman was full of secrets, perhaps some of them dark and haunted—but those were the secrets I must bring to light, whether I used them in print or not.

Linda started to leave, but Monica nodded to her graciously. "Please stay. I want you to hear this."

I almost wished Linda would go, now that she'd begun to waver about the book, but she hesitated, and Monica spoke more sharply.

"Sit down, do. And don't fidget. After all, you're the one who knows where every picture and paper is kept, and you may help me fill in when there are things I've forgotten." She pursed her mouth at me. "At my age, there's so much that I forget."

Even as she spoke, I knew this was no admission of her years, but her own little joke. This woman would forget nothing that she *chose* to remember. She was merely producing an act for whatever she wanted to dismiss.

Linda sat down, still uneasy. "What about *him?*" She nodded toward Ralph.

"He doesn't matter. Goodness knows what happens inside his head—if anything ever does."

Linda sat in a chair across the room where she wouldn't intrude, and Monica took her place again on the beige sofa, stroking Annabella with one hand and picking up the famous iris with the other. She hadn't troubled to lower her voice as she spoke, but if Ralph heard her he gave no sign, teetering back in his chair and smiling slightly, as though the world and everything in it amused him. More than anyone else in this house he made me uncomfortable, and I mustn't make the mistake of discounting him.

I'd brought a loose-leaf notebook and soft pencils, and I got ready to make notes. There'd been no time to jot down questions ahead of this interview, but I knew that enough would occur to me. I mustn't be too provocative to start with, lest I alarm her.

"What do you want to know?" Monica asked. "Where do you want to begin?" Annabella made one of her plaintive remarks, and Monica tapped her lightly on the skull. "Now, now, Annie," she said, "tell me later." And then to me, "Annie does tell me things, you know. I'm sure she has second sight. Of course she's had a lot to say about you.''

I wasn't sure how to take this. "For instance?'' I prompted.

"Oh, just that you spell TROUBLE in capital letters. But I expect she's jealous.''

Annabella regarded me balefully and began washing a paw with a raspy pink tongue. I suspected that no one else would dare call her "Annie.'' Close to the sofa, Cherubim cuffed Seraphim, or perhaps it was vice versa, but neither made a sound.

"I'm glad to see you're wearing my ring,'' Monica went on. "It should be seen, and not hidden away in a jewel box.''

"I'm proud to wear it. But just for a little while. Then I'll return it. Right now perhaps we can start with your childhood. I know very little about your early life, so I'll be glad of anything you want to tell me.''

The iris nodded in emphasis as Monica waved it. "I don't want to talk about my childhood. All that bores me. Linda has plenty of printed information out of the past. Ask *her*.''

"Some of it may not be accurate,'' Linda objected mildly. "Studios used to make up what they pleased for publicity releases, and not all the fan magazines based their stories on fact. Not any more than Hedda and Louella did. Rumor was good enough.''

I had to persist. "Just a few details. You were born in Desert Hot Springs, not far from here?''

"It's all a matter of record,'' Monica said impatiently. "Even the dates. I've never lied about my age.''

Linda helped me. "She was born on her parents' ranch near where Desert Hot Springs is now. It didn't exist as a town until the forties.''

"My mother told me that you grew up there until your mother took you to Hollywood?''

"What difference does it make? My life didn't really begin until I got into pictures.''

"Something made you ambitious, drove you. I remember reading about how gutsy you were as a young girl. You always did the unexpected—things that brought you attention in the right places, so you could prove your talent. What do you suppose gave you that drive?'' I was always more interested in *whys* than in *wheres* and *whats*.

"Being a child wasn't a happy time for me. I don't want to think about it."

A sense of kinship touched me. I hadn't had a happy childhood either, and when I was growing up, *she* had been my beacon.

"Who did you look up to?" I asked. "What drew you to Hollywood?"

She considered for a moment. "I suppose it was having the right sort of face that took me there. And wanting to get away from where I was."

Again she let the question drop. Perhaps I could find someone around Desert Hot Springs who would remember her family—my family—and remember her. If there was concealment of her girlhood, then I had to dig it out. But right now I must find a way to start her talking more freely.

"This morning I saw that marvelous bronze bust of you in the museum."

She smiled almost warmly. "I suppose you know that Peggy Smith did that? It's considered her best work, though I'm afraid she only used her talent when the whim moved her. A great natural gift, but untrained. Everyone kept telling her that. Once she did a little stone nymph and a fawn that I always liked. They used to stand in the garden of Cadenza—my home in Beverly Hills."

"The same ones that are in your garden on the mountain here?"

"You've seen them then? Yes, I brought those two with me when I moved here for good. Peggy spent too much time on me. She was the only one who stood up against my—my enemies."

"Why should anyone be your enemy?"

Monica shook her head darkly. "That was a precarious world. And terribly hard for women. It wasn't always talent that gave you the first step up. We all walked tightropes, even after we were established. The studios owned us, and they could discard us if we lost our popularity. I fought for all my chances. One slip and you started down. Then, suddenly you had no friends.''

She must be remembering the time after *Mirage*.

"But you never slipped," I said quickly. "*Mirage* was your greatest role. You could have gone on as long as you wished."

"No! I was always tied to Saxon—to those sentimental comedies. If it hadn't been for him . . . Anyway, I didn't want it anymore after that horrible thing happened. I suppose I blamed myself afterwards. And that's been hard to live with."

It was time to be provocative, and she'd given me an opening. "You mean your friend Peggy's suicide?"

Monica closed her eyes and let the iris droop. "That's what everyone called it—suicide. But I was never convinced."

"What do you mean?" I asked, startled.

"Never mind now. Let's go on."

Ralph left his chair and came in from the balcony. "Hey," he said to Linda, "what's that blue car doing down by the gate? It's been there on and off ever since morning, and just now the fellow driving it got out and disappeared toward the gatehouse."

Linda gave me a quick look that said, *Don't upset Monica,* and stood up. "I'll call the guard at the gatehouse right away, just in case. I can use the phone in my office."

"Maybe I should go down there and see what's up," Ralph said.

"Yes, you do that." Monica dismissed him with a wave of the iris.

When they'd both gone, she sat silently, staring at nothing. I still wanted to know what she'd meant in her hint about Peggy's death.

"You were talking about Peggy Smith," I reminded her gently.

She seemed to shake herself mentally and come back to the present, but she didn't pick up her doubts about Peggy's suicide that she'd thrown at me so tantalizingly.

"I have a few other small things Peggy did. Look over there."

I went to the bookcase shelf Monica indicated and examined a small ceramic group. The pieces were cunningly wrought and formed a famous scene from *Mirage*. The same one in the restaurant where Monica and Saxon were seated at a round table, the little Swiss clock between them, ready to pop out its cuckoo. What laughter and tears they'd managed in that scene—before the whole thing had turned into anger and bitterness between them. A bitterness they'd never have dared to portray in their earlier, more lighthearted pictures.

Now I recalled that in the Mirage Room, where Keith and I had dined, there'd been a small cuckoo clock on the wall. Saxon had remembered every detail. So here was the clock again in these ceramics created in delicate color and miniature detail.

"Peggy Smith seems to have done such a variety of things. So why *didn't* she develop her talents?" I asked. "Why didn't she become famous in her own right?"

"Perhaps she might have—if she'd lived. You recognize the scene, don't you?"

"Of course. I don't know how many times I've seen *Mirage*."

Monica didn't seem particularly pleased, and I was beginning to glimpse the ambivalence in her. The past was lost and over, and she must sometimes resent the fact that it was regarded as far more important in her life than the present could ever be.

"Do you ever watch your old movies?" I asked.

She flapped the iris at me angrily. "I don't watch them at all! I can't bear to. But I do want to talk about Peggy. Not about her death, but about her life as it affected me. I owe her that."

I was willing to listen, wherever she led. I'd long ago learned not to be so intent on my questions that I missed new openings.

After a slight hesitation, as though she sought for words, she went on. "Peggy grew up with too many dreams she couldn't fulfill. I'm afraid she didn't work very hard at being successful. She just wanted results. She found she could attach herself to a star and live vicariously." Monica's tone had turned faintly scornful in speaking of her old friend.

"What about her creative gifts?"

"She was young and I don't think she realized what she had. In some ways she was foolish. I suppose creating in clay and stone, painting a little, making jewelry, were just things she'd always done rather easily. Hobbies. She never worked at these things very much unless they were connected with me. I've never known anyone since whom I could trust as I did Peggy. Not even Linda. Linda has outside distractions. Her brother, for instance, who doesn't approve of Monica Arlen. Oh, I know! And that ridiculous friend of hers—Wally Davis. I don't trust him at all. For one thing, he works for Saxon Scott."

I needed to know more about anything that rankled in Monica. "Why don't you trust Wally? He seems a pleasant man."

"He's not good enough for Linda. What he wants is to make a lot of money as quickly as possible. He wants to climb—in any way he can. And Palm Springs is a good place for that. We have the rich, the very rich, and the super rich. He'll succeed all right, since he knows how to make himself useful. Though who knows at what?"

I wondered where the poor and middle people came in. Probably they served the others. There was a certain shrewdness in this old woman whom Monica had become. She might be a recluse, but she knew what was going on.

Moving along at the bookcase, I read random titles. They were mostly novels—a mixture of old and new . . . books that had been best sellers. Next on the shelf set into a space was the framed photograph of a house. I recognized it at once—Cadenza, Monica's former home in Beverly Hills. I picked it up and studied the rather grand architecture. Pseudo-Italian, and thoroughly pretentious.

"You didn't build Cadenza, did you?"

"Thank goodness, I didn't have to. All those dream palaces built by early stars like Valentino and Swanson, Mary and Doug, Harold Lloyd, and the rest, were already going out in the thirties. After the depression, movie stars began to live more like other people. Even here in Palm Springs there aren't many estates—unless you're an Annenberg. It was Peggy who found Cadenza and talked me into buying it. It had belonged to a woman whose career had collapsed in tragedy. A rather nasty shooting. You wouldn't know her name, probably. She's hardly remembered any more, but she spent millions during her brief fling. Peggy thought it was the right setting for me. That black marble staircase—ridiculous!''

"Didn't you like Cadenza?"

"I loved every inch of it. But it was like living in a permanent stage set. Not exactly cozy. Saxon never liked it at all. He built himself a beach house in Santa Monica, and that's where we went to be cozy."

"But you still own the house?"

"Not because I've wanted to keep it. I don't have any illusions about it anymore. Those places are anachronisms today—dinosaurs from the past. The upkeep is terrific and the taxes high. Sometimes Linda has been able to rent it, but it's closed up now, with just a caretaker. You can hardly give those houses away today. Some of them have been turned into schools or hotels, or given to institutions. The bulldozers have taken others to make way for building lots. Now I *need* to sell it, for whatever I can get, and Linda has put it on the market again. But who is there to buy?''

I set the picture back on the shelf, feeling a little sad. ''I'd like to have seen the house.''

"That's easily arranged. Tell Linda."

She seemed in a gentler, more reminiscent mood, so perhaps this was my opportunity to do what Linda wished. I must move quietly, persuasively. If I shocked her, she would withdraw at once.

"Linda's brother took me into the Annenberg Theater at the museum, and Wally was there. You've never seen the theater, have you?"

She shook her head emphatically. ''Never! Oh, it's not for want of being asked. They'd give their eyeteeth to get me down there—exploit my name for some of their fund raising. Even though all those committees know that I never make appearances, or attend public events, they never stop trying.''

She was making everything clear, but I still sought for a chink in her armor, a tiny crack I might get through.

"Saxon Scott was there with Wally. I met him this morning."

There was a definite freezing quality in her stillness, but she asked a surprising question, opening the crack unexpectedly.

"How does he look—Saxon?"

I had to be careful. I mustn't wound her vanity. "All right, I suppose. He's heavier and older than he used to be, of course."

She sighed. "Don't try to spare my feelings. Men wear better than women do. Their faces don't fall apart. When we're old, we get too fat and lose our figures. Or we get thin and angular, which is just as bad. And our faces—disaster!"

"You still look wonderful," I said softly, and I wasn't lying. What she achieved was an illusion of beauty, perhaps only the echo, the ghost of beauty long past that she could still evoke when I looked at her. It was the actor's genius to present what wasn't there.

She must have sensed something in my voice—the sort of admiration she'd responded to in Peggy Smith, and again in Linda. It was our willingness to believe in the dream, to lose ourselves in rapt adulation, that offered food and drink to Monica Arlen. Much more so than with Saxon, I thought. I suspected that he didn't really care for any of that. Nowadays Monica must receive very little of the nourishment that had fed her so richly in the past.

"What was Saxon doing there with Wally?" she asked, and I felt that her guard against me had lowered a little.

"They're going to show *Mirage* for a very special gala evening," I said. "Wally's doing the publicity and has a hand in some of the plans. He wants Saxon to appear onstage after the showing of the picture."

This time she flung the iris on the floor and poked it irritably with her toe. No wonder it looked bedraggled. The poor thing must have led a hard existence.

"How dare he?" she cried. "How dare he!"

Did she mean Wally or Saxon? I suspected the latter.

Annabella stood up on the green cushion and growled at

me deep in her throat. Monica put out a soothing hand, but she was still angry.

"I really don't think Mr. Scott will do it," I said. "Not unless you're there with him to share the stage."

"That's impossible! Ridiculous! As he very well knows. Does he understand that you're going to write about me?"

"Wally told him. Mr. Scott has agreed to let me interview him."

Monica's face had grown quite pink, but except for putting one foot on the iris, she restrained herself. "What else did he say to you?"

I tried to sound casual. "He suggested some people I might talk to, who knew you in the old days. Your former cameraman and makeup woman."

"Alva? Nicos?" She spat out the names. "If you go near them I won't talk to you at all! That Alva—she even turned around and married Saxon! Though I knew it would never last."

I decided to play a risky card. "I want very much to write about you, Aunt Monica. But I can't do it unless I have a free hand."

She flung up her arms in an explosive gesture, making wings of the white caftan, and sprang to her feet. Annabella stood up again and spat her own indignation.

"Go away!" Monica cried. "I don't want to talk to you anymore! You're already on his side. Every woman always fell for him, and you're doing the same thing, even though he's a fake. He always was a fake! Now you'll run and tell him everything I say, and I don't want to talk to you at all!"

I picked up my pad with its very few notes and went quietly to the door. "I'm sorry I've upset you, Aunt Monica. But I can't help the way I feel. It would be so wonderful to see you and Saxon Scott together again, even for one evening. You'd be honoring that classic film—honoring yourselves."

She burst into sudden tears just as Linda came into the room and ran to comfort her. I was in wrong with everyone, including Annabella. Only the white cats regarded me with kind interest.

"You've upset her, Carol," Linda accused. She put her

arms around the suddenly frail and trembling old woman. "There now, dear, you needn't talk anymore if it disturbs you. I'm sorry I went out and left you alone." Again there was reproach for me—an edge of resentment that was growing stronger.

Monica refused to be comforted. "I can't trust anyone! Annie is right about Carol! So just leave—both of you. I'm going up the mountain and sit in the sun."

She picked up a big straw hat from a chair and tied its ribbons under her chin—a slim, dramatic figure in her gold and white. Without another glance in our direction, she strode toward the back stairs that led to the hillside above, her gown sweeping about her. I was left wondering why she'd wanted to talk about Peggy Smith at all. Was there some feeling of guilt in her that she wanted *me* to expiate in my writing? This would bear exploring—if she ever talked to me again.

EIGHT

WHEN SHE'D GONE I TURNED TO LINDA. "I TOLD HER ABOUT THE benefit, as you wanted me to. I guess there was no way to let her know without upsetting her. I'm sorry."

Linda managed to suppress her indignation. "Oh, it can't be helped. I wouldn't have dared to tell her myself. She always reacts emotionally and calms down later to see things more rationally. Not that she'll go up on that stage. I never really thought she would. But she does want this book written."

"She was also upset because I wanted to talk to Nicos and Alva Leonidas. I can't write about her without outside sources. I *must* talk to other people who knew her."

"Never mind. It will work out. Anyway, I have something to show you. I've kept an Arlen room in this house and it will be useful to you now. Let's go have a look."

She led me downstairs to a room tucked away behind her office. A single window at the back was shaded by the steep rise of the mountain, and Linda turned on a lamp.

The room was crowded, filled to the brim with Monica

Arlen. A small red chair—adopted from a picture—offered a place to sit and read from this treasure store, and there was a desk for Linda's work. Shelves along one wall held scrapbooks, and magazines bound into files, as well as volumes that contained pieces about, or references to Monica Arlen. There was, of course, an endless collection of photographs. I realized that some of them must never have been published and would be wonderful to use in a book.

One wall was solid with such pictures, and I studied them eagerly. Many of the shots were of Monica and Saxon together—looking stunningly young and appealing, before life itself had lifted that early air of valor from their faces. There were photographs of other stars as well, all signed lovingly to Monica. Pictures of Bette Davis, Joan Crawford, Barbara Stanwyck, and other women stars of Monica's time. What anecdotes she could tell of those Hollywood years! Nor were the men omitted in her personal collection. There were poses with Cooper, Stewart, Fonda, Gable, and with David Niven and Charles Boyer and others. Some were merely informal snapshots and all the more interesting because these people had been her friends.

Linda stood at my shoulder. "Most of them used to come to Palm Springs in the old days to play and escape. I've heard her talk. They stayed at the Desert Inn or La Quinta Hotel, or El Mirador. The Desert Inn is gone, of course. It stood right down there near the museum, where the Desert Inn Fashion Plaza is now. La Quinta is still as beautiful as ever, and the main part of the El Mirador Hotel is still standing. I believe it's to be preserved. It was used for a scene in *Mirage*, if you remember. That's a picture of it over there."

I looked at a shot of the familiar tower and low white building that I'd seen in the film. "I'd like to visit El Mirador," I said, and moved on to another picture of Cadenza. "Monica told me a little about her Beverly Hills house. She thought you could arrange for me to visit it."

"Of course I can take you there. Perhaps after Christmas. I'm afraid decay is setting in, as it does with these neglected places. It's a shame because they'll never come again, and they belong to movie history and should be preserved."

"Cadenza is an important part of my book, since Monica lived there during the great years."

Linda was thinking of something else. "Carol, when I was out of the room, did she say anything about the telephone call from Saxon?"

"No, she never mentioned it."

"Please ask her about it. She won't tell me, and I need to know why it upset her so badly."

"If I get a chance, I'll ask," I said doubtfully. "I've upset her enough for now, so I don't think she'll talk to me for a while."

"Yes—I was afraid of that."

Linda sounded critical, and once more I was aware of her ambivalence toward me—something I'd sensed from the beginning. It might take very little to turn Linda against me altogether.

Again I moved about the room, stopping beside a glass-covered table, where various memorabilia from Arlen-Scott pictures were on display. There I found the original cuckoo clock, cracked and broken, just as it had been when Monica threw it on the floor in the restaurant scene.

"She kept that," I said wonderingly.

"Her secretary kept it. In fact, Peggy brought together most of these early things, and she made the first scrapbooks. I've pasted up the later ones, using whatever I could find here and there. Most of this was actually collected at Cadenza. I just brought it here, catalogued everything, and put the collection in order. It should give you valuable source material now."

"Do you know anyone in the Desert Hot Springs area whom I could talk to?" I asked. "Everything Monica became later began there. Even the fact that she doesn't want to talk about those days makes me feel there's something about them I should know."

"I suppose I could ask Saxon." Linda sounded doubtful.

"You know him quite well, don't you?"

For once she didn't flush or evade my question, though there was a hint of defiance in her response.

"You might as well know that I worked for Saxon Scott in

his L.A. office when I first came to Hollywood. He was the one who told me he'd heard from Palm Springs friends that Monica was looking for a secretary. He asked me to apply for the job.''

This was surprising, and I wondered if Monica knew.

"Why would he do that?"

She looked away, not meeting my eyes. "I'm not especially proud of this, but at the time I wanted to please him. I suppose he was hoping for a—a sort of spy in Monica's house. He wanted me to keep him posted on everything she did." Linda broke off and went to sit behind the desk, drumming on its surface with nervous fingers. The earlier tension I'd seen in her was back more strongly than ever.

I couldn't help feeling shocked, and I suppose this showed in my face, because Linda snapped at me.

"Don't stare at me like that! It wasn't as bad as you think. Monica needed me, and I got a lot of satisfaction from being useful to her. In the beginning I was just sorry for her— because of the way she used to be. Because of all she'd lost. Saxon never needed sympathy or pity. He's fine as he is. I suppose I've always been a sucker for being needed. Carol, anything I've told Saxon is harmless. I haven't betrayed any of *her* secrets. And now I'm entirely on her side. She doesn't know how I came to her, and I don't want her to know."

"I won't tell her. But why did Saxon ask you to do such a thing?"

"Perhaps"—she sounded almost wistful—"perhaps he never really got over losing her. I've always felt there's a young part of him that still remembers."

I could better understand Linda's ambivalence now. Her loyalty to Monica would have been tempered by a need to talk to Saxon now and then. She'd always admired them both—as they used to be. Nevertheless, what Saxon Scott had asked of her seemed strange and a little ominous. It was hard to believe it had been done out of old love for Monica Arlen.

Linda rumpled her short hair and grinned at me defensively. "You see what happens when I get into this room? I turn romantic and start making up happy endings. Which I know very well aren't going to come about. Saxon has no idea what she's like now. I haven't told him, and sometimes I feel I don't ever want them to meet again. I want to spare her that. You'll need to watch these swampy places, too, Carol. Otherwise, you can get mired down and sink in sentiment. The reality isn't sentimental at all."

She lapsed into brooding silence, and then stirred herself once more.

"You'll find most of your own articles in this room—the ones I've been able to collect. They're in a special file under your name."

"My articles? Why?"

"Because you're related to her. Because I've wanted all along to get you out here. You seemed to be a part of this. Though sometimes I'm not sure, now that you've arrived. I'll tell you one thing—in a showdown I'll be on Monica's side, not Saxon's. Sometimes I do dream about their being together on that stage at the Annenberg, and I make up things I know can't happen. It's just daydreaming. She's such a lost, unhappy lady, and perhaps a lot of this is his fault. Never mind. Let me show you a few other things."

She went to a shelf and brought out a file of clippings. "There are some good *Photoplay* articles about Monica here. That magazine was one of the more accurate ones. Though I love the old gossipy things too, since they were seldom unkind to her. Here's one you'll like." She found a clipping and held it out to me. I read the schmaltzy words:

"Hooray! Hooray! That darling Saxon Scott (don't you adore him in *New Wine?*) has finally popped the question to his beloved Monica Arlen. I've seen the curiously carved emerald ring he's given her—I must know more about that! They've both promised that I'll be the first to know when they set a date. Then of course *you'll* be the first to know what I know. I must say it's about time for our favorite romantic lovers."

Linda smiled. "That's Louella, of course. Hedda didn't gush as much, but she could be nastier if she got mad at anyone. There was a time when she had a feud with Monica. You must ask Monica about that.''

"I want to know especially about what Monica was like when she wasn't on screen. What she thought and felt, and *cared* about. What happened between her and Saxon that made her give up everything, throw over her career and wreck her life?''

"Neither one will tell you that.'' Linda sounded positive. "Anyway, this book ought to be a record of Monica's successes, what she thought about her craft, her art. What she and Saxon created together in their films.''

"Of course that's important. But it wouldn't make a book of any substance by itself. I want to know about the struggles and defeats, even those failed marriages. Whatever their magic was on screen, it grew out of what they were. A man and woman in love, perhaps falling out of love. *Pain* is part of that story. There's very real human tragedy here, but, before I can write about it with any understanding, I need to know a whole lot more. All that seething, hidden emotion—how do I get at it, so *I* can feel? Linda, I need to be strongly involved in what I put on paper, and right now my feelings about Monica are pretty mixed.''

Linda's antagonism and her resistance were growing. "I can't help you,'' she said.

I tried to explain further. "In this sort of writing there needs to be a strong human thread—a feeling for real people. That's what readers relate to. Not just how many movies she made, or how good or bad they were. Besides—and this is personal—in understanding Monica, perhaps I'll come to understand myself a little better. In a strange way, she's been part of me for so long.''

In her look of unswerving, stubborn disapproval, Linda could resemble her brother—unshakable in her private convictions, unswayed by reasoning. She would approve of what *she* wanted to see in my book about Monica, and not what I was talking about.

"I don't want to hurt her,'' I said. "Have you ever considered that it might be better for her? You know—if she opened everything up and then worked through those painful memories until she could free herself of them.''

"*No!* She's too old to tear herself apart all over again. I wish she hadn't given you that ring!''

I stared at my hand, startled. "I told her it was only a loan.'' I pulled the emerald off my finger. "Here—you can give it back to her, if you like.''

Linda shook her head, refusing the ring. "It's up to her. You'll have to give it to her yourself.''

I was putting the ring back on my finger when Ralph Reese appeared in the doorway.

"So this is where you've got to!'' he said. "What happened? Did her majesty throw you out? Did one of the cats scratch you?''

Linda stared at him angrily, and I broke in. "What happened down at the gate?''

"Plenty.'' His manner was only a shade short of insolence. "I found out about the man in the blue Chevy. His name's Gack, and he works for your ex, Mrs.—uh—*Miss* Hamilton. He's a tough hombre, and you'd better watch your step.''

Anxiety swept back in an instant. Owen had insinuated himself into this house without ever setting foot in it, and I was helpless to keep him out. "What does this fellow want?''

"Just to talk to you.''

"I've no intention of seeing him.''

Ralph was clearly enjoying this. I suspected that he would be entertained by any animosities he could discover or stir up.

"He says you snatched Mr. Barclay's son and took him away from New York without letting his father know.''

I had no need to defend myself to Ralph, or explain anything, but my sense of helplessness grew.

Linda came to my rescue, advancing so determinedly from behind her desk that Ralph stepped backward in mock alarm. "Just get out and leave us alone,'' Linda told him. "You've done what you were asked to do, but if you cause any trouble for Miss Hamilton, I can make it hard for you with Miss Arlen. You understand that, don't you?''

Ralph shrugged and went off, managing another sly look for me.

"How I'd like to get rid of *him!*" Linda cried. "But even if Monica knew everything he's been up to, she might not let him go. She needs a man around to make her believe she's still Monica Arlen. How different she must've been when she was young—before everything was spoiled for her. I wish I could have known her then. Now all I can do is try to protect her, save her from—from marauders. Are *you* a marauder, Carol?"

The sudden challenge was disturbing. "I hope not. I'm sorry if you believe that."

Linda went on, musing to herself. "If I tell her too much about Ralph it will only hurt her. And besides, then I wouldn't have anything left to threaten him with."

"What *are* you holding over him?"

"Pilfering. Theft. He's taken pieces of Monica's good jewelry. When I caught him, he said she'd given him the jade ring, and I expect he's sold it by now. Just the same, he got a bit nervous when I threatened to talk to Monica. At least he agreed not to tell her you were here until I could manage it myself. That was the trade-off. She's already missed the ring, and perhaps she even suspects. Though the loss of a little jewelry wouldn't be enough to send her into one of her retreats. The phone call from Saxon did that."

"I don't like Ralph's talking to one of Owen's men."

"Nor do I, Carol. At least he did it outside the gates. Gack can't get inside. You know I've warned the guards again about strangers. They don't like Ralph and they'll report to me if he tries anything."

I could make no pretense of concentrating on the clippings I'd been leafing through. Again the present loomed too dangerously close. Every minute that passed played into Owen's hands. By this time, all sorts of schemes would be fermenting in his brain. He never left anything to one point of attack.

"I still don't know what to do, Linda. Keith and I can't hide here forever, yet the moment we step outside, we're right where Owen wants us."

"Perhaps you could at least tell the police chief about Gack?"

I had gone to the police more than once before, when

Owen had threatened me or been abusive, and I had no confidence in gaining their help. Unless a real crime was committed, their hands would be tied.

"The police don't like to get mixed up in child custody cases," I said. "Especially not when a man as powerful as Owen is involved. I'm not breaking any law. The courts gave me the right to take Keith anywhere I please. But what good does that do me when Owen will simply override the law?"

"You need a change. Maybe the ranch will do you good."

"I don't know. It's not safe to take Keith outside the gates."

"Jason will work it out. Though I'm a little surprised that he's invited you."

"Surprised?"

She sighed. "I suppose I'd better tell you. Then you can go out there with your eyes open."

This sounded ominous and I waited.

"Jason was divorced last year, after being married for a number of years to a perfectly dreadful woman who fooled him completely. Someday there'll be an inheritance for both Jason and me. That's what she married him for in the first place. The money. She's even admitted it, thrown it in his face."

"How awful," I said. It was awful for anyone who had to go through the pain and betrayal of a broken marriage.

Again Linda hesitated. "This is the hard part to tell *you*. They have a child—a little girl named Gwen. She's only a year or so older than your Keith. Beryl, Jason's ex-wife, has taken her away, though Jason has custody, and she and Gwen have been moving from state to state for more than a year. There's a man in the picture somewhere who's helping her out."

I felt sick with shock as I listened.

Linda saw my expression. "Take it easy, Carol. It's better for you to know all this. Laws differ everywhere, so Jason hasn't been able to touch her, or get Gwen back. Beryl won't even talk to him. By the time he finds them, if he ever does, Gwen may be grown up and poisoned against him. Perhaps damaged for life. Beryl's psychotic enough to make her own child the victim in order to punish Jason."

How well I knew what that was like. I could feel Jason's pain as I'd felt my own when Keith had been taken from me by his father a few months ago. Now I could understand Jason's feeling against me. From the first, I'd sensed not only his disapproval, but at times a real hostility, though I'd put this down to my relationship to Monica Arlen. It was a lot stronger than that. How could Jason help but be automatically on the father's side in a divorce case? To him, I would be duplicating his wife's behavior.

Yet even as I understood and sympathized with Jason's viewpoint, a small core of resentment started to grow in me. I *wasn't* like Beryl, and if Jason judged me without a hearing, he was being totally unfair.

"You'll still go to the ranch, won't you?" Linda asked.

"I'm not sure. I'll have to think about it."

She seemed suddenly eager. "Of course you must go. He asked you himself, and that means he's had second thoughts about you. Besides, Keith really does need the trip."

Her words sounded a little too urgent. The "tune" was somehow wrong, and I wondered uneasily if there might be some reason Linda wanted me away from the house.

I hated to distrust her. "I'm glad you told me," I said as I moved toward the door. "I wouldn't want to go out there blindly. Right now all I want is to breathe a little fresh air. Maybe I'll take the boys outside."

I left her putting away scrapbooks and folders, and looked into the dining room. Keith and Jonah were squabbling in normal small-boy fashion over the end of a game. At least this was progress from the solemn, withdrawn state my son had been in for so long.

"When can we go for a ride, Mom?" Keith asked. "Jonah wants to show me where he lives."

"I'm afraid we can't drive anywhere right now."

His disappointment was clear, and in the face of it, my resentment against Jason increased. I understood perfectly well how he felt, but I hated it that his own mistaken reactions should cut Keith off from an interesting experience. I had to face the issue.

"We've been invited to visit Jason Trevor's ranch tomorrow,

113

Keith. I wasn't sure we should go, but if you want to we will. Do you think Jonah would like to come too?''

Both boys were immediately excited over the idea, and their pleasure strengthened my determination. Even though Jason had invited us, I'd sensed at the time that he'd half regretted the gesture. That was *his* problem. I would simply ignore his misconceptions and prove him wrong when the chance offered.

In the kitchen I stopped to speak to Jonah's grandmother, and she gave her permission readily, so the trip was set.

The boys came with me outdoors and ran ahead to climb the steps leading up to where the smoke tree grew. I lingered for a moment on the narrow strip of brick walk between house and mountain, staring up at the formidable peak that cut into the sky directly above. What I saw up there caused me to freeze in apprehension.

Near the crest of the shoulder, two men in bright shirts were climbing the mountain's rocky side. There was a moment when they looked down and I looked up, and though they were tiny figures, I sensed an awareness between us. Of *what* I didn't know.

"Linda!" I called. "Linda, come here!"

She came out of her office at once. Above us, the two men were climbing toward the top.

Linda wasn't upset. "They're probably just kids. There's not much rock climbing around here—too crumbly and dangerous. Mostly backpackers go up the canyons, or follow trails on top of the mountain. But you know kids like to test themselves. That's all those two are probably doing."

"Couldn't they climb right down here into the garden?"

"Not without killing themselves. They'd have to use ropes. That's sheer rock rising straight above this house. I've told you—at night our alarm system is turned on and no one can get inside the house. Monica's as edgy about that as you are, Carol. If you worry about everything, you'll go out of your mind! Now run along and play with the boys. It will do you good."

After she disappeared inside, I stood for a moment longer staring up at the spectacular peak. The slope above me didn't reach the mountain's highest point, but it was high enough, and that was a long way up. Which might mean nothing to experienced climbers. Ropes were easily come by, and Owen could hire anyone he chose. Rock climbers, cat burglars, kidnappers!

The two men had disappeared over the crest and nothing moved up there. I could hear birds in the garden, and faint sounds from the town below. Loudest of all was the thump of my fast-beating heart.

Restlessness drove me for the rest of the day. I let the ranch trip stand, though I felt increasingly unsure about everything else. Once I'd thought that anger would sustain me. But anger was never enough. Owen would move, as I knew very well. He was already having me watched. But from what direction would the real attack come?

Before Keith went to bed that night, I taught him Monica's phone number. I made him repeat it over and over again. He was good at memorizing, and he knew how to dial. This was one more small protection, if ever he became separated from me. Though I prayed he'd never need to use it.

When he was asleep I returned to the upper garden. A few lights from the house showed me the way. My need was to be quiet and alone. High above me the mountain stood silhouetted against dark blue silk, and a sliver of moon was pinned against the sky. The moon and all those stars seemed more brilliantly close here in the desert than I'd seen anywhere before.

When I reached the pool I stretched out in a chair and closed my eyes, willing myself to be still, to empty away all tension. It was no use. Even with my eyes closed, an inner panorama flowed endlessly through my mind, and the questions wouldn't be quiet. How was I to find answers that would enable me to order my life and protect Keith? Right now, all I seemed to do was live from day to day, from hour to hour, and this was anything but satisfying. How was I to plan for the future when the next minute might be filled with peril? Tonight the emerald ring weighed heavily on my finger, and I turned it absently.

The touch of it brought more questions—about whether I

115

could ever write the book about Monica Arlen that should be written. Questions about what she was really like *now*—and not only in the past. Since she was angry with me, perhaps nothing would come of this book anyway.

Night doubts. How disturbing they could be, with answers always moving farther away than ever.

After a time, I left my chair to stand beside the pool, watching a reflection of the slim moon in rippling black water. Up on the mountain the wind had risen and shrubbery in the garden swayed and sighed. Once more I searched the dark crest far above, but nothing stirred against the sky, and all the rest of the mountain was as softly black as the pool itself, deep beneath that gilding moon. Anything could hide up there. Once a tiny shower of stones slid on the slope above me, as though some night animal had struck them loose. Or had they been kicked by a stealthy foot?

Such thoughts were unsettling, and I circled the pool and stood with my back to the summer house, still staring upward. If it hadn't been for the mountain sounds and the soughing of the wind, I might have heard a step upon the tiles as someone left the summer house. I was still searching the black slope, however, trying to make my eyes penetrate whatever secrets the mountain held. I had no warning at all when something struck me violently in the back, and thrusting hands shoved me headfirst into the water.

Stunned with shock, I went under completely. When I recovered the power to move, and my head broke the surface, I realized in horror that something dark swam in the pool beside me. Before I could strike out and escape, hands clasped around my ankles. In an instant I was pulled to the bottom of the pool. With all my strength I tried to break free and swim, but the awful weight crept up my legs and wrapped around them like chains, once more pulling me down.

There was no air left in my lungs. They were bursting. At the last instant, my legs were released and I kicked myself desperately to the surface, to gulp air. Immediately my feet were grasped again, and I barely had time to hold my breath as I went under, pulled to the bottom, my ankles pinned in that steely grip.

I don't know how many times it happened. I was allowed to reach the surface, teased with a chance to breathe air into my lungs, and then pulled under again, mercilessly. Each time I felt this would be final, and I'd be held under too long.

When my head broke the surface for the last time, I managed a single wild scream before I went under, swallowing water.

Consciousness can go quickly, and I have only a blurred memory of what happened next. Someone must have heard my scream, for sudden floodlights dazzled the water. Voices shouted and running feet clattered on the tiles. My head was above the surface—if only I could breathe, and the bands around my body were gone. Only succoring hands held me now, and I was being unceremoniously hauled out of the pool by Ralph Reese.

After that I lay face down on the tiles, while Ralph pumped water out of my lungs. I seemed to hurt all over, but I was breathing again and air was the most wonderful element in the world. When I opened my eyes, I found Ralph bending over me, and Linda beside him, both dripping wet. She had jumped in too, to help me out.

The water had been warm from the day's sun, but now I was aware of sharp air chilling me to the bone. My teeth chattered and I shivered with cold and shock.

"Quick!" Linda cried, pulling me to my feet. "Let's get you to your room where you can change to something dry. I'll fix you a hot drink. I'm frozen myself. How on earth did you fall in, Carol?"

Ralph was made of sterner stuff. No shivering for him. "Do you always go swimming with your clothes on, Miss Hamilton?" he asked. "It was a good thing I was around to fish you out."

I pulled away from his supporting arm, dazed, but not trusting him. "Someone—someone t-t-tried to d-d-drown me!" I gasped, and then made an effort to steady my voice. "Someone pushed me into the pool and tried to hold me under the water!"

"That's impossible!" Linda cried.

"She's off her nut." Ralph was scornful. "There was no

one else around when I got here. She was just yelling and flapping around in the water."

I had no strength to argue, to deny. There *had* been someone in the pool with me. Ralph, of course. Or someone else who had eluded all the barriers—someone sent in by Owen?

Between them, Ralph and Linda half carried me toward the house, our shoes squelching water and clothes dripping. At the top of the steps, Linda paused with an arm around me, looking down toward the rear balcony at this end.

Monica Arlen stood at the rail, her face white above her long dark robe as she stared at us.

"What is it?" she cried. "Linda, what's happened? I heard shouting."

Linda answered her unhappily. "Carol says someone pushed her into the pool and tried to drown her."

Monica clutched at the balcony rail with both hands, too shaken to speak. Then she made a low, moaning sound and fled into the bedroom behind her.

At once Linda abandoned me. "Ralph, see that Carol gets back to her room. Monica's frightened and she needs me."

"Hah!" Ralph said. "Maybe it's Miss Arlen who pushed her in!"

For an instant I thought Linda might slap him, but she restrained herself with an effort. "There were some men climbing the mountain today. Maybe you were right, Carol. Maybe Owen Barclay has a longer arm than I thought."

She hurried off and once more I moved from Ralph's touch. "I'm safer walking alone."

His look seemed to know all and tell nothing. When I stumbled into my room, I found Keith still asleep, and I shed my wet clothes in the bathroom and put on a warm robe. Then I got into bed, still shivering.

In a little while Linda appeared with a cup of steaming soup. She'd changed her own clothes, and had managed to quiet Monica.

"I'm sure it was Ralph. It must have been Ralph," I said as she sat down near my bed. "But why would he try to drown me?"

She was already shaking her head. "I can't believe anyone would try to do that. Not even Ralph."

I supposed she was right. It was only Owen to whom I was a threat. If I were dead, Keith would go straight into Owen's hands—as I already knew. This returning thought was even more chilling than water closing over my head. Now there had been a real threat to my life. If I hadn't been able to scream . . .

Not until I was finishing the soup, did I become suddenly aware of my hand. I held it up for Linda to see. "Monica's emerald! It's gone!"

Linda's expression told me that losing the ring was worse than nearly losing my life. "That's awful! You should never have worn it up there, Carol. It probably came off in the water. Now it's too dark to search for it. In the morning I'll send Ralph to look for it in the pool. I won't dare tell Monica."

"No," I said dryly, "don't tell her anything more to upset her. I'll be all right now, Linda. Thank you for the soup."

She looked at me doubtfully, perhaps rehearing the wrong emphasis of her own words. Then she took my cup and went off, leaving me to my own shattering thoughts.

An hour or two went by while I tossed, growing more and more wide awake, living over those terrible moments in the water. At least I was warm again, and eventually I got up and stood for a few moments beside my sleeping son. Then I wrapped my robe more tightly around me and went to the open door of the balcony at the front of the house.

Outside it was cold and bright and very clear, with all those stars looking down on oasis and desert. The lights of Palm Canyon Drive followed the mountains. I'd noticed that all this area had the appealing custom of using palm trees for streetlights, so that illumination glowed up through the branches. What had once been a dirt track called Plank Road now stretched for a long way through the little "cities" strung together at the base of the San Jacintos.

Beyond the house, beyond the town, loneliness seemed part of the vast landscape. Nighttimes were always lonely for me now. How foolish I'd been, how starry-eyed, only a few years ago, when I'd believed that something wonderful and

119

treasuring had come into my life, bringing me a man to value and love, and who valued and loved me. I couldn't have been more blindly stupid. Yet I couldn't regret what had happened, because I had Keith. No, for Keith, as well as for me, I must stay alive.

I wondered if Jason Trevor ever stood out there beneath the desert stars and thought about loneliness. Probably not. He would think only with anger of the loss of his daughter. I had already sensed in him that deep, hot rage, and I'd known, though I hadn't understood, that at moments some of this had been for me. A judging anger.

My hand looked bare on the balcony rail, and I thought again of the missing ring. It *had* to be found in the pool. The emerald was precious beyond its value—in a sense symbolizing much that had happened in Monica Arlen's life, and it could never be replaced for her. Or even for me. We must find it quickly.

At last, in spite of too many fearful thoughts, the peace of the night and of the sleeping city began to quiet me so that I was ready to return to bed. Ready until I caught movement on the lighted terrace. Ralph Reese stood at the far end of the stone wall, smoking. The hour was late—two o'clock, my watch told me. Was he there because he couldn't sleep either, or because he waited for something? Or had met someone?

Perhaps I made a slight sound, or perhaps he had an animal's sense of being watched, because he turned and looked up at my balcony. Terrace lights fell on his face and the insolence was there again—even bolder and more open than before. He gave me a slight salute of finger to temple, ground out his cigarette on the bricks, and went through a door near Monica's end of the house. No alarm sounded.

Which only meant that of course he could turn the system on and off at will, if he wanted to come outside at night. That too was far from reassuring.

Once more feeling chilled, I went back to my own bed, but not to sleep for a long time.

NINE

THE TWO BOYS DIDN'T UNDERSTAND WHY THEY WERE BEING SMUG-
gled out concealed under a blanket in the back of Jason's
station wagon, but they regarded it as a game, and stifled
their giggles. I was more apprehensive as I sat beside Jason in
the front seat. No blue Chevy was in sight at that early hour,
however, and after what had happened last night it was a
relief to get away from the house. I was no longer safe in
Monica's fortress.

In a little while the boys were able to sit up and look out.
We drove along a main road called Tahquitz-McCallum, and
when I asked about the name, Jonah was full of information.
The boy's bright, dark eyes and slightly cocky manner were
appealing, but I suspected that he could easily get out of
hand.

"Tahquitz is a real bad Indian spirit who lives in a canyon
on the mountain," he told us. "That's what they call the
canyon too. All the little Indian kids are scared of him. But
I'm not."

121

"I'm not either," Keith said.

Jason smiled. "The canyon sometimes trembles and rumbles so Indian mothers used to blame that on Tahquitz and used him as a warning to naughty children."

"Was McCallum somebody bad too?" Keith asked.

"Hardly," Jason said. "The McCallum family practically started Palm Springs. The place had other names in the old days—Palmdale and Palm Valley. Though out here the old days aren't that long ago. Agua Caliente is what they called the hot springs. John McCallum—he received the courtesy title of judge when he was old—planted fruit orchards. He's the one who brought water down from the mountains in a canal. His daughter Pearl did a great deal for the city to keep it beautiful. It's a name that's respected in this town."

I sensed that Jason was talking to cover my own disturbed state of mind. When we'd started out, he'd asked if I was all right, and I'd managed to assure him that I was. I don't think he believed me, but I couldn't speak out in front of the boys. Anyway, I wasn't sure I wanted to tell him what had happened last night. Linda would take care of that. I just needed to escape from the house and put everything behind me for a while. It felt good to be driving into the desert.

Today Jason looked comfortable in jeans that were faded and a bit worn at the knees, his blue shirt open at the throat, and short, scuffed boots of tooled leather on his feet. He still seemed a stern, remote man, and I was intensely aware of the circumstances that stood between us.

A recently risen sun flooded the desert, so that palm trunks and the mountain itself glowed with a pink light. As we left Palm Springs behind, the warming scents of mesquite and creosote drifted in the car windows. On every hand the desert rolled away—not flat, empty land, but with high rock formations, shifting dunes, gullies where water must sometimes flow. I began to have a feeling of familiarity. All those stories I'd heard from Mrs. Johnson when I was ten were part of my own fantasies, always connecting with Monica, who also lived in the desert. This morning the country around me no longer looked strange and frightening as it had seemed when I'd driven here.

Jason pointed out feathery gray smoke trees growing in a wash, and a few rounded paloverdes with their green bark. I had a sense of recognition in everything I saw.

"Desert Hot Springs is off that way." Jason motioned toward the north. "You should drive Keith out there sometime to see Cabot's. It's a pueblo-type building full of local history. You can learn from it yourself."

"I know," I said. "Monica was born in the area, so I'd especially like to go there. For some reason she doesn't want to talk about her childhood, though I need to know a lot more about the years before she went to Hollywood, if I'm to write this book. Right now, she's banished me, though Linda doesn't think it will last."

Jason looked straight ahead through the windshield and offered no comment, his very silence suggesting disapproval. Yesterday's resentment of being judged began to stir in me again. This was a disapproval to which he had no right!

"Why don't you like the idea of my writing about Monica?" I asked bluntly.

"It doesn't matter to me, one way or another. It's none of my business."

Now that the subject had been opened, I wanted to smoke him out, force him to talk about what was bothering him. My earlier notion of ignoring what he felt toward me wasn't going to work. I couldn't, after all, stifle my own resentment against his prejudice. Monica wasn't the true subject I wanted to open, but perhaps she was a way past his prickly guard.

"You *do* disapprove, and I'd like to know why," I challenged him.

"Maybe it's because Hollywood biographies usually turn out to be glorified gossip. Rather cheap gossip, at that."

"Gossip *isn't* what I want to write. I'm not looking for tidbits of scandal. It's the human experience that fascinates me. Monica had a spectacular success—I've seen all those old films of hers. Yet she threw it away overnight to live as a recluse. Other people survive broken love affairs and go on. Why didn't she? Perhaps it will even help *her* if I can get her to open up honestly with me. I'd like to write about her with understanding and sympathy."

123

"Then it'll be pretty bland, won't it? Isn't gossip what your readers are likely to want?"

His argument wasn't really about Monica. It concerned all the other things he held against me. "Why not wait and see what I'm able to write?" I asked. "It isn't fair to leap into judgment." *I* wasn't talking about Monica either. "I think you're baiting me," I added.

He slanted that sudden smile at me—reminding me of his sister—a flash that lighted his desert tan. He *was* baiting me, yet the truth behind his hostility wasn't a subject I could open up with him directly. Not yet.

"What about your article on the museum?" he asked. "Have you already dropped that?"

"Of course not. I've been making notes, setting down impressions. I need to know more before I write."

As we neared the ranch, he pointed out to the boys a few low buildings occupying an empty space of desert, with no houses nearby. Buildings that included a house, a barn, and a fenced corral with three or four horses inside. Along the western boundary tall eucalyptus trees made a handsome windbreak.

Keith sat up and exclaimed. His interest in animals was always lively, and his very excitement made me glad we'd come. Never mind about Jason Trevor and his prejudices! I must thrust away the thought of water closing over my head, arms pulling me down. For this little while I must escape from all tension—for my own sanity.

"It's not a real ranch anymore," Jason explained. "In my parents' day it was a working ranch. They've moved to a coast town now. But Linda and I grew up out here, and since I've always liked to come back, I've kept a bit of it up. I stay here whenever I can, though I have a small place in town."

The house was a weathered brown, low and wide, with a front porch that boasted several old-fashioned rockers. Jason led us into the long living room, where an early morning fire burned in a rock fireplace. At the far end, open double doors led into a dining room, and another warm hearth. Mrs. Sanchez came to greet us, smiling and plump, her English flavored with the Mexican "tune" that was to grow familiar to me. The lilt of the words was different from the Puerto Rican cadence I was more accustomed to.

Breakfast was ready, and we sat at one end of an enormous oak table that must have served ranch hands in the past. When sizzling ham with hash brown potatoes on the side was brought in, and a plate of thick toast slices from home-baked bread, both boys went eagerly to work. Watching Keith, I could forgive Jason anything. What he thought about me didn't matter. Somehow, I must hold to that and swallow my resentment.

After we'd eaten, he took us out to the corral with its rail fence, and introduced us to the horses. Keith and Jonah were lifted to the back of an elderly mare, and led cheerfully around the corral by Mr. Sanchez, who appeared to like small boys.

Jason and I sat on the top rail of the fence and watched in comfortable silence. Gradually, a sense of peace I hadn't felt for a long while began to envelop me. The sky was pale blue and cloudless. Already the sun warmed the morning, but at this time of year the warmth was kind, and I raised my face gratefully to the light, and to the westerly breeze. Fall in New York could be the best time of the year—invigorating. This was different, more languorous, and very pleasant. The horror of last night seemed far away.

Jason watched the two boys, one so fair, the other dark; he watched Keith particularly. "His father must miss him a great deal," he said quietly.

My sense of languor vanished. Now it would begin. The remark, for all his quiet tone, was deliberately provocative, and I plunged into an answer.

"As you miss your daughter? No, I don't think so. If I believed that, I wouldn't have run from New York."

Jason said nothing, and even his silence was hostile, skeptical. I slid down from the rail, feeling better braced with my feet on the ground.

"Linda's told me about your wife and daughter. I'm terrible sorry, Jason. I felt sick when I heard what had happened. I know what it's like. Owen stole Keith from me a few months ago, though I got him back that time—by law. Next time I might not.''

"Yet you can't see what it might be like for Keith's father?''

I looked at him on the fence above me, seeing the grim lines about his mouth, the coldness of his eyes, and I almost faltered. I might never be able to convince this man, but I had to try.

"It *isn't* the same. It isn't like that for Owen! If Keith were truly happy with his father, I would let him go on visits whenever Owen wished. In fact, I was willing to do that from the first—until I began to see what was happening.''

Jason's laugh dismissed my words. I heard deep bitterness in the sound. We were a long way from any mutual understanding, and I tried to suppress my own rising anger. He had reason. The hurt he'd suffered over the loss of his daughter was something I felt and understood. Yet only I could know how different it was from anything Owen was capable of feeling.

"Fathers don't always come out fairly after a divorce,'' I said quietly. "Not any more than mothers are necessarily right, just because they're mothers.''

He heard me as if from a distance, and said nothing.

The quiet of the desert closed around us. Only the horses, neighing and stomping, and the boys' laughter made a tiny core of sound in the midst of a great silence.

Jason said, "Would you like to ride a little way into the desert?''

I shook myself out of a depression that had taken hold. "I'm not much of a rider, but I'd like to try.''

My jeans and sturdy shoes would serve, and I was boosted into a saddle. Jason mounted his own palomino—a real beauty—and led the way out. The boys were having so much fun they hardly noticed our going. They would be safe with Mr. and Mrs. Sanchez.

The western saddle was comfortable, and the mare they'd given me moved smoothly. There was something exciting about sitting in a saddle above the world, and being borne along by an animal instead of an indifferent machine. For a little while trouble couldn't touch me. Not even Jason's silent disapproval could touch me.

Away from the shelter of the ranch the wind blew steadily. It always blew out here in the desert, Jason said, though this was a calm morning, comparatively. Sand foamed around the horses' hooves in little eddies, but didn't rise in the air, as it could in a real storm. For the first time it was possible to see the desert in a way that a moving car never allowed.

"We'll just go a little farther," Jason said, "so you won't get too sore."

He rode easily beside me, moving as one with a horse that seemed aware of his slightest touch. My feeling of elation grew—a feeling that was purely physical—and I was happy to indulge it.

"There used to be large bands of wild horses roaming all this area," Jason said. "You can still hear coyotes sometimes at night, though unhappily the horses have been hunted out. Up in the mountains there are a few bighorn sheep left, but they're wary of men. Men are the marauders. Too many, too brutal, too careless—spoiling the land wherever they go."

The word he had used caught my ear because his sister had used it to me just yesterday. Why had she asked if I were a "marauder"? The thought intruded on my lighter mood, and I tried to thrust it away.

We were riding toward a nearby rock formation that rose like a miniature mountain ahead of us, and when we reached it Jason helped me to dismount. After we'd tethered the horses to a mesquite bush, we climbed the rough rock to the top, where we could look out across the sand in all directions. For a little while even Jason's prickliness seemed to subside.

Since we were so different, and came from opposite backgrounds, I found it surprising that there were moments when I felt almost comfortable with Jason Trevor. As though— and this was a startling thought—we were more alike than we were different. The air hadn't cleared between us, but at least friction had lessened for a little while, and we could feel at ease with each other.

He pointed into the distance. "That's where the San Andreas Fault goes through. You can hardly see it from the ground, but from a plane, or from the mountains, it makes a ruled line straight across the desert where the fracture cuts through. Some of the mountains around here were pushed up because of the Fault. Not that we have many real earthquakes. The last bad shake just east of Palm Springs was in 1969.''

There had been predictions of new quakes along the Fault, but Californians seemed to live rather casually with their earthquakes, putting out of mind what couldn't be helped. The way East Coasters lived with the threat of hurricanes. A submerged uneasiness that it was better not to look at too often.

In the west the Little San Bernardinos rimmed the horizon, as bare and burned-out in appearance as the moon. The distances seemed endless, and I found a human need to focus on what was near and tangible. From a clump of mesquite a quail made its chuckling sound, and the marvelously clear air was aromatic with growth that I hadn't known existed on my trip by car through the more western desert.

"This is a good time of year," Jason said, sounding relaxed and peaceable now. "Not as beautiful as spring, when everything blooms, but the mountains have stopped radiating heat, and everything revives, including those of us who live here. It's still early in the season, so the tourists haven't appeared in full force yet."

"I don't have much of a sense of the life in Palm Springs," I said. "Monica lives in a rarefied atmosphere of her own."

Amiably, he tried to explain. "There are all sorts of levels. So many different and extreme lifestyles. The rich and the tourists come here for playtime living. Or for retirement. Most of those who come in from outside to build expensive homes have made it big somewhere else. It's not a competitive place like Los Angeles. All those movies you admire have their source in a lot of bloody infighting that takes place somewhere else. With an eye on the dollar, and the hand sometimes in the till. When somebody like Cliff Robertson blows the whistle, he's put into limbo for years."

"But good movies *are* made."

"In spite of, maybe. I don't put down the creative people, the dedicated writers and directors and actors. A number of

them hold to their own vision. They can leave competition behind when they come here to soak up the sun. Though that's make-believe too—as though the rest of the world ceased to exist. There can be a lot of heads in the sand here in the desert!''

''What about you?''

''I belong to the working types who put down roots and like it here. Some of us even stay through the broiling summers because the desert gets under our skins and this is where we want to make our lives. People stayed here the year-round even before air conditioning.''

''There's a wonderful feeling of space,'' I said. ''I even like all the sand colors. But the desert's awfully big, and sometimes it scares me.''

He smiled again. ''It's not a kid's sandbox. I suppose it takes a certain toughness to survive, and it can be pretty savage at times. There are still sidewinders—rattlesnakes to you—though they're small and nocturnal, and they avoid people. Then there's the wind. Even though a lot of the valley is cultivated now, the earth can rise into the air and bury everything. Winds that tunnel down through San Gorgonio Pass blow it our way. San Gorgonio's the big mountain standing up there north of Palm Springs. Farther south, at the end of the Santa Rosas, there are wastelands and real desolation. Moon country. You'll see it when you fly over by the southern route.''

I could almost like him in this expansive mood. He held out his hand and we started down from our rocky summit, his grasp firm and impersonal.

''I suppose you know about that secretary of Monica's?'' he asked as we reached the ground. ''The one who killed herself years ago?''

''Peggy Smith? Yes, of course. I found that bust she did of Aunt Monica in the museum.''

Jason pointed again. ''It was right at the end of these rocks that her body was found. They say she brought Monica's gun with her and drove out here deliberately to kill herself. Her car was nearby. Of course Linda's obsessed by anything that

129

concerns Monica Arlen, so she's talked about it. There's some gossip for you.''

He was baiting me again, but I didn't rise to the challenge. Monica's curious hint that perhaps Peggy Smith's death hadn't been suicide returned to me at the sight of the very place where she had been found.

Jason boosted me into the saddle again, and we rode back to the ranch. A long-ago death had reached out to touch the present, and we were silent all the way.

The rest of the morning was spent in a leisurely fashion that suited me well. At lunch Mrs. Sanchez's beans and rice were devoured with enthusiasm by two hungry small boys. Everything could seem almost "normal" out here. This simple ranch life seemed far happier than life at Smoke Tree House. Yet the need to return to the mountain was always there at the back of my mind. However pleasant this escape, it couldn't offer us the security we needed right now. Gack, the man in the blue Chevy, would grow doubly watchful, since we'd given him the slip this morning.

For a little while I'd been able to stop thinking about what had happened in the pool, but it *had* happened, so that even Monica's fortress had been breeched. Nevertheless, we would have to go back, and if there was an enemy within the walls, then I'd have to deal with that too.

After lunch, when I suggested that we'd better start home to Palm Springs, Jason vetoed this calmly.

"I'll drive you back at sunset," he said. "There'll be an early moon over the desert tonight, and you have to see our best attractions if you're going to write about us."

Even though his words were faintly derisive, he seemed good-natured enough. Perhaps this day in the open had relaxed him too.

He had work to finish at his desk in the library-study, and he asked if I would mind.

"I'll find something to read," I said, and followed him into a big room with a touch of the Spanish in its dark furniture, and of the Indian in colorful rugs and wall hangings. I liked the spacious room with its whitewashed walls, doors that opened onto the wide porch, and books everywhere.

I found myself contrasting Jason with Owen, who hated to read. Owen always demanded center stage, and someone else's attention on a book irritated him. All my writings had been done when he was out of the apartment. Owen's angers were always explosive—he never held anything back. In Jason anger could run still and deep, though it hadn't seemed directed against me today. I no longer considered him arrogant, as I'd done at first. Now I understood why he was angry, and why he'd been critical of me.

I studied titles along a bookshelf and smiled to discover a similarity in our tastes. He too liked Adam Hall and Le Carré. There was even an early Stephen King that had given me shivers. But he read a lot of other things too—books about the Middle East, and China. A volume on South Africa that I'd found fascinating and disturbing. Clearly, Jason didn't live with his head in the sand.

I finally selected something on desert animals, and settled down in a corner of the room. Once, after I'd been reading for a while, I looked up to find Jason watching me speculatively.

"Linda said you weren't sure you wanted to come here today," he said.

"That's right. At first I didn't want to come. Not after Linda told me about your wife and daughter. I could understand how you'd feel toward me, though there didn't seem to be any way I could defend myself. I don't mean that I haven't done things I've regretted and been wrong about. But it isn't the way you probably thought."

"Why did you change your mind?" His tone seemed casual.

"I wanted Keith to have the trip. Besides, I kept getting indignant whenever I thought of how you'd condemned me without a hearing. I suppose I wanted to stand up for myself, in spite of what you thought. Now it doesn't seem to matter much, though perhaps it will again. Why did you ask me to come?"

"I'm not sure. Mixed reasons. Maybe I thought—oh, never mind."

"Perhaps you wanted to speak up for my husband's viewpoint?"

This time he laughed openly, naturally. "Maybe you're

right. Neither of us can help being prejudiced by our own experiences. So it could be safer if we avoid explanations and accusations. Look—if you need to go to Desert Hot Springs for your research, I can drive you there.''

The sudden offer was a truce, but I wondered if a truce was what I really wanted. A truce meant that we'd put aside our points of disagreement and not talk about dangerous topics. It meant only a postponement of facing the real issues. For right now, I accepted that.

"If you would really drive me somewhere, there's a town in the mountains that I'd like to visit—Idyllwild. Monica doesn't want me to meet the couple she used to know who live there. So I can't ask Linda to take me. Yet I really need to talk with them both, if I'm to write honestly about Monica.''

"Honestly? That usually means somebody's going to get hurt.''

A truce might be difficult, after all.

"Look, Jason," I said, "I can't work if I have to analyze myself and my motives every inch of the way. I need to go into this with an open mind and not set up barriers. If I'm to develop insight, if I'm to find my own viewpoint, I can't worry about who might be hurt. I don't even know that yet. All I'm after is to discover as much as I can learn. Enough so I can take sides.''

"Between Arlen and Scott?''

"If necessary. Of course I'd like to be on Aunt Monica's side. But sooner or later I must understand what happened in the past. So much hinges on that.''

"After all this time, isn't that a trivial question?''

"Not to me it isn't.''

"Who do you want to see in Idyllwild?''

"Nicos and Alva Leonidas. Both were old hands at Monica's studio in her great days. Linda wants me to write *her* kind of book—glowing with praise for Monica's achievements. That's fine, but I have to find the woman as well as the actress. There's a great deal of material about the actress, but I'll have to hunt for the woman. The best way to do that is through her friends and enemies.''

"All right," he said. "I know their restaurant in Idyllwild—

132

the Lindos. So I'll take you there. You can bring the boys again, if you like.''

"Thanks, but I'd better not take Keith away from the house too often. Even though we managed this today, it might not work next time. Owen won't stop at anything when he goes after what he wants. He can be—dangerous.''

"That sounds melodramatic.''

Anger leaped in me again, taking me by surprise. I'd thought myself so calm.

"Yes—it is melodramatic. Last night someone tried to drown me in Monica's swimming pool. It was very melodramatic.''

He swung away from his desk. "What are you talking about?'' So Linda hadn't told him.

I related the whole thing as quietly as I could. I didn't want terror and fear to rise in me again, but they came anyway. I had to hold on to myself hard in order to finish the story.

Before I was through, he came to sit near me, clearly shocked and concerned. "You can't stay up there any longer,'' he said when I paused. "We'll find some other place—''

"What other place? Monica's house is still safer than anywhere else. I can't believe that your sister is mixed up in this, and I have to stay there for now. If it was Ralph, he can be guarded against. I never thought I wouldn't be safe going up to the pool—with Monica's walls all around. I was wrong.''

Jason got up and moved restlessly about the room. This time I'd convinced him, and I was grateful for his concern. But there wasn't anything he could do for Keith and me right now.

"Why didn't you tell me sooner?'' he asked. "I sensed right away that something was wrong.''

"What was the point in telling you? I meant to leave that to Linda. Until you said I was being melodramatic.''

"I'm sorry. I'm afraid we haven't understood each other very well.''

I wasn't sure we did now. "Please go on with your work. I'm all right. And I'm very glad you brought us out here today.''

"I won't be much longer,'' he said and returned to his

papers. Though now and then he looked over at me rather doubtfully.

I read on absently about the desert wood rat, which preferred human belongings to trim his nest. And I learned that since date groves had been established in the area, raccoons had come down from the mountains, extending their range. I wished I could care. Now that I'd stopped holding away the memories of last evening, I kept feeling hands around my ankles, pulling me under the water.

In the end, I gave up trying to read and took my book back to its shelf. A framed photograph on the bookcase caught my eye and I picked it up, realizing it must be Jason's daughter. A bright-faced little girl with long brown hair looked out at me trustingly in the color print. I put the picture down and turned to find Gwen's father once more watching me.

"She's beautiful," I said, and could find no easy words to express what the sight of Gwen's picture did to me.

"She belongs here," Jason said grimly.

What if I repeated the same thing he'd said to me? What if I asked if his child's mother wouldn't miss her daughter a great deal if she had to give her up? But I couldn't speak the words. I was willing to make an intuitive leap that he couldn't make toward me and to believe in his "truth."

"My daughter is why I'm on leave from my regular post at the museum just now," he said. "I take out classes now and then, and work on free-lance projects. That way I can leave for any part of the country at a moment's notice. I have a good agency looking for her, and I've made several futile trips so far, but lately we've come a little closer."

"To snatching her back?" I asked.

Anger was hot in his eyes, but he said nothing. There was nothing more I could say, and I wandered outside, where the boys were chasing each other around the house, whooping exuberantly. *I* was lucky. I had Keith, and he was beginning to sound like any normal, obstreperous little boy. It had to stay that way. I knew how Jason felt, but the rights and wrongs were no longer as clear-cut as I'd thought.

The rest of the afternoon slipped by quietly, and around four o'clock Jason said he would drive us back. With the sun

going down beyond the western mountains, Mt. San Jacinto stood black and massive against a golden sky. The promised early moon sailed over the desert, and its beauty held an aching quality for me. I hated to return to the tensions of Smoke Tree House and the new threat it now held for me, but that was where reality waited—a reality I had to face. Jason's quiet ranch was only part of a fantasy I mustn't think about. It had no meaning for the future, no substance or connection with the frightening possibilities that faced me. I'd had enough of building my life on make-believe, and I mustn't indulge that weakness again.

The light on top of the tramway up Mt. San Jacinto beckoned us for miles, like a blue star. When we reached Palm Springs, the mountain already cast its shadow across the town. Soft lights glowed upward through palm trees that lined the streets, and when we crossed Palm Canyon Drive its bright shop windows shone like jewel boxes in the dark.

At the gatehouse, the man called Gack sat in his car waiting, and he gave me a knowing grin as we drove by. We followed the road through the upper gate, to find Wally's car parked on the bricks of the terrace. I held out my hand to Jason.

"Thank you for a beautiful day." Feeble words, but all I could offer in gratitude.

"Thank *you*." Then he added, "Take care of yourself, Carol."

For all our edgy exchanges, a certain fellowship had been established between Jason and me. Perhaps we were on the same side, after all.

Helsa took the two boys in charge and told me that Linda had gone out. Miss Arlen had left word that I was to come to see her the moment I arrived.

Did that mean she'd forgiven me? I wondered. And why was Wally here, if Linda was away? I hurried upstairs, to find Monica's carved door ajar, and when I tapped she called to me to come in.

I walked into her living room, totally unprepared. Owen Barclay was sitting on the sofa beside her.

135

TEN

Owen stood up, bowing with mock courtesy, and Monica smiled a warm welcome—which I wouldn't have expected, considering the way we'd last parted. I could only stare at them both, stunned and shocked.

Monica was in full "costume" again, dressed in something of filmy azure, and once more wearing the chestnut wig that had seen service in *Mirage*. She seemed younger, and strangely eager, as though new hope had come unexpectedly into her life.

"Ah, Carol! I'm glad you're home. Linda has gone off somewhere—such a nuisance!—but her young man was kind enough to bring Mr. Barenklovich to see me." She turned to Owen. "This is my great-niece, Miss Hamilton. Carol is going to do a biography about me. Wally, do come in here and explain to Carol."

I was still too stunned to speak, and I looked around to see that Wally Davis stood beyond the glass door to the balcony, talking to Ralph. He came cheerfully into the room to greet

me, closing the door carefully behind him. I saw why at once. All three cats had been shut outside on the balcony, and I noted Owen's look of aversion in their direction as Wally came in. Monica did well to protect her pets.

Moving carefully, I walked to a chair and sat down. I'd been completely betrayed, and I still felt too alarmed to say anything. My one clear thought was to hide my inner trembling from Owen. He would know very well how frightened I was, but I didn't mean to show it outwardly.

"Hi, Carol," Wally greeted me. "Saxon sent Mr. Barenklovich to me, since he was finding it difficult to see Miss Arlen. I phoned Linda this morning and she made the arrangements."

Monica broke in delightedly. "Carol, what do you think! Mr. Barenklovich proposes to buy my Beverly Hills house!"

There was a tightness in my chest as I stared at Owen. He looked as he always did—handsome, with his tightly curled gray hair, penetrating dark eyes, and a mouth that would never again seem anything but cruel to me. As always, he had the lithe, predatory look of a tiger on the prowl. Monica had no idea of the danger, but his overpowering presence was making her behave in a keyed-up way. Usually, *she* was in control, but with Owen present, everyone snapped to attention, a little off-balance.

He smiled at me sardonically. "I'd like to tell you what I have in mind, Miss—uh—Hamilton."

I looked away from him, focusing on the iris that lay across Monica's knees. Not for a moment longer could I bear to watch him, but I had to hear whatever it was he was planning. I had to listen above the quick beating of my heart.

"I've needed a West Coast house for a long time," he went on blandly. "My agents out here have been looking around, and when they told me that Monica Arlen's famous home was on the market, I flew right out to make an offer. I've suggested three million dollars."

A fit of coughing shook me, and I was glad to be sitting down. It was true that even in a lowering market, houses in the Los Angeles area could sell for still larger sums. But not one of these white elephants like Cadenza, no matter who had lived in it.

"Wally, get Carol a glass of water," Monica said, regarding me kindly. "Isn't it wonderful, dear? I've been wanting to sell the house for a long time, and I do think Mr. Barenklovich's offer is very generous. I can't wait to tell Linda what has happened."

With an effort I found my tongue, and when I spoke it was with an intensity that made them all look at me.

"Don't believe any of this," I told her. "It's true that his name was Barenklovich when he was born, but it's Owen Barclay now, and you've all been *had!*" I flashed an angry glance at Wally. "Owen is my ex-husband and Keith's father. Aunt Monica, I came here to be protected from this man."

Monica started to fall apart quite visibly. The hand resting on the iris trembled, and her deep-set eyes looked suddenly wild. Wally's mouth had dropped open, and Ralph, watching through the glass, came quickly into the room. Even the cats were staring in, though they stayed safely outdoors, beyond Owen's malevolent reach.

"Hey, Miss Arlen," Ralph said. "It's okay. You're all right now. What do you care who he is, if he pays you a lot of money for the house?"

"Exactly," Owen said. "That I was once married to Carol hasn't any bearing on anything. I've made you a genuine offer, Miss Arlen."

He sounded utterly and completely convincing, though I didn't think for a moment that he really meant to hand out three million dollars for a Hollywood mansion that no one wanted.

Under Ralph's ministering, Monica rallied and spoke to Owen with that impressive dignity she could command.

"Thank you for coming to see me. I'll have to think about this. Please give me a little time."

"All the time you want," Owen said cheerfully, and moved toward the door. "I'll leave now, but I'm staying with friends in Rancho Mirage, and I'll get in touch with you when you're less upset. Of course my offer stands."

He beckoned to Wally and went out the door. Wally, still

in a state of confusion, gave me a displeased look and hurried off in Owen's wake. I ran after them both. If Owen made the slightest move toward Keith . . .

He didn't. I stood rigidly at a terrace door downstairs, and watched as Owen got into Wally's car and they drove away. Keith and Jonah were safe in the kitchen with Helsa, busily licking a frosting bowl, unaware of Owen's alarming presence. What I was to do now, I didn't know, but first I must return to Monica.

I found her sitting on the sofa weeping helplessly, with Ralph beside her, offering a shoulder. The very sight of him gave me a chill. It had surely been his hands in the dark water last night, pulling me down. Who else could it have been?

I sat on Monica's other side, and patted her arm. A cruel trick had been played on her, and the result was devastating.

"I'm terribly sorry," I said. "But you mustn't believe anything Owen Barclay tells you. He's trying to use you to get at me. You'd better not see him again, Aunt Monica. He'll only hurt you in the long run."

She looked up from her weeping. "He seemed such a nice man—a charming man. And I know he has all that money. Three million dollars won't even mean much to him, and it means everything to me right now."

I thought of something that might reach her. "He's far from nice, though he can seem to be charming. I saw him kill a kitten once by throwing it from our apartment terrace."

She was as shocked as I'd expected her to be. "How awful! How wicked! He did seem to dislike cats, so I had Ralph put them on the balcony."

"That was good—to put them out there, where he couldn't hurt them."

The balcony door was open now, and Annabella, followed by the Persians, stepped gingerly into the room—as though she walked on burning coals. Her fur stood up along her back, her tail was twice its size, and even her ears looked angry.

Annabella leaped onto Monica's knees and the white cats rubbed their heads against her legs, all three offering more comfort than either Ralph or I could give.

"Just the same," Ralph said, "this man wants to buy your house. You don't have to see him again to pick up his offer."

"Don't listen to Ralph, Aunt Monica," I said hotly. "He doesn't know anything about Owen. Besides, I don't think you can trust Ralph. I think he was the one who pushed me into the pool last night. He tried to drown me!"

Monica's face seemed to crumple all over again, and she flung out her hands with a wild gesture that the old Arlen would never have used. "I'm so awfully sorry about that, Carol. I've been sorry ever since it happened. Sometimes I'm just too impulsive."

I stopped patting her arm and stiffened. "What are you talking about?"

"I only wanted him to give you a scare—that's all. I wanted him to make you go away and leave me alone. I could tell that you were going to do my book all wrong. You were just going to tell the old lies about me over and over again."

I caught her flailing hands and held them tightly. "Did you tell Ralph to push me into the pool? To drown me?"

"No—no! Of course I didn't! All I told him was to give you a good scare so you'd want to leave. That was all. I never thought of the pool, and I never wanted to harm you, Carol."

"Ralph?" I challenged.

He didn't trouble to speak to me directly. "Miss Hamilton's crazy. I never went near that pool last night, until I heard her yell. I wrecked a perfectly good watch jumping in after her—and look what thanks I get."

I knew he was lying, but in spite of her own words, Monica believed him, and suddenly she was furious with me.

"You've spoiled everything! Ever since you came, you've caused nothing but unhappiness. So now you can take your troubles and your child and go somewhere else. Just go away—*now!*"

Ralph grinned at me triumphantly. "You better go, like she says."

I stood up to face him. "I'm going to talk to Linda about this. And if you lay one more finger on me I'll call the police.

Or she will. You don't want the police asking questions, do you?''

He made an effort to shrug off my words, but I'd reached him. I didn't think he'd try anything more—for a while at least.

Monica was weeping into her handkerchief again, but I had no more comfort to offer her. I walked out of her apartment, leaving her to her cats and Ralph. I felt thoroughly shaken, and not a little terrified.

As I followed the upper passageway, I found the door to Ralph's room ajar, and I looked in. He was my enemy now and out in the open, so I wanted to know all I could learn about him.

His room had an almost spartan appearance, its only decoration the rifles and handguns displayed above the bed. He *would* be a collector of lethal weapons. I went past quickly, feeling a little sick.

I wished Linda would come home. She had helped Wally make the arrangements for Owen's visit, and we had some serious talking to do. Owen had found exactly the right approach to Monica, and had cut into the heart of my defense with one clever stroke. What was worse, his identity might not matter in the least to Monica, if she chose to believe that he would buy her house for all that money.

Nevertheless, I wouldn't pack up and leave right away. My terror was laced with anger that made me feel stubborn. This was exactly what Owen wanted—to smoke me out of Monica's house, so that I'd be at his mercy. When Linda returned we'd decide what should be done. I wanted to believe that she too had been fooled. Besides, an hour from now, Monica's feelings toward me might change again. There was still the book she wanted me to write and that might keep me here.

As for Ralph, I must simply be on guard against him, and he wasn't clever enough to know much else but the use of force. He would have enjoyed pushing me into the water and making me think I might drown. But he had also pulled me out in time, and he wouldn't go so far as really killing me. There'd be no profit for him in that.

Moving idly, seeking something to distract me, I went into

the Arlen room, where Linda had collected so much material about Arlen and Scott. Without much interest, I began to look through the files. I needed something powerful to quiet my racing heart and jangled nerves.

A large folder on Saxon Scott caught my attention, and I took it out and sat in the red chair. With an effort, I made myself concentrate. For the first time, I learned that Saxon's real name was Crofton Scott, and that he'd worked under that name in a few roles on Broadway. He'd made no great stir until he'd come to Hollywood. Even then, he hadn't been noticed particularly until Monica asked for him as a leading man. By that time she'd made several successful pictures, and the studio gave her what she wanted. Crofton had changed his first name to Saxon, and once they began making films together, he'd emerged as an actor to be respected in his own right, to say nothing of becoming a new heartthrob for the country. The rest was movie history.

It was curious that after so many years of silence, Saxon should be making a gesture in Monica's direction, even to the point of phoning her. I must see him soon, if I was going to stay—if I was really to write Monica's story.

When I'd replaced the folder in its file, I started looking at titles on the nearest shelf. One book was about the great tragedies and scandals of Hollywood, beginning with the Fatty Arbuckle affair, continuing with Mabel Normand, and on to Paul Bern, who had killed himself soon after marrying Jean Harlow. Even the Olivier-Leigh story was here, but the book wasn't recent, and it ended before Marilyn Monroe's death.

Searching the index, I found Arlen and Scott listed, and turned to the page number, only to discover that the entire chapter had been torn out. Just ragged edges showed where the pages had been. I was standing there with the book in my hands when I heard a car coming up the mountain. Linda had come home. Carrying the mutilated volume, I went into her office and sat down to wait.

In a few moments she breezed in cheerfully. "Oh, good— there you are! I've some interesting things to tell you. How was your visit to Jason's ranch?"

"Fine," I said. That wasn't what interested me most now. "We do need to talk right away, Linda. About that man you allowed Wally to bring here to see Monica—"

"Mr. Barenklovich? How did they get along? Wally told me what he has in mind—to buy the Beverly Hills house. I think it's wonderful. You can't imagine how hard it is to move those old Hollywood mansions these days. I wonder what sort of offer he's made."

"Listen to me," I said. "It's *not* wonderful. Mr. Barenklovich happens to be Owen Barclay, my ex-husband and Keith's father. What you did, Linda, was to invite the man I'm trying to escape straight into this house!"

For a moment she looked as Wally had, with her mouth open, but she collected herself quickly, threw off her shoulder bag, and dropped into the chair behind her desk.

"Carol! How awful! I didn't dream . . . He must have fooled Wally completely, and then *I* bought it too. What happened? Is he still here?"

"No, he's gone. I told Monica who he is, but Owen said the offer still stands, and he means to get in touch with her later."

"I'm sorry, Carol. Truly I am. How did Monica take all this?"

"It's upset her, of course. She's ordered me out of the house again. And now that it's no longer safe here . . ."

"Of course it's safe! Now that we know who this man is, he can't possibly get back in."

"There's more," I said, and told her about the directions Monica had given Ralph—to frighten me so I'd leave. "Only, after he'd pushed me in the water, he followed his own brutal instincts and tried to torment me. Linda, if anything else happens to me, you're to go straight to the police. I've told him you'll do that, so perhaps he'll leave me alone."

To my astonishment, Linda began to laugh. She choked on the sound immediately and apologized. "I'm sorry, Carol. It's just that I'm so relieved."

"*Relieved?*"

Again she apologized. "Oh, I know how that sounds. But I was so upset about what happened. So afraid that someone

143

had managed to come in from outside that I've been a little crazy with worry. I want to protect Monica, as well as you, you know. That's my main job."

Not merely a job, I thought—it was her career, her purpose in life, and I didn't think that was a healthy way for her to live. For the first time, I was beginning to understand her brother's concern.

"Ralph we can handle," she said. "I really am relieved."

"Did you have the pool searched for Monica's emerald?"

"Yes. I went out there with Ralph this morning and we both couldn't see a thing on the bottom of the pool. He dove in and searched, but he didn't come up with anything."

More ramifications. If Ralph had pushed me in the pool, then he could have pulled the ring from my finger. So now of course it wouldn't be found. And that was terrible to contemplate.

"We simply can't lose that ring," Linda went on. "I haven't dared to tell Monica that it's missing. You're sure you were wearing it last night, Carol?"

"Of course I'm sure."

She was silent again, and I waited. "You know," she said at last, "if your ex-husband would really buy that house, it would solve all Monica's problems for a while. How much did he offer?"

My exasperation sounded in my voice. "The offer was for three million dollars. But it doesn't mean a thing. He won't buy it. He'll just stall and keep trying to see her. Then she'll let him in again, and—"

"Not necessarily. I can fix it so that any further transactions take place away from the house. Not even Monica has to see him."

Linda was falling into the trap too, and I felt increasingly helpless. "Right now there's nowhere else I can go. Yet if Monica wants me out of her house—I've got to think of something."

"She'll come around. Monica likes you, really. And she wants her book to be written in a way she can control. Now I've something to tell *you*. I've just had a long talk with Saxon Scott, and a few things have been cleared up. That's

where I've been—at his house. And I know why he telephoned Monica. He actually asked her to go on the stage with him at the benefit affair, when *Mirage* will be shown.''

I couldn't care very much. "What did she tell him?''

"That she wouldn't do it, of course. But he's being persistent. I don't really know what's got into Saxon. It makes me uncomfortable because it's out of character for him to do this. Why *now?*''

I thought of the mutilated book I still held. "I found this in the Arlen room. The pages about Arlen and Scott have been torn out.''

I handed her the volume of Hollywood tragedies, and it fell open to the gap. Linda sat looking at it blankly.

"I checked the index," I said. "The missing chapter is about Monica and Saxon. Do you suppose *she* tore them out?''

Linda clapped the book shut indignantly. "Of course not! But perhaps I can guess who did. Though I haven't the faintest idea why.''

"Who do you think it was?''

"Saxon himself. He was here in this room a couple of days before you arrived. I brought him up to the house on the chance that I could persuade Monica to see him. I thought it might be good for *her*. Just to patch up old quarrels. I left him in the Arlen room to wait while I talked to her, because I thought he might be interested in looking through what we've collected. Only she went into a terrible tizzy and took to one of her retreats. It wasn't just the telephone call he made to her later that upset her. It was because he came *here*, and she was furious with me for letting him in. I only did it for her. Their feud has gone on too long, and she's unhappy. I didn't know about the plans for the benefit then.''

"Why didn't you tell me that Saxon had been here?''

"Oh, it's all such a kettle of fish! You had enough to worry about without this upheaval Saxon was causing.''

"But why would *he* tear out those pages, even if he happened to see the book?''

"I haven't a clue. I'll have to ask him about this.''

"Could you get hold of another copy?''

145

"Probably not. It's long out of print."

She ran a finger down the index, checking names, and then looked up at me.

"There was something about Peggy Smith in the missing pages. Though that probably doesn't mean anything. She was likely to be mentioned now and then in connection with Monica."

"Her name keeps cropping up," I said. "Today when Jason took me riding in the desert, he showed me where her body was found—not far from his ranch. And Monica hinted to me that her death might not have been suicide. There's something awfully strange here. Do you have any of the old newspaper accounts of what happened?"

"Of course there was something strange!"

Startled, Linda and I looked around to see Monica in the doorway. She had changed from filmy azure, discarding the wig and the iris, and had put on tan slacks with a yellow shirt. She looked surprisingly trim and slender, and her natural pageboy hairstyle became her. She'd washed the makeup and tears from her face, and now that I'd stopped expecting her to look like the Monica Arlen of the screen, I no longer felt shocked by her aging. With the passing years she had gained a dignity, perhaps even an autocratic arrogance, that compensated in its way for the loss of youth and beauty. She was a *personage*—someone to be reckoned with—and now a smoldering excitement seemed to move in her.

"Have you been working on our book?" She regarded me amiably, as though she'd never ordered me from her house.

Her switches of mood left me more unsure of her than ever. Linda brought her a chair and she sat down, waiting for my answer.

"I've been looking through the files." I glanced at Linda, who shook her head slightly—a warning not to mention the missing pages. "What do you mean, Aunt Monica, about Peggy Smith's death being strange?"

She leaned back in her chair and let a trousered leg swing gently at the crossed knees. "Please, Linda." She reached out a hand.

"You're not supposed to smoke," Linda said. "It's not

146

good for your heart. Oh, all right. Just one." She opened a drawer in her desk and brought out a pack and a lighter.

Monica inhaled deeply and with pleasure. "There was a lot that was kept out of the papers at the time. Of course Saxon and I talked to the police and told them what we could. Or at least we pretended to."

She paused, her bright look tantalizing me.

"You might as well go on," Linda said.

"Yes, perhaps it's time. Peggy died at El Mirador."

"But she was found out in the desert!" Linda cried.

"She was taken there, and her car left nearby. Of course by the time she was discovered by the Desert Patrol—that's the sheriff's mounted posse, not the Palm Springs police—the wind had shifted the sands, destroying any evidence that might have been left. Anyway, it happened at El Mirador."

"Why are you so sure?" Linda asked.

"We'd just filmed a scene for *Mirage* on location there. In those days nearly everything was still built on the sound stages or the back lots, so that both lighting and sound could be controlled. Now, I understand, that's all been changed because of fast film and better recording methods. Pictures can be made anywhere."

Linda nodded. "Though it's come full circle. Some companies are going back to those big sound stages and back lots in order to save money. Go on, dear, please."

"Well"—Monica seemed to collect her thoughts—"our director had a thing about realism, and he decided to use the real El Mirador. He wanted to catch that feeling of vanished glamour and nostalgia. Of course this was after the war, remember. It wasn't a hotel anymore." She sighed, thinking back.

I wished she would return to Peggy Smith, but there was no hurrying her.

"El Mirador means the lookout," Linda said. "It became Torney General Hospital during the war. It's owned by Desert Memorial Hospital now."

A fire of high excitement burned in Monica's eyes, and when she went on, it kindled in her voice, whispery no longer.

"Linda, we must take Carol to El Mirador! I can show her just where those *Mirage* scenes were shot. Then she can write about them properly. Besides—*I* want to see it again."

"That's a good idea," Linda agreed. "When would you like to go?"

"Why wait? Tomorrow morning would be perfect. Carol really must see the place firsthand. For our book!"

I noticed that the possessive pronoun had changed. She would help me all the more willingly if it began to seem *her* book. Besides, whatever role I played, the story really did belong to Monica Arlen.

"I'd like to go," I said. "But after what's happened, I don't want to leave Keith alone, and I don't want him away from the house."

Monica regarded me sympathetically. "I understand how you feel. But Ralph won't try anything else. I've had a talk with him. And now that I know who that man is who came here, I won't have him in the house again. So it will be all right. Linda, can you make arrangements with the hospital so we can get in?"

"I know someone I can call at home," Linda said, and picked up the phone.

Monica sat watching me with that curiously bright look that made me uneasy. "I'm sorry you were disturbed about Mr. Barenklovich coming to see me, Carol. But it really has nothing to do with you."

"It has everything to do with me! Owen tricked his way into this house because his one purpose is to get hold of Keith. He was stopped this time, but he won't give up. You have to understand that what he told you was entirely false. He will never carry out any of his promises."

She waved a thin hand at me, unperturbed. "It doesn't matter. I can see him away from Smoke Tree House if I want to. What I came down here to tell you is something else. I've made up my mind."

Linda had hung up the phone. "About what?"

"I've decided that I will appear at the Annenberg Theater. So you can tell Wally that, Linda. At first, when Saxon phoned me, I was terrified. I simply shut everything out. But

I've had time to think about it now, and I'm sure I can put on a good show.'' She looked a little mischievous. ''After all, I've been trying out for you lately, Carol, and it's worked, hasn't it?''

''Beautifully,'' I admitted. ''You can create the old illusion whenever you wish.'' Nevertheless, what she was saying worried me.

''I'll do it better on a stage, of course, with proper lighting and makeup. I'll show Saxon! He doesn't really believe I can do this!''

She was beginning to tremble with excitement, and she'd smoked her cigarette to a stub. In spite of my concern, I didn't think anyone had a right to stop her if what she wanted to do was bringing her to life.

Linda responded by applauding. ''Good for you! Of course you can do it, if you decide to. And tomorrow we'll visit El Mirador. It's all arranged. This time, Carol, you can bring a camera, if you like.''

''Not to take pictures of me!'' Monica said quickly. ''Cameras used to love me, but not anymore. It's too hard to fool a camera.'' Suddenly she began to wilt. ''I'm tired. This has been an exciting day.''

Too exciting, I thought—in all the wrong ways. But I couldn't let her go without finishing what she'd opened up about Peggy Smith.

''You were going to tell us about Peggy's death,'' I reminded her.

She looked piteously at Linda, who shook her head at me and spoke firmly. ''Another time. Monica needs to rest now. I'll help you upstairs, dear.''

For once Ralph wasn't around. Perhaps he was sulking in his balcony chair, after Monica's scolding.

I watched them leave, Monica leaning a little too heavily on Linda's arm, and felt more uneasy than ever because of Monica's frailty and the possibility that she was taking on more than she could handle. Apparently she had some difficulty with her heart, and sometimes she seemed far older than her years. There were also my growing doubts about what Saxon Scott might be up to.

When they'd gone, I turned again to the damaged book. Peggy Smith's name was mentioned only once in the index among those pages that were missing. Tomorrow, when we were on the scene—if we really went to El Mirador—it might be possible to question Monica and get an answer.

The phone rang in Linda's office, and after three unanswered rings, I picked it up. The voice was Jason's.

"Carol? I've had an uncomfortable feeling about you—so I thought I'd check it out."

"Linda's upstairs with Monica," I told him. "Shall I buzz her?"

"No, it's you I want to talk with. Is everything all right?"

I liked the sound of his voice on the phone, and I liked his concern. "It hasn't been all right. Owen Barclay managed to fool everyone by using his real name to get into Smoke Tree House. When I came back this afternoon, he was with Monica, waiting for me. He's offered to buy Cadenza for three million dollars. He won't stop. He'll never stop!" I could hear my voice rising.

"Easy does it," Jason said quietly. "You have friends here. I'll talk with the police chief tomorrow."

"If Owen breaks any laws, he'll do it fast and get out of the state before anyone can stop him. I doubt if your police chief will help. But thank you anyway, Jason. I wish there were something practical to do. Linda says no one else is going to get in here, and that it will be all right."

"She's pretty dependable," Jason said. "Stay away from places where you'll be alone."

"I will. I'm glad you called, Jason."

"I've been thinking a lot since you were here," he said. "I'll see you soon."

I hung up and went back to the Arlen room. I would pick out some books and a file and carry them upstairs, so I could read in my room after dinner. More than anything else, I needed to throw myself into work. No more walking in the garden at night.

Yet I stood before the shelves for a long while without seeing the titles, remembering my ride in the desert with Jason. Out there I'd been able to pretend that everything was fine and that I was free to enjoy whatever I liked. All of which was just the sort of fantasy that had brought me to disaster. There could be no more such self-indulgence.

I put the desert—and Jason—firmly from my thoughts and looked for the files I needed to begin my task of writing about Monica Arlen.

ELEVEN

THAT NIGHT I WORKED—TRIED TO WORK—UNTIL NEARLY ELEVEN, while Keith slept quietly across the room. There had been fewer nightmares for him since we'd come to Smoke Tree House. He still didn't know about the new danger, and the nightmares were all mine.

That evening, Linda had tried to assuage my worries by taking me down to the lower gate. The night guard had just come on, and the day guard was about to leave. She introduced me to both men, and explained the situation to them carefully. No one who was a stranger and unauthorized by Linda herself was to be allowed through the gate. Miss Arlen was in an emotional state right now, and if she gave any countermanding orders, they were to be checked with Linda first.

I began to feel more reassured. Clearly it was Linda who ran things at Smoke Tree House; she who hired the guards and made the rules. Neither man questioned her authority, and both were sympathetic when she explained the danger that faced me and my son. They assured us that no one would get through, and they had direct contact with police head-quarters, so I needn't worry. There would be no more epi-sodes like the one today. Not with Mr. Barenklovich or anyone else.

I felt as reassured as it was possible to be. Of course there was always the possibility that Owen might make a bold move, send in his armed goons, storm the gate, and take Keith by force. However, I didn't think he'd chance that at this time. He'd been in some hot water lately, with an investi-gation pending, and while he considered himself safe enough, he wouldn't want to call down the law on his head by so open a move. His action, when it came, would be more subtle. Like sending someone in to drown me? But Monica had said it was Ralph, and I couldn't allow myself to be made a prisoner in this house—not if I was to work.

This evening I'd begun to fill in items concerning Monica's Hollywood years. Already a more detailed picture was evolving, and my old star-worship was giving way to solid interest and respect.

From the letters of friends she was emerging as a generous, kind, and admirable woman—which made her present state all the more pitiable. What had hardened her? What had happened to change her? When I had the key to that, I would know how to write about her. The years, of course, had taken the toll they did with everyone. But something in particular had happened to Monica, and I had a growing feeling that it dated back to the taboo subject of Peggy Smith's death. Today Monica had almost opened up about it, and that was something I must work toward—getting her to tell me the whole story. Or if she wouldn't, perhaps Saxon Scott would.

Before I turned in, I pulled together my museum notes and set down further impressions. After my day at Jason's ranch, I wanted more than ever to write about the Desert Museum. Not only because it was remarkable in itself, but because I wanted to please Jason.

Just as I was putting my notes away, I heard a car coming up the mountain. I turned off the light in my room and stepped out on the balcony to watch as it drove past to the garage. The terrace was lighted, and I could see Linda at the wheel. She got out and the car door slammed. Keys clinked as she turned off the alarm system to let herself in from the garage. Quickly, I went out my bedroom door and stood in the glassed upper passageway. Linda, of course, must have her own social life, and there was nothing to be uneasy about. Nevertheless, I waited as she came upstairs. She looked both excited and angry, and when she saw me waiting she came toward me at once.

"Come in my room for a minute, Carol," she said, pushing open the door. "We need to talk again."

It was the first time I'd been in her room, and I saw that she had the same rather simple tastes her brother had, with an emphasis on the Southwest. There were authentic ornaments of Indian pottery and basketwork, and the painting of a local canyon scene.

I sat down, while she threw herself wearily on the bed.

"I'm glad you're still up," she said. "I went to see Saxon again tonight, and I don't want Monica to know. Perhaps I shouldn't have gone, but I had to. Wally is all steamed up about this affair at the Annenberg, and I was beginning to feel good about seeing Monica come out of her shell. When you found those pages missing, however, I started to feel uncomfortable about what Saxon might be planning. So I phoned him and he said I could see him tonight."

She moved restlessly and sat up, once more driven and nervous, the way she'd been the first time I'd met her.

"I asked him straight off about those pages. He said he hadn't touched a thing the day I left him in that room. He didn't own the book himself and had never seen it. I can't be sure he's telling the truth. I've seen him lie expertly when it pleased him. He's behaving rather strangely, and I'm worried about what he may be scheming. I've known him longer than I have Monica, and as I told you, he sent me to this job. I've always liked him, but now I'm not sure I do. *He* can take care of himself, and I'm not sure that Monica can. I have to look out for her. *We* have to look out for her. She may walk straight into some trap of Saxon's, and I won't have that."

"What do you mean—trap?"

"That's the trouble. I don't know, and he isn't talking. It wasn't a pleasant visit this time. I've always thought him a kind and sensitive man. Now a sort of hardness is coming out in him that I've never seen before. In the past, even when I knew sometimes that he was lying, he's done it in a light, rather appealing way. You know the man he used to be on the screen. But now it's as though something he'd been brooding about for years has surfaced, and it's pushing him into action. I'm afraid for Monica."

"What can he do that hasn't already been done to her years ago?"

"He can hurt her. I often think she's still half in love with him. There's never been anyone else. They wounded each other badly, and he's not the same man she used to know. Any more than she's the same woman he knew. If he chooses, he can humiliate her if she goes out on that stage with him. The very contrast between the two of them breaks my heart. I mean the way she's aged, while he still looks marvelous, even though he's older."

"She can create enough of an illusion to get by on a stage," I pointed out. "She can play the old Monica Arlen beautifully. We've both seen her do it."

Linda shook her head. "The trouble is, she doesn't really see herself. She never puts on glasses unless she's reading. She decided long ago that putting distant things in focus wasn't a good idea, so she sees a soft-focus image in her mirror. She can make that image up so that it really looks very good, and she's kept her slender figure with regular swimming. But, Carol—she looks *ancient* beside him, and she may not realize this. I'm afraid of what will happen when she has to face the truth—as he might force her to face it."

"If they both choose to go ahead, there isn't much you can do to stop them, is there?"

"I'd like Saxon to stop the whole thing. I tried to sound him out a little this evening to find out how he really feels about her. He only turned cold and not very friendly. He wasn't sympathetic when I told him about her wanting to visit El Mirador tomorrow. He called that a lot of romantic nonsense."

"Perhaps it really is," I said.

Linda jumped off the bed and took a nervous turn around the room. "Hasn't she a right to that? She *earned* everything the world wanted to give her years ago. So hasn't she a right to a little nostalgia now?"

"When does life ever play fair and allow us *rights?*"

She hardly heard me. "People are always complaining about the huge sums performers are paid. No one seems to consider that these big talents often earn for only a few years, while their work generates fortunes for others. So why shouldn't they have their share of what the world is willing to pay? The complainers would jump at the chance, if they could."

I agreed, but this discussion was leading nowhere. She had nothing more to tell me, so I said good night and returned to my room.

When I fell asleep I dreamed I was on a runaway horse tearing over desert sands toward a barrier of mountain rock that I was certain to smash into. I woke up just short of the crash and lay awake for far too long.

In the morning, a shower revived me, Monica came downstairs early, with Ralph in attendance. Apparently he was to accompany us to El Mirador, though this was something I didn't relish. Keith would stay at Smoke Tree House with Helsa.

At least Monica wasn't playing the Star this morning. She wore trim beige pants and a sweater to match, with a green scarf at her throat. She'd put on dark glasses and a straw hat that shielded her face. If it was still her fancy that strangers might recognize her, I could feel only sympathy and concern for the delusion.

It was a sympathy that had grown during my reading of her personal correspondence last night. In this short time, I'd learned more about Monica Arlen than I'd ever known before. If Saxon had once been a kind person, so had she. Her generosity to beginners in her field had been well known, and several young actresses, who were to become successful in their own right, owed much to her sponsorship. I wondered how many of them remembered. Apparently studio crews had adored her. She'd never put on airs, and she knew everyone by name and could ask about personal problems with genuine interest.

This time we took the old white Rolls-Royce, and I asked if I might sit in back beside Monica. Whether she was pleased with this attention, I couldn't tell because of the dark glasses that hid her expressive eyes. Ralph was driving, and Linda sat beside him.

This morning, Monica seemed young in spirit—not playing a role, but touchingly eager for the first trip she'd made away from the house in a long time. Her state of excited anticipation made me apprehensive. She reminded me of a child who becomes stimulated to that height of nervous tension that always ends unhappily. Linda, too, was aware of this, and she spoke over her shoulder as we drove along Palm Canyon.

"Don't expect too much, Monica," she warned. "El Mirador won't be the way you remember it."

Monica paid no attention, and her excitement didn't abate in the least. Suddenly, she leaned toward the car window. "There it is! El Mirador's tower. Do you see it on ahead?"

A square bell tower, open on four sides and crowned with a pointed roof, rose above the low white building—a steep roof decorated with whimsical scallops of yellow and blue.

A strange anticipation began to rise in me. A different anticipation from Monica's. She was returning to the past, while I had a strong feeling that something significant was to happen in the present. Whether good or bad, I didn't know.

When we'd turned onto Indian Avenue and parked, Ralph went to fetch the keys from the hospital down the hill. We waited before the main entrance, where a huge mat still lay. On faded maroon were white letters that read: EL MIRADOR HOTEL, and I thought of all those vanished stars who had crossed this threshold when Monica Arlen was young.

"Do open the door, Ralph!" Monica cried as he reached us, and slipped her hand through the crook of my arm. I sensed by her touch that something a little fearful had begun to lace through her excitement. She was suddenly afraid of going back.

Ralph unlocked the big doors, and I heard Monica's breath catch in a long, soft sigh.

Where once western chandeliers had shed their brilliance over stunningly beautiful women and handsome men, the same copper wheels now lay twisted upon the floor among an assortment of hospital fixtures—come to an inglorious end.

Ralph touched one rim with his toe. "Junk," he said.

Monica didn't hear him because she was far away in another time. "I remember the thirties—before the war. John and Lionel Barrymore used to come here then. And Constance and Joan Bennett. Spencer Tracy came, and Charlie Farrell, before he founded the Racquet Club here in Palm Springs. Janet Gaynor, of course. They both live here now. Olivia de Havilland came, Paulette Goddard—and so many others. I could go on and on. Now it's all gone, and those of us who are left are so terribly old."

I tried to draw her away from sadness. "Tell us about filming the scenes from *Mirage* that were made here."

Linda moved to take her arm, but Monica shrugged us both aside. She crossed the floor, seeing none of the clutter, her eyes aglow with memories.

"It was after the war when we came here to make those scenes. We cleared out the hospital things and tried to restore it to the way it used to look. Though first we filmed the last scenes, when the place was filled with wounded soldiers. Oh dear—I'm going to cry. Come through to the terrace, Carol. I want to show you the gardens."

Linda spoke quickly. "They're gone now, dear."

Monica paid no attention, and when Ralph opened the rear doors for her, she went through to a terrace whose wide steps led down to a sloping lawn. The lawns had been well kept, though the luxury of what had once been gardens was gone.

"Nothing's left!" Monica cried. "There were bungalows over that way, and a swimming pool. Tennis courts. And a wildflower garden. Everyone came!"

She whirled about, looking up at the gallery a story above. A flight of white steps at the far side led up to where the gallery curved around to run past upstairs rooms.

"Come!" Monica commanded, and to my surprise she ran up the steps with one light hand on the rail, moving like a girl in her eagerness.

"I'll stay down here," Ralph said, taking out the inevitable cigarette. He stared morosely into a pit of crumbled earth, where there must once have been a planting, or even a fountain.

By the time I'd climbed to the upper gallery, Monica was running past the rooms, peering in one window after another. The bedrooms were empty now, but she must be refurnishing them in her imagination—remembering.

"In the script we occupied adjoining rooms, Saxon and I. *That* room and *this* room! Only of course we didn't stay in our own rooms!"

Her mouth had a mischievous lift again, and I wondered whether she was talking about the film or the reality.

I drew the camera from my shoulder bag and snapped pictures here and there, even catching one of Monica, when she wasn't looking. It was only a distance shot as she peered through a window, so I didn't think she'd mind.

After a moment she came back to the rail and looked out across empty grass. "Over there is where the bungalow stood, where we stayed one night. How well I remember. The moon was shining on the black mountain that's always so close, and El Mirador's lights were soft. Everything was almost the way it used to be."

We stood at the rail on either side of her, Linda listening and as rapt as Monica. The fantasy had never really stopped for Linda, even though there were moments when she recognized it for what it was. Both of us were so intent on watching her, that we didn't notice what was happening below. Not until Monica stepped back from the rail in alarm, covering her mouth with her hand. I looked down and saw Saxon Scott climbing the steeply sloped bank of grass. He looked stunningly handsome, his white hair styled longer than in his film days, his face fuller, more mature, yet still unlined. In contrast, Monica looked like nothing at all. A woman whose clothes were out of style, whose face was old in the morning light.

She turned angrily to Linda. "You told him I'd be here! You arranged this!"

Linda put an arm about her shoulders. "No—I *didn't*

159

arrange anything. If I mentioned our coming here, I didn't dream Saxon would show up too."

Monica turned her back on the man who climbed toward the terrace, and I knew that Linda had been wrong. Monica knew very well how she would look in his eyes. There was no place for her to run, nowhere to hide. All the doors of this upper gallery were locked and there was no way down except by the outside stairs.

Saxon had seen us. He climbed the steps to the terrace and stood looking up, while Ralph watched him speculatively.

"Good morning," Saxon greeted us.

For a moment longer, Monica stood with her back to him. Then she moved from the support of Linda's arm and stepped to the rail. "Why did you come here?" Her voice sounded harsh, and I sensed her terrible despair. How awful this moment must be for her, when Saxon remembered her only as beautiful and young.

He answered with quiet courtesy. "I wanted to see you. I've wanted to talk with you, and you've always refused me. So I chose this way. Don't blame Linda. She had no idea I meant to come."

"We haven't any need to talk—not ever again!"

"Let's not play Romeo and Juliet," he said, teasing almost gently. "We're neither of us young anymore, and we needn't hide from each other. Will you come down, or shall I come up?"

Ralph edged closer to him. "You want him to go away?" he asked Monica.

"I'll come down." Monica made her decision, and went toward the stairs, disdaining Linda's arm. Now that her earlier excitement had drained away, Saxon had all the advantage. She couldn't play her old role under these circumstances of wrong clothes and brilliant sunlight. Only her dark glasses and her brimmed hat offered hiding. I glanced at Linda and knew by her own look of despair that neither of us could help Monica now.

As she reached the bottom step, Saxon came toward her, holding out both hands in a gesture that was purely Saxon Scott. Monica hesitated, reluctance showing in every inch of her

body. Then she put her thin, veined hands into his strong ones. He leaned over and kissed her cheek, skillfully avoiding glasses and hat brim—an actor's practiced gesture. At once she snatched her hands away and stepped back from him.

"Don't make fun of me! I'm old, but not foolish. I know what the years have done to me. You've been luckier."

She wasn't acting now, but I sensed that he was. For whatever purpose he'd come, I found myself angrily suspicious of his motives. He meant to hurt her, and there was no way to stop him.

Since there were no chairs on the terrace, as there must once have been, he led her to the wide steps and lowered her gently onto the top one, sitting down beside her. Linda drew Ralph aside, and we moved back to the lounge doors, though not out of hearing, lest she need us.

Saxon must have been shocked by her appearance, yet I was stunned to see him reach out and remove the sunglasses. With another gesture, equally, merciless, he lifted off her hat, so that her hair looked dingy under bright sunlight. She sat beside him with all her defenses gone, and her shoulders rounded as though against repeated blows. I hated him in that moment, and I know Linda did too. Yet Monica could still summon her own hard-won dignity, and now that she had been stripped of any defense, she looked straight at him.

"What do you want of me?"

He picked up the hand that had worn the emerald ring and examined it as though it had been the most beautiful hand in the world.

"I want you to join me onstage at the Annenberg on the night when they show *Mirage*. Linda told me how marvelous you can be as the Monica Arlen everyone remembers. It's time we made this gesture before we're both in wheelchairs. Let's do it and give the world one last thrill!"

She drew her hand away, shivering. "No—no! I thought I might do it, but I can't."

"You *will*," he said. "Because I want you to."

Linda moved beside me. She'd heard the note in his voice—as though underneath the gentleness and courtesy he threatened in some subtle way—and in an instant she was across the terrace, dropping down beside Monica.

"I know you could do it, dear, but now I don't think you should," she said urgently. "Saxon, I won't let you hurt her. I won't have that!"

"Why on earth should I want to hurt her? We both remember the quarrels, the bad times. But that was long ago. I remember the other times as well. Have you forgotten them?" He spoke only to Monica. "Do you remember the bungalow down there—before everything changed?"

She looked at him intently. "I remember, but I didn't think you'd want to."

"Of course I remember. I remember how beautiful you were, how enormously gifted and brilliant. All that doesn't die, you know. Don't be afraid of what you see in a mirror now. Remember—I'm older than you are."

She couldn't accept his words as anything but mockery, and she rose from the low step—rose easily by sheer power of will.

He stood up beside her quietly. "When I met Carol in the museum the other day, she was wearing the emerald ring. I'm glad you gave it to her."

I remembered guiltily that I no longer wore it, and hoped they wouldn't notice. I still felt dreadful about the loss of the ring.

Monica said nothing. I had the feeling that she was simply holding on now, enduring and hoping for this ordeal to end.

"This is enough!" Linda cried. "I'm taking you home, darling. I think you've been horrible, Saxon. She doesn't need any more of this. Help her to the car, Ralph."

Saxon, however, was not ready to let her go. As she turned away he put one hand on Monica's arm. "I want to see you on the stage of the theater that night," he said. "You'll be there, won't you?"

She flung up her head with the old Monica look, suddenly challenging. "How can *you* dare risk it?" she cried, and then pulled away from him as Linda and Ralph helped her through the lounge and out to the car.

For an instant Saxon had looked startled, but when I would

have followed them, he stopped me. "You really are going ahead with a book? The Monica Arlen story?"

"Of course," I said.

"And you want to talk to me? So why not now? Let me drive you to my house, and you can ask anything you want. Almost anything. Perhaps it will help you to see some of the things I've kept from those Hollywood days."

Even though I disliked him intensely at that moment, I still needed the interview. The opportunity was *now*, and I would be on my guard against him if he tried to say unkind things about Monica. After what had just happened, I was thoroughly on her side.

While I had the chance, I flung down a challenge of my own. "Tell me one thing right now. Monica has hinted that Peggy Smith might have died here at El Mirador. If that's true, where did it happen? And where do you come in?" A little while ago I never could have spoken so bluntly to Saxon Scott—nor have wanted to.

For once, I'd surprised him, and the role he'd been playing fell away. He too could put on a mask, but when it was dropped he looked an older, harder man.

"I don't know anything about that," he told me curtly. "She was found out in the desert."

He was lying, of course, and I made one more attempt. "I know that's where she was found. I saw the place yesterday. But Monica says it happened here."

"Then you'd better ask her. Do you want to interview me or not? There's just one taboo. I won't discuss Peggy Smith."

"All right," I said coolly. "I'll accept your taboo. I'd like to see whatever you've collected. Wait a moment, while I tell them where I'm going."

When I reached the Rolls, Monica was already in the back seat, weeping silently, while Linda tried to offer comfort. Ralph watched my approach with his usual insolence, and I ignored him to lean in the window beside Monica.

"Mr. Scott has invited me to see his memorabilia, and I'm going. I do need to interview him. You understand, don't you, Aunt Monica?"

She ignored me completely, and I turned to Linda. "I want

163

to go with Mr. Scott. Please check on Keith for me and tell him I'll be back soon."

"All right—go if you have to. I'll tell Keith. But when Saxon brings you back, don't let him onto our road. Phone me from the gate and I'll come down for you. Don't trust him, Carol. I don't anymore."

Monica put down her handkerchief, the look in her eyes lost and tragic. She wasn't acting now. "*He* killed her!" she wailed. "I've never told anyone in all these years, but he killed her!"

Before Linda could stop me, I reached in to take Monica's hand. "Saxon? *He* killed Peggy?"

"Just leave her alone!" Linda snapped at me. "You can see how upset she is. She doesn't know what she's saying."

Still tremulous and shaken, Monica pushed her away. "Just ask him about Peggy! Once I loved him, but he destroyed everything. He betrayed all of us. He's a dangerous man, so be careful, Carol."

Linda gestured to Ralph and he pulled the car away from the curb. I watched as it joined the traffic on Palm Canyon Drive. Then I walked over to Saxon's Mercedes, parked a little way off. He couldn't have heard Monica's words, though he'd been watching us.

I felt deeply shaken as I got into his car. The past had been so embroidered over with fiction, so cleverly concealed, that it was going to be difficult to sort truth from fantasy. Yet I knew one thing. Monica's voice had trembled with real emotion as she'd made her accusation. However wild her words had been, she was a frightened woman, and I had the very real feeling that she was telling the truth.

TWELVE

WE LEFT MT. SAN JACINTO BEHIND AS WE DROVE THROUGH THE string of little "cities" that had been incorporated along the base of the mountains. Away from Palm Canyon, country club communities clustered around their golf courses, and expensive homes climbed canyons into the lower hills, or spread out with their swimming pools and gardens to displace the desert in the east.

Except for the Annenbergs and a few others, this was not an area of big estates. Ex-movie stars, or current ones, lived in comfortable luxury, but without the ostentation of the past.

Farther on were date groves—great areas of trees growing in tall columns and overspread by a solid roof of foliage. The ground beneath was eerily dark, except where bands of sunlight slanted through between the trunks. The groves were man-made forests with even, geometric aisles.

Saxon Scott lived in one of the wealthy enclaves in Indian Wells—the Eldorado Country Club, set close to the foot of the Santa Rosas, and guarded by a mountain called "Ike's

Peak." A reminder that the area had long been a haven and playground for presidents.

We were recognized at the main gate, and drove through into broad avenues lined with palms and thick tropical growth. Low houses of redwood and stone were set apart from one another, all edged with green plantings and well-watered lawns, their inner patios and swimming pools out of view from the street. The encroaching desert was held away, and only the bare, baked-looking mountains, their sides slashed with deep canyons, suggested that nature could take over harshly whenever it chose.

Like the others, Saxon's house was low and wide, with a generous overhang of roof all around, and a great deal of glass that looked out toward the mountains.

When he'd parked the car, he took me into a stunningly beautiful living room. Its spacious carpet was a soft, rosy cinnamon, and the cherry and brown flowered upholstery had obviously come from a fabric designer's shop. Those walls that were not made of glass, and the slanted ceiling as well, had been painted a soft shell color that offered light and airy space. Central air conditioning controlled the interior climate.

"It's heavenly," I said. "Peaceful and beautiful."

Saxon smiled. "Carefully contrived, and not very real. If you're going to write about us, don't be taken in. We live in decorator homes and dedicate ourselves to play and happy make-believe. When you live here, it's easy to forget there's a real world out there, and that it takes a great deal of money to live this way."

I thought of Jason Trevor and his ranch in the desert, and of the work that absorbed him. Lately, I'd begun to compare Jason and his way of life with that of other men.

"You do have a business," I said. "We had dinner in your restaurant the other night. You're not exactly idle."

"More make-believe. To serve the sunbathers. May I get you a drink?"

I shook my head and sat down near glass doors, where I could look out at the stark fissures of the mountains. There were no houses climbing these canyons. Not yet.

"If you don't mind, I'll have one," he said. "Will you stay for lunch? I'd like you to."

Again I shook my head as he poured himself a stiff whiskey and soda. "No, thank you," I said. "I'd rather talk."

"I need this after what happened this morning," he said, tossing the drink down thirstily.

"What really did happen?" I asked. The image of Monica crumbling at the mere sight of him still haunted me. "You planned it cruelly. Why should you torment her now, when she's old and terribly miserable?"

He sat opposite me, and I thought him far more interesting, with a more mature appeal than he'd had as that young man on the screen. I remembered the dangerous, exciting roles he'd played, and wondered if he'd only been playing himself. I couldn't really like him, but I found him fascinating.

His expression hardened. "You're here to interview me, if you like, Miss Hamilton. But not to interrogate."

"That's a pretty fine distinction." I bristled in the face of his male arrogance. "Have you thought about how awful it was for her this morning? She was totally unprepared, with all her defenses down. She didn't even have her props to get her by."

Saxon's healthy tan could flush even darker. Nevertheless, I rushed on, more indignant than I'd expected to be.

"You've weathered the years well, Mr. Scott. She hasn't. And while there are times when she tries to fool herself, she understood only too well what you were seeing. How could you do that to her, when once . . . a long time ago . . ." I broke off, surprised that I was becoming so personal, so impassioned in Monica's defense. This was hardly the way to conduct an important interview. "I'm sorry," I said lamely. "I shouldn't have—"

He spoke more gently. "Yes, you should. I'm glad you want to defend her. I deserve everything you've said. I haven't seen her in years, and while we get used to our own faces in the mirror, we remember those we don't see exactly as they used to be. Besides, Linda has always played her up, so I really didn't expect what I saw."

Linda would have, I thought, wondering if her own protectiveness had hurt Monica in the long run.

"In any case," Saxon went on, "none of this is your real story. *I* am not your story."

"Of course you are! If I write about her, I must write about you. I want to. One of the things I need is the answer to what changed her. Not just what happened in the years that make the connecting bridge. It's the terrible occurrence—whatever it was—that blew everything up before you finished *Mirage*. You were part of that."

He shook his head emphatically. "There's no use asking about our celebrated breakup. I'm not going to talk about that. And I don't think she will either."

"You're wrong!" I told him with new conviction. "She's going to be ready soon. I can feel it coming. Monica needs this book to free her from the past. Not just as a record of her achievements, but as a revelation of her as a real woman."

"And who's to tell the difference between the actress and the woman? Or the actor and the man? In the beginning, perhaps, there's a distinction and some of us try hard all our lives to keep the person separate from the personality. But that's not what the public wants, so don't count too much on honest revelations. We're apt to forget where the distinctions lie."

I shook my head. "Opening up will be a catharsis for her. She needs that."

"You don't know what you're talking about!" He was suddenly angry. "You don't know what dangerous currents you may stir up."

If what Monica had said was true—that Saxon had killed Peggy Smith—then he must of course protect his own secrets.

"Are you afraid?" I asked, forgetting diplomacy again.

He was still actor enough to control himself and his outer anger subsided. After a moment, he went on more quietly. "Let's get back to Monica—the way she used to be. That's the real heart of your story. Not the old woman I saw this morning."

Secure in the way he himself had aged gracefully, he was being cruel again, and with sudden longing I wished that he could see Monica put on her "performance." For her sake.

"That's unkind," I said sharply. "And very unfair."

His look softened, as though he was remembering a different, younger woman. "She had a natural acting talent—more than I ever had. I had to learn to be a good actor—which was fairly easy, playing with her. She was born with a genius to perform, and she brought her own natural gifts to everything she did on the screen. She had instinctive timing and a flair for pace. Most of all, she possessed that special, mysterious spark that the great ones have. When it's there, it can last a lifetime. Hepburn has it still, and so does Bette Davis. When they're on a screen, they're the ones you watch. Age doesn't matter. Perhaps they don't like their faces now either, but they aren't afraid of being seen as triumphantly old. So why is Monica concerned?"

"She seems so—so vulnerable," I said. "So open to wounding."

"That's another gift—vulnerability. Usually only the very young have it. I remember it in Garbo. Of course in Marilyn Monroe. And today, especially in Meryl Streep. It's that aching quality that reaches out and twists your heart."

"I didn't see your heart breaking today."

He didn't hear me, still musing aloud. "I remember her hands. So beautiful, so graceful. The things she could do with that iris she used in so many of her pictures."

"She still has it," I said. "Or anyway, a version of it. And she can gesture with it as marvelously as ever."

This seemed to disconcert him. "The iris—in those hands?"

"You're being condescending and vain!" I cried. "You might have a little compassion."

He looked startled. "I'm sorry, Carol. That was a heartless thing to say. It's just that I remember the first silk iris she ever carried—because I gave it to her. I started her off with that little affectation, and I was proud of what she did with it, how she made it her own."

"I didn't know you'd given it to her."

He went on musing. "She used to have an inner sweetness, a generosity that I've never seen so strongly in any other woman. All lost now. Because I made a stupid mistake that I've been paying for ever since. A terrible mistake."

I waited, hoping he would go on in this more unguarded vein. He broke off, however, recovering himself.

"There's a photograph of her over there on the piano. My favorite picture."

I went to pick up the portrait in its silver frame, and saw the lovely, faintly exotic face of the young Monica Arlen. She was smiling warmly at the camera. Smiling, not only with her lips but with her eyes—lovingly. Feeling as he did, it was strange that he should keep her picture out.

"I used to play around with cameras a bit," Saxon said. "That's a picture I took myself, with her eyes made up in that exaggerated way she used for the screen. Hers were more convincing—not like Theda Bara's or Myrna Loy's as they did their eyes in the twenties and thirties."

So she had been smiling her love at the photographer? There was even a tender inscription in her famous scrawl. My moment of heat subsided. If Saxon Scott still felt strongly enough to keep her picture on his piano, how could he hurt her now?

"I grew up making believe about her," I said. "I suppose I turned her into my whole family. I couldn't know her in reality, but I could identify with all those roles of hers that I saw in movies. I never accepted the fact that what I built existed only in my imagination."

"So you came running out here to California when you needed her?"

"I came running because I was desperate, but I was still dreaming. Of course she doesn't understand any of this. *Her* reality is quite different, and now I'm trying to match mine to hers, since perhaps she needs me by this time. Yet even though nothing real has been taken from me, I feel a sadness, a sense of loss."

I hadn't meant to say any of this, and I didn't expect him to understand. Yet when he spoke his expression was almost tender.

"I hope you won't mind, but Linda's told me a little about you. I can see how much the writing of Monica's story means

170

to you, and I really would like to help—if you'll ask me questions I can answer. I'd like to see this book published."

He cocked an eyebrow at me in that familiar way, and I felt that flip-flop of response that a very young heart had given him long ago. But now I must be wary, even in the face of his seeming gentleness. I must remember his moments of cruelty. At least his present mood would make the interview easier. I went back to my chair so I could write in my notebook.

"Let's begin then. Tell me about when you made *Mirage*."

He smiled, thinking back as though something amused him. "You might ask Monica if she remembers the restaurant scene."

"The one with the cuckoo clock? Do you know that she still has that broken clock? Linda showed it to me yesterday."

"Interesting. I wouldn't have expected her to keep it."

"I don't think she's had much to do with what's been kept. Peggy collected things first, and then Linda."

"I see. Ask her if she remembers what's inside the clock. Perhaps it will start her talking."

"All right, I will. When you were making that movie, did you sense how good it was going to be?"

He shook his head. "Nobody can tell much about any picture while it's in the making. Even the rushes you see every day can't give you the overall feeling. The actors in *Casablanca* thought it was run-of-the-mill while they were making it. We had a similar experience in not knowing what the *Mirage* ending would be until we got to it. Scenes are done out of sequence and it's remarkable that we can even present the proper emotion on screen, when we aren't always sure where we are chronologically. Of course it's the public who decides in the long run. Audiences respond or turn their backs—and that's all that counts."

"The retakes didn't feel right, did they?" I said.

"They almost spoiled the picture. It was a good thing there were so few. Everything had changed by that time."

I ventured a statement, rather than a question. "Because Peggy Smith had died."

He forgot his own ruling in a sudden burst of anger. "She

171

was a terrible woman! Though I didn't have the sense to realize it at the time. She had her own gifts, but she was more interested in winding Monica around her little finger. Monica believed in her, trusted her, and she even fooled me for a while. But it was her influence that destroyed Monica.''

I took a long chance, counting on his anger to keep his guard down. "Monica believes Peggy was murdered.''

He shied away visibly, and I could feel the wall go up between us. At once I backed down. "I'm sorry. I shouldn't have said that, but I keep coming back to Peggy Smith—to her relationship with Monica. Somewhere along the way I have to learn what her influence was. Certainly she must have been a talented woman to do that sculpture in the museum.''

"Leave it alone for now," he warned sharply. "I can't talk about her. Not yet."

"Then tell me about the way Monica was when she was young. Tell me more about her acting. I've seen all your pictures, of course, but I'd like your view.''

"She had a strong drive in those days. She wanted to be the *best*. Though she was never arrogant about it. She not only wanted to entertain—she wanted to enchant, to entrance, to charm everyone, on screen and off. She could never bear to be disliked.''

And she could still do that, when she chose, I thought, writing quickly.

He went on, half to himself. "Perhaps that was her greatest weapon and her greatest weakness. It's not safe—or very real—to go through life wanting everyone to love you. She needed to grow up, to stop her make-believe off screen." He smiled at me. "You see, she was guilty of that too. She needed to get tougher in order to protect herself and survive.''

And now that she had, I thought, it wasn't especially becoming. Or did she use this to conceal a new vulnerability that age had brought?

"Not that she wasn't capable of mischief," he went on. "She was always capricious, and sometimes she could play pranks that hurt people, when she didn't in the least intend to. She had a disregard for scandal and gossip too, and oddly enough she didn't invite it in those days, even when her behavior verged on the outrageous. She had a quality that made everyone want to protect her."

"She still has that—for Linda," I said.

"Hah!" The sound rang with his scorn. "Remember that woman I suggested you see—she's Alva Leonidas now. Once when Alva didn't get Monica's makeup right, Monica threw a whole box of face powder at her. It went all over the dressing room, and Alva nearly died laughing. Of course, in two minutes, Monica was laughing too."

He could laugh at the young Monica himself, yet show only a hard impatience toward the one who was old.

"I'm planning to see Alva Saturday, if I can. Jason Trevor has offered to drive me up to Idyllwild. I haven't called her yet, however, to make an appointment."

"I've already spoken to her, and she's willing to talk with you."

"Thank you. For some reason, Monica doesn't want me to see Alva and her husband."

"No, she wouldn't. But you'd better go. Just remember that Monica wasn't all sweetness and light in the old days either. We had some bang-up fights on occasion."

And one bang-up fight that has never ended, I thought. Again I ventured a pointed question, since those were the most likely to bring a response.

"How could you give up Monica Arlen and marry someone else?"

His gentler manner toward me vanished in an instant. Saxon Scott had a temper himself, but before he could demolish me, I went on quickly.

"Look—I really can't tell where the worst quagmires lie. If I don't ask provocative questions I'll never get anything to tell me what *you* are like."

He stood up, and I thought for a moment that he was going to dismiss me without another word, but he merely changed the subject.

"Perhaps there are some things around the house I can show you—pictures and objects that will touch on your story. Perhaps they'll even give you a few safer questions to ask. I don't keep everything in one place. What I've collected is part of my life, and it's spread throughout the house."

When he led me into his study, my eye was caught by a wall of photographs behind the desk. I stepped over to it at once. An enlargement that occupied central space was of a smiling young woman with an impish face, and short curly hair. She sat in a chair beside a swimming pool, with a terry wrap around her, and a small child in her arms.

Saxon noted my interest. "My wife," he said. "My ex-wife, Alva. And our boy."

No one had told me there'd been a child. Saxon went on.

"Our son died when he was a year old."

"I'm sorry. I didn't know."

"It was a long time ago. Though there are always tender places. We've remained friends of sorts—Alva and I."

"What was she like—your wife?"

"A good scout. A good friend."

"But she wasn't Monica."

"No, she couldn't be. I suppose it was our mutual affection for Monica that drew us together. It was a mistake for us to marry—a mistake for both of us. She's been a lot happier with Nicos Leonidas. Would you like me to call her now and set up a definite appointment?"

"That would be fine. Perhaps I could see her tomorrow."

Saxon picked up the phone on his desk and dialed. "Hi, Alva. I told you about Carol Hamilton, Monica Arlen's niece. She'd like to come up tomorrow to talk with you."

The woman at the other end asked a question.

"Yes, of course it's all right. At least with me. I'll trust you to be discreet, Alva. There's a lot you and Nicos can tell Miss Hamilton that will help with her book. Any stories you remember about Monica."

When he hung up he smiled at me. "There you are. She can give you a great deal. Though perhaps not everything you want."

"Not when you've suggested discretion. There's to be a conspiracy of silence, isn't there? So how do I break through?"

He was no longer smiling. "You won't need to. It will all explode by itself one of these days. When the right time comes, the volcano will blow its top. And we'll all be wiped out in the ashes.''

He sounded ominously prophetic. "You *are* scheming something. Linda said you were.''

With an effort he shook off the brooding mood that had settled upon him. "I have a plan—not a scheme. And nothing volcanic. I'd like Monica to join me in making a gift to El Mirador when it's restored. All these things I've saved, and that Linda tells me Monica has collected, ought to be preserved after we're gone. They're movie history, I suppose. I've thought of presenting an Arlen-Scott collection to El Mirador, if it seems appropriate. There'll be other stars to honor, as well, if I can sell this idea. Perhaps we could even announce it at the benefit, when *Mirage* is shown.''

Why didn't I feel reassured? There was nothing here to disturb Monica. She too should want to see these collections preserved. Though it occurred to me that Linda might guard them more jealously than Monica herself, and I wondered if *she* would be willing to give them up to more impersonal care. I'd seen instances where a privileged caretaker became the possessor who would part with nothing.

"Will Monica really appear at the theater with you?''

"She'll come. She won't be able to help herself. In a way, we're still bound together. Perhaps by our own fears and distrust of each other. She won't want me to go out on that stage without her.''

I was still moving from one photo to the next. A small snapshot had been tucked between two larger pictures. In it Saxon stood with two women, one of them a young, laughing Monica. The other woman was fair-haired, wore dark glasses, and looked slightly dowdy. Even in the small print I could see her sullen expression.

"Who is this with you and Monica?'' I asked.

Behind me, Saxon was silent for a moment. When I looked around, he grimaced wryly. "She's your mystery woman— Peggy Smith. That was taken at El Mirador when we were shooting *Mirage*.''

I studied the snapshot with more interest, but I could tell

nothing about the second woman except that she'd been in a bad temper when the picture was snapped.

"I saved that because it's so good of Monica," he said, as though some explanation was necessary.

Door chimes sounded, and I heard steps in the tiled foyer as Saxon's man went to answer the door. When Wally's spirited voice called out, Saxon sighed.

"I'll have to see him. Do you mind?"

We returned to the living room, where Wally waited, looking as colorful as ever in green slacks and a Hawaiian shirt.

He beamed at us. "Hi, Carol. Hello, Sax."

It was the first time I'd seen Wally since he'd brought Owen to Monica's house yesterday, but he was behaving as though we were on the most affable terms. His relationship with Saxon, however, had taken on an edge.

Saxon grimaced at the familiar shortening of his name, and he was clearly impatient with Wally's unexpected appearance. A fact that was not lost on Wally. For all his good cheer, I suspected that a growing resentment lingered just beneath the surface in Wally Davis.

Now, however, he sounded exuberant as he spoke. "Sax, you have to be the first to hear that Monica's agreed to appear with you at the benefit. Linda called me a little while ago. I can't wait to start the wheels turning! The date is set for early December, so we can go into high gear right away. Can't you see the headlines? Scott and Arlen together again! We can name our price for the tickets. All Hollywood will come. We're lucky there's been a cancellation, so we can step in fast."

Saxon glanced at me with a hint of triumph in his eyes. In spite of Monica's near collapse this morning, she'd apparently changed her mind with equal swiftness and agreed to appear. Perhaps, as Saxon said, she wouldn't let him go out on that stage without her.

"Fine," he told Wally. "I knew she'd agree. Though coming on right after the picture, the audience is likely to see us as a couple of antiques."

176

"They'll love you!" Wally cried. "They'll be soppy with emotion. How could there be a dry eye in the house?"

"When Monica steps out on that stage," I said, "she'll make everyone who sees her believe the legend again. She may even make you look old, Mr. Scott."

Saxon smiled with no real pleasure. "Thanks for coming to tell me, Wally. Anything else?"

It was a clear dismissal, and I caught an edge of rancor in Wally again as he started for the door. I stopped him before he went out, and this time I couldn't keep my own feelings from showing.

"Do you know what Owen Barclay is planning next?"

Wally glanced at me in surprise. "I'm hardly in his confidence. Have you told Sax that this Barenklovich fellow he sent to me is your ex-husband?"

Saxon looked astonished. "I didn't know. Carol, I'm terribly sorry. This puts a new light on everything. Sit down a minute, Wally, and let's talk about this. I didn't like the man particularly, but he seemed to have legitimate business with Monica. What's this all about?"

Wally came back into the room, though he didn't sit down. "It's simple enough. He's made an offer for Monica's Beverly Hills place. A cool three million. Considering how hard it is to move those old mansions, it's pretty generous. So how can she refuse, no matter who he is?"

To my surprise, Saxon responded with a greater anger than I'd seen in him before. This was far beyond mere irritation.

"I want this stopped!" he told Wally. "She mustn't be allowed to sell Cadenza. Get busy and find a way to stop him!"

Wally looked surly. "How can I do that? Even if I wanted to, there's no way."

"You'll get a commission, of course?"

"Look," Wally said, "this is already out of my hands, and I don't want to make waves. Even if I am working for you—"

"If you don't scotch it, you may not be working for me much longer," Saxon warned, sounding as arrogant as he

177

could be on the screen. "And don't forget—I know a few things."

The threat was there, and Wally turned beet red. "I'll do what I can," he blurted, and almost fled for the front door.

I hated what Saxon had done, and I didn't want to stay in this house a moment longer. Nor did I want Saxon to drive me back to Palm Springs.

"Wait, please, Wally," I said. "I'm ready to leave, so perhaps I can go with you?"

"Sure." Wally was curt, still smarting under Saxon's words. "Come along," he added, and went out to his car.

"Thank you for seeing me," I said to Saxon.

He held my hand for a moment. "I'm sorry this session hasn't gone well for you. If you like, we can set another date."

"I'll phone you," I said stiffly.

All I wanted was to escape. I couldn't forget Saxon's treatment of Monica that morning, and he'd been equally cruel just now to poor Wally Davis. Saxon Scott was no more like his gallant screen image than Monica Arlen was like hers. Only the picture he'd created on the screen of a some-times dangerous and hot-tempered man seemed to ring true. Everything else was illusion, and it's always depressing when illusions dissolve.

He walked to the door with me. "Would you like to know why I don't want to see Monica sell her Beverly Hills house?" he asked.

His tone had turned surprisingly gentle again, and I glanced at him quickly. "I haven't thought much about it. It was the way you treated Wally just now that struck me."

"Perhaps I have a feeling that Cadenza ought to be yours someday."

This was an astonishing idea. "Why should it? What in the world would I do with it? I certainly couldn't afford to keep it."

"You might give it to a foundation—where *she* wouldn't. Too many of those old dream palaces have been bulldozed. Yet they're a part of movie history, California history, that will never come again."

178

"It's all academic, anyway," I said. "I don't suppose I'm even in Monica's will. Besides, I don't believe for a moment that Owen will carry through on his offer. Of course he'd make the amount large, so he can keep her dangling for a while. It's all a way of getting to Keith and me."

"I'm very sorry I played a part in this," he said again, and I could almost believe the ring of sincerity in his voice.

Being diplomatic didn't matter to me anymore, and I asked the one point-blank question I'd never expected to put to him.

"This morning Monica told me that you killed Peggy Smith. Was she making that up?"

All the life seemed to drain out of him, and with it the last shreds of pretense he might keep up. When he spoke, it seemed to be out of old pain, no longer concealed.

"It's true enough," he said. "I destroyed Peggy Smith in more ways than one, and I will never forgive myself."

"You mean you caused her to kill herself?" I asked softly.

"I pulled the trigger of that gun," he said, and opened the door for me. "Wally's waiting, Carol."

"But I can't leave everything like this!" I cried, completely shocked. "If it's true, why would Monica have been willing to keep still all these years?"

"Because she loved me," he said grimly. "For a time."

I went out to Wally, not daring to ask another question.

THIRTEEN

WALLY AND I TALKED VERY LITTLE ON THE DRIVE BACK TO PALM
Springs. His surly, unhappy mood was understandable, and I
felt sick with shock over Saxon's words. He was an actor,
and actors could exaggerate and dramatize. They were often
onstage. Yet he had spoken at the end with such devastating
calm that I had to believe him. Sometimes today I'd almost
liked him, and at other moments I'd found him detestable.
But the quiet pain that had wrenched out those words of
admission had been real. What horrors had he and Monica
lived with for all these years?

I began to seek a cause. Some reason that might have
driven him to such an act. Peggy Smith must have done
something awful to bring out this violence in Saxon. Probably
only Monica could tell me, and I didn't know if she would
ever speak.

Shakespeare's memorable line beat through my mind: *Truth
will come to light; murder cannot be hid long*. Yet here was
murder that had lain hidden for thirty-six years! Only to

surface now. But *why?* What catalyst had set the ugly past stirring for Saxon and Monica? Not my presence, surely, for all this had begun before I came. In any case, this was something I wouldn't speak about to Linda right away.

As we neared Smoke Tree House, the frightening present began to surface again—more threatening than the past. Owen Barclay was the *now* for me.

Wally said he'd rather not come up to the house, and would I mind phoning for someone to pick me up at the gate? I didn't mind, and he drove away, lost in his own gloom.

In a few moments Jason's station wagon came down the road, with Jason at the wheel. A feeling of pleasure and relief rose in me at the sight of him. He looked healthy, without being one of the lotus-eaters who lay forever in the sun. He had his own private tragedy, yet he appeared to deal with it without letting it destroy him. His cheerful greeting told me that all was well with Keith up at the house.

"Hello, Carol." He reached over to open the car door for me. "We've finished lunch, but Helsa can get something for you if you haven't eaten."

He was glad to see me, and I was unexpectedly glad to see him. I could let it go at that for now.

"Linda told me what happened at El Mirador this morning," he said as we drove up the mountain. "I'm afraid Monica has gone into another of her retreats, as Linda calls them."

"Just the same, she's agreed to appear with Saxon at the Annenberg," I said. "Even though what Saxon put her through today was pretty bad, she's given in."

When we reached the house, I went first to look for Keith, and found him in the garden with Jonah having a picnic. Ralph was with them, sharing sandwiches. In spite of my uneasiness where Ralph was concerned, his liking for Keith seemed genuine, and that, for me, was his one appealing quality.

"Thank you, Ralph," I said. "You're very good with small boys."

He grinned at me. "I'm good with little girls, too."

I should have known better than to speak to him at all. I kissed Keith and went back to the dining room, where Linda and Jason sat with me at the table while I ate a light lunch.

"What Saxon did this morning was horrible!" Linda cried the moment I appeared. "I never dreamed he'd pull a thing like that."

"Hey—calm down," Jason told her. "Monica can't feel so bad if she's said she'll go onstage with him."

"That's only because he's threatening her in some way," Linda said indignantly. "She won't tell me what she's afraid of, but I know there's something. . . . I don't want her to do this—it's too risky."

A reluctance to betray Saxon's "confession" held me silent. In spite of everything, in some way I didn't understand, I felt I owed him my silence.

I could tell Linda something else, however. "Wally came in while I was at Saxon's and he brought me home. He seemed very excited about Monica's consenting to appear."

Linda shook her head regretfully. "I can't even talk to Wally these days. There was a time when I thought it might be a good idea for Monica to come out in public. Now I'm afraid it will tear her apart. She hasn't the strength to handle it."

"Perhaps she has," I said. "Perhaps you ought to give her a chance to show Saxon the woman she can still be. That could mend her pride and re-energize her more than anything else."

"Carol's right," Jason agreed. "All this coddling and protection you go in for isn't a good idea. Not for you, Linda, or for Monica. It's nonsense to think of her as a great star whom you have to preserve. She's not a lab specimen! I'll bet she's a lot tougher than you give her credit for. If she's all that great, let her come out and prove it!"

Linda looked outraged, and I suspected that nothing we said would change her mind. She really *was* the conservator of a museum, in which the most valuable artifact was still alive. Nevertheless, I was grateful to Jason for telling her the truth, and I remembered ruefully that only a little while ago I'd have sided with Linda against him. By this time perhaps some sort of clean desert wind was blowing through *me*.

"Saxon didn't know about Owen's offer to buy Cadenza," I told Linda. "Wally opened all that up while he was there, and Saxon seemed upset. I wonder why."

182

"Who cares?" She was still fuming. "Monica will have to take Owen Barclay's offer, though I hate to see that house go. It's where Monica lived during her great days, and of course Saxon was in and out of it constantly, so he may have a proprietary feeling about it."

I didn't dare tell her what Saxon had said about the house coming to me. That was nothing I wanted to have happen, and it was ridiculous. What I wanted *not* to happen was that they should all take Owen's offer seriously. No one would believe in my warnings. The sound of three million dollars was enough to smoke screen anything I might say.

I spoke to Jason, changing the subject. "Saxon has made arrangements for me by phone to meet Alva and Nicos Leonidas tomorrow morning. If you're free, it would be fine if you could drive me up there."

"I can manage it, and I'll be glad to." His words and his look warmed me. I had one friend, at least.

Linda spoke sharply. "Monica doesn't think it's a good idea for you to talk to those people. And neither do I."

"If Saxon doesn't mind, why should she?"

"She's upset about everything right now."

Contradicting this, just as I finished my lunch, a call came to Linda from Ralph. The message was for me. Monica had decided that she wanted to see me right away.

Jason rose from the table. "Suppose I pick you up around nine tomorrow morning. I've got to be going now."

I told him that would be fine, and when he'd gone, I hurried upstairs, hesitating before I knocked on Monica's door. I couldn't help remembering with a cold wash of fear that moment when I'd walked into her rooms and found Owen waiting for me. But he wouldn't be there now.

Ralph came to the door and stared as I walked past him. He could convey more silent insolence than anyone I'd ever known. This I could ignore, as I could not ignore what had happened in the pool.

The living room was dim and empty, with draperies closed. I followed her voice and found her in a pleasant bedroom done in white and soft gray-green. Shaggy white rugs on the polished floor looked as though they'd come from the Andes, and tiny green orchids bloomed on curtains and chaise longue. Somewhere in the past, Monica had abandoned early Hollywood for something exquisitely simple.

The three cats were again in attendance, seated near the bed, and Annabella's haughty regard followed me as I came in. Propped against huge pillows, Monica looked old and frail, and not at all like the valiant, eager woman who had run up the stairs at El Mirador this morning. Her dark eyes, sunken in their sockets, stared at me through a twilight of pulled curtains.

"I have to know!" She reached out a hand to me. "Come here—sit down close to the bed. Tell me what he said to you!"

She could mean no one but Saxon. I pulled a chair over and sat down, taking her hands in mine. Pity welled up in me because of all she had once been, all she had lost.

"He really didn't have much to say," I told her falsely. "I saw some of his photographs, and we talked a little."

She closed her eyes, and I didn't know whether she felt relief, or was just concealing her own emotions.

"Never mind," she said. "If Mr. Barclay buys Cadenza, I'll be saved after all."

"Don't count on it, Aunt Monica. Please don't count on it."

Her expression changed to one of alarm—as though I hadn't been saying the same thing all along. "I *must* sell that house. It means everything to me now. My life! Of course there will be other offers, but nothing as large as this. Or as immediate."

I doubted that there would be any offers, but there was no point in arguing further, since she was determined to deceive herself. When the whole thing fell through, they would all believe me. But by that time, Owen might have succeeded in his main purpose—to abduct Keith.

"I suppose Linda has told you I mean to appear at the benefit?"

"Yes. She's upset because you've agreed."

"Sometimes"—there was a hint of venom in her voice—"sometimes I enjoy upsetting Linda."

"How can you possibly want to upset anyone so loyal to you?"

"Victims try to find other victims," she said, unexpectedly astute.

"You don't strike me in the least as being a victim."

A sudden fierce light glowed in her eyes. "You're right—I'm not! Or never for long. And I try not to fool myself *all* the time. Oh, there'll be a stir when I walk out on that stage. It may even last for a little while. But I'm out of all that now, and Hollywood can be a lonely place if you're not on the right lists and don't get invited to the right parties."

"Do you care about that sort of thing?"

"I used to. What did Saxon say about my consenting to appear with him?"

"He didn't seem surprised. He was sure you'd be there."

"And I will be! This one thing I'll do!" Once more a valiant determination rang in her voice. "I'll show him who and what I am. I'll show him I'm not afraid of him, or of anything he might do. If he's smart, he should be afraid of *me*. We've been tied together by the past for much too long, and I mean to break that tie."

I remembered what Saxon had said about being bound to Monica through the years. "Why *should* you be afraid of him? I don't think he means you any harm." Yet I wasn't sure that was true. I didn't know *what* was true.

"He means me every harm. Even though *he* is to blame for all that happened, he still wants to punish *me*. He's waited all these years, and now he means to try. But when I go out on that stage, he won't dare. Whatever it is he plans, he won't dare to carry it out. Not if *they* fall in love with Monica Arlen all over again. I can do it—I know I can!"

She was growing excited, and I held her hands tightly, trying to calm her.

"Don't, Aunt Monica. You need to stay as quiet as possible now. This has been a difficult day, and you must try to rest."

Her strength was surprising as she wrenched her hands from mine. "Did you tell Saxon I said he'd killed Peggy Smith?"

I nodded unhappily.

"Did it upset him? Did he admit it?"

Faced with her point-blank question, I had to answer. "He admitted that he was responsible for her death. He said he'd pulled the trigger."

"That's something! It's the first time he's admitted anything in all these years. Did he tell you the rest?"

"That was all he had to say."

She lay back upon her pillows again, but her eyes were open, as if she looked into the past and saw again a scene so terrible that it had destroyed two careers, as well as a life. When she spoke, it was as if to herself, as if she'd forgotten I sat beside her bed.

"It happened at El Mirador. I was there. We had to do something to save Saxon from the police. There'd have been a whopping scandal. I helped him to clean up the room in the bungalow where she died. Then we took her out to the desert. I drove *her* car, and Saxon took her body in his. We left her there, with the gun in her hand. She'd meant to kill *him*. I saw the struggle when the gun went off. Even the powder burns were right for suicide. It was an accident, but if we hadn't acted quickly, he'd have been charged with murder. Even if he'd been cleared in a trial, the damage would have been done. Saxon lost his head, so *I* was the one who had to think what to do."

I listened to her with shock and sorrow, feeling pity for them both. It would have been better if they'd risked the scandal and gone to the police. The guilty secret they'd contrived together had divided them anyway, as well as doing permanent damage to themselves as human beings.

"Why did Peggy try to kill him?" I asked.

"Because she was jealous. Because she thought he loved *her!* When of course *I* was the one he cared about all along. Because I loved him no matter what he'd done, I had to help him. We fooled everyone. By the time she was found, our plans were made, and we never cracked under questioning. We meant to save ourselves, and save those great careers as well. How foolish we were. How blind."

She was quiet, her eyes closed, while a trickling of tears came from beneath her lids. In the end, they hadn't saved anything, but now I could begin to understand how it must have been. With the guilt of Peggy's death between them, the guilt of what they'd done in destroying a life, they might easily have begun to hate each other. Neither must have been without conscience. When they played those retake scenes together, the ugliness that lay between them had shown all too clearly on the screen. She had never forgiven him for an affair with Peggy that had led to what happened. And he had never forgiven her for what she made him do. The awfulness of their actions together would always haunt them.

"He wouldn't believe me," she said softly. "He wouldn't believe that I never stopped loving him, no matter what had happened. His blame for himself carried over to me, so that he became my enemy—as he is now. Though he needn't have been. We could have helped each other."

"Perhaps he's grown more generous by this time. If he wants to make a gesture of reconciliation, shouldn't you accept it?"

"That's not what he means to do. He has an actor's ego! He can never forgive me for being strong and taking charge, when he was weak. He really believed in that image he projected on a screen, and the truth was more than he could take." She broke off and closed her eyes. "I'm very tired. But I'm glad we talked, Carol. Now you'll understand why you must never trust him."

I drew the coverlet over her, disturbing Annabella, who glared at me. "I'll sit here for a while, Aunt Monica," I said. "I'll be right here if you want anything."

She roused herself to look at me—the old Monica Arlen look that could warm with affection and gratitude. "Thank you, my dear. I haven't been much of an aunt to you, have I? But I'm glad you've come. I need you now."

My own quick tears came straight out of my childhood, when I'd have given anything to hear such words from *her*. Perhaps in some strange and circuitous way, we would come to love and appreciate each other yet, Monica and I. That old concealment of what hadn't really been a *crime* was so long ago, and both she and Saxon had paid for it over and over again. So now I consoled myself for knowledge I'd wanted, but couldn't live with comfortably, because it was going to haunt me too.

Monica reached out to stroke the Siamese. "Annie's been warning me," she murmured. "She's always sensitive to things the rest of us can't see."

In that case, she ought to warn Monica against Owen, I thought. But Annabella only curled up contentedly and began to purr under the stroking hand. After a moment or two the Persians joined her on the bed, and went prettily to sleep at Monica's feet.

Perhaps a half hour passed before Linda knocked on the door, and I went quickly to answer ahead of Ralph.

She looked pleased and excited as she came into the room. "Saxon just phoned me," she whispered, with a glance at the bed. "He seemed concerned about you. But mainly he wanted to tell me about his idea for an Arlen-Scott room. I think it's wonderful, and I'll tell Monica about it as soon as she wakes up."

But Monica wasn't sleeping. She opened her eyes and commanded us to stop whispering.

Linda burst out with her news, while Monica listened sleepily. I had misjudged Linda. She wouldn't be possessive, after all, of the Monica Arlen collection.

Monica, however, took the whole thing calmly and rewarded her with a yawn. "Let's not get excited until this really goes through. How do we know he means it—or that anyone will care? There were a great many movie people coming to El Mirador in the old days, so why *us?*"

Linda only beamed. "You're always too modest. You've never realized how much you and Saxon meant to a whole country because of your films. Thanks to television, you're far from forgotten."

"It doesn't matter anymore," Monica said sadly.

"Of course it matters! You'll see."

"I've outgrown all those fantasies about fame," Monica said. "There are more important realities to be dealt with now."

It occurred to me that there was one reality that hadn't been dealt with yet, and perhaps this was the time, while she was in a down-to-earth mood.

"Has anyone told you that we discovered some pages torn from a book in the Arlen collection?" I asked.

At once Monica was wide awake, alert. "What pages? What are you talking about?"

Linda looked daggers at me, but I paid no attention, driven by a growing feeling that Monica shouldn't be kept in ignorance about what went on in her home. She was not as fragile as Linda believed, and it was the tough, unvanquished side of her that I was beginning to respect. Perhaps her "retreats" were a way of renewing her will to fight.

"The index showed Peggy Smith's name," I went on deliberately. "However, the chapter that referred to her, and to you and Saxon, has been removed from the book. Have you any idea why?"

She blinked rapidly. "How could that possibly happen, Linda? Unless it was done long ago, when all those things were kept at Cadenza."

"No," Linda said. "It had to have happened recently. I remember those references vaguely." She hesitated, and then gave in with another dark look for me. "I didn't want to worry you about this, but since Carol has told you, you might as well know. That time when Saxon came up here to try to see you, I left him in that room. I thought he'd be interested in looking around. He's the only person who could have torn out those pages. Though he claims he didn't do it."

"Do you remember what the pages were about?" Monica asked.

Linda frowned. "They were innocuous enough, as I recall. There was some mention of Peggy as a talented sculptor."

"I know why he might have torn them out," Monica mused. "No—don't ask me now. I don't want to talk about it. It doesn't matter anymore. None of this matters now, when so many other problems face us."

She lay back and closed her eyes again. At a sound, I turned and saw that Ralph had come to the door and was listening openly to every word. I didn't know how long he'd been there. He might very well be a collector of small details, filing them away, in case he could use them to his advantage one day. It wouldn't be the first time that an employee in a famous household had sold intimate knowledge. I wished both Linda and Monica would regard him less as a fixture and more as a possible source of future trouble.

I remembered something else Saxon had told me, and since it wouldn't be any great tidbit for Ralph, I mentioned it.

"Saxon told me to ask you something, Aunt Monica."

"Yes—go on."

"He wanted to know if you remember what's inside the little cuckoo clock that was used in *Mirage*."

She countered with her own question. "Do you remember how that clock came to be in the picture?"

"There was an early scene shot in Switzerland—"

"We filmed it on a studio sound stage," she corrected.

"All right. It was supposed to be in Switzerland. There was a romantic little chalet, with the clock on the wall. And in the picture you had to take the clock with you when you left. You said the cuckoo clock knew too much about you to be left to talk to anyone else. So the character Saxon played bought it from the woman who owned the chalet. And in the big restaurant scene later in America, you brought it to the table deliberately—to remind your love. But there wasn't anything in the picture about something being hidden in the clock. What did he mean?"

She bristled. "He needn't think he can get around me that way! Of course I remember what happened in *real* life. Just don't let Saxon get to you, Carol. He's probably still a great charmer."

She didn't mean to tell us what had been hidden in the clock. I gave my place by her bed to Linda and returned to Keith.

Young Jonah had gone home, and for the rest of the day Keith and I played games together. I read aloud to him, and sometimes we just talked—the way he used to love doing. He was becoming much more like the little boy I remembered.

I didn't see Linda alone again until after Monica had retired that evening. She and I sat in the cheerful upstairs sitting room, looking out at the lights of Palm Springs. Tonight she seemed oddly sad and subdued. As I sat reading and making notes, she paged absently through a magazine, until she came to a decision and tossed it aside.

"Monica told me everything tonight," she said abruptly. "I mean about that terrible time at El Mirador. How horrible it must have been for her. It's a good thing she was strong enough to save them both—Saxon and herself."

"Peggy Smith *died*," I said. "And I don't think Monica saved either of them."

"That's because things didn't work out as she expected. Besides, if Jason is driving you to Idyllwild, then it's necessary for you to be armed with the whole story."

What was the whole story? I wondered. "Tell me about Alva and Nicos," I said. "How much do they know?"

"I can't tell you that. They were both close to Monica. Nicos was the only person she trusted behind a camera. And Alva was the one who could make her look as beautiful as she wanted to be. Of course they loved her, like everyone else. Until after the breakup, when everything changed."

"How did those two happen to marry?"

"Nicos always wanted Alva, I gather, but she couldn't see anyone in those days but Saxon. After he parted with Monica, Saxon began to take Alva out. I suppose Monica was really the pivot around whom they all turned. When she removed herself from them, they had only each other. Of course it didn't work out because it wasn't really Alva that Saxon wanted. Perhaps if the baby had lived . . . After the divorce, Saxon set her up in the restaurant she still runs with Nicos in Idyllwild. And her second marriage seems to have worked out fine. I still wish you wouldn't go up there, Carol. What can you hope to get from them?"

"Anecdotes, memories—anything they can give me. I never know what I can use until I put it all together. Right now I'd better get back to my typewriter and set some of my notes in order."

We said good night, and I stood for a few moments in my bedroom doorway, making certain Keith was asleep. I really didn't feel like working now, and I couldn't settle down. Too much that was terrible to think about had been opened up for me today. I couldn't stop those scenes at El Mirador from running through my mind. Peggy Smith senselessly dead, and those two working so desperately to conceal her murder!

Accidental, or not, that's what it had been, even though I'd wanted to make excuses for them, and it had become worse through concealment.

If it hadn't been for Monica's machinations, they might have weathered what had happened far better than they had. Hiding everything, contriving false trails, had only set ghosts rampant in both their lives; ghosts on whom they'd never been able to turn their backs. Perhaps Saxon was trying to lay those very ghosts now—and that frightened Monica, yet at the same time caused her fighting spirit to rise.

It was hard to think about anything else, but the book with the missing pages still tantalized me, and I began to wonder if pages on either side of the missing chapter might tell me something. Moving quietly, so I wouldn't disturb Linda, I hurried downstairs. When I reached Linda's office, I saw that a light was on in the adjoining Arlen room. When I looked in, I saw Ralph Reese working at something he held in his hands. I watched, ready to run if he made the slightest move toward me, but still curious.

It was the little cuckoo clock he was working on, and I saw that the back was open. I made no sound until he fumbled inside, drew out a folded slip of paper, and started to open it.

Then, still ready to run, I spoke to him sharply. "You'd better give me that."

He whirled to stare at me, but it took him no more than a moment to recover from his surprise.

"Snoopy, aren't you, Miss Hamilton?"

"Exactly what are *you?*"

"I'm only obeying orders. Miss Arlen told me to come down here and bring her what was in the clock. So that's what I'm going to do. But now that you're here, we might as well have a look together."

Before I could stop him, Ralph opened the slip and read the penned words aloud:

" 'Darling, I'll see you on the ninth in Acapulco.' "

Nothing earthshaking. Only a lovers' rendezvous.

"What do you suppose they were up to in Acapulco?" The leer in Ralph's voice was exaggerated. "She must have been quite a gal in her day."

I couldn't be sure whether he'd really come to look for the note because Monica had sent him, or because he was curious on his own. In any case, the time had come to retreat. The house was too empty down here with just Ralph and me.

"You'd better take her the note," I said. "I'll check with Monica later about this."

He stopped grinning and scowled at me. I waited for no further response, but fled upstairs, and heard his laughter ringing after me. He really did enjoy scaring people.

In our room I stood looking down at my sleeping son. The soft curve of his cheek, the way damp locks clung to his forehead, the dewy look of young skin—all wrenched at my heart. I bent to kiss his cheek lightly, and then sat down to talk to myself at the typewriter.

There were things I wanted to set down about Monica. Not so much the new facts I'd collected as my new feelings toward her. Today we'd moved a little closer together, and I had glimpsed her with her defenses down. The words Saxon had written so many years ago tucked into the back of a clock saddened me all over again.

I knew one thing. On the night of the benefit I would stay as close to Monica as I could. If she wanted support from me, I would give it. It was possible that I could find a new affection for the real woman, and forget my fantasies of the past. In spite of all that was devious about her, in spite of the terrible things she had done, she was trying now in her own way to face the past with something like honesty and courage. To these I could give my allegiance.

FOURTEEN

UNFORTUNATELY, MONICA'S MOOD HAD CHANGED COMPLETELY by morning. I was up early, to be ready for Jason, and Keith and I were having breakfast when the call came. Once more it was an imperative summons.

I hurried upstairs and found her waiting, dressed in a flowing India print of saffron and black. She sat regally in a high-backed chair, and I knew at once that she was ready for fresh battle. Yesterday's softening had been the mirage.

Annabella sat at her feet, on watch as usual, while the two Persians curled together asleep on a cushion. Apparently Ralph wasn't up at this early hour, and we were alone.

"You're not going to Idyllwild," Monica announced the moment I came into the room. "I've just telephoned Saxon. I've told him that I don't want you stirring up things that are better left alone, and he has agreed. He'll let Alva know that we don't want you bothering them."

"Do you mind if I sit down?" I asked.

She waved carelessly, and I saw how bright her eyes were, how ready she was for a fight.

"I don't understand," I said. "You've already told me what happened to Peggy, so why are you concerned about my talking with Alva and Nicos?"

"They're not my friends. Not anymore. I don't want you to see them."

"Because there's more than you've told me?"

"That's none of your business!"

"Maybe you're right. I'm beginning to think that from your viewpoint none of this book is my business."

"If you don't want to write it my way, I'll get someone else to do it. There are dozens of ghost writers who would jump at the chance."

"I'm not a ghost writer. I can only write a story as I see it."

She was fuming, but I wondered if she might also be bluffing a little. Perhaps I could bluff too.

"Then it's settled," I said. "If you won't help, if you must keep blocking me, I'll have to go ahead on my own. I'll find the people who knew you in Hollywood. I can work from printed material too. Of course I won't be able to write as good a book as I might with your help. And I won't be able to check details with you. But I *am* going to write about Monica Arlen, one way or another, and I'm going to Idyllwild today."

I started for the door, hoping she would stop me. When she let me go, I returned to breakfast feeling both defeated and strangely freed. The threat of Monica's censorship had hung over me from the first. I didn't want to write what the trade called an "authorized" biography. I had to go my own way, or not do this book at all. Not that I meant to be unkind or merciless. Hatchet writing wasn't my thing. But I didn't want to write something colored by Monica's own rosy self-deceptions. Yesterday she had spoken to me frankly, and those confidences were not ones I would betray. Nevertheless, even though I might censor my own words, I first had to know as much as I could. So Alva was an important link.

Linda looked up as I rejoined her and Keith at the table. "You're not going to Idyllwild, are you?"

So she was in on this too. "I haven't changed my plans," I told her quietly.

I was just finishing my coffee when Monica swept into the room in her saffron silk, her hair freshly brushed, and a touch of coral on her lips.

"We were both too hasty, don't you think, Carol dear?" she said as she sat down at the table.

I didn't mean to be beguiled as easily as I had been yesterday. She had something up her sleeve, and I waited for her to go on.

When she spoke, it was to Keith. "Since your mother plans to be away this morning, perhaps you can spend some time with me, young man. After all, you're my nephew, a few times removed, and we ought to get better acquainted. I've some interesting things I'd like to show you."

Keith was still in awe of Monica, and he looked at me, questioning and uncertain. I decided to accept her offer at face value. Perhaps she was having second thoughts about the book, and this was a way of making an overture.

"That should be fun," I said to Keith.

"I've collected a good many things in my travels," she went on, "and I'd like to show you some of them. Of course there are still treasures packed away in my Beverly Hills house, and I'll need to sort them out one of these days before I sell the place. Perhaps you and your mother can go there with me. I haven't seen Cadenza for years, but it's a fascinating house, and I think you'd like it. But today I'll just show you some of what I have here."

She gave me a sudden smile, and I knew she wouldn't mention who it was that had made an offer to buy her house. Her reversal of moods didn't reassure me, since I knew she was still up to something, but at least she would entertain Keith while I was gone.

When he'd finished breakfast, Monica took him off with her, leaving me with a bright, slightly malicious smile.

Linda sighed, looking after her. "You've really upset her this morning, Carol."

196

"She seems to rally very well. Maybe you've kept her packed in cotton batting too long."

Linda glowered a bit, but said nothing.

I was ready to leave, and as soon as Jason arrived, I hurried out to the car, eager to be on my way. Just as I was getting in, Linda came running from the house.

"Telephone call for you, Carol. It's Alva Leonidas."

So here it came! I went inside and picked up the phone. "I'm sorry, Miss Hamilton . . ." Alva's voice was light, a little breathless. "Nicos and I won't be able to see you after all today. We've a big luncheon party coming here, and we'll be tied up for hours. Perhaps some other time."

I knew there wouldn't be another time. Monica, via Saxon, had taken care of that. No wonder Monica had been willing to distract Keith, playing her games, because she knew I wouldn't be going anywhere anyway, and she needn't take him for long. Now I would have to play a game of my own.

I told Alva I was sorry, and went back to the car, where Linda was waiting, talking with her brother. When she turned with a question, I shrugged.

"It was nothing. Just a word about when we should be there. We'd better get started right away."

Linda looked bewildered, but I smiled at her and waved from the car window as we left the terrace. Not until we'd driven through the gate at the bottom, did I tell Jason what had happened.

"If you're willing, I want to go," I finished. "I can't let Monica get away with this, or it will be impossible to write the book my way. I'll just have to play it by ear with Alva and Nicos when we get there, and hope I can talk with them. I wonder what Monica said to Saxon to change his mind?"

"All right—we'll go," Jason agreed, but he sounded curt and I had the quick impression that he had removed himself to some distant mental place this morning.

I'd been looking forward to being with him again, perhaps more than I'd admitted to myself, and his new remoteness depressed me further. This wasn't going to be an easy day.

We followed Palm Canyon Drive with silence growing between us, and I tried to give my attention to our route. All through this area there seemed to be numerous places called "palms," "springs," "desert," and "canyon," with combinations and variations that completely confused the newcomer.

At Palm Desert, near the southern end of the San Jacinto range, the Palms-to-Pines highway began, and we left the valley floor to follow a road that wound toward the crest.

For the first time, Jason offered a terse comment. "We're taking the long way around, so you can see more of the country."

As we climbed, leaving towns and desert below, the vegetation changed and I found that I could identify some of the growth, both because of books I'd read and because of Mrs. Johnson, who had so long ago filled my head with her own desert memories.

"I can tell the creosote," I said. "And I think that's cheesebush and dyeweed growing out there."

Later these gave way to larger plants like juniper and scrub oak, which grew at a higher elevation.

"How do you know these plants?" Jason asked. "Have you been boning up?"

"A little. Linda loaned me a book about the valley. Mostly, though, I remember the stories Mrs. Johnson used to tell me. She loved the Southwest, and she made me want to see it. She could sketch a little and she used to draw pictures for me in pencil. That was the best place I lived in as a child. When she moved away and I went to someone else, I kept all her drawings—a lot of them of plants and animals. But I don't really *know* anything—I'm just guessing and remembering."

"You're doing all right," Jason said gently.

His change of tone put me on guard. I didn't want him to be sorry for me because of foster homes in my background, and I became as quiet as he had been.

When the car had climbed fairly high, we stopped at a point where we could look east over the entire Coachella Valley—an enormous sandy stretch, broken here and there by oases, where little towns clustered. Mostly there was sand, rimmed in on the far horizon by brown mountains. I remembered the diorama at the museum. It had indeed been true to life.

When we drove on and reached the crest, Jason parked again, and we followed a path on foot to a lookout point, from which we could see the San Bernardinos. Plumes of smoke rose above them in ominous columns. I'd heard on the radio of new brush fires burning near Los Angeles.

"It's such beautiful, terrible country," I said.

Jason stared off at the smoke, lost in his own moody thoughts. I was sharply aware of him beside me, his sun-streaked hair blowing over a tanned forehead, his look concentrated more on something inner, than on the scene before us.

"You're troubled this morning," I ventured. "Has anything happened?"

He took a folded sheet from his pocket and held it out to me. "I received this from my daughter yesterday."

I took the paper, sensing his pain. For a child nearly seven years old, Gwen's letters were well-formed, and she expressed herself briefly and clearly: *Dear Daddy, please come and get me. I want to come home.* Words to wrench the heart.

"I've been too full of my own troubles," I said. "I'm sorry. Can you tell where it was mailed?"

"The postmark was a small town in Arizona, but I have no idea whether they're staying there, or just passing through. She must have known that her mother wouldn't let her write to me, because the envelope was addressed in an adult hand. Some kind person must have seen her need and mailed it for her."

"Is there any way to follow it up?"

"I've sent the envelope to the detectives I've hired. It's at least an indication of where they've been recently. The fact that the law's on my side doesn't help as long as they keep moving. The police only say that if I can find them, they'll slap on a court order good within the state. There's a national law coming, but that doesn't help much now. Or protect you. Though it may be a deterrent to others who try to snatch their children."

How well I knew. And no comfort existed for him except to recover his daughter. I could only murmur how sorry I was.

Perhaps he sensed something of the feeling I couldn't put

into words, for he held my hand for a moment as he took the note, and his own words had a rueful sound.

"When I first heard about you from Linda, I sided against you, Carol. I've already told you that. Because *you* were a mother holding your child away from his father. But it isn't as simple as that, is it? Everything depends on the individual case. We seem to be parents in the same boat."

More than anything at that moment I wanted to turn my palm in his and clasp his fingers, cling to the lifeline of his warm brown hand. Perhaps he sensed the sudden surge of need in me, for he let me go abruptly and turned to leave. The rejection was slight, but it hurt. Not that I blamed him. We'd both been burned very badly, and he was no more given to trusting than I.

"Let's get back to the car," he said, and I went with him in silence. The road had leveled and we passed a mountain lake before turning north. Now the pines—ponderosa and white fir and cedar—grew cathedral tall. The sight was a contrast after the dead browns of sand and rock. Pines, instead of palm trees! Yet, strangely, I missed the desert, to which I was finding an affinity. Or perhaps the affinity was also to the man.

Jason, of course, knew about everything that grew, every tree and plant—and about the animals as well. Assured now of my interest, he was willing to talk about topics that opened no threatening quicksand under our feet. In spite of the fact that I liked him very much, and wanted to know him better, I was on guard too. This time I must be very careful of my emotions, so they wouldn't get out of hand. The thought made me smile to myself. When had I ever managed such caution?

Now, as we followed the top of the San Jacinto range through parklands, an anxiety I'd been holding away moved in again to occupy me. Ever since Owen had appeared at Smoke Tree House, Monica's "fortress" had grown less safe. Once he'd made his connection with her, his attack could get in almost anywhere. Perhaps even through Linda? I didn't think his reach could touch Idyllwild as yet—though I wasn't even sure of that. I could believe that both Linda and

Monica would protect Keith. But what about me? If Owen knew of my trip to the mountains, how vulnerable might I become?

It was late in the day to think of that, and probably foolish anyway. Jason was with me, and I was safe enough. I mustn't let my too ready fears and vivid imagination make me a prisoner.

We traveled now through the beautiful green belt high above the desert. Small communities and isolated cabins offered desert-dwellers an escape from summer heat, as well as skiing in winter. Yet whatever was built up here also had to weather storms, and many of the houses were built in the A-frame style, with steep roofs to shed the snow.

Idyllwild was a small mountain town tucked in among the pines. Jason had been to the Lindos, and knew the way, turning off the main road as it ran through a rustic business section. The building perched on a ledge halfway up a steep hillside. Nicos Leonidas, as Jason told me, had come originally from the Isle of Rhodes, and he'd named his inn rather whimsically after Athena's temple on the rocky cliffs of that Greek island.

My uneasy anticipation grew. I still had no idea what I might be getting into by coming here against the wish of these people, or how I was to persuade them to talk to me.

The Lindos was alpine brown, and looked like anything but a Greek temple, built low and wide, with an encircling porch glassed in on three sides, forming the main dining area. Wide steps led up to double screen doors, and when Jason had parked the car, we got out and climbed toward the entrance.

Sitting on the top step, smoking a pipe and watching our approach, was Wally Davis. All my vague self-warnings began to clamor through me at once.

He stood as we came up the steps. "Hi," he said, sounding surly. An unwilling messenger? "I've made a lunch reservation for you, since you decided to pay no attention to Alva and come up anyway. I'd better warn you that you're not exactly welcome. You won't get what you want, Miss—uh—Hamilton."

So Wally had taken sides against me. With whom, and why?

I stopped where I was, staring up at him. "How did you know? How did you get here?"

"You came by the scenic route. There's a shorter way up. And I knew because Linda phoned this morning and asked me to come."

Wally led us into the dining area, and while many of the tables were occupied, obviously no large affair was in progress that would take all of Alva's attention. From across the room, she saw Wally and came toward us, her manner cheerful but a little forced.

She must have been a very young woman when she'd worked at Monica's studio—younger than Monica or Saxon. Now she was frankly plump, and her hair, twisted on top of her head, was an interesting shade of near-red. Her face seemed more youthful than her years, and her manner was vigorous, lively, uninhibited.

"You weren't supposed to come," she told us frankly. "But since you're here, we have a table for you." She greeted Jason, whom she knew, and then led the way to a table beside a window overlooking the tops of pine trees.

"Mind if I join you?" Wally asked, clearly acting under instructions not to let us out of his sight. There was nothing we could do but accept his glowering presence.

As I studied the menu, Alva bent to speak to me. "Nicos is out right now, but he may be back before you leave. When you've finished lunch we can talk about Monica a little." Wally scowled and she grinned at him. "With certain guidelines, of course."

I was inclined to like Alva, even though she was bowing to Saxon's wishes.

The restaurant offered Greek and Mideastern dishes, and I ordered felafel and a salad with feta cheese, while Jason asked for something exotic wrapped in vine leaves. It was hardly a festive occasion.

Jason, as I was coming to realize, could be a quiet, listening presence, not demanding attention, but missing nothing. When we'd ordered, he spoke directly to Wally.

"What's this all about? Why are you really here?"

"Believe me, I wish I wasn't. I've got other things to do in Palm Springs. Monica sent word through Linda that I was to get up here pronto and keep an eye on things. I'm supposed to make sure Alva doesn't get carried away and talk too much."

"About what?" Jason asked quietly.

"I'm not sure. Just no talk about El Mirador. That's what Linda said."

"And no talk about Peggy Smith?" I put in.

"Right. But I've been handed another mission as well. As it happens, I was having breakfast with Owen Barclay at Saxon's restaurant when Linda tracked me down."

I could feel the fine hairs rise at the back of my neck. I'd felt earlier that there might be some connection with Owen, and this was disturbing. I didn't want my perceptions to be so right.

"Why were you seeing *him?*" I demanded.

Wally grinned at me, almost amiable now. "Because he invited me. I may be leaving Saxon's employ, you know, and Mr. Barclay pays rather well for—well, you might call it messenger service."

Jason put a quieting hand on my arm. "You'd better explain, Wally."

"I couldn't just run off when word came from Linda, leaving Mr. Barclay without an explanation, could I? When he knew I'd see you, he asked me to give you something from him, Carol."

Wally reached into his pocket and drew out a thick envelope, handing it to me across the table. When I didn't reach for it, Jason took it from him.

"Do you want me to open it?" he asked me.

I answered quickly, "No! Whatever it is, I don't want it. Just take it back to him, Wally."

"Oh, I can't do that," Wally said airily. "Mission unaccomplished? Never! Not for Owen Barclay."

I took the envelope reluctantly and slipped it into my handbag. I had no intention of opening it while Wally watched—and could report my reaction to Owen. The fact that Owen knew I was up here in the mountains was more disturbing than ever.

"I want to make a phone call," I said.

Wally indicated a public telephone, and I dialed Smoke Tree House. When Linda answered, I told her that Owen had been able to reach me through Wally, and that he knew I was away from the house without Keith.

She spoke soothingly. "Don't worry, Carol. Everything's fine here. Keith is having a wonderful time with Monica, and Owen won't be allowed into this house again. You really can trust me on that, Carol dear."

Perhaps I could. But how could I trust Monica, who often seemed motivated by sudden impulses that she followed on the spur of any moment?

"I won't stay away too long," I promised Linda. "We're finishing lunch, and as soon as I've talked to Alva, we'll start for home."

I went back to our table, and when we'd finished a pastry of sesame seeds and honey, Alva invited us to have coffee in the living quarters back of the restaurant.

The big, slightly shabby room was done in soft shades of green and yellow that matched the outdoors with its pines and patches of sunlight. Nicos had not yet returned, and I sat down uneasily and tried to relax enough to conduct a sensible interview.

Jason stood near a window, leaving the floor to me, but I sensed gratefully that he was listening and would be ready to step in if I needed help. Wally hovered restlessly, never out of earshot.

Alva remembered well the old, great days, and if part of me hadn't been preoccupied I'd have enjoyed her stories more. The package from Owen was always there in my mind.

I hadn't expected her to show the warmth of affection she revealed in talking about Monica Arlen. Perhaps she had made a separation between the time she remembered and the present. Saxon came into her stories too, though here she hedged a bit delicately, as though her own more personal memories might get in the way. Listening, I found myself wondering if she'd ever really fallen out of love with him, and if Monica had always stood between them.

"You've probably no idea how strong it was—the Arlen-Scott wave that swept the country when those films were new," she said. "Young men began to dress casually like Saxon Scott, and they tried to imitate that macho image he projected on a screen. Women copied Arlen's hair, even to the way it swept over those marvelous cheekbones when she turned her head. And of course they copied its color. There was a company that put out Arlen wigs long before Eva Gabor wigs came along. They even tried to imitate that exotic tilt of her eyes that came off so well on the screen."

"Her eyes still look like that," I said, "but I understand you helped them along for the camera, Alva."

"I never wanted to do that. I thought she was perfect the way she was. But she insisted, so I did the best I could to gild the lily. They never make pictures like that anymore, and something's been lost to America. The magic is gone. What we have is teenage stuff—horror and occult and space. Sex and brutality and violence. Dreadful pictures!"

"There are good movies being made today—a few," I said. "Though of course they're different. The make-believe glamour is gone. The myths aren't accepted anymore. When we look at the old pictures on television now, we know they're make-believe."

Alva almost snapped at me. "We needed the relief of make-believe when the country was in a terrible depression. And when the war came along. We *needed* heroes and heroines! We could come out of a movie house with a lift to our spirits, instead of feeling depressed."

Jason turned from the window. "But didn't that sort of make-believe do a lot of damage too? Kids grew up expecting life to be like the movies."

"Yes!" I said. "I went a long way down that road myself. If all those silver dreams hadn't been in my eyes, perhaps—" I didn't finish the thought out loud—that perhaps I'd never have married Owen Barclay.

"You really are going to write about Monica Arlen, aren't

205

you?'' Alva said, as though she hadn't quite believed, even while she was telling me stories.

"Of course I am. That's why I must talk to a great many different people."

Alva shook her head. "It's a wonder *she* will let you go ahead."

"She can't stop me."

"What's she like now—the woman she's turned into?"

I hesitated, and Jason spoke from his place near the window. "She's still living her make-believe. Smoke Tree House is her fantasy now—cut off from the real world."

"Yes. I suppose that's the only way she could live."

I had to protest. "If she comes out for this benefit appearance, she may surprise everyone. She'll give them her special magic and make them believe whatever she wants them to believe."

"I hope she doesn't do that. It's too risky. I mean Saxon—" Alva jumped up to run across the room. She picked up a framed picture—an enlarged shot of herself and Monica, and brought it over to me. "Nicos took this a year or so before *Mirage* was made."

Monica wore pleats and a cashmere sweater, with a scarf tied jauntily at her throat. She had been hamming a little, the smaller Alva exaggeratedly adoring beside her.

I looked sadly at Monica's laughing face. "There isn't much fun left in her. I wish I could have known her when she was like this. Why did you say it might be risky for her to appear at the benefit?"

Alva took the picture from me and replaced it. When she spoke it was over her shoulder, not looking at me. "Legends should be allowed to stay legends. Besides, I don't like cruelty under any circumstances, and I think Saxon is being cruel."

"I think so too," I agreed. "Just the same, Monica has decided to go through with it, and perhaps she'll fool him, if he thinks he's going to humiliate her. Tell me why you think he's being cruel?"

Wally came to life. "Saxon said there was to be no talk about the benefit."

"But why ever not?" I demanded.

"Yes, Wally"—Jason backed me up—"why doesn't Saxon want any talk about the benefit?"

"How do I know?" Wally sputtered. "He never tells me anything. And it was Linda he talked to."

"We don't owe Saxon anything anymore!" Alva was suddenly vehement. "We can talk about anything we please!"

"No, we can't." A man's voice spoke from the doorway. "We still owe Saxon plenty! More than I like to owe him. You'd better remember that, Alva."

Nicos Leonidas had come into the room. He was a lot bigger than his wife—massive in an overpowering way. He wore a full black beard peppered with gray, and his gray eyebrows made tremendous overhangs above dark eyes that seemed to challenge whatever he saw. I found it difficult to imagine him as the young photographer who had known better than any other how to bring out Monica's beauty with his camera.

"Now then," he boomed, "what's all this about? You weren't supposed to let them come, Alva."

"Hello, Nicos," Jason said. "Carol's a free agent. She can go where she pleases. Scott has nothing to say about that."

"I've only told her about the way it *used* to be," Alva assured her husband. She hurried to introduce me, sounding like a child caught out in some misdeed, clearly ready to be submissive, now that Nicos had appeared.

He shook hands with me stiffly, and I made a small effort to disarm Alva's husband. "I've seen every one of those Monica Arlen pictures when you were the cameraman. You made that camera love her."

He stared at me somberly, and I was startled to see moisture in his eyes. "Everyone loved her," he said, and the angry boom was gone from his voice.

"Will you tell me about her?" I asked.

He sat down across from me and began to talk quietly about Monica Arlen, reminiscing with affection.

I made notes until he paused. "I wish she could hear you," I said. "It would do her good."

His emotional shifts could be immediate, and he was at

once brusque again. "All that's over! What she used to be. You shouldn't have come here at all."

"But we are here," I pointed out. "And I'm glad you've both shared some of your memories with me. I'd like to do her justice—as honestly as I can."

He only scowled. The interview was at an end, and it was time to go. I thanked them both, and Jason came with me to the door.

Wally followed as we left, as though he didn't mean to trust us from his sight until we were safely on our way. When we drove toward the road, he stood staring after us.

Out of sight of the Lindos, Alva Leonidas was waiting near the road. Jason braked beside her, and she handed me a slip of folded paper.

"Take this, Carol. And don't tell anyone I gave it to you." Her words came out in a rush. "Go and see this man in Desert Hot Springs. Maybe he can tell you more about what you want to know. I can't talk, because Nicos would have a fit. He's the reality I must live with. The Monica Arlen part of our lives was so long ago, and we can't get involved now."

I thanked her, and as we drove away I opened the paper and read aloud what she had written:

> You must try to see Henry Arlen. He's Monica's cousin, once or twice removed, and he knew her when she was growing up on her parents' ranch near where Desert Hot Springs became a town. He still lives there, and he works part time at Cabot's pueblo.
>
> Saxon and Monica are trying to bluff each other, and you'd better be prepared. Henry should know. I'm sorry I can't talk to you.
>
> Alva Leonidas

"I suppose you'll want to see him?" Jason said.

"Yes—though I didn't know Monica had another living relative. That means I do too."

Now, however, something else was uppermost in my mind.

The thought of it had never been far away, nagging at me ever since Wally Davis had handed me the package from Owen. As Jason turned the car onto the highway, I took the envelope from my bag and opened it. I found it filled with tissue—and suddenly I knew. I knew before I unwrapped the protective packing that Owen had sent me Monica's emerald ring.

FIFTEEN

I TOOK THE RING FROM THE TISSUE AND SLIPPED IT ONTO THE fourth finger of my right hand. All the ramifications of what this meant were springing at me.

I knew Ralph had pushed me into the pool, even though he denied it. So it must have been Ralph who had stripped the ring from my finger and taken it to Owen. Perhaps as proof of what he'd done? If this was true, he could very well be in Owen's pay, and my last shred of safety at Smoke Tree House was shattered for good. To close the circle, knowing how it would devastate me, Owen had used Wally as his messenger and returned the ring.

Jason glanced at me. "Do you want to stop for a while, Carol?"

"No—I must get back to Smoke Tree House as quickly as possible!"

"We're taking the route along the top," Jason said. "It's a lot shorter. So just hang on."

The sound of his voice, calm, reassuring, helped me. I

found myself watching his hands on the wheel as he drove—
brown hands with long fingers, squared at the tips. Exciting
hands. But I didn't dare think about that.

"I haven't any commitments right now, so I can drive you
to Desert Hot Springs tomorrow, if you like," he offered.
"Then you can talk to Henry Arlen—if you think that will
help. We can bring Keith with us. I know he'll like Cabot's
Hopi pueblo. I took Gwen there a couple of years ago and she
decided that was where she wanted to live."

I knew how he felt when he spoke of Gwen because I'd
been where he was, and was terrified of being there again.
Jason's words had drawn me back from the edge of horror
that the ring had brought me to, and I knew that I must go on
with what I needed to do, and somehow protect Keith at the
same time. It would be better to have him with me tomorrow.

The miles went by and we descended once more to the
desert, to meet the highway cutting through the pass from Los
Angeles. Mt. San Jacinto stood apart from the mother range,
dominating it in height, but separate from it. Named, I'd been
told, by the Spaniards after a St. Hyacinth. The White Water
River rushed along it course beside the road, and wind tunneled
down from the pass, pushing at the car from behind. The gale
was so fiercely habitual here that signs had been posted to
warn of high winds. As the road turned south around the
mountain's flank, we were once more in the valley, approach-
ing Palm Springs.

Its palm-lined avenues were a welcome sight in my eagerness to reach the house. No blue car waited at Monica's gate,
and the guard waved us through.

Linda came hurrying out to greet us, her expression anxious.
"You shouldn't have gone!" she wailed. "Monica is furious!"

I got out, not stopping to argue with Linda. "Where is
Keith?"

"He's all right," she said impatiently. "Monica kept him
busy all morning, and this afternoon Helsa went up to the
pool to watch him swim. That's where they are now. Keith
isn't the problem—*you* are!" She turned to her brother. "Will
you stay, Jason? I need to talk to you both."

He shook his head. "Thanks, not this time. I want to get back to the ranch. Will you be all right now, Carol?"

"I'm fine." I had to be fine, for Keith's sake.

"Then I'll pick you and Keith up around nine in the morning."

"Thank you, Jason. For everything."

He seemed to understand, and he held my hand for a moment, as he'd done before. "We'll see it through, Carol," he said, and I knew he had come completely over to my side. This comforted me a little as he drove away.

I turned back to Linda. "I'll go talk to Monica at once."

"No, you won't, because she's not here. Ralph has driven her into town to see Owen Barclay and his lawyers. About the sale of Cadenza, of course. She wouldn't let me go with her, but I got hold of her attorney and sent him over right away. So she can't do anything foolish."

I held out my hand with the ring for Linda to see.

"Oh, good—you found it!"

"No, I didn't," I said. "Wally had breakfast with Owen this morning, and Owen gave him the ring to return to me."

Linda's eyes widened. "What's going on?"

"That's what I'd like to know. I'm sure Ralph is behind this."

"Oh no! I can't believe—" She sounded shocked.

"We'd better believe."

I started past her upstairs, but she stopped me. "What's this about a note in the cuckoo clock? Ralph found something and took it to Monica."

"I don't think it matters one way or another."

"Of course it matters. Monica read it and tore it up. After that she was terribly depressed for a while."

"There are more things than that for her to be depressed about."

I left Linda to her worries, and went to the pool to find Keith. For the rest of the afternoon I stayed with him, listening to his chatter, trying to respond.

Apparently Monica had shown him some pictures of Cadenza and I wondered why she seemed to be building it up in Keith's imagination. Was Owen somehow pulling more strings?

But I mustn't be suspicious of everything and everyone. It was natural for Cadenza to be important in Monica's mind. But the ring burned my finger with its warning.

When Monica and Ralph came back later in the afternoon, Keith and I were playing checkers in the little drawing room downstairs. I could hear Linda at her typewriter in her office, with the door closed, and she didn't come out.

The state of Monica's temper was clear as she stormed into the house to confront me. She dismissed Ralph with an imperious hand, and sat down beside me on the sofa. She'd dressed for town somewhat conservatively, for once, in a light beige frock and green scarf. Nor had she worn the chestnut wig. By now she'd probably discovered how little Owen cared for movie people—unless he could use them.

"Keith, go outside and play for a while," she ordered. "I want to talk to your mother."

She could still intimidate him, and though he went reluctantly, he obeyed. At once she turned indignantly to me.

"So! You went to Idyllwild this morning directly against my wishes!"

"If you're not going to help me with the book, then I can't think about your wishes," I told her.

She pursed her mouth, but let the anger flow out of her as easily as it had risen. How much was real, how much was acting, I couldn't tell. Perhaps not even Monica knew.

I watched her with a mingling of admiration and pity that added up to reluctant affection. I felt revolted by everything she and Saxon had done. Yet she'd paid over and over again through the years. There must have been a terrible, secret torment as she shut herself away from all that mattered to her. Now she was fighting—perhaps for the very right to live. Even though this had been a right denied to Peggy Smith, I couldn't despise this pitiable woman. Even her play-acting was desperate, and sad to watch.

"I don't like people talking behind my back," she went on more mildly. "You and Alva—"

"You needn't worry about anything Alva told me. She still has a tremendous admiration for you, and she said nothing that wasn't flattering. It was the same with Nicos when he came in. Neither of them has forgotten that you were the most wonderful thing that ever happened to them. So when I asked questions they didn't like, they both put up barriers.''

This didn't seem to comfort her. "It doesn't matter anymore. It was all so long ago.''

"It matters to this book. I don't want to write it without your help, Aunt Monica.''

She opened her beautiful eyes very wide and looked straight at me with an honesty I'd seldom felt in her. "I spoke too quickly, Carol. Of course we must work together. I owe it to—to the people we all used to be. To Monica Arlen and Saxon Scott. To Peggy Smith.''

"I'm glad you've changed your mind,'' I said, and she returned my smile tremulously. There was more I had to tell her, however.

"Tomorrow Jason is driving Keith and me to Desert Hot Springs—to see Henry Arlen. Since you won't talk about your childhood, perhaps this cousin will fill in the blanks.''

For a moment she was silent and I feared another outburst. Then she collected herself and answered sadly, perhaps again lost in unhappy memories.

"Growing up in a place I hated was pretty boring. I had to fight my mother every inch of the way to get *out* of there, to get *to* Hollywood. I hate gray streets and nothingness.''

"Gray streets?'' I picked up her words.

"Any street is gray if you want to be somewhere else.''

For a little while she sat thinking, lost in the past. Then she made up her mind. "If you're going to look up Henry Arlen, I'll go with you. I haven't seen him for a good many years, but if it's reminiscences you want, perhaps I can jog his memory.''

Once more she opened her eyes wide, but her mood had changed again, and now her look was one of triumph. As though she'd moved one of the men on the checkerboard successfully. A look that made me uneasy.

"That's fine,'' I said. "I'm glad you'll come with us.''

I didn't know whether she'd be help or hindrance, but it might be useful to see her out in the desert region where she'd grown up.

She closed her eyes and went through a ritual Linda had told me about. She inhaled to the capacity of her lungs, and then released her breath slowly. An exercise to achieve calm. When she looked at me again, however, her eyes were snapping with life, and I wasn't sure the deep breathing had worked. As usual, she could change subjects without notice.

"I can see why you married Owen Barclay. I can also see why you divorced him. A totally fascinating, impossible man. Probably a vicious man. But in a little while I had him eating out of my hand."

I doubted that, but said nothing. Perhaps each had been conning the other.

"Carol," she went on, "you must understand the relief I feel over this sale of Cadenza. You were wrong to have misgivings. Mr. Barclay really does mean to go through with it. Oh, of course everything hasn't been signed on the dotted lines yet, but we're well on our way. My financial difficulties will be over. So perhaps your coming here has been good for me in several ways."

She had a marvelous talent for self-deception. All Owen Barclay really meant to her was the sale of a house. The injury he had done to Keith and me in the past, and meant to do in the future, simply didn't penetrate the protective shell of her ego.

I drew the emerald ring from my finger and held it out to her. "Please take this back. I don't want the responsibility of keeping it, Aunt Monica. We haven't told you, but it was lost for a while."

"What do you mean—lost? I couldn't bear for it to be lost!" She took the ring from me and sat turning it about in her fingers.

I told her exactly what had happened. That Ralph had pushed me into the swimming pool, and that he had certainly taken the ring from my hand and delivered it to Owen.

She slipped the ring on with fingers that were shaking. "That's awful! Really dreadful, Carol! How could Ralph do such a thing? I can't bear to think of what's happening."

"What are you going to do about Ralph?"

Her look was oblique. "I'll talk to him, of course."

215

And he would deny. We were getting nowhere.

"Everything was so peaceful and quiet before *you* came," she said.

"I'm sorry if I've disturbed your quiet life."

That look of mischief that was perhaps an echo of her girlhood curled her lips and lighted her eyes. Yet now it was a look colored by a hint of malice.

"Perhaps it's been too quiet. There was so much that was exciting in the old days. Now Linda protects me. Protects me from being alive! Sometimes I even wonder if I might do something with my life again—starting with my appearance at the Annenberg."

"You're not afraid of Saxon anymore?"

"Afraid? If anyone's afraid, it's Saxon. We're still tied to each other, and we always will be, whether we like it or not. That night we'll put on a good front and prove to an audience who we are. If we fail, we fail together. But we won't, you know!"

I wished I didn't feel that this new Monica was a woman who balanced on a high rope. After years of avoiding dangerous heights, if she should falter up there . . .

My doubt must have showed, for her fervor of excitement died as suddenly as it had risen.

"You don't believe I can do it!" she wailed. "There's no one to believe in me anymore. Not even my own mirror!"

"I believe you can do whatever you set your mind to," I assured her. "It's Saxon I distrust. I hope he won't try to humiliate you in some way that night. I do want to be with you in the theater, Aunt Monica."

"Of course you'll be with me. You'll be in the wings—so you can write about it properly afterwards. Saxon won't hurt me. If he should try, he'd only destroy himself. So he won't dare."

I wasn't sure she was right. I had seen in Saxon Scott a man consumed by old, deep hatreds. Perhaps a man who would sacrifice himself if he could carry out an act of revenge— because of wounds that had been festering for too many years.

"What did *you* do to Saxon?" I asked softly.

She answered without hesitation. "I saved him from himself.

And I suppose that's the most unforgivable sin of all. He's not really like that screen image of his, you know. But I loved him anyway.''

"You mustn't torment yourself. Perhaps when you and Saxon walk out on that stage together, you'll go back to when everything was right between you.''

"I wonder," she said. "I wonder if I could . . ." Quite suddenly she put her head on my shoulder and wept, while I held her, not knowing how to help and strengthen her, not even believing in the sentimental solution I'd offered.

At a sound I looked toward the door. Linda was watching me with an oddly blank expression on her face, and Ralph stood just behind her. I didn't know how long either had been there, or how much they'd overheard.

Linda came to draw Monica gently from my arms. "You're tired, dear. Let me help you to your room. Ralph can bring your tray upstairs, and when you feel better you can tell me about your trip to town."

I sensed that Linda was asserting her guardianship again. This was what she lived for—Monica's need of her—and she must resent it when Monica turned to me. She was probably glad when I was out of the house.

Even as I watched, Monica gave up. All her rising courage and determination, her excitement over a life that might be lived again, died away. As she went with Linda, leaning on her arm, an old and defeated woman, indignation surged through me. It might be a lot better for Monica Arlen to take defeat in a valiant fight than to give up without even trying. Perhaps my words hadn't been so empty after all. Perhaps they'd supported Monica in the very course of action she ought to take.

Ralph continued to lounge in the doorway.

"Lots of rivalry around these days, isn't there?" he said. "Looks like everybody's trying to be top dog. You know you've put Linda's nose out of joint since you came, don't you?"

I went past him to the terrace, not wanting to dignify his words with a retort, though he'd been shrewder than I'd have expected.

"I know about the ring," I told him. "I know exactly what you did with it."

"Do you now?"

"Yes. And I've told both Linda and Monica."

I didn't wait for his lies, but went outside to join Keith. At least I'd served notice on him that we knew about his double-dealing.

Linda didn't appear for dinner that night. Ralph carried trays upstairs for all of them, and Keith and I dined alone. Afterwards, I went to work on my notes, elaborating on some of the stories Alva and Nicos had told me, before they could grow cold.

When Keith was asleep, I went to stand on the balcony, looking out over Palm Springs, thinking of the time I'd spent with Jason. We had seemed to come closer in understanding during those hours of travel in his car. He wasn't a simple man to know, yet I felt that we had become friends.

It was all too easy to imagine Jason's hands touching me, his arms holding me. Harmless comfort to think of in a dangerous world.

SIXTEEN

THE NEXT MORNING LINDA DIDN'T COME DOWN FOR BREAKFAST.
Helsa said she had a headache and had stayed in bed. Monica,
however, came blithely to the table to join Keith and me.

She had decked herself out in a long-skirted, sun-yellow
dress with a boat neck—vintage almost any year. Over this
she had draped long strands of amber and topaz beads that
gave her a gypsy look. Her hair was covered with a large
straw hat, tied under her chin by a scarf of braided orange
silk, and she kept the hat on through breakfast. Its brim gave
her an advantage, since she could hide her face simply by
ducking her head.

I must have stared when she walked in, for she laughed
good-naturedly. "Do I look like a movie star? I dug this out
of a chest of clothes I acquired from old pictures. I can't even
remember what film I wore it in. Henry Arlen hasn't seen me
for years, so I'll need to make an impression."

"You look very impressive," I said. Even Keith was
staring, stunned by the effect she could produce.

I mentioned Linda's headache, and she shrugged it off. "Linda's peeved because I don't want her to come on our little trip this morning."

"Why shouldn't she come, if she wants to?"

Monica shook her head playfully. "Today I'm escaping all my keepers!"

I didn't trust her. I knew very well why she was coming with us. Alva Leonidas had told me in her note that Henry Arlen "knew" something. So Monica had invited herself along in order to prevent him from saying anything she'd prefer I didn't hear. It was as simple as that, and as complex.

"We'll have fun, won't we, Keith?" she went on, ignoring my doubtful expression.

"Sure," Keith said and finished his glass of milk. "Can I go outside, Mom, and watch for Jason?"

The bruise beneath his eye had yellowed, and the swelling was gone, but the mark of Owen's fist still made a patch of sickly color on his cheek. I nodded and he left the table.

Jason came for us just as we finished breakfast and we went out to his car. He helped Monica into the back seat, which she preferred, while Keith sat in front between Jason and me. If her appearance and her presence disturbed him, he showed nothing.

As we drove off, I glanced up at the house and saw Linda standing on her balcony watching us—unsmiling and resentful. Monica saw her too, and waved gaily.

Once more Jason had turned remote. After asking how I was, he had little to say, as though he'd withdrawn from any gesture that might have been made between us on the trip to Idyllwild.

I wondered if he would always be like this—so that I must start anew with him every time we met. For a little while yesterday we'd seemed comfortable with each other, but now he was holding himself away again. Why should I mind? Why did I continue to feel drawn to this disturbing man? I seemed to have learned nothing at all.

Yet when I looked at the harsh lines drawn down from his mouth—lines that always tempted my fingers—I wanted only to offer comfort, where no comfort was wanted or needed.

220

The road to Desert Hot Springs pointed north across more stretches of sand, to where a town of spas had grown up at the foot of the Shadow Mountains.

At least Jason talked to Keith as he drove, telling him about the place we were to visit.

"A man named Cabot Yerxes built this house in just the way the Hopi Indians built their pueblos a thousand years ago. He hadn't any money, so he used his own labor and whatever materials he could pick up free. He found old railroad ties for the roof beams and floors, and he hauled rock and sand and earth for the cement and adobe he made himself. He never stopped adding rooms, so the house was still unfinished when he died some years ago. He and his wife lived there for a long time, and now the house has been preserved so people can visit it—still the way it used to be."

Keith's interest was caught, and when we reached the quiet, unspectacular little town, and the pueblo came into view, he was eager to explore. The moment we left the car, he ran toward a redwood statue that rose on the grounds of the rambling white building. It was an Indian head carved from a sequoia that had been felled by lightning, Jason said, and it reached several stories high, the feather that topped it carved from a single cedar tree. The man who had created the carving was putting up one of these Indian statues in every state of the union.

Keith looked tiny beside the tremendous head, and the strong, stern face seemed not to see him, the eyes looking far out across the desert.

"Let's get out of the sun," Monica murmured from behind the shelter of sunglasses and hat. "Let's see if we can find Henry Arlen, since that's what we've come for." Again I sensed an excitement in her voice that made me apprehensive. She was quite capable of unpleasant surprises.

We walked across sandy earth toward the strange memorial of a building that Cabot Yerxes had built, and which was now called by his name. It looked rather like a castle, its square adobe towers and flat roofs rising against bare mountains beyond. Unlike the usual pueblo construction, Jason pointed out, where each room had only one door or window, Cabot had put in as many windows and doors as he pleased, many of them looking out from a four-story-high vantage point. Everywhere, the brown beams of roof supports protruded, adding to the southwestern look.

Near the entrance an elderly man dozed on a bench, and Monica nudged me. "I think that's Henry. My goodness, how old he looks!"

She walked toward the sleeping figure with an arrogant tilt of her chin and prodded him awake. He looked up, startled, staring at her without recognition.

"You want to go through?" he asked.

Monica whipped off her dark glasses. "Don't you know me, Cousin Henry?"

"You—you're *her*," he said incredulously, and rose to his gaunt height, staring down at her in obvious astonishment. His hair was white and he wore it in what had once been an Indian style, cut straight over the forehead and above the ears, and his eyes were a faded blue.

Monica's arrogance vanished, as though she realized that no challenge of this elderly relative was necessary.

"You've gotten old, too, Henry," she said testily. "We haven't seen each other since I came here that last time—before the war."

"Yeah," he said. "I remember." The gaunt face softened a little. "A crazy one you turned out to be! You wanted to set me up in some kind of business."

She sniffed. "Yes. And you told me just where I could go and what I could do with my money! It was a foolish idea, anyway."

"I never did much like being tied down," he said sheepishly.

Monica drew me forward. "This is Carol Hamilton, my great-niece. She's related to you too. Distantly. And this is Mr. Trevor, my secretary's brother."

Henry held my hand in his long, bony one. "I didn't know there was anybody left, except me and Frog Face here. I thought everyone was gone."

Monica looked annoyed, and Henry laughed. "You never liked to be called that, did you?"

"I wasn't crazy about the name, but I remember I called

222

you Pack Rat to get even. Carol wants to talk to you, Henry. She's writing a book about me, and she wants you to tell her all about when I was a little girl. Think you can remember that far back?''

Henry Arlen considered. ''Sure, I can remember. After a while, if you want, you can come over to my house, and I'll show her some old pictures and stuff I've hung on to. Who's the kid?''

''My son,'' I said. ''And I'd like very much to visit your house.'' Keith was tugging at my hand. ''But first, we'd enjoy going through the pueblo.''

''That's my job—taking people through. The boss isn't here right now, but there's a lady inside who'll sell you tickets.''

Monica sat down on the bench that Henry had vacated and waved Jason and Keith and me on toward the door. ''Go ahead. I'll stay here. I've seen the place and I don't like all the steps up and down. Henry, you should have accepted that offer I made. Then you wouldn't be doing this now. After all, I owed you something.''

Jason and Keith went ahead, but Henry paused in the doorway with me. ''What're you talking about?''

''That time on the ranch, when I was about six, and you were ten—remember? That sidewinder? You saved my life. My mother always talked about it afterwards.''

Henry shrugged. ''I just moved faster than that ol' snake, and I got you out of the way. Nothing much.''

''It was to me—I'm still alive. You didn't even kill it.''

''Why would I do that? Maybe the critters have more right to the desert than we do. It used to be better in those days. Not crowded like now.''

''Crowded'' seemed a strange word for this sun-baked town drowsing at the foot of the mountains, but Henry was remembering another day.

''You don't mind staying here while we go through?'' I asked Monica.

''Run along. I'll be fine.'' She looked thoroughly pleased with herself, as though she was still plotting something.

The building was filled with different levels of tiny rooms

223

that had been added on at whim. They were crowded now with articles that had once been part of a man's life. On a table near the doors I saw strange fossils from the nearby Salton Sea, a handful of mesquite beans, a handsome Indian bonnet that some warrior had once worn. A Sioux war lance leaned against the wall in a corner.

"He was especially interested in everything about Indians," Henry said.

There was so much, crowding tables and ledges—the rare mixed in with the merely curious—that it would take weeks to examine it all. Perhaps of most interest to me were the old photographs of Indians. Before the Spanish came, those Indians had owned most of California. Some of their descendants locally were rich because of land around Palm Springs that the white man still couldn't touch.

I was quickly lost as we took unexpected turns, and climbed up and down steps, always discovering new rooms at different levels to explore. Jason managed to keep up with most of Keith's questions and paid him a quiet attention. Both man and boy had grown easy with each other—as Jason and I were not.

At my elbow, Henry spoke. "She sure looks *old*," he mused. "I thought them movie stars got their faces ironed out or something."

"Monica hasn't been a movie star for a long time. She left all that years ago. You knew her parents, didn't you?" My own great-grandparents, I thought.

"Sure. Her ma, especially. A real nice lady. She used to feed me oatmeal cookies when I was a kid."

Monica, after all, had decided not to stay behind. She spoke from a doorway. "My mother was hateful and mean," she said sharply. "Everything I ever did, I had to do in spite of her."

"Aw go on!" Henry said. "Your ma was never mean to anybody."

"You didn't know. No one knew. I had to run away to get to Hollywood."

Her sudden intensity seemed to alarm Henry, who clearly preferred a less emotional atmosphere. "Hey," he said to

Keith, "you notice the window glass in this house? It's scrap glass that Cabot picked up wherever he could. That's why the panes are in all different colors and pieces. He just mounted each piece in whatever size he found it and fitted it in."

Monica closed her eyes and leaned against a crowded counter. Her small outburst had shaken her. "I don't like this place. It's too dark and crowded. It reminds me too much of things I want to forget."

Like memories of her mother that disturbed her?

Keith had seen all he could absorb inside. "Can I go look at the Indian head statue, Mom?" he asked. "I like it better out in the sun."

"I'll keep an eye on him," Monica offered. "I've had enough of this too. Come along, Keith—we'll go downstairs."

Jason spoke to Henry. "You needn't come clear to the top. I've been up there before, and I'll show Carol Mrs. Yerxes's apartment."

Henry seemed glad enough to return to his bench, and Monica and Keith followed him down. If there was something she wanted to warn Henry not to talk about to me, she would now have her chance. But there was nothing I could do to stop her, and I climbed the narrow stairs after Jason.

The room at the top of this square tower was in contrast to the rest. It was less of a museum, and some effort at old-fashioned luxury had been attempted.

"Cabot's wife was a theosophist and she used this as her retreat," Jason said. "She liked to come up here to meditate. In fact, they used to hold meditation classes, and people came from all over to attend."

It was a small room, with a bed, a dressing table, a washstand, and many more pictures.

"Carol," Jason said, "I want to talk to you."

"Has something new happened?"

"A lead, that's all. I have to check this one out myself. Gwen and her mother may still be in Arizona, so I'm going there tomorrow."

I knew how much I would miss him. Just having Jason within reach by phone had become something I'd come to depend on.

"Of course you must go," I said. "I hope you find them."

"I'm not counting on it. I may be away for a week or more if I have to move around. Will you be all right now, Carol?"

The remoteness he seemed to put on so easily had lessened for the moment, and I wondered if he were as torn about me as I was about him.

"I'll manage," I said. "I'm on guard now. Though we can't go on indefinitely living like this. I must try to see Owen soon. There's a way I might be able to fight back."

"How can you do that?"

"I've been thinking about it. Perhaps I can bluff a little and scare him off. I know how close to the law he's always operated. There were one or two things . . . If I could build them up and make him believe I know more about some of his deals than I really do, perhaps I could frighten him off."

"It sounds risky. But perhaps worth trying. When do you plan to see him?"

"Right away, if I can work it out. I don't want to ask Wally, so perhaps I can manage it through Saxon."

I wanted to reach out to Jason in some way, and didn't dare. Too many barriers stood between us. Whenever he took a step toward me, he drew quickly back, and that was something I couldn't deal with. I might want him in my life, but not with all that baggage of distrust he carried. He was on my side now, yet still on guard himself.

I went to the high window of the room, where I could look out upon the Indian head that was nearly as tall as this tower. Keith stood in the sand near the great carving, and both Monica and Henry were with him. So was a stranger—a burly-looking man I'd never seen before was talking to Keith. Monica waved her hands as if in protest, but the stranger suddenly snatched Keith under his arm, pushed Monica away, and ran toward a car near the road. Almost in the same instant, Henry Arlen hurled himself at the man's legs in a flying tackle, bringing him down.

I screamed to Jason. "Quick—downstairs! Someone's got Keith!"

Jason went out of the room and down the stairs with me

close behind. We tore past the woman at the ticket counter and rushed outside.

Henry lay on his stomach in the sand, while the husky man dashed for his car, Keith squirming under his arm and screaming for me. Jason caught him at the road's edge and swung a hard-muscled arm around his neck. In an instant Monica was beside Jason, beating the fellow around the head with her silver-mounted purse.

Free to run, Keith rushed into my arms and I caught him up and carried him to the bench beside the pueblo. He clasped both arms frantically about my neck, his whole body trembling. When I looked back I saw that Jason's pent-up rage was being released on the man he'd captured. Owen's man knew his danger. He struggled from Jason's grasp and fled to his car. Jason would have gone after him, but Monica sagged suddenly against him, and he caught her before she slumped to the ground.

Dusting off his pants with a jaunty air of satisfaction, Henry Arlen swaggered over to join us on the bench.

"Hey, kid," he said to Keith, "it's okay now. We fixed him good, we did!"

Keith hid his face against my shoulder. He was shaking, and I could feel the same killing rage in me that had possessed Jason. But I had to soothe my son.

"He's gone. It's all right, darling. Hush, now. We'll never let him take you."

The car was speeding down the road, and Monica righted herself and stepped back from Jason.

"You'd have finished him off, wouldn't you?" she said.

"I might have, at that," Jason told her grimly. "I suppose I should thank you."

They came toward us and Henry nodded at Monica. "You still got plenty of spunk, Frog Face."

"Now you can see what Owen's like, Aunt Monica," I said. "He won't stop at anything. But who told him we'd be here?"

She was still breathing quickly, still angry. "Believe me, Carol, I didn't. Is the boy all right?"

I held Keith close. Who had known we were coming to

Desert Hot Springs? Linda, Ralph, perhaps Wally? Even Saxon?

"I'll talk to Owen Barclay!" Monica cried, getting excited again. "I'll tell him just what I think of him."

Though I was glad of her concern, I had to keep her from seeing Owen. That would do no good.

"Stay away from him—just stay away! I'm going to see him myself. I'm going to stop this once and for all." I looked at Jason. "I'm going to see him tomorrow."

As her indignation died, Monica's spirits began to droop. "I've had enough. I want to go home."

I was beginning to realize that her stamina would hold up just as long as she wanted it to. After that, she could collapse in a moment.

"We'll start back right away," I told her. The purpose for which I'd come here no longer mattered. Henry didn't have anything to tell me that Monica wouldn't prevent.

He surprised me, however, by having other ideas. "You ain't going to pieces now, are you?" he demanded of her. "Not after the way you went after that kidnapper! This lady"—he nodded at me, his eyebrows abristle—"this lady, she's come all the way to see what I can show her at my house. So let's go there now, and you can rest. I'll give you something to eat, if you're hungry. You used to like chili when you was a kid."

Monica gave in. "I just want to go somewhere and lie down."

Henry spoke to the woman inside the pueblo and came with us to Jason's car. It was close, he said—he usually walked. On the way he told Keith stories to distract him.

Inside the sparsely furnished house, the living room was spanking clean, with everything in order. Henry was a good housekeeper. Monica lay down upon the lumpy sofa and stretched out with her eyes closed.

"She should never of left here in the first place," Henry muttered. "Look what it got her—all that movie stuff!" Monica gave no sign that she'd heard as he pulled a crocheted afghan over her.

When he'd dished up bowls of hot chili that had been

simmering on the stove, we sat down to eat in the kitchen. Monica didn't stir, but she could hear us through the open door as Henry rambled into long stories about the past. Whatever it was that Alva thought Henry "knew" had never emerged and no longer seemed important to me. I just wanted to get Keith back to the relative safety of Smoke Tree House. As we ate, Henry brought old photo albums to show me, and I found a number of snapshots of Monica as a little girl. Even then she'd been pretty, though often a bit rebellious-looking.

Henry pointed out a picture of Monica's parents—my own great-grandparents. The first pictures of them I'd ever seen. The print was blurry, but I felt an unexpected kinship for those two who stood against the very mountain slope that rose behind this house. Here was a real connection for me with my family past.

"You can have that, if you want it," Henry said.

The snapshot had been fitted into slots, and I removed it carefully. One of these days when Monica was in a good mood, I'd try to learn more about her parents. And not only for the book.

When we'd finished eating, Henry was reluctant to let us go, and he invited us back with a gusto that seemed faintly wistful. When things were better, I thought, I would come to see him again, and not just to talk about Monica.

The drive across the desert seemed longer than when we'd come out. Keith slept in my arms, exhausted, and Monica dozed and muttered in the back seat. The moment we reached the terrace, Linda rushed out to help her from the car, filled with anxiety as she assisted her upstairs to her room.

"Please wait," I said to Jason, and took Keith off to bed. Helsa brought him hot milk, and when he fell quickly asleep, I rejoined Jason.

"I don't want to talk directly to Owen on the phone," I said. "Saxon should know how to reach him, and perhaps he'll set up a meeting between us. Will you stay until I've called Saxon?"

Jason listened while I talked on the phone. After some hesitation, Saxon agreed to see if he could set something up for me with Owen. In a few minutes he called back and told me that Owen had agreed. Saxon had suggested his restaurant early in the morning as a meeting place, and a time was set.

"I don't think you should see this man alone," Saxon said. "Let me pick you up and drive you down in the morning. Then I can stay within hearing, if you like."

"I'd like that very much," I told him.

It was done.

"When are you leaving?" I asked Jason.

"Early tomorrow. Be careful, Carol. I don't much like any of this. I'll call you in the evening, if I can."

"Yes—fine. Jason, if it hadn't been for you today—"

He gave me the smile I'd begun to watch for. "Monica and Henry helped," he said, and touched my shoulder lightly.

I watched as he drove down the mountain, wishing he didn't have to leave immediately. But he must fight for his daughter, as I must for my son.

When his car was out of sight, I went upstairs and sat with Keith for a long time. In my mind I went over and over the words I would say to Owen tomorrow, trying to prepare myself. This was a desperate try, and I had just one chance to get it right.

SEVENTEEN

IN THE DARK HOURS OF THAT NIGHT MY FEAR OF FACING OWEN GREW so strong that my courage was nearly submerged. I began to question everything. I even wondered about Saxon. He had been surprisingly kind to me, yet I didn't really know him, and couldn't be sure how far I could trust him. He had agreed readily enough to do as I asked, yet when it came to Monica's affairs, there seemed a murkiness about everything concerning Saxon—a fog of concealment that kept me worried.

Night hours are always the longest to get through. I slept only a little, and was glad to see dawn shining on the mountain and into my room.

First of all, I had to deal with Keith, who didn't want me out of his sight for a moment. I tried to make him understand.

"Darling, what I'm going to do this morning will stop anyone from ever taking you away from me again. So you must help me now, honey. Stay with Helsa, or Linda, or Aunt Monica all the time. Don't go anywhere by yourself. Not even into the garden."

"Can I play with Ralph?"

"Not until I come home. Promise me, Keith."

He clung to me and cried a little. Yet there was a sturdy courage he could summon, and in spite of yesterday's nightmare, he did his best.

Linda joined us at breakfast. Apparently she'd heard about our day from Monica, and was sorry and concerned—more like my old friend of the letters. The one point that she disapproved of was my reliance on Saxon.

"I don't trust him anymore, Carol. He's turned into someone I don't know."

I tried to reassure her, in spite of my own misgivings. "After all, we'll be in the restaurant, and at that hour the help will be around getting ready for the day."

She accepted that doubtfully. "Jason's going away. I wish he could be there too."

No one wished that more than I, but this was how it had to be.

Saxon came for me at ten and we drove down the mountain to his restaurant. We were there well ahead of Owen, and Saxon seemed especially considerate and kind.

"Look, Carol, I'm going to stay right here with you," he promised. "I don't think you should be alone with this man for a moment."

My mental picture of Saxon Scott in this strongly protective role was a familiar one, and I was thankful to have him here.

He took me into the empty Mirage Room and turned on a few lights. We sat at a round table—right out of the film— and a busboy brought us coffee. I had a sense of déjà vu—as though *I* were playing a movie scene with Saxon Scott. He seemed sure of himself, and strong and young, yet I didn't know whether he was acting a role from one of his pictures. Perhaps he never knew himself. His consideration for me seemed genuine, and I began to feel a little more confident. Until he spoke of Monica.

"Is she getting ready?" he asked.

I knew what he meant—ready to walk out on a stage with her hand in Saxon Scott's.

"You'll see," I told him. "She'll be beautiful that night. She'll make everyone believe in her. Even you! Perhaps you'll be able to look at her—and remember."

"All I want is to forget," he said grimly.

"Don't hurt her. Let her have her moment on that stage."

He didn't have time to answer, because someone brought Owen into the room, and Saxon rose to shake hands with him. I must have tensed every muscle, for my arms and shoulders began to ache. Owen looked as striking as ever, and he was immaculately dressed in his usual conservative suit and tie. The sensual mouth that had once attracted me looked cruel and merciless. Everything about him frightened me, yet he mustn't guess that I was afraid.

"Well, Carol?" he said, and I heard the challenge in his voice, knew how furiously eager he was to best me, punish me. Of course he would come to this meeting expecting to have me completely at his mercy.

He took his place at the table across from me, and I caught the scent of his after-shave lotion and found it sickeningly familiar. Saxon sat beside me, but when Owen glared at him his virile role slipped a little, and he looked away, not meeting Owen's eyes.

"Do you know why I'm here?" Owen demanded of Saxon, and then spoke to me without waiting for his answer. "It's your move, Carol. Are you willing now to talk about sending Keith back to me?"

I swallowed hard. "What I plan, Owen, is to send you to prison."

His laughter had the terrifying ring I remembered. How could I ever have been captivated by that hard sound—a sound that meant total confidence in his ability to vanquish anyone who stood up to him. I mustn't let that laughter freeze me, even though old conditioning died hard.

"Just how do you propose to do that?" he asked. "Because of course I'll get my son back, and when I do I'll see that you never come near him again. And perhaps not near anyone else, dear Carol."

He was so sure of himself that he was willing to threaten

me in Saxon's presence. I glanced quickly at Saxon, who tried to rise to the occasion.

"Now, see here—" he began.

"You keep out of this," Owen said.

Saxon flushed and stared at his coffee cup. This scene was going wrong, I thought wryly, and I didn't look to Saxon again for help. I had to lie now, and I must put my heart into it.

"I have some records that I've been keeping over the years, Owen. They're safe in a bank vault where even you can't find them. I've told others of their existence, and if anything happens to me the box will be opened. I never wanted to use them. For Keith's sake, I've never wanted to expose you. But now you've gone too far. If you kidnap Keith, or if you even *try* to take him away from me again, I'll put all my information into the hands of a district attorney."

I recognized the dark flush of fury that rose in his face—a sign of danger to anyone who displeased him, the sign of violence to come. For a moment longer he held himself in hand.

"You're lying, of course. I always made sure you could never put your hands on anything that would hurt me. Don't think you can pull a nutty bluff like this on *me!*"

I stared at him without blinking, dredging from somewhere inside me all the conviction I could manage. "Try me, if you want to find out."

As I'd seen in the past, Owen could move faster than anyone I'd ever known. He was on his feet in an instant and had reached across the table to drag me up by the collar of my blouse. I was choking and helpless in his hands. Saxon made no move at all. He sat there staring at us as though all will to move had gone out of him.

I was struggling and gasping, when something astonishing happened. Someone had come into the room from the doorway behind us. Owen was dragged away from me, and I saw Jason's fist catch him squarely on the chin. Owen went down with a crash that echoed through the room, and lay very still. It wasn't like a movie fight that could go on and on, while the breakaway furniture smashed and the fighters took a terrible beating. Not a tablecloth was pulled, not a coffee cup spilled. Owen simply lay on his back on the floor, out cold, while Jason stood looking down at him and rubbing his knuckles.

Waiters came running in, but none of Owen's goons. Apparently he'd been so sure of dealing with me easily, he'd left them outside. Saxon sat at the table with a stunned look of betrayal on his face. Self-betrayal. In this real life moment when he should have risen to my defense, he'd done nothing. Perhaps in that instant of speeded-up action he'd realized for the first time that he was an old man—and finished. He had let the villain of the piece frighten him into doing nothing.

"You'd better get him outside," Jason told a waiter. "Barclay's got a car waiting, with a driver in it." Then he came to put his arms around me.

"It's okay now," he said, and I knew I was shaking as hard as Keith had. Jason put a hand gently to my throat. "Did he hurt you badly?"

I shook my head, finding that I could breathe again. "I thought you'd already left."

"I couldn't leave until I knew how this meeting would turn out. I just stayed out of sight, in case you didn't need me here."

"I needed you," I said.

"I'll take you back to Monica's now."

I couldn't leave without speaking to Saxon, but he waved my words aside and got to his feet. For once, he seemed unable to play any of those gallant parts he'd done so well on the screen. There was nothing to be said, and I could only feel sorry for him. In that instant I knew how much Saxon Scott had always wanted to be a hero.

Neither Owen nor any of his men were outside when we reached the street, and I suspected they were already on the way to the hospital.

Jason helped me into his car. "I heard what you told him, and you put a ring of truth into it that's going to keep him worried," he said.

"He can be violent on the spur of the moment. He's never been able to control his rages."

I stared at Jason's hands on the wheel as he turned the car

away from the curb. There was broken skin and traces of blood on his right knuckles. It was the same hand that had caressed my throat just now, making sure I wasn't hurt.

"When he cools down—" Jason began as we started up the mountain.

"He never cools down! And he never forgives! Jason, he'll have it in for *you* now."

Jason braked the car on the road up the mountain towards Smoke Tree House, and put an arm around me. "Listen to me—you stopped him cold. For now, anyway. I know how much courage it took to go through with what you did. I like courage."

I didn't care about those barriers between us anymore. I only wanted the comfort and safety of his arms. He kissed me—not too gently—and held me for a moment longer.

"There are things I have to work out, Carol. Just as you do too. I must go ahead with this trip, but I'll keep in touch by phone. Will you be all right now?"

I hadn't felt so all right in a long time. When he drove up to the terrace and left me there, the warmth of his concern stayed with me.

I gave Linda an account of all that had happened, except about Saxon's humiliation. She was appalled, and also a little angry with me because of Jason's involvement. I couldn't feel reassured by her reaction.

We were into December, and it seemed strange to see Christmas decorations blossoming in the midst of palm trees and sand. The center mall at the Desert Inn Fashion Plaza burst into dazzling white trees, silver bells, and scarlet poinsettias. Palm Springs shop windows took on a festive look and a few Santa Clauses appeared.

Linda promised that we'd have a tree and try to make this a happy time for Keith. I was still afraid to take him away from the house, though no word had come to me about Owen. I wasn't even sure if he was still in town. Saxon had been silent ever since that meeting at his restaurant, and I had the feeling that he would never forget that I'd witnessed his shame.

For any other man, this wouldn't have mattered, but Saxon had gone on playing his screen self long after his film days were over. He hadn't really faced the truth until now—I'd seen that in his face. I wished I could tell him that he really didn't have to be that stupendous movie hero anymore.

Our preparations for Monica's big night began in earnest, and as we shopped in elegant Palm Canyon Drive stores, I began to feel a sense of unreality. What we were doing seemed so *normal,* and we were being so lighthearted about it. Yet underneath—under all our happy pretense—I could feel a spreading apprehension. Neither Monica nor Linda was really confident about what was going to happen, and their own forebodings infected me. And what about Saxon now? What if he tried to recover his old macho image by doing something unexpected on the stage—something that might crush Monica?

More and more, as we moved toward that zero hour, I found myself drawn to her with a strong new feeling. I began to long for her appearance to be a triumph, after all these years of sadness and neglect.

Trying on gowns from one shop to another, she finally selected one that seemed exactly right. It was a lustrous panne velvet in a deep shade of garnet. With its bright touches of gold, which would show up well in stage lights, she would look magnificent. She rejected the somewhat shabby chestnut red wig, and Linda found her a new one—ash blond, as she'd bleached her fair hair even lighter for early pictures. Nothing fluffy. The style was sophisticated and suited her, piling pale coils on top of her head. Stunning.

Unhappily, I began to feel that Monica's meticulous preparations were, in fact, intended for Saxon first of all. Whether she would admit it or not, she was still emotionally involved with Saxon Scott. Which would be fine, if they stepped out on that stage holding each other's hands warmly, affectionately. But I wondered if that could happen.

The bright spot for me during those days was when Jason telephoned. He called nearly every day, and once twice in one day. Nothing was going well with his quest, but he felt he must continue, moving from town to town in Arizona, searching for evidence that Gwen had been there. At least there were enough leads to keep him going. Always I sensed his discouragement and distraction, but took comfort in his need to talk with me. As I needed to talk with him.

In spite of everything that had happened, Monica refused to cancel the sale of Cadenza to Owen. I could understand how much she needed the money, but I was still sure that he would never go through with paying her a cent. *He* didn't want that house, and in the end she was going to get hurt. No arguments would change her mind, however, and she was being secretive. She wouldn't even acknowledge if he was still in town.

I hadn't meant to tell her what had happened at Saxon's. I still felt sorry for him. But Linda told her with some enjoyment, and Monica seemed to relish every word.

"Saxon has always been like that," she said scornfully. "He's hidden behind that facade he built up until he convinced himself it was real. But when there's a crisis, he's lost. *I* know." This new recognition of Saxon's weakness seemed to make *her* stronger, until I wondered if what I'd feared might happen in reverse. Not that Saxon would hurt Monica—or could hurt her. But that she might in some way destroy him. In spite—or perhaps because of—her own unreciprocated feeling for him.

In any case, wherever he was, I knew Owen was marking time, waiting, and undoubtedly scheming. For this little while we were being left alone, but I couldn't count on such peace forever. How much of my desperate bluff he believed I had no idea, and I had no confidence in his staying away from us permanently. His own smoldering rage would see to that. It was always Owen's nature to lie in wait—that tiger I considered him to be—lurking in shadows until he could come in for the kill.

During this time, Keith had grown increasingly cross and restless, and it was hard to keep him occupied. Unfortunately, Ralph had regaled him with an account of the famous Palm Springs tramway, until Keith began to tease me to take him up the mountain. I could only promise that we'd go "sometime," and put him off. After his fright at Cabot's he understood a little better the need to stay within the safe boundaries of the house, but that didn't make him content to be a prisoner.

I made an arrangement for Helsa to stay with Keith the night we would be away, and I asked Linda to put the guards on a special alert. She even promised to have one on duty up at the house itself—something we usually dispensed with. Nothing reassured me, and I began to look toward the night of the benefit with growing anxiety.

And then, the day before the benefit, Saxon Scott came to see Monica.

EIGHTEEN

SHE'D BEEN PSYCHING HERSELF UP FOR A WEEK. BOTH LINDA AND I had seen it happening. She'd taken to living the impersonation of her former self, wearing the clothes and the makeup, concentrating on the moment when she must walk out on a stage and convince a sophisticated audience of her peers that she was forever young, vital, beautiful—a STAR.

"Her mental state is half the battle," Linda told me. "It's what makes a performance work. Like an athlete who keys himself into a winning state of mind."

When Saxon phoned, Linda put him through to Monica. Monica wouldn't tell either of us what he'd said, but later in the day she sent Linda on an errand and ordered me down to the gate to get Saxon past the guard. She had talked to the guard imperiously on the phone connection—yes, she knew they were supposed to check all visitors with Miss Trevor, but *she* was away, and this was perfectly all right. Miss Hamilton would come down herself and bring Mr. Scott in.

For once it was a drizzling day, but I wrapped myself up

and walked down the road to the gate to meet Saxon, who sat at the wheel of his car. Mists lowered over the mountain, dipping into pockets close to the town, yet allowing the peak to stand free—so it looked like a Japanese print. Palm tree tops bloomed like eerie flowers in the drifting mist. Their long fronds dripped moisture, and dried and broken bits of palm skittered on the ground.

Saxon opened the car door and I slid into the seat next to him. "I'm your escort," I told him. "She doesn't want to be left alone with you, but she's sent Linda away."

I hadn't seen him since the time in the restaurant and I didn't like the change in him. He'd accepted his age at last, but in the wrong way. Even his shoulders had lost their jaunty look. I wished there was something to say that would let him know I understood what had happened. Jason was young, and Owen still in his prime. How could a man of Saxon's age be expected to stand up to one, or equal the other physically? I might wish secretly that he'd at least tried, but I could understand very well why he hadn't. Only I could say none of this, because it would only hurt him more.

He greeted me with a wistfulness I'd never seen in him before. His very look was an apology that I had no way to acknowledge.

When we reached the terrace, he turned off the engine and sat for a little while in silence, while drizzle streaked the windshield. When I started to get out of the car, he stopped me.

"Wait, Carol. I want you to know what I'm going to do. I think it will be a relief to her, really. I'm going to call the whole thing off. I find I don't want to walk out on that stage with her tomorrow night, and I want her to join me in canceling the whole thing."

For a moment I was too shocked to speak. Then I burst into words. "How can you do that to all the people who have worked for this? You can't cancel at the last minute—that's a terrible thing to do!"

"Oh, I expect the rest of the show will go on. They'll present *Mirage,* and they'll get others who were connected with the picture up on the stage, as they've already planned."

"But you and Monica are the big attraction. Everyone will be terribly let down and disappointed. They'll be furious with you."

"I don't care much about that."

"You may not, but Monica will. I don't believe she'll go along with this. Why are you backing out, Saxon?"

"Because I was going to do a pretty rotten thing. I was going to go out there and give them a real show. Even if it landed me with a trial that should have taken place long ago. Monica, of course, would be an accomplice."

I felt sick over his words. "This is what Linda has been afraid of. But you couldn't go through with it, after all, could you?"

"No," he said. "Not because I'm full of loving kindness, but because I don't have that kind of nerve. That's what I found out about myself the other day in the restaurant."

"What happened that morning doesn't matter," I said. "You don't have to mix yourself up with those old movie parts. Now you can be *you*. But can't you perform with Monica this one last time? She's counting on it so."

"No," he said. "That would be the final hypocrisy. Let's go upstairs and talk to her."

Ralph let us in and then disappeared—undoubtedly on orders. The room was ready. Draperies had been pulled against the gray day, and the warm yellow glow from a few lamps gave a flattering ambience. I knew what she was going to do before she walked into the room, but I had no idea how well she'd do it.

Saxon and I were sitting together on the sofa, talking quietly about nothing important. The Persian cats had taken to him, and one was already on his knee. Annabella disapproved, and sat across the room with her tail twitching. Her blue eyes with the black oval down the center looked like marbles, with a hint of yellow reflection from the lamps. She watched Saxon intently without blinking.

I saw his face when Monica appeared—saw it before I saw her. He looked stunned, shocked, and I turned my head.

I'd never seen her look more beautiful. She'd put on another of her "costumes," and this one couldn't have been more perfect for facing Saxon. I remembered how striking it had been in the Switzerland scene from *Mirage*. For a lounging robe she'd adopted a stunning Japanese kimono, and it was that garment she wore now. A true kimono of the ancient style—a rich silk, with sleeves that hung nearly to the floor. The color was a dark navy blue, and the V of the neck closing was piped in white silk that stood away from the nape in the traditional, seductive style. At the hem white chrysanthemums bloomed all the way around in a glorious print. In her ears were emeralds, and on her finger the emerald ring. Always there was the refrain of emeralds.

But it was the *woman* who graced the kimono. Her neck rose, slim and graceful, to a head crowned with chestnut hair. The soft light of the room flattered and smoothed away her years. She hid the betrayal of her hands demurely in flowing sleeves, and the lightest of smiles touched her lips, warm and soft with color.

"Hello, Saxon," she said, and the old magic was in her voice. He had never believed, and he was totally unprepared. Her laughter mocked him gently, triumphantly. "You see? You didn't think I could do it, did you?"

"My God!" Saxon said, and the words had an angry ring.

Monica came toward him, and he backed away as though she alarmed him. He turned to me, still angry.

"Just forget everything I told you!" he said. "I'll be there!" And he walked out of the room without another glance for Monica Arlen. We heard him running down the stairs, and a moment later his car started down the mountain.

Monica looked completely dismayed. "What's the matter with him? Why did he run away?" She came to sit beside me, and I felt her trembling.

"Never mind," I said. "You just took him by surprise."

"But why did he come to see me? He *asked* to come!"

I couldn't tell her the whole truth. I couldn't crush her with the threat he'd intended, and had withdrawn, only to contradict himself again. Now he meant to go through with it after all.

"He wanted to cancel his appearance with you at the benefit, and he wanted you to cancel, too," I said.

"That's outrageous! And if I didn't?"

That was what I couldn't tell her. Annabella came out of the shadows making remarks of her own.

"Never mind, Annie," Monica said. "I can guess what he meant to do. Only *I* am not going to back out. And Saxon won't do one thing about it! I'm still strong, and underneath all that make-believe courage, *he* is the weak one. He always has been, and that's what he chokes on every time."

"It might be safer to cancel," I said uneasily. Though if Saxon had any plan to tell a story that had been suppressed all these years, he would be the one to suffer most. Could he really face that?

"I wouldn't think of canceling," Monica said, and her trembling had stopped. "I'm going to give everyone who comes tomorrow a performance they'll remember. I'm going to show them who I am and what I can do, whether Saxon appears with me or not. Besides, *I* am the one they'll come to see."

There was an excitement in her that disturbed me. I wondered why I'd ever believed that Saxon might hurt her. It was much more likely to be the other way around. Perhaps he knew that now and it was this that made him angry.

She rose with Annabella in her arms and moved about the room. Not with the mincing steps that should have matched the kimono, but with a bold, assured stride.

"Go away, Carol," she said. "I don't need your long face staring at me."

She needed nothing from me, and I went downstairs to the Arlen room and immersed myself in more reading, to take up time until Linda came home and I could tell her what had happened.

It was during the next hour that I unearthed a treasure that especially delighted me. It was a folder of the old photographs, and among them was one of a very young Monica—probably taken when she first came to Hollywood.

The picture wasn't a close-up, but full figure, with Monica in a simple sweater and skirt. She looked very young and utterly lovely. Her wide, exotically tilted eyes looked out at the camera—not altogether innocently. Even then there must have been a certain awareness in her, and a knowledge of the struggle she must make. Her hair in those days had been short and blond, with a slight curl to it, and it fluffed delightfully about her face. She had already matured a great deal from the girlhood snapshots Henry Arlen had shown me.

By the following night we were all balanced on an edge not far from hysteria. Linda gave Ralph the afternoon and evening off. Neither she nor I wanted him around dropping remarks that might upset Monica. Linda herself would drive her down when the time came.

I had told Linda of Saxon's visit and she'd been upset. Who knew what Saxon meant to do? If Monica was right, he would do nothing, but Linda didn't believe that.

Wally was to drive me down to the theater early, so I could watch for Saxon. When he came, I wasn't to let him out of my sight, and I was to gauge his mood, so that if it seemed threatening in any way, Monica could be protected, even at the last minute. Linda decided that she mustn't appear at the theater until the picture was nearly over. I agreed to whatever she wished, and hid my own misgivings.

In midafternoon a messenger arrived at Smoke Tree House with a long florist's box. I carried it to Monica's bedroom, where she lay in darkness, resting, with Linda nearby on guard. Annabella met me suspiciously at the door, and I had a feeling that the tension pervading the house had reached the cats as well. Even the white Persians seemed restless as they followed Annabella around.

Monica put out a hand as I came into the room. "This is all wrong!" she protested. "Linda's keeping me prisoner, when I should have had a dress rehearsal. How do I know the lights will be right? I ought to have gone down early to check everything out. I don't even know what the stage is like, whether there are steps . . . I don't know anything!"

"It's not that complicated," Linda assured her. "You'll go out on the stage from the wings and accept the ovation they'll give you. Saxon will say a few words, because it's expected. You needn't say anything unless you want to. Just give them your special smile and they'll love it. They'll be at your feet, darling."

I held out the florist's box. "A messenger just brought this for you, Aunt Monica."

Linda, still watchful, would have intercepted the box, but Monica sat up in bed and snatched it away. I think both Linda and I knew what she hoped for as she opened the box and looked for a card. There was none, and she spread pale green paper to reveal the single long stalk the box contained. It was a blue iris—a real one—perfect, exquisite. No card was needed.

Monica lifted the stalk from the box wonderingly. "He remembered! He always sent an iris on special occasions." Yet she sounded sad—almost afraid.

"It's going to be all right, dear," Linda assured her. "He wouldn't have sent this if he meant to hurt you. Now you can relax and rest."

I wished I could feel as sure as Linda sounded.

Monica burst into tears and fell back on her pillow.

Linda rescued the iris as Monica dropped it. "I'll put this in water so it will be fresh for you to carry when you go out on the stage tonight." Then she spoke to me. "You'd better go now, Carol. Let her sleep. She hardly closed her eyes last night."

For the rest of the afternoon, Linda kept everyone away. Only she was allowed to help when the time came for Monica to dress.

During the afternoon I answered the phone in Linda's office, to hear Jason's voice on the line—a wonderful, reassuring sound! The sound of sanity in a world gone askew.

"Carol, I'm home, and I want to see you tonight."

There was nothing I wanted more, yet I couldn't have been more tied up.

"There's the benefit tonight . . ." I began.

"Yes, I know. I plan to be there. Could you come a little early and meet me in the garden of the museum? Perhaps near that bronze bust of Monica?"

"Of course," I told him warmly. "I'll be early anyway, so just tell me when."

In the late afternoon, Linda drove out alone, leaving a note that Keith brought to me.

> Monica's asleep, thank God. I have an errand to do and I'll be away an hour or so. Don't disturb her.
>
> Linda

I had an uneasy feeling that she might have gone to see Saxon herself.

Keith and Jonah and I were eating a light supper in the dining room when her car came up the drive. I didn't see her because she parked near Monica's end of the terrace and went straight upstairs.

At least I was grateful for the lively presence of Helsa's grandson. He was good for Keith and I could leave the two of them in Helsa's care with confidence. It was a relief to have Ralph away.

After supper I put on the one gown I'd packed in my hasty flight from New York—a white Halston in a toga style that draped over one shoulder and fell about me in soft silk folds. Gold earrings, a cuff bracelet, and white sandals set off the dress, and I was female enough to be glad that Jason would see me looking my best for once.

Keith and Jonah admired me, and waved me off from the upper balcony when Wally came to pick me up. He seemed anything but his usual cocky self tonight, and I knew the tension had reached him too.

On the way down, I told him about the iris Saxon had sent, but he didn't seem especially impressed or pleased. "Saxon likes to put on a good show. I saw him yesterday and told him I wouldn't be working for him anymore. A funny thing happened while I was there. Your ex-husband phoned and made an appointment to see Saxon today."

I hated that. It meant that Owen was still in town, or close by. And he hadn't given up.

We reached the museum well ahead of the evening crowd, and a guard told me that Jason would be with me soon in the garden. I sat on a stone bench in the softly lighted area and waited. The moon was full tonight—big and close—a disk of silver, reflected in the quiet pool beside me. I remembered the last time I'd seen the moon in water, and shivered.

As she had done that other time, a bronze Monica stared at me with the same concentration I'd felt before. Shadows moving in the night air made her seem almost alive, as though some enigmatic expression flickered across her face. Peggy Smith had managed to convey in her sculpture the same secret look I'd caught now and then on the real Monica's face. This work, I remembered, had been created the same year Peggy had died. I could only hope that Monica Arlen, whose world had crashed around her then, would regain something of her own tonight. Whatever wrong she had done in the past, nothing must happen to defeat her tonight. I knew very well—and so did Linda—that this was her last chance.

Jason came out of the museum, and for a moment stood looking for me, the strong planes of his face cast into relief. I remembered my early feeling about him—that here was a man with banked fires that burned deeply, and I knew as I'd known then, that these could be dangerous fires. I no longer cared whether they burned me.

He sat beside me on the bench. "How are you, Carol? I wanted to see you alone for a few minutes before all this begins tonight."

In the distance we could already hear a murmur of voices as early members of the audience arrived. By now the television cameras outside would be watching celebrities as they entered. The showing of *Mirage* would continue for nearly an hour and a half before Monica and Saxon must go out onstage.

"I'm all right," I said. "Did you have any luck at all on your trip?"

He shook his head, but he didn't want to talk about this now. "What are your duties here tonight?"

"I'm supposed to watch for Saxon when he comes."

"He hasn't arrived yet. I saw Wally just now, and he's looking for him too. Carol, I couldn't stop thinking about you while I was away. I got through all the disappointments *because* I could think of you. I wanted to tell you that tonight."

"It's been the same for me," I said softly. "I keep wanting to tell you about everything that happens. Only now I can't seem to remember what I wanted to say."

"I think we need each other. Though I don't know whether I'm ready for this, anymore than you're ready. Perhaps right now our need is mainly to explore, to know each other better. To move slowly."

I understood all too well. In both our marriages we'd rushed in, throwing caution to the winds. Yet now we knew that neither was entirely sure of the other—or perhaps of ourselves—and that in a good many ways we were still strangers. In this there was some safety, even though my own foolish instinct was to plunge without heed or caution.

He drew me up from the bench, kissed me lightly, and let me go. At that moment I could have clung to him all too eagerly—and knew that I mustn't. He still needed space around him, and if I was to hold him, I must allow him that—as he would allow me whatever space I needed.

"You look beautiful tonight," he said. "Your dress is exactly right."

The long folds moved about me as I walked, and his words gave me assurance, as the gown gave me grace. This was something Owen had tried very hard to take away, once he considered me a possession.

Together we went inside to where tangerine carpeting on the Grand Staircase brought an audience in evening dress down to the theater level. The starburst glass chandelier sparkled on women's jewels and coiffured hair, on black jackets and men's jewelry as well. For a few moments we stood apart, watching that beautiful, fabled crowd, picking out well-known faces. I felt like a young movie fan watching from the sidelines. Everyone really was turning out for Monica Arlen and Saxon Scott.

Wally came bustling over, more anxious and uneasy than I'd ever seen him, as though Linda's anxieties had infected him.

"Neither of them is here yet," he whispered.

"Linda wants to bring Monica down when the picture is nearly over," I reminded him. "And now it looks as if Saxon means to arrive late too. Perhaps it's better that way. More dramatic." Or perhaps he would return to his earlier plan and not come at all?

"I suppose so." He hurried off, driven by those inner tensions that wouldn't let him rest.

Jason had an aisle seat in the last row, and he took me to it. "Sit here for a while, and I'll watch outside. I'll let you know when either of them arrives."

When he'd gone, I reminded myself that I was working on a book about Monica, and began to take note of all that I saw. Or overheard. The chatter of excitement ran high with anticipation.

The famous director who had worked on *Mirage* was dead, but the producer was here, and when he walked out on the lighted stage, the audience applauded. After a few anecdotes, he introduced the film. The house lights dimmed, the audience began to stir again, then settled down as titles for *Mirage* began to slide across the screen, and the wonderful Max Steiner music began.

It was hard to sit quietly watching. I kept thinking about Jason's words, and wondering if we could ever trust each other completely, without haunting, unsettling doubts.

I thought of Monica as well, and of how she would weather this night. How Saxon would *permit* her to weather it. And what would happen after tonight? Could Monica take the anticlimax? I wished Saxon would come, so that I could look into his face and see what he meant to do. Or perhaps his not being here was the answer—he meant to do nothing. Not even appear.

As I watched the action on the screen, I saw again how marvelous those two had been together in their youth. Monica's face seemed so alive, so eternally young, so filled with hope and anticipation, all part of her role—only to be deadened in the retakes of the two or three scenes that weren't right. Once more I was moved to tears—this time because I knew the woman she was to become, and that added almost unbearable poignancy.

Before it ended, I slipped from my seat and went to find

Jason at the back of the theater. Wally was with him, and he grabbed me excitedly.

"Monica's here! I was just coming to tell you. Linda's taken her backstage. But Saxon still hasn't showed up. I'm going to go phone him."

I spoke to Jason. "I'll join them now. Monica said she wanted me with her. Jason, they've loved the picture all over again!"

I touched his arm and went away quickly.

Several notables were in the green room at the side of the stage, and in spite of Linda's efforts to keep her alone and quiet, Monica was holding court with her electric presence. She saw me and held out her hands.

"Carol darling! Have you seen Saxon?"

"He hasn't come yet, but he should be here any moment—if he's coming. Wally's gone to telephone. The picture is nearly over, and they've loved every minute of it."

"That doesn't matter," Monica said. "What matters is *me*—the way I am now. That's what I have to show them."

"And you will," I whispered.

She looked utterly beautiful. The new blond wig was soft and natural, sweeping her coiffure high. Her garnet velvet gown with the spray of gold leaves running diagonally across shoulder and breast flowed to the tips of golden sandals, clinging where it should cling and hiding what should be hidden. The sleeves were wisely long and came to a flattering point over her wrists. Long earrings of gold filigree hung from her ears, and the intaglio emerald gleamed on her left hand. She'd chosen to wear it on her engagement finger tonight, and I felt both moved and a little frightened at the sight. In the other hand she carried the real iris stalk with all her old grace, using it to punctuate her own animated words. Under artificial light her makeup did exactly what it was supposed to do, and she seemed ageless. When she moved I caught the scent of her perfume—light, but faintly mysterious. A scent I didn't recognize—perhaps something she'd kept from a long time ago.

Wally came to tell us that it was nearly the moment for Monica to go on. "Saxon didn't answer my call, so he must

PHYLLIS A. WHITNEY

be on the way. Perhaps we can give them an intermission to gain a little time.''

"No!" Monica's voice had tautened, and I knew how keyed up she was. "I can't bear waiting any longer. If I'm to do this, I want to go out there and get it over. If Saxon is so inconsiderate as to be late, I'll go on alone.''

Saxon must have returned to his earlier plan of not appearing at all, I thought, and knew this was probably the better way. Let Monica have this triumph she had earned, and let her have it alone.

Wally flew off to consult with the actor who was to introduce Arlen and Scott, and get things started.

"You can't do this!" Linda wailed. "It will be too hard for you. You didn't plan any speech, and without Saxon—"

Monica gave her a withering look. "What do you think I've been doing all afternoon, a prisoner in my room? Of course I've been thinking of what I might say. This is *my* night, with or without Saxon. He's probably been planning this all along—forcing me to either face an audience alone, or back down. Well, I'll show him!''

There was nothing more to be said, and we followed Monica's slender, valiant figure into the wings. The famous actor had begun his introduction at the lectern, explaining that Saxon Scott had been delayed in coming to the theater (a moan from the audience), though he was still expected to arrive. Nevertheless, Monica Arlen was here (applause). He went on with a few words about the famous pair who had done so much for films, and then turned to welcome Monica.

Linda clutched me desperately as Monica went out to face the lights. She moved gracefully, proudly—every inch the woman they'd just seen on the screen. It didn't matter that her face had grown older; she gave them her impersonation of youth—she gave them herself. The response was tremendous. All over the theater men and women rose to their feet applauding a long-lost star, and Monica raised her iris to them in salute, and smiled her famous smile.

Standing easily center stage, she began to speak. Her voice had grown older, but tonight she knew very well that she must sound like the Monica they'd just heard. She lowered

252

her tones to the old inflections—playing herself, as I had seen her do at Smoke Tree House. If the performance could not be entirely true because of the passing years, it was so close that for those who watched and listened, the sight of her brought tears to their eyes.

The few words she spoke were of no special significance—just a memory or two from the past, a mention of the acting years with Saxon, an expression of her feeling that tonight she had come home again. It was enough. This time the applause was wildly emotional. This was the homage such an audience could give generously when they were touched and delighted by one of their own. Monica bowed graciously, waved the iris again, and walked off with her chin in the air and her step steady.

Linda flung both arms about her, weeping, and Monica shook her off sharply. "Stop that! I did it, and now I want to go home. Saxon didn't even come. He didn't even see me out there at all. Oh, Linda, look what's happened to my iris!"

We both looked, and saw that the strain she'd revealed in no other way had caused her fingers to snap the iris stalk, so that blue petals hung limply from a broken stem. Linda took it from her and began to cry harder than ever.

People were crowding backstage now, reaching for Monica, embracing her, and I knew we needed to get her away at once. Reaction was setting in, and I saw by the slightly wild look in her eyes that she'd had all she could take. For once Linda was no use at all, but fortunately Wally and two museum guards managed to get Monica through the crowd and out of the theater.

Jason was waiting outside, and he came with me to the white Rolls. "Maybe I'd better drive," he said with a look at his sister.

Linda managed to pull herself together. "No—Wally will get us home. I'm afraid something's wrong with Saxon. Monica wants you to drive out to Indian Wells and see if you can find out what's happened. Maybe his man will know."

"I'll go with you, Jason," I said quickly. "Look in on Keith when you get home—please, Linda?"

She nodded and got in beside Monica. "It's not Keith I'm

253

worried about, but I'll look in on him. Call me when you get to Saxon's.''

Jason and I talked very little on the drive, self-conscious with each other now, and somehow a little wary. He spoke admiringly of Monica's appearance tonight, and some of his criticism of her had lessened, as appreciation of her courage grew. She had been a gallant lady out on that stage, and perhaps none of us could fully realize the strain she must have been under. Even though, once she was out there, the adrenaline, the old exhilaration, had seen her through.

When we'd been checked in through the entrance to the club grounds, we went at once to Saxon's house, only to find it dark and apparently empty. Not even his houseman was home tonight. Though the streets were lighted, there were no lights near the house. Jason placed a hand against the door, and at once it swung inward. It had been ajar all along, and we stared at each other.

"We'd better go inside," Jason said.

A switch flooded the entry hall with light, and he found another to turn on living room lamps. Everything seemed quiet and undisturbed—as luxurious as I remembered. Draperies had been pulled, shutting out the mountains.

"Look in his study," I said. "Over there."

Jason went through the dark doorway and again turned on a light. I heard him gasp and hurried into the room. I had only a glimpse of Saxon, flung forward across his desk, but it was a glimpse I would never forget.

Jason spoke to me over his shoulder. "Stay in the other room, Carol, while I call the Riverside sheriff's office. I'm afraid he's dead."

NINETEEN

WHILE WE WAITED FOR SHERIFF'S DEPUTIES, JASON PHONED LINDA and said she must decide whether to break the news to Monica now, or wait until tomorrow. He would try to persuade the sheriff to let Monica rest tonight. They would undoubtedly want to question her because of her planned appearance with Saxon on the Annenberg stage this evening. Saxon had been shot, but Jason had seen no gun, and it didn't look like suicide.

I felt numb with shock, unable to believe. Tonight I had seen Saxon Scott young and heroic again on a screen—an artificial image. Now I found it was the stricken man, with all his failings, whom I liked best, and I remembered his kindnesses to me.

The deputies and coroner came quickly and began their terrible routine. Though Jason and I could tell them little, it was well after midnight before we were allowed to leave.

Jason drove me back to Monica's, and by that time I could cry a little. Tomorrow's headlines would blare the news, and even before that the airways would be full of Saxon's murder. The fact that it came on the heels of Monica Arlen's triumphant appearance at the theater would keep reporters and columnists busy for days to come, and Monica would be bombarded unless Linda and I could fend them off. The house would really become a fortress now.

When I saw Linda, however, I wasn't sure she could take care of herself, let alone Monica. The light was on in her office, and Jason and I went in to find her sitting at her desk, looking pale and ill. The cup she was drinking from clattered as she set it down in the saucer.

"Are you all right?" I asked, thinking how foolish it is that we always ask that of people who are anything but all right.

She stared at us blankly for a moment. "Nobody's all right. I had to tell Monica. The telephone's hardly stopped ringing, even though we're unlisted. Not because of Saxon, but because of her appearance tonight. But the other news will come through at any time, and she was picking up the phone. I've given her a sedative, and I stayed until she fell asleep. What's going to happen now?"

"We'll face it out together," Jason said. "I can stay for the rest of the night, if you like."

"How did Monica take it?" I asked.

"She fell apart." Linda's voice cracked with emotion. "You'd have thought she'd just lost him, instead of when she really did all those years ago."

"Perhaps she hoped secretly that something would come to life between them tonight," I said sadly.

"I don't know about that, but she's ready now to build a new grand passion out of his death. She's always lived in a dream world. I suppose that's the only way she's kept from being hurt more than she could bear."

I knew all about dream worlds—they had been mine for too long. But if a person kept on trying to live in one, it could destroy everything that was real.

"How can we help her to stop that?" I asked.

Linda shook her head. "I don't think we can."

She reached for the coffeepot and Jason took it from her hand. "No more. You need something to help you sleep, not coffee. I'm going to stay and bunk down on a sofa somewhere. Better take the phones off the hook."

Linda relinquished the pot and accepted gratefully. "You can have my room, Jason. I'll sleep in Monica's extra bed."

We heard the sound of a car reaching the terrace, and Jason went to look out. It was Ralph, and when he'd parked he came inside to join us. It was clear that he'd been drinking, though I'd never thought that one of his vices.

"I just heard," he said. "About Scott, I mean. What happened?"

Jason answered him quietly. "He was murdered. We don't know anything more than that."

Ralph showed no emotion one way or another. When he put out a hand to steady himself it was because of the liquor. "How's Miss Arlen?"

"She's asleep," Jason told him. "Just go to bed and stay away from her for now."

A little of Ralph's cockiness returned. "Okay. I got something to sleep off myself." He left without further questions and I was relieved to see him go.

Linda still sat at her desk staring blankly at nothing. "I was glad when Saxon didn't come to the theater tonight. I was *glad!* But I never wished him dead."

Jason moved quickly to draw her up from her chair. "You're heading for bed right now."

Unlike her usually independent self, she leaned on him heavily as he helped her upstairs. I followed them to Monica's door. There she rallied a little and turned us away, so she could go in alone.

Jason came with me to my room, where Helsa sat beside my sleeping son, the radio on, murmuring softly. She had heard and she looked at us in alarm.

"I'll tell you tomorrow," I said.

She nodded her understanding, and refused Jason's offer to see her home. "I have my car, and it's only a little way."

When she'd gone, Jason and I sat on the balcony for a while. Not talking. Just waiting to get sleepy. I wanted to shut out the horror, the memory that was etched on my mind, but there was no way. It would stay with me forever. Jason's quiet presence was my only comfort. It would take very little to send me into his arms tonight, but neither of us took the step that would make this happen. False solace that skipped over everything that was real wasn't what I wanted now, and he didn't offer it.

For the next few days Linda's requiem was what we heard over and over. Everyone had liked Saxon Scott—no one wished him dead. But someone had come to see him that afternoon. Someone who had definitely wished him dead, though so far no murder weapon had been found.

It developed that two people were known to have visited him that day, and both had checked in at the gate to the Eldorado Country Club at separate times. Linda Trevor and Owen Barclay—in that order. Both claimed they'd talked with him, left him alive. Both said he'd seemed tense and keyed up, anticipating the evening ahead. Owen had apparently been the last one known to have visited Saxon, and he talked readily and glibly to the police, claiming that he'd wanted Saxon to intercede for him again, so that he could talk with Monica in her own house concerning the sale of Cadenza. Apparently she'd refused to see him there, and he thought Saxon could manage this.

How much of anything Owen said could be believed, I didn't know. Murder out of passion might well be Owen's style, but it wasn't Saxon who had knocked Owen out in the Mirage Room that day, and since he had no apparent motive (and could pull a lot of strings), the police didn't hold him.

Linda had gone to see Saxon simply to plead with him not to embarrass Monica that night. This I could believe, since it was exactly the sort of thing Linda would do. And since Owen had seen him alive later, she was only questioned briefly.

At Smoke Tree House, Keith's young ears quickly caught the undertones of tragedy. I tried to regale him with stories of Monica's appearance at the Annenberg, but he knew something was terribly wrong, and he had to be told. Jonah had gone home again, and it was harder than ever to keep Keith occupied. Once more, however reluctantly, I accepted Ralph's help. He seemed genuinely fond of Keith, and though he was back on duty with Monica, he spent what time he could with my son. I was never far away, keeping an eye on them both.

All the following morning Monica had stayed in bed, still drowsy from the medication Linda had given her. When a police officer came, she woke up sufficiently to see him, but Linda said she cried all the way through his visit. She had little useful information to offer, totally absorbed in the high tragedy she was now creating in her own life. She had looked forward to being on the stage last night with Saxon, and it had grieved her when he hadn't come. Now that she knew what had happened, she hardly wanted to go on living. Moment by moment, Linda reported, she was convincing herself that she had just lost the great love of her life. These were California police, and they were able to allow for emotional performances. Not that her feelings weren't genuine—she was clearly suffering. It was just that gifted performers could suffer in a very high key.

That afternoon, to my surprise, Monica sent for me with instructions to bring my notebook. When I walked into her living room, only Ralph was present at his usual outdoor post. Keith was swimming, while Helsa watched.

Monica sat cross-legged on the floor, wearing plaid slacks and a pullover. Spread on the floor before her was an array of glossy publicity shots—all either of Saxon alone, or of Monica with him, and all dating back to their great days on the screen. Nearby, Annabella and her fluffy friends watched with interest, but when one of the white cats put a tentative paw on a photograph, she was cuffed by Annabella.

Today Monica obviously cared nothing about her appearance. Her cheeks were still tear-streaked, and she looked up at me with swimming eyes.

"Sit down, dear. I can't stand Linda's long face for another moment and I've sent her away. My own is bad enough. I've got to get myself in hand. I'll weather this as I've weathered every other terrible loss in my life. The only thing to do is keep busy. That's why I told you to bring your notebook. I want to talk to you about Saxon. I want to pick out photographs you might use in the book."

The transformation from the Star I'd seen on the stage last night to this fragile-looking old woman saddened me. Nevertheless, she was showing more spirit than Linda gave her credit for.

The stories she told me for the next two hours were fascinating. Her memories were rich and colorful, and far more useful to me than any research I could do in the Arlen room. *She* was my best source. Though she still wanted no tape recorder.

"I don't want to leave anything on tape, since I sound the way I do now," she admitted. "Last night I made an effort to breathe properly and control my voice, so I wouldn't sound too different from the film. But it was a strain, and I can't keep it up."

Linda was still taking phone calls in her office downstairs, and I could hear the distant ringing through open windows. No calls were put through to Monica's phone for a long while. When it did ring, Ralph came in from the balcony to answer.

"It's that lawyer—Aldrich," he said. "You want to talk to him?"

Monica held out her hand, and he brought the phone to her by its long cord. She got up from the floor, stretching wearily. As she listened, her face brightened, and she nodded at me cheerfully.

"That's fine, Bill. I'm glad it's settled. I don't really need to see him again until the closing. So just go ahead. . . . No, don't worry about me. I'll be fine. Come and see me when you can."

Ralph returned the phone to its place, but when he would have gone outside again, she stopped him. "Will you pick up those photos for me, please? I know them all by heart anyway."

A hint of color had come into her face as she sat down beside me.

"Wonderful news, Carol! Owen Barclay called Aldrich today and said that a check for the down payment was in the mail. So the closing can now be set. What an enormous relief this is! I don't know what I'd have done if he'd backed out.

There's good news for you, too. Owen has gone back to New York, since the police didn't require him to stay. Bill says he'll be there for some time. Until he's ready to move to the Coast and into my house. Of course he'll return, dear, but for a little while you're free of him. Bill said he didn't think you'd need to worry about being followed anymore. Owen's got a lot of other things on his mind.''

Had my bluff in trying to frighten Owen worked, after all? I didn't dare take too much comfort in the thought. It would only be a matter of time until he found some other way.

"If it wasn't my house he bought," Monica said, sounding apologetic, "it would be someone else's. And I do need the money."

"I know," I said. "I wish I didn't still feel so doubtful about this."

The call had distracted her, but now her attention returned to the photographs Ralph was putting into a box. She snatched up one of the pictures with a dramatic gesture, and began to cry in great wrenching sobs.

"You better stop that," Ralph told her coolly. "Your face is a mess, and if you're going to be a millionaire, you better get yourself back in one piece."

She blinked at him, blew her nose, and sat up straighter. His direct words had cut through her grief as my sympathy couldn't.

"Ralph is right. Anway, I've done enough talking for now, Carol. I just wanted you to know more about Saxon the way he used to be. He's a terribly important part of my story."

"I know," I said. "Thank you for telling me about him."

"What about your kid?" Ralph said to me.

"What do you mean?"

"I mean you better get him out of this house while you can. He's going stir crazy, and he needs a change. If you want, I can take him up on the tramway this weekend."

"Not without me. I'll think about it."

Monica nodded impatiently. "Yes, of course Keith must go up the tramway, Carol. Everyone makes that trip. Get Jason to take you. I have something else for Ralph to do."

"Sure," Ralph said. "What?"

She dabbed at her cheeks with tissue, and got up to move nervously around the room. Sometimes she reminded me of one of her own cats.

"I want you to go to Beverly Hills, Ralph—to Cadenza. I want you to pack up everything there is in the house except the furniture, and have it shipped here. Bill Aldrich said I'd better get it cleared out right away, though Owen Barclay may want to buy some of the large pieces. Perhaps Carol and I will drive out before you finish the job. She really ought to see the house. Right now, I only want to rest."

She leaned on Ralph's arm as he helped her toward the bedroom. At the door she looked around at me with a sudden radiant change of mood.

"Carol, I did it, didn't I? Last night! They loved *me!*"

I knew what she meant. The audience had accepted more than the Monica Arlen they'd seen on a screen. They'd responded to the beautiful and courageous woman she'd given them on that stage. A woman who had been created out of her own determination, but who could hold them in her hand, nevertheless. That was the reassurance she needed more than anything else. Perhaps it would help her get past her loss.

"Of course they loved you," I told her.

Her moment of exhilaration faded as she remembered Saxon, and she promptly wilted. Ralph got her to the bed and looked around at me.

"Hey," he said, "who do you think did it?"

His complete insensitivity angered me. "I have no idea," I said coldly.

Monica tilted her chin. "Don't keep anything from me, Carol. If you or Linda learn anything, you're to tell me right away."

A number of things happened in the following days, though nothing conclusive was discovered about Saxon's death. The police were still investigating, but if anything useful had emerged, they weren't talking, and in a few days Saxon's body was released for burial.

Though Saxon Scott had no family left, old friends stepped in to take care of the funeral arrangements and the burial was to be at the Forest Lawn in Glendale. There were two other Forest Lawns, but famous movie stars were usually taken to Glendale. Saxon had been a wealthy man, and there was no problem about money, though his will asked for a simple funeral. To me, it seemed especially sad that he had even less family than I did.

Neither Monica nor Linda went to the funeral. Monica wanted to go, but Linda put her foot down and wouldn't allow her to face the strain of what might happen. There would be crowds at the gate and the usual delirium, and Monica mustn't become part of a spectacle.

In the end, I was the one who went. Paul Webster, who had been Saxon's friend and attorney, sent a car to meet me at the Los Angeles airport, and I was driven to Glendale. When we reached the cemetery, it was to find the anticipated crowd gathered outside the gates. Hollywood funerals were a specialty here, and our car was ushered through slowly, while strange eyes peered at me, wondering if I was "anybody."

Listening to the service held in Wee Kirk of the Heather, I found the fact of Saxon's death still impossible to accept—as sudden death always is, especially when shrouded in the horror of violence. Two or three of Saxon's friends spoke, including his attorney, but the ceremony was kept brief, as Saxon himself had wished.

Before it was over, I found myself crying. In a sense, I was an old friend too—like some of those who stood outside at the gate—and I had been ever since I was a child. My tears were for Monica as well—for wasted lives and useless feuds that should never have been, and only injured the living. I wept as well because it was too late to mend anything, and Monica would now carry an added scar forever. She, at least, had wanted to make up with him that last night. It was he who rejected her.

Afterwards, just as I was leaving, Mr. Webster disengaged himself and came to speak to me. He was an impressive man whose rugged, weathered look gave him an air of assurance and dignity.

"I'm very glad you came, Miss Hamilton. This is an appropriate place for Saxon. He picked it out himself because he said he wanted to look down into Burbank and thumb his nose at the Warner studios.''

I liked Mr. Webster, and was glad to have him escort me back to my car.

"I've been wanting to talk with you," he said as we walked along. "Would it be possible for you to come with me to my office before you return to Palm Springs? You'll be driven to the airport in time for your plane."

The invitation surprised me, but I agreed, and went with him to his long black Lincoln. We were whisked down to Wilshire Boulevard, and I was brought into a beautifully muted and expensive office high above the street.

Seated in a leather upholstered chair, I faced the attorney across his polished desk. Why I was here at all puzzled me.

"Saxon spoke very warmly of you," he told me. "He liked you very much."

This too was surprising. "I hardly knew him. Of course I'm glad if he felt that way, since I grew up watching him on the screen—along with my great-aunt, Monica Arlen."

Mr. Webster nodded. "A few days ago Saxon called me to Indian Wells to add a codicil to his will. He has left you rather a large sum of money, Miss Hamilton, as well as an important property."

While I listened in astonishment, he explained that Saxon had left me half a million dollars, and had willed me his restaurant as well. Saxon's and the Mirage Room! When I could recover from my first shock, I asked Mr. Webster hesitantly—not sure of the propriety—if anything had been left to Monica. He didn't mind my question, but told me that she had never been mentioned in Saxon's will at any time.

I still felt stunned and thoroughly bewildered. "Why—why in the world did Mr. Scott do this? I'm a stranger. It makes no sense."

"He gave me a reason," Paul Webster said, "though I don't fully understand it. He said you were related by blood to Monica Arlen, and he had cared more about her—*when she was young*—than for any other woman in his life."

"Yet he didn't speak to her for the last thirty-six years!"

"That wasn't altogether his doing. Something happened long ago that Monica could never forgive him for."

I found the courage to ask about the episode when Peggy Smith had died. "Did he ever tell you about that?"

Mr. Webster hesitated so long that I was afraid he might not answer. When he did, he told me little more than I already knew.

"He said that he was to blame for her death. But that he never meant to kill her. This was confidential, of course, since he'd escaped a murder trial."

"Then you know Monica's role in this?"

"Yes. I expect that what they did together built the barrier that grew up between them. Neither could forgive the other."

"I think Monica was ready to forgive, but that he wasn't," I said.

There was nothing more to discuss. Mr. Webster told me he would be in touch shortly, and I left for the airport.

I was glad for the flight back to the desert, since it gave me a quiet time to think. There was so much now to consider. My money problems would be resolved in an unexpected way, though this would make little difference in how I would live right now. I would continue to work on Monica's biography, of course, and when that was done, I'd find other writing projects. With new money coming in, it was even possible that I might help Monica, if the sale of the house fell through. Was this, I wondered, the real reason why Saxon had put me in his will? Because, though he wouldn't leave anything to her directly, he knew I would look after Monica?

In Palm Springs I took a taxi and reached the house in time to have dinner with Linda and Keith. Jason had gone back to work, and Monica was dining upstairs again.

Linda took little interest in my account of Saxon's funeral, her resentment against him still high. All her sympathy was for Monica, and I said nothing about the will. The time wasn't right and she might even resent this act of Saxon's.

The next day Jason took Keith for a tour of the museum, and my son came home filled with excitement about all that he'd seen. Now that he'd had a taste of freedom, he wanted more, and he returned to the idea Ralph had planted in him of a trip by tramway to the top of Mt. San Jacinto.

Jason said, "Why not Saturday? I can take you both up, if you like."

It was difficult to give up my worry about every step Keith took away from the house. However, there did seem to be a lull in Owen's moves against us, and I gave in. Even the newspapers spoke of his being in New York, and we hadn't been watched by Gack or anyone else in a long while. So we began to plan almost lightheartedly for the trip. Ralph would be in Beverly Hills by that time, and Keith was disappointed that his friend couldn't go up the mountain with him.

I was only relieved, and began to look forward to a day spent with Jason. We hadn't seen much of each other, though he'd been in touch with Linda every day. I knew he was still holding a distance between us, sorting everything out. To what end, I couldn't be sure. Sometimes I wished I didn't care as much as I was beginning to, but there seemed no help for that.

The afternoon before the tram trip, Linda asked me to come into the garden with her. She wanted to talk to me away from the house, where no one could overhear. Her edgy manner made me uneasy, but I left my typewriter to go with her, not knowing what to expect.

When we reached the upper level, she cast an anxious look toward the house, but Monica wasn't visible. We sat on a bench in the little summer house, and bougainvillea shielded us from view, draping purple blossoms over latticework.

"I'm terribly worried," Linda said. "She's carrying on much too much. Perhaps she feels guilty because she was out on that stage having a marvelous time, while Saxon was lying dead. But it's more than that. She's got a new notion in her head that I don't know how to deal with. She's saying that something dreadful is going to happen to *her*. She says Annabella is forecasting terrible events. This is really crazy, and I don't know what to do about it."

My fingers played with a handful of dried petals. Bougainvillea was so beautiful, so brilliant, but it never lasted away from the nourishing vine—like Monica Arlen. For her, Hollywood and her years in films had been the vine that kept her young and alive. Away from the source, she had faded and dried up, as Saxon had not. The movies had never been his life's blood. But then, he'd never been the actor that Arlen was. So there was much more for her to lose.

"Is there any way to get her back to work?" I asked. "I don't mean playing major roles. That would be too much for her—at least to begin with. But look what Bette Davis is doing. And Myrna Loy and Claudette Colbert. Janet Gaynor is making a hit in summer theaters, and Mary Martin is co-host on a television show. Perhaps Monica could start with a cameo bit now and then, where her name would mean something. They'd jump at a chance to get her, especially with all this publicity surrounding her now."

"There's publicity, all right." Linda sounded irritated. "Have you any idea how many papers and magazines want to do pieces about the two of them? Yet she won't talk to anyone. She won't stir out of this house, and she's working herself up into a state of fear."

"I'm sorry," I said. "I hadn't realized—"

"Oh, I don't blame you for not seeing what's under your nose! It's important for you—and for *her*—that you bury yourself in this book. Besides, you have Keith to worry about. . . . Carol, do stop playing with those petals!"

I brushed them from my knees in surprise. I'd never seen her quite so tense. "You're not taking this seriously, are you—about something happening to Monica?"

"If I don't take it seriously, I have to believe that she's really going out of her mind. That's why you want to distract her, isn't it? All this talk of getting her back to work?"

"Why not? Work could turn her in a healthier direction. Even the college circuit might want her, if she won't think of a play or movie."

Linda stood up impatiently. "Go and see her! Go and see her right now. Then tell me what you think."

"Wait, Linda. Of course I'll go. I've been trying to see her for a couple of days, and she keeps putting me off. First, though, I have to tell you something. Then you can help me to prepare Monica."

She sat down again and listened as I told her the astonishing news of my inheritance from Saxon. She heard me blankly at first, then in dismay, and finally with rising anger.

"How could he do such a thing? Didn't he ever understand how much she loved him?"

"Listen to me," I said. "It won't do any good to be upset by Saxon's will. It's a fact. I don't understand why anything has been left to me, but it has. So now we must go on from there. If Owen backs out on buying her house, I can still help Monica. She won't have to give up this place, or go anywhere else, unless she wants to. There'll be income from the restaurant—or I can sell it—and when my writing begins to earn something again, we'll be in a strong position—no matter what."

"And you think she'll accept your charity? When she should have been his wife! Everything he has should have come to her!"

Linda didn't live in a real world, anymore than Monica did. Each looked at her own "reality," and refused the larger picture. I wondered if Jason could talk some sense into his sister. There was no point in my saying anything else now, and I stood up.

"I'll go see her at once. Please come with me."

She wanted to come, obviously. At the moment, I think she trusted me less than ever.

We found Monica sitting outside, looking off at distant mountains, though I suspected that she saw very little. She hadn't dressed for the day, but still wore an old bathrobe that made her look even older than her years. Her hair seemed grayer than I remembered, and today it was disheveled, as though she'd been running her hands through it frantically. Not one of the cats was in view—ominous in itself. Animals can sense disaster and get themselves out of the way.

"Come inside, dear," Linda said. "Carol wants to talk to you."

Now that I'd seen her, I knew how impossible it would be to talk to her at all. I couldn't bear the look of pain in those once wonderful eyes. I couldn't bear the thin, tight look of her lips, as though she kept from screaming only by great effort. If at first she had played a tragedienne's role, it had become real now, and it was frightening to see.

She rose obediently at Linda's words and came inside, allowing herself to be made comfortable on a sofa with pillows at her back and her feet up. But when Linda looked at me, challenging, I found nothing I could possibly say. After a scornful glance in my direction, Linda spoke the words she wanted me to speak.

"Carol doesn't believe anything terrible is going to happen to you. *She* doesn't believe that Saxon's death has anything to do with you."

Monica seemed to pull herself together, and she turned her head to look at us with quiet dignity. "It has everything to do with me. Blood always sheds more blood."

I'd heard her say those words once in a movie, and I dropped to the rug at her knees and took her hand in mine. There was no emerald ring on her finger today.

"You mustn't think such things. Movie plots aren't real life. *You* are real and alive, and you need to start living again. Really living."

The movement of her head back and forth was slow and negative. "There's nothing for me anymore. Not with Saxon gone and my own life in danger. Besides, I think you were right about Owen Barclay. His lawyers are becoming evasive about a closing date. I won't be surprised if he backs out completely."

"It won't matter if he does," I told her. "I may come into some—some money. I can take care of us. Even take care of this house for a while until the biography begins to earn. Then a share of that money will be yours. You're my family, Aunt Monica."

At least she wasn't beyond snatching at a straw, because she opened her eyes and looked at me with an affection I'd glimpsed only now and then.

"You almost give me hope, Carol. But there have been signs. Last night I saw Saxon. I saw him standing in my bedroom, and he was trying to tell me something. Something frightful. He was trying to warn me."

Linda bent over her soothingly. "You had a bad dream, dear. It's natural to dream vividly when you're suffering."

Monica pushed us both away and sat up. "He blames *me!*" she cried. "If I had behaved differently, he might never have died. And he's right!"

Linda spoke to me sharply. "Go away, Carol. You can't talk to her now."

I let myself out of the apartment and stood where I could see Keith playing happily with Annabella in the garden level above me. Already the air was growing colder, as the sun made its early dip behind the mountain, its shadow creeping slowly out across the town.

Monica's state of mind seemed as frightening as Linda had indicated, and I wondered about its cause. Who was it that might be threatening her—and why? No longer Saxon. Only in her dreams would Saxon Scott ever speak to Monica Arlen again.

TWENTY

SLEEPLESS, I WORKED UNTIL AFTER MIDNIGHT IN THE ARLEN ROOM.
There was still so much I needed to read, to make notes
about. Work was the one thing that could distract me from a
present reality I could do nothing about: Monica's state of
mind. So I threw myself into that deep concentration every
writer can summon when the need is great.

Already I'd made lists of questions that must be asked
about Arlen and Scott's film-making days. I'd made lists of
people I must seek out and talk to—if they were still alive.
Before long, I would need to go to Hollywood itself—that
nebulous place that everyone said was so much more an idea
than a locality. I'd glimpsed a little of it at Forest Lawn,
where the crowds of fans had gathered, and where so many
famous stars had been buried.

Since I could think better with a pencil in my fingers, I
usually made my notes in longhand, and I'd invented my own
system of abbreviation that only I could read.

When my writing hand began to cramp and my eyes blurred,

I put my books and papers away and went through Linda's office to an open terrace door. There were two alarm systems in the house, and Linda had taken care of setting the one that covered Monica's end of the house. She had left the alarm off at this end, and I knew how to set it when I was ready for bed. So the door was still open to the cool night air. There were no guards up here, but only at the lower gate that opened onto the road.

As I looked out, I saw in surprise that someone occupied the lighted terrace at night. A man sat on the wall, silhouetted against the starlit view beyond.

Ralph? But Ralph was in Beverly Hills. He had phoned today from Monica's house, and talked to Linda. In spite of Monica's growing concern that Owen meant to back out, Linda was pushing the project of emptying the house. It must be sold—if not to Owen, then for a lesser sum to someone else, and Ralph might as well do some of the physical work of packing.

I stood in the doorway, startled and uncertain. Except for Keith and me, this end of the house was supposed to be empty. Linda had moved into Monica's apartment while Ralph was away, and of course Helsa went home after dinner. I had only to reach for the key to the alarm system, and with the doors open, I could set it off. But first I had to know who was out there, and I called.

The man left the wall and came across the terrace. "Hello, Carol," he said softly.

It was Wally Davis, and I didn't feel reassured. "How did you get here? I didn't hear a car."

"I walked up," he said. "The guards down at the gate know me, and Linda has left word that I can come in whenever I like. I didn't want to wake the house by driving up the road."

"I'll call Linda," I said. "She's with Monica tonight, and I suppose they're both asleep by now."

"No, don't call her. I didn't come up to see anyone. I was feeling restless and uneasy. So I drove to the gate and walked up to make sure everything was all right. Since what happened to Saxon . . ."

What he was saying sounded reasonable, and he seemed less bouncy and excitable, less pushy than usual. When he put off the veneer of excessive exuberance, he could be quite likable.

"Did Linda tell you?" I asked. "Monica thinks something is going to happen to her."

"Yes, I know. Maybe she's right." Then he shook his head despairingly. "I don't mean that. Linda's got me doing it too. But someone *is* around who shot Saxon. Sax was a secretive man, and he had his own fears and concerns— apparently justified. But he didn't talk to me about them, or, I think, to anyone else. I understand you're working hard on the book about them both?"

"I'm trying to get it organized. I'm not ready to write yet."

"This may be a more colorful book than you expected. Now they'll buy it for the murder alone."

"If anyone buys it, I hope it will be because I've done justice to both Monica Arlen and Saxon Scott. I'm not interested in the sensational."

"You don't need to be. There's no way to keep it out of an account of their lives. If you write about either of them, it will be there. Beginning with whatever it was they covered up when Peggy Smith died."

"What do you know about that?"

"Linda's told me."

"Did Saxon ever talk to you about that time?"

"Once. He said he'd made the worst mistake of his life, and that he'd spend the rest of his life paying for it."

"Because of his affair with Peggy Smith?"

"So you *are* interested in the sensational?"

Wally could get under my skin, whether he was being jolly and affable, or pricking me with verbal pins.

"I'm interested in finding out the truth," I said.

"Ah, truth!" He began to walk up and down the terrace, flapping his arms. Then he paused to grin at me. "Don't worry—I won't expound on the subject of truth at this hour! Do you want to know why I came up here tonight?"

I waited, and when he went on he wasn't grinning. "I came to pay a call on Ralph."

"He's at Cadenza."

"I know. That's why I came. I didn't know if I could get past the house alarm system, but luckily you were working late. So I went up to Ralph's room."

"To Ralph's room! You had no business coming inside the house without letting Linda know!" This argument might be reasonable with anyone else, but Wally wasn't likely to be bound by convention.

"Let me ask you something," he said. "You know about Ralph's collection of firearms?"

I nodded.

"Did you know it's gone? He's taken every one of those guns down and stashed them someplace else."

"I'm sure he has licenses for them."

"No doubt. But why are they gone—and where?"

"Why does this worry you?"

His cocky air returned. "Oh, no reason at all. Just idle curiosity."

"You mean you'd do something that outrageous—sneaking in the house on your own on a mere whim?"

He stared at me for a moment—soberly. "No, Carol, I don't expect you to swallow that. I do have Linda's interest in mind, remember. I wanted to know about those guns, and I knew she wouldn't let me search."

"But I don't understand why—"

"Don't try to. I got what I came for, so I'll leave now. It might be better if you don't mention this to Linda."

"I can't promise that."

"Okay. Do as you like. I understand Jason is taking Keith and you up the tramway tomorrow. Have fun." His salute was mocking as he left the terrace.

I went inside, closing doors and windows, setting the alarm. Then I climbed the stairs and looked into Ralph's room. Wally was right. The collection of firearms, new and antique, had been removed from the walls. The fact seemed ominous, though I had no idea what it meant.

Back in my room I stood looking down at my sleeping son.

Tomorrow I would see to it that he'd have a wonderful time. He was excited about the trip, and I knew that Jason would make it live up to his expectations. I hoped the day would go well between Jason and me too. So much of the time now there was an underlying uncertainty in me about Jason. Not about myself—not anymore.

In the morning we drove north on Palm Canyon, curving around the mountain to the straight-lined road that rose steeply to the foot of Mt. San Jacinto. The Valley Station, where the tram started, was 2,820 feet above sea level, and there would be another rise of nearly 6,000 feet to the top.

When Jason had parked the car, we climbed wide steps to the lower building. Jason carried the picnic basket that Helsa had packed, so that we could have lunch in the pine grove on top of the mountain. Trams ran frequently, and we could return whenever we pleased.

It felt wonderful to be free of Smoke Tree House and out in the open with only Jason and my son. This morning Jason seemed more relaxed than I'd seen him in a long time, and easier to be with. It always pleased me to see how well he got on with Keith, who liked and trusted him. Both Ralph and Jason were helping Keith to overcome his suspicion toward men. That, at least, I must give Ralph credit for.

We'd caught the first car up the mountain and we stood at the front in order to watch the precipitous rise up the canyon. The blue and white car filled quickly and we started up, with Keith wildly excited by the adventure. The steep lift upward was spectacular. Tramway towers, connected by long ribbons of cable, had been built straight up Chino Canyon, with sharp rock cliffs rising on either side. Far above the gorge we could glimpse the Mountain Station that was our goal at the top. It would take about fifteen minutes to go up, and while the car was never more than eight hundred feet above the floor of the canyon, the ground seemed farther away as we rose, because of those towering cliffs. As our elevation increased, the vegetation that seemed to grow out of sheer rock changed in character.

"It's much colder and wetter at the top," Jason said, "so

desert plants won't grow up there. And the high elevation growth doesn't take root below. So this is a special place where you can see plants at different levels all the way up—depending on the climate of each level.''

As we reached the five towers in turn, our suspended car would teeter for a moment, and then move upward again, with Keith squealing over the slight disruption to our balance. Sheer granite pinnacles seemed very close as we neared the top, and looking backward through rear windows, we could see the canyon and all of the Coachella Valley falling away below.

''Mom, look!'' Keith was pointing ahead, and I saw a wide fall of ice encasing the lip of the mountain, where water had spilled. From desert to ice in a few minutes' time!

The building at the top housed a restaurant and seating areas, but we didn't linger inside. Jason took us first to a lookout point where we could see the entire spread of the valley with its distant rimming of mountains. On a morning so marvelously clear, we really could see forever. Jason pointed out the San Andreas Fault, where it struck its own line of demarcation across the desert—a natural dividing line where barren sand met darker soil.

Up here in the clear, cool, pine-scented air, we seemed far removed from all that troubled us in the world below, and I wanted to savor every moment with Keith and Jason. For this little while I could feel safe and carefree.

When we could absorb no more of the view, we turned to the heart of the mountain, where tall Jeffrey pines filled a steep-sided, hidden valley. Here the pine bark smelled strongly like vanilla. Railed cement walks led in a steep zigzag to a grove below, where rustic tables offered pleasant picnicking. Keith, finding this freedom heady, ran ahead down the walk. He'd been penned in for so long, and I had no wish to keep him on any tight leash. Few people were about at this early hour, and those in our car had dispersed in different directions—some with backpacks for a day of hiking.

Lower on the walk, Keith shouted, pointing upward. ''Look, Mom—a real cave over there! Ralph told me there was one up here. Can I climb up to it?''

"Later," I said. "We'll see."

We left our basket on a table, and roamed among tall pines. The trees were well spaced, so we could see out between them. Yet in this little pocket of a valley at the top of the mountain, where no distant view was visible, I had no disturbing sense of enclosure.

A stream ran among the trees, and Keith found a small bridge he could run across, his feet pounding on the planks. All around, rocky hillsides cupped us in, and the Mountain Station overlooked us far above. We could see straight up through dark branches to where an intensely blue sky sent morning sunlight slanting down in shimmering bands of gold.

While Keith explored the bank of the stream, Jason and I sat on a boulder and watched. It seemed desecration to disturb this lovely place, but what had been happening at the house must be faced, and I couldn't put unpleasantness off forever. So while we had these moments alone, I plunged in and told Jason of Monica's new aberration.

Jason was still more concerned about Linda than about Monica. He was deeply worried over the way his sister had been caught up in what he felt was the dangerous make-believe of Smoke Tree House.

"Saxon's death wasn't make-believe," I said.

"Yet it must have been some sort of strange fantasy that led to it. Someone imagining Saxon as a threat. I wish Linda would marry Wally, if she's going to, and move away. She's letting her own life slip by, and it's growing harder for her to leave, as Monica becomes more dependent upon her. Now your book ties her there all the more."

"I want to write it," I told him quietly.

"I know. I might feel a little better if the sheriff would turn up a lead in Saxon's death. I wish Linda hadn't gone to see him that day."

"But Owen saw him alive after she left." I heard the hollowness in my own words. Who knew what Owen might say or do, if it served his purpose? Or if he became angry enough to lie.

I asked Jason about Gwen, and he told me of another lead he'd received, though it hadn't been solid enough to follow at the moment. The awful thing was that the entire country was available to them, and Gwen and her mother could cross any state line they chose.

The FBI had kept a hands-off policy until now. "They've been more interested in snatched cars than snatched children," Jason said. "Even when kidnapping parents have been caught, it's only meant a contempt of court charge. But there's a new law that will make it a felony and the FBI will come into such searches actively. This may even stop a few parents from making that first move. Just the same, people who want to disappear usually can, and children grow up all too quickly."

Yes, I thought. If it took him years to find Gwen, she might no longer recognize him, and she would certainly have been prejudiced against him.

I shivered and looked around for my son. He was no longer by the stream, and I jumped down from the rock. "Where's Keith? Jason, do you see him?"

He was nowhere in view, though I was sure no one could have come into that grove without our being aware of the fact. I called for him, trying not to feel foolishly frantic. Strangely, there were no echoes up here. Perhaps the pines absorbed sound, so my voice had a flat ring. Nevertheless, Keith heard me and answered from a distance. When I looked upward in relief, I saw him high above us on the zigzag path, climbing toward the cave he'd noticed earlier. His red jacket stood out vividly against the pines, and he waved at us, laughing and mischievous.

"Come and find me!" he called. "Up on top!"

"Keith! Don't go up there alone!" I shouted.

He only laughed again and ran on up the path.

Jason and I started after him, but it was some distance to the top, and his young legs had a good start. When we reached the entrance to the building above, Keith was nowhere in sight.

From the first, I was frightened, though Jason pointed out that he could be anywhere at all, teasing us. As soon as he got hungry he'd come out and join us, with no real idea of the fright he'd caused me.

When our shouting brought no response, however, we

returned to the building and asked questions of ticket sellers and other attendants; even of people who had been out on the mountain. No one had seen a small boy in a red jacket.

The tramway authorities pointed out that with an entire mountain to roam, Keith could have gone in any direction, and it was possible that he had fallen and hurt himself. Now a real search began. The forest rangers were notified, a few hikers enlisted, and the nearby woods and mountain were combed. With no result at all.

Hours later, we found a woman who remembered Keith's red jacket and claimed that she'd seen a little boy getting into a car with a man up near the road. She couldn't remember what the man looked like, or the make or color of the car. She had noticed Keith and could describe him clearly.

I knew almost from the beginning that the police wouldn't find my son. There was only one answer. Owen Barclay had reached out across a continent and scooped him up.

TWENTY-ONE

DURING THE NEXT FEW DAYS A FULL ALARM WENT OUT—WITH NO results at all. If this were an "ordinary" kidnapping, then all authorities would be interested. On the other hand, if Keith's father was behind it, there could be a backing off. So I said little about Owen, and let the general alarm go out. The unknown man in the unknown car had vanished into anonymity. All he had to do was remove Keith's red jacket and become less conspicuous at once. We couldn't even tell which route they'd taken along the top of the mountain.

Jason was with me as often as he could be, and now we had a mutual grief in common. Most of all, I was haunted by the thought of Keith's terror. His father would inflict on him all the fury he felt toward me. Not only for the past, but because of what had happened at Saxon's. That would be something he would never forget or forgive—and *I* would be to blame.

My anxiety was made all the more intense by a state of helplessness. My imagination worked overtime, creating pictures of Owen and Keith that tortured me. I ate little and slept less.

One thing I did was to put through a call to Owen in New York. I was unable to reach him, since no one would tell me where he was. And that alarmed me even more.

Sometimes I stood in our room at Smoke Tree House and touched Keith's clothes, his toys and games that waited for him so innocently. And when I could stand the pain no longer, I drove myself into futile action. Christmas was a week away, and I wrapped packages feverishly, as though this would assure that my son would be here to open them.

Linda tried to be helpful. She took messages for me and offered vague counseling, but I felt farther away from her than ever. Her obsession was with Monica Arlen, and nothing else mattered enough to her as long as she felt that Monica might be in danger—even if it was only from herself.

Strangely enough, it was Monica who finally took me in hand. One morning I climbed up to the garden, just to be out in the sun and open air. I was sitting on the marble bench where the stone nymph stood in a tangle of neglected growth nearby when Monica joined me.

This morning she wore an old pair of slacks, a tan shirt, and scuffed loafers. Her hair was smoothly combed, her face clean of makeup, so she looked like the woman she was—as though she'd stopped pretending. At least her fear of unknown disaster had lessened.

For a few moments she said nothing, staring past me at the stone nymph. When she spoke, she directed my attention to the little statue with the fawn at its feet.

"I can remember when Peggy carved that," she said. "I knew by then that she was foolishly in love with Saxon. Yet she threw herself into the work of carving that piece, and I recall something she said at the time. A cliché, of course, but very true. She said, 'Work is the only cure, the only force that heals.' "

"I can't concentrate," I said. "I don't think I'll ever work again."

In bright sunlight, the wrinkles that come so easily to women in a desert climate were evident, with little trace of her former beauty left. She seemed not to care anymore about the illusion she could assume so easily when she chose. Her own escape into work had been lost long ago. Nevertheless, she seemed to have become wiser, as well as older—perhaps in the effort to surmount her own demons.

She went on as though I hadn't spoken. "I wish I'd listened to Peggy. When Saxon turned away from me, I decided there was nothing more to live for. I gave up everything and hid from life. I destroyed myself in those years. Every single thing I've done since then has been horribly wrong."

Her pain broke through my own barrier of anguish, and I made an effort to respond. "I'm sorry. I haven't been able to think about anything but Keith since this happened."

"Yes, you're being as foolish as I was. Sooner or later, you need to face the fact that you may have to live without your son. The sooner you work at *something*, the better for you. You needn't give up the search, but you still have a book to write."

What she was saying was true, but I didn't know how to stop thinking of Keith.

"Look at me, Carol," she said. "Do you want to wind up like *me?* With nothing? Do you want to throw away the rest of your life? Look at me and tell me what you see."

I looked at her and saw exactly what she wanted me to see—a wasted life. A life without value, thrown away because of a painful loss that she'd thought she couldn't endure.

"For me, Saxon really died thirty-six years ago," she said. "Yet now I've let it seem as though he had died all over again. If I'd tried to go on living my own life from the start, I wouldn't be feeling like this now."

She had brought me out of preoccupation with my own pain. "You proved what you can do the other night."

"Yes, I know. The strange thing is that I *do* care. When you're young, you think that whatever happens when you're old won't really matter. That's stupid. Whatever your age, life always matters. Perhaps more than ever for me now, because there's so little time left."

I touched her hand gently, but at once she drew away,

as though she had built a dam against emotion, against affection.

"You're young, Carol. You'll marry. You'll have another child. I never had one at all. Just the same, this time I *must* come to life. Carol, I *want* to live!"

My eyes had been dry with rage ever since Keith was taken, but now I began to cry. She didn't touch me or speak. She offered neither affection nor sympathy. She waited until my weeping stopped, and then she stood up.

"We have a book to write," she said, and I heard the old note of command in her voice.

Part of me understood what she had done. Perhaps she had lost the habit of true generosity that she'd known as a young woman; perhaps she behaved generously only when she wanted something for herself. It didn't matter. I was grateful anyway.

"Thank you," I said, and stood up beside her.

I knew that I still wanted to write about Monica Arlen. Not just of the imaginary woman whom Linda adored like some goddess on a pedestal because of what she'd once been, but the real woman who had suffered pain and loss and tragedy, and yet was now making a last effort to salvage something of her life. I could understand better now what it had cost her to go out on that stage and enthrall an audience, when she knew her real self so well.

"Work and pain aren't exclusive of one another," she said as we walked together toward the house. "Though I used to think they were. Of course you won't give up your search for your son, but in the meantime you'll work as hard as you possibly can because work is the only anodyne there is. I've found that out—perhaps too late—but there's still time for you."

I'd started after her down to the house level, when Linda came running from her office.

"Carol! Come to the telephone quickly. It's Keith on the line, asking for you. Hurry!"

With Monica following, I flew through the house to her office and snatched up the phone with a hand that was shaking, fearful that he might hang up before I could get there. The voice was my son's, and he had waited.

283

"Mommy—is that you?"

I tried to keep my own terror from reaching him. "Yes, darling, I'm here. Tell me where you are."

"Mommy, this is a bad place. Come and get me—please come and get me!"

My knuckles were white with my grip on the phone, but I held on to my control somehow. "Wait, darling. Don't hang up, and don't go away. Tell me where you are and I'll come right away to get you."

His words rushed out in a tumble. "It was only a game! I didn't mean to run away. He said it was just a game. He said there was a cave he could show me. But then he brought me here."

"Where, Keith—tell me *where?*"

He took a deep breath and I knew he was trying to get his own fear under control. "I'm at that house. Aunt Monica's house—with the funny name. You know!"

"Cadenza? In Beverly Hills? Is anyone with you? Who brought you there?"

"Ralph brought me. But he's gone now. Everybody's gone from inside."

This was no time for questions. "It will take a while to get there, darling, but I'll come as fast as I can. Listen to me, Keith. There must be neighbors . . . can you go and stay at the closest house until we come?"

"I'm afraid. They might be waiting outside. Mommy, I hear something. I've got to go now. Come and get me *fast!*"

He hung up and I stared at Linda and Monica. "I must go to Cadenza at once! That's where he is, Monica."

Linda took the phone from my hand, dialed the museum and spoke to Jason. When she'd hung up, she told me he would be here right away. "He'll drive you there."

"I'm coming with you," Monica announced.

Linda started to protest, but Monica hushed her with an imperious wave. "Look," she said.

Annabella had come into the doorway, and she sat staring at us, her blue eyes wide with mysterious knowledge. The black tail twitched ominously.

"Annie knows more than any one of us", Monica said softly. "Linda, get her carrying case."

A strange thought cut through my distraction: *The witch's familiar?* I shrugged it off and fled to my room to put a few things into a bag for Keith. Monica was the last person I wanted along, but to dissuade her would take too much time.

When Jason arrived, we were ready. Linda had reluctantly agreed to stay near a telephone while we were gone. She put Annabella, already restless in her traveling case, into the passenger seat. But we weren't to leave easily, for the cat promptly set up a loud howling.

Monica flung up despairing hands. "She won't go without the others. Hurry, Linda—fetch them!"

The whole thing seemed wickedly absurd, but as soon as Linda brought out the two white cats in their own travel case, Annabella stopped yowling, and we set off in peace.

We drove toward Los Angeles, turning our backs on Mt. San Jacinto. This was the route I'd followed in bringing Keith to Palm Springs. Only a little while ago—a hundred years ago! So many awful things had happened in this space of time. I was thankful especially for Jason's calm strong presence—a man I hadn't even known at the time of my flight from New York.

It seemed as though my heart would never stop its frightened thumping, and once Jason reached out to cover my hand with his own. "We'll find him, Carol. Just hang in there." Now I knew that deep anger which burned in him existed against whatever threatened me as well, and I was glad. I could count on him to help me deal with whatever waited for us at Cadenza.

The drive seemed endless before desert and mountains were left behind, and we followed the San Diego Freeway. Most of the city of Los Angeles was made up of thousands upon thousands of single-family homes—small houses that had nothing to do with the high rises now going up on Wilshire Boulevard, or with the ostentation of former movie millionaires.

North of Sunset, the car followed a winding road into canyons above the city, and into the area known as Beverly

Hills—a tiny enclave in itself, surrounded by the city of Los Angeles. Up here, the homes built by the long-ago movie stars had been large and fantastic. Most of the more conventional Georgian and Tudor styles came later. In the twenties and thirties, those with Hollywood riches had not only imitated Europe; they had enlarged and combined and adapted with great extravagance and eccentricity. At that time, studios wanted their stars to live like stars, and these had indeed been dream palaces where fantasy lives could be played out for the public to see in fantastic settings. Now many of them were gone, and with the passing of time what had once seemed architectural monstrosity became fascinating to a world that lived on a smaller scale.

Monica had driven this way so many times that she knew every inch of the way, and she guided us up a winding road that led to her private eminence on a hill. At the entrance, far below the house, an iron gate beside an extravagant gatehouse stood open.

Monica rolled down her window. "This shouldn't be unlocked! Where's the guard?"

There was no one in the gatehouse and we drove on through rows of palm trees and acacias, past what had once been rolling lawns, now overgrown in neglect. The gardener had been let go recently, Monica said, because of her straitened finances, but there was always a caretaker. He lived there, so where was he now? An ominous circumstance that he appeared to be missing, with the gate left open.

The driveway wound and climbed until it reached a wide crescent before the pillared facade of an enormous house, Italianate in its romantic conception—an "ornamental flourish" indeed, this Cadenza.

The central section of the house was like a small Roman temple, with marble arching above the front door, and two Ionic columns on either side supporting a pediment decorated with the figures of a frieze. On either side of the "temple" stretched long arcaded wings roofed in red tile. An Italian country villa in Beverly Hills!

Monica left the car the moment we stopped, running toward one of the two stone lions with long curly manes that posed at either end of a terrace. She flung her arms around a stone neck and called out to us.

"Saxon found these and brought them here from Tuscany!"

I had no time to waste on furbelows, but when I would have run toward the front door, Jason stopped me.

"Wait, Carol. The door's open, and we don't know what that means. Let's look around outside first."

Monica left the lion and stood staring at the shadowed arcades of the nearest wing. "You'd better listen to Jason," she said. "I have a feeling something's wrong."

Everything about the place seemed too quiet and empty. Unnaturally quiet. No one appeared at the open door, and no face looked out at us from any window. The stillness was like death, with only the distant hum of the city to break the quiet. A stillness that frightened me. If Keith were inside, he would have heard us by now and come running out.

We left Annabella protesting in the car with her Persian friends, and started around one end of the immense building. Once there had been ornamental gardens at the back, and a greenhouse and swimming pool. All too expensive to keep up, Monica said, and all gone now. A shutter or two dangled, ready to fall. I tried to peer through a rear window, but it was set high, and the rear and side doors were all locked upon inner silence. It was an intimidating house—too widespread, too gloomy within its long arcades, too hard and cold with stone and marble, and the evidences of neglect. When I thought of Keith, perhaps trapped inside and alone, I felt more frantic than ever.

"We've got to go in!" I protested.

"We will," Jason said, and when we'd made the complete circuit without being challenged and without finding any sign of life, we returned to the front door. Monica took both cat hampers from the car, insisting on carrying them like suitcases herself, and she hurried ahead of us up the wide marble steps. We followed her into a hall of rose-tinted marble, its proportions so vast that its beauty was like that of a museum, stupendous, but haughty and chill.

"How on earth could you live in a place like this?" I whispered to Monica, not wanting to rouse the echoes.

"It was good publicity copy. But we rattled around. Upstairs we sectioned off some rooms and made them a bit more cozy."

She set down the cases and let out the three cats. Annabella stepped gingerly onto cold marble, her fur bristling, her tail aloft, as if she sensed with her own radar what lay about her, and didn't like it. The white cats stayed close to her and to each other, clearly fearful.

The enormous hall was two stories high, with a vaulted ceiling decorated with cherubs and clouds. Marble balusters railed an upper gallery, shadowed and empty. On our far right a black marble staircase curved grandly down from the floor above. I had read about that famous staircase, and it would take very little to imagine Gloria Swanson coming down, lost to reality in *Sunset Boulevard*, or perhaps a frightened Ingrid Bergman in *Notorious*. Yet Monica Arlen, who had really gone up and down those stairs a thousand times, gave them hardly a glance, her attention still on the cats.

"You're all right now, my darlings. Nothing will hurt you. What's wrong, Annie? Tell me what's worrying you."

Annabella's mewing was insistent and more querulous than ever.

"She doesn't like it here," Monica said—a deduction that took no great powers to interpret.

I'd had enough of caution, and I ran across rosy marble, forgetting the echoes, and shouting for Keith. His name was flung back at me from hard surfaces, and painted faces on the ceiling seemed to look down at me in scorn. No young voice answered me.

"He won't hear you," Monica said. "This is a huge house, and if he's here he could be anywhere. We'll have to look. Let's start over here."

She strode through a door at the right of a marble fireplace, and Annabella, still bristling suspiciously, led the other cats after her into a drawing room that might have graced a palace. Here a parquet floor shone like satin as sun poured in through windows topped by fanlights. Rugs had been removed, and in one corner marks in the wood showed where a grand piano must once have stood. The few pieces of furniture that

were left looked elegantly French, but lonely. Over a doorway were Grinling Gibbons carvings of fruit and flowers,
imported from England, and highly esteemed by the California of another day.

The ceiling displayed a design of green leaves in great
painted rays and wheels of foliage, from the center of which
hung a chandelier, splendid and dusty. The wall in one corner
was water-stained.

Once more, Monica reacted. "What parties we used to
hold here!" she said sadly. "Everyone who mattered came.
Everyone! Marlene Dietrich sat on that very piano and sang
"Falling in Love Again.""

I had no time for nostalgia, or for beautiful, empty rooms.
I found double doors leading into a corridor, and I rushed
along it, opening door after door, calling for my son. Very
quickly I lost my way. Rooms seemed to open from other
rooms with little reason or pattern. There was an enclosed
patio at the heart of the house, to further confuse any sense of
direction. Jason came with me and our feet sounded alarm-
ingly loud on bare floors. Anyone who hid from us would be
warned well ahead of our approach.

When we entered one room we found a marvelous portrait
of Monica Arlen on the wall. She held a blue iris in her hand
and smiled at us enigmatically with eyes and lips. The real
Monica was there ahead of us, along with her cats, and she
was staring at the picture she had posed for so long ago.

This had clearly been a room given over to movie memorabilia, though Linda must have removed most of its treasures
to Smoke Tree House years ago. There were a few things
left—books on a shelf, a number of ornaments, a pair of
ballet shoes from a picture in which Monica had portrayed a
dancer who could dance no more. Two cardboard packing
boxes stood in the middle of the floor and were half full, so
Ralph must have been at work here. His role in whatever had
happened was still a mystery, and seemed all too threatening.

"I always hated that portrait," Monica said. "I never
wanted to pose for it. They *made* me!"

A strange thing to say, but I couldn't puzzle about it now.

"We've got to find Keith," I said, still sure that he must be here somewhere in these vast reaches.

We wandered on through a banquet hall ornate with more cherubs and tarnished gilt. Beyond it a butler's pantry opened into a kitchen nearly as large as the dining hall. Here, for the first time, was evidence of human presence. A partly eaten meal for two had been set at one end of a table. An overturned chair lay on its side—again an ominous warning of some disaster.

"Keith *is* here," I said. "He was here in this room—I can feel it!"

"Owen Barclay must be back of whatever has happened," Monica said, putting into words what we all knew very well. "But where is everyone? Anyone? And why would Keith have been left alone to phone you?"

"We haven't searched upstairs yet," Jason said. "Will you show the way, Monica?"

She shook her head. "Not yet. There's another room we haven't looked into yet. I remember telling Keith about it."

We had circled the patio into the opposite wing, and she led the way to a carved door that she opened upon a library. A musty smell of long neglect rose to meet us. If there had been renters in this house from time to time, they'd been little interested in books. Though the books were still here— thousands of them, probably installed by the original decorator, since Monica had chosen to take few of them to Smoke Tree House. Along one wall of shelves ran a ladder on a track, and above the opposite wall an overhanging gallery housed still more dusty volumes. It was a room of dark paneling and heavy, dark furniture.

Once more I shouted for Keith. By this time I expected no answer, but a creaking sound reached us from the gallery. I tore up narrow stairs to the railed overhang above, and saw at its far end a Spanish chest covered with intricate carving. As I stared, the lid moved upward an inch or two, and eyes peered out at me through the slit.

I rushed to fling back the top, and Keith climbed out into my arms. He clung to me, sobbing, and I carried him down to the cracked leather sofa in the library.

"It's all right, darling," I soothed. "We're here. Everything is all right now." I was crying too, in my enormous relief. He looked as though he had been fed regular meals, but his face was very pale.

Monica sat beside us, and Jason leaned over to place a quieting hand on Keith's arm. "Can you tell us what happened? We need to know right away."

I'd forgotten Annabella and her forebodings, but now the Siamese sprang past me to sit on Keith's lap, and her presence seemed to reassure him. He took a deep, gulping breath and raised his wet face from my shoulder.

"Is he gone? Is he really gone?"

"Do you mean Ralph, darling?" I asked.

"No—my father! He came here with two men. They came this morning at breakfast, and I was scared."

Though I'd expected this from the first, now that it was certain, all my fears swept back full force. We were open to attack in this house—completely vulnerable from almost any direction, and I wanted only to leave.

"There's no one in the house now," Jason told him gently, but Keith was still frightened.

"They hurt Ralph. My father beat him up, I think, and then one of the men said they'd better get out of here fast. Dad told them not without me. Only they couldn't find me, because I hid in that big box up there, where they never looked. I waited for a long time before I got out and telephoned you, Mom. I remembered Aunt Monica's number, like you said I should."

I held him tight. "That was good, darling. You've been a very smart boy."

"Do you know if they took Ralph with them when they left?" Jason asked.

"I don't think so." New terror came into Keith's eyes. "They—they said he was dead and they better get out real quick. Dad told them to hide him somewhere so he wouldn't be found right away. Mom, I wanted to look for him, but I was too scared. The house makes noises like it's talking. And it hides things. So I got back in that box after I phoned you. But I know an easy place where maybe they could have put him. I don't think they took him a long way off, because I heard the car leave pretty quick.''

"Show us where," Monica said.

Keith was used to obeying her no-nonsense orders, and he led the way into the hall, with Annabella and the two white cats following. The Siamese had stopped puffing up her fur, which seemed a good sign.

At the far end of the hall Keith indicated a closet for cleaning equipment. When Jason pulled the door open, Ralph slumped out upon the floor. His hair and face were covered with blood, and one arm appeared to be broken. Jason knelt and felt for a pulse in his neck.

"He's still alive. Monica, where's the nearest phone?"

"In the library," she said, and he hurried off.

Monica stood looking down at Ralph. This was no longer her strong young bodyguard.

"Can you hear me, Ralph?" she asked.

He groaned and opened his eyes.

"You had to be greedy, didn't you?"

"It turned out—wrong," he said faintly.

Monica continued to press him. "You were selling information to Owen Barclay, I suppose?"

Ralph only blinked at her.

"You even told him when we went to Desert Hot Springs, didn't you? And when you pushed Carol in the pool you took my ring from her finger and gave it to Barclay?"

"Sure—why not? I did all of that." He closed his eyes and his breathing seemed barely perceptible.

"There's a fur rug down the hall," Monica said to Keith. "Bring it and we'll cover him."

I went with Keith to help with the moth-eaten throw rug, and we drew it over Ralph. Monica dampened towels in an adjacent washroom and cleaned some of the blood from Ralph's face, gently, efficiently. The wound on his head was serious, and still bleeding. She sent Keith for more towels to stanch the flow. Through all this she was behaving remarkably well, and doing so without Linda's support.

Jason returned in a few moments. "The police and an

ambulance are on the way. Keith, can you tell us what happened? How did you get here?''

At the end of the hall a cushioned bay window extended over a side lawn, and we went to the window seat, where I took Keith onto my lap. Monica remained cross-legged on the floor beside Ralph, and now and then she patted his arm and spoke to him reassuringly.

By this time Keith was eager to talk. His voice broke now and then, but he told his story with sturdy determination.

''It was only a game at first. Ralph said we'd fool you for a little while, and then I could go right back to you. Before he even left Aunt Monica's for this house, he planned what we'd do. He said he'd drive up the mountain on the day you took the tram trip, and he told me where to meet him, up near the top. He said he'd come in his car and I wasn't to tell anybody. It was our secret, and he would show me a wonderful cave.''

Keith shivered and broke off, remembering how it had really been. I held him tight and he went on.

''It wasn't like he said. He never showed me the cave, and it wasn't any fun at all. He just grabbed me and took me away in his car. He made me get down out of sight in front, and he didn't like it when I started to cry. He—he scared me. But after a while, when we were off the mountain, he was nice again—like he used to be. He said he was taking me to an interesting place, and as soon as we got there he'd phone you. Sometimes he laughed in a sort of crazy way. He was talking about having a lot of money and showing everybody how smart he was. He said it was a big adventure, and I'd never guess how big until it was over. So I should just relax and enjoy it. Mom, I couldn't help going with him!''

''Of course you couldn't, honey. You're telling us very well. Is this the place where he brought you?''

''Yes, he said it was Aunt Monica's old house. And after that he began to act nice again. I think he really likes me, Mom. So it began to be fun. He said he'd phoned you and it was all right. But he never did, did he?''

''No, Keith, I'm afraid he didn't.''

''There was a man here when we came, taking care of

things. Ralph gave him some money and said it was from Aunt Monica, and he could take a week off. Then Ralph did something to the burglar alarm wires, so they wouldn't go off and call the police. I sort of liked the house at first. Aunt Monica's already told me about it. It's spooky and full of big rooms. Ralph said I could explore all I wanted if I didn't go outside. At first he came with me when we went in and out of rooms, because he said we might need a place for me to hide. He told me there were some bad people, and if they ever came I should get into that chest in the library and not make any noise. He wanted to talk to them before they knew I was there. At first I didn't want to hide, but he said it was Dad who might come, so then I did what he told me.''

At the thought of Owen, Keith started to shake again, and I soothed him until he was quiet.

''The police will be here soon, Carol,'' Jason said. ''Everything's okay now.'' And then I realized that I was shaking too.

Monica pushed herself up from the floor. ''I think Ralph's getting worse.''

There was nothing more we could do, however, until the ambulance arrived.

''When did your father come?'' I asked Keith.

''This morning, Mom. We were eating breakfast when the doorbell rang. Ralph told me to go straight to the library and get into that box. So that's what I did. The carving on top has holes in it, so some light comes in, and air. I could hear them talking because they came right into this room looking for me. I guess they were searching everywhere. But the box is up there in a dark place, and they never saw it. Dad was awful mad at Ralph.''

I hugged him again. ''You did very well, darling. I'm glad you hid from them.''

''Did your father tell Ralph to bring you here?'' Jason asked.

Keith shook his head vigorously. ''No! I listened real good when Ralph was phoning yesterday. I didn't know he was talking to Dad then, or I'd have run away. He told whoever it was on the phone that I was with him, and if somebody

294

would pay him a lot of money, he would deliver . . . but then he saw me in the doorway, and started talking soft, so I couldn't hear the rest. I guess it was all Ralph's idea—to do this."

And Ralph had been playing out of his league.

"Then they beat him up when they knew?" Jason prompted.

"Dad was awful mad, and I guess he hit Ralph a couple of times. He fell and knocked his head on one of those iron dogs by the library fireplace. It fell over, and when I found it later, there—there was blood on it. Then one of the men said, 'I think you killed him, Mr. Barclay. And the kid's run away. So we better get out.'

"They gave up looking for me after that. They took Ralph out of the library and I heard them going away in a car. After a while I phoned Smoke Tree House and talked to you, Mom."

Sirens were coming up the canyon, and Jason went to the front door. I took a moment to telephone Linda, and told her what was happening—though not in detail. "I don't know when we'll be home, but I hope it will be soon."

Her concern, as always, was for Monica. "How is she? Has she gone to pieces? Maybe I should come. . . ."

"No! Stay where you are, Linda. She's stronger than I've ever seen her. So don't worry. She should be home by tomorrow at the latest."

"I'm leaving right away," she told me, and hung up.

When the ambulance had gone with Ralph, we went through a long session talking to the police. Keith was excited, and only too willing now to tell his story to anyone who would listen. A police officer said Ralph would be held for kidnapping, and they wanted to know all about the way Owen Barclay had nearly killed him. They weren't, however, much interested in the fact that Owen had tried to take his son. The boy was here, they pointed out. Nothing had really happened, but they would put out warrants for Owen's arrest on assault charges. Which could be a lot more serious if Ralph died. With that, I had to be satisfied.

Monica put on one of her best shows, without her props, and even the police seemed impressed by her great name, and her grace and charm under trying circumstances.

"Yes, of course we'll stay overnight," she told them, consulting none of us. "This is my house and we'll stay right here. Though you might leave someone on duty to guard us."

I hated to stay in this echoing museum. Nothing was really over—not with Owen out there free. I didn't think the police would be clever enough to pick him up. He'd never take the obvious routes out of town under these circumstances. Word would be out through all the news media that he was wanted, and he would take every precaution until he'd had time to pull strings in high places. Though if Ralph died, perhaps even Owen's strings couldn't save him.

Monica continued to astonish me. By the time the police were gone it was late afternoon, and we were all hungry, never having bothered with lunch. She went into the vast kitchen, found that Ralph had stocked the refrigerator, and proceeded to whip up a passable meal. We sat down to eat at a table in the kitchen. She ate little herself, and I began to watch her feverish air uneasily. I knew she was driving herself. If Linda was coming, I hoped she'd get here before long.

A red sun slipped down through city haze and disappeared into the Pacific, leaving the lights of Los Angeles spread like a great electric carpet below our hilltop. Every city has its own voice, and this one came to us softened by distance—not the vast, throaty roar of New York that was funneled through concrete canyons—yet still a strong hum of sound. The view had its own special distinction. Lights reached out to the west, and then dipped suddenly off into blackness. The curving line of demarcation was as distinct as though someone had drawn it with a pen—that scalloped line where the land ended and the dark ocean began.

Monica insisted on doing our few dishes, and she commandeered Keith to wipe them. Annabella, her stomach full, roamed about the kitchen, while the white cats slept. She seemed to be trying to warn Monica about something, but her mistress was far off in some keyed-up place of her own and paid no attention.

When we'd eaten, Jason and I went outdoors to stand at a stone parapet in dusky light. Trees hid the houses on lower levels, and this hilltop seemed a world of its own. We were aware of the police officer patrolling at intervals, but there was a lot of ground to cover.

"You won't have to stay on with Monica now," Jason said. "Owen will have his hands full for some time. I understand there may be some government charges coming up."

I wished I could feel as confident, but he didn't know Owen as I did. He would have the ingenuity, the money, the power, to get himself free of almost anything.

"He's out there somewhere," I said. "It could be that he's right down there now in the woods around this house."

"There'll be someone on guard all night, and tomorrow we'll get you and Keith back to Smoke Tree House."

"Yes. I'm beginning to worry about Monica. She did fine for a while, but if she keeps on like this she's heading for an explosion."

"Let's talk about you," Jason said. "About you and Keith leaving Smoke Tree House for good."

"I still have a book to write. And where would we go?"

"Anywhere you please. How about my ranch? You could write your book there."

I looked at him quickly. "I can't think of anywhere I'd rather be. But not yet, Jason."

He drew me to him and I didn't want to be anywhere else but in his arms. It was Keith who broke in upon us.

"Mom, you better come. Aunt Monica's acting funny! She says Annabella is telling her awful things, and we're all in danger."

TWENTY-TWO

KEITH RAN AHEAD OF US TOWARD THE KITCHEN, BUT WHEN WE reached the big, sunny room, Monica wasn't there. Everything had been put neatly away and the sinks were clean, but there was no Monica in sight.

Eventually, Annabella's high-pitched meows, sounding down a hallway, led us to her. Monica had returned to the room where her portrait hung, and she was picking random volumes from a shelf and dropping them on the floor, one after another. A single lamp burned on a table, and in the shadow-filled room her eyes looked wild and her hair had been tangled by nervous fingers tugging through it.

The two Persian cats were mounds of terrified fluff huddled together in a corner, while Annabella sat on a table, mewing excitedly—as though she directed Monica's uncontrolled behavior.

"What is it?" I cried. "What are you looking for?"

"I can't find it! I know it must be here, but I can't find it!"

"Tell me what you're looking for, and I'll help," I said.

She stared past me to the doorway, where Jason and Keith stood watching. "Please, Jason, take the boy upstairs and put him to bed. He's had enough for the day. Just stay with him. I must talk to Carol."

I nodded at Jason. Surely Linda would get here soon and help me to calm her down.

When Jason and Keith were gone, she waved me to a chair, though she didn't sit down herself. She went to a table and began to smooth Annabella's fur. "It's all right now, Annie. I'm going to get everything straight as soon as I can find the book. I'm sure there's a second copy. So just calm yourself."

It was eerie to see the cat grow quiet as Monica stroked her.

"Cats are very smart, you know," she went on. "Especially when it comes to instincts. They react to all sorts of stimuli."

She looked up at herself in the portrait and shook her head. Wistfully? Regretfully?

"I didn't realize how Cadenza would make me feel. I thought all that was behind me. But I can still remember the days I sat for that picture, hating it. You can see that I'm smiling a little—because I was thinking scornful thoughts about the artist. The silly man was falling in love with me—and that was only make-believe. Like everything else! He didn't know anything about me, really. So I was mocking them all in my smile."

As I studied the portrait again, I could see the hint of wickedness and mockery.

"There are too many memories here!" She was suddenly vehement. "Too much guilt, and I can't stand it any longer. Everything I've done—the good things and the bad—have all been accidental. They were just *accidents*, Carol. I never planned anything before El Mirador. The good I just fell into, and so I did with the bad as well. Even when that awful thing happened at El Mirador, I improvised. I went from moment to moment making it up. So of course it didn't work."

She sounded mournful, lost in a past that was too tragic for her to bear. Then with one of her swift changes, she turned her back on the portrait and glared at me.

"Everything might have worked out, if *you* hadn't come! Sit down, Carol. Stop fidgeting."

I obeyed, though I sat on the edge of my chair. Her moods seemed too high and low in their extremes, and for the first time I wondered if she could be dangerous. Perhaps too far gone in her delusions to distinguish between fact and fantasy. I measured the distance to the door warily.

"I'm not your enemy, Monica," I said.

"You don't mean to be, but you are. Listen to me now, and listen *good!*"

"I'll listen. Take it easy, Monica."

She had no intention of taking it easy, and she began striding about the room, while the Persians huddled against each other in fright, and Annabella's tail curled in excitement as she watched her mistress with wide blue eyes.

Monica's voice rose another notch, all the cadences of her youth lost in the shrill sound.

"That terrible thing that happened at El Mirador all those years ago—I never intended that, Carol. Oh, it's true that Saxon tried to get hold of the gun, and he shot her by chance. But it was *my* fault. And it was my insane idea to conceal it all afterwards. If he'd been a stronger man—really like the roles he played—he'd have stood up to me, stopped me. Then *he* wouldn't have died!"

I stiffened in my chair, but I didn't speak. The door seemed very far away.

"You never guessed, did you? I could always be so clever—so stupidly clever! I badgered poor Linda into driving me to see Saxon that afternoon before the benefit. I hid under a blanket in the back of her car, so they'd think it was only Linda going through the entrance at the Eldorado. But I was the one who confronted Saxon in his study that day. I'd brought one of Ralph's guns with me, because I couldn't trust Saxon not to expose everything at the Annenberg. I tried to win him that day he came to the house, when I dressed up. But he was sick of his own guilt, and he hated me. So he was going to destroy us both in one terrible, dramatic gesture. I had to stop him. But all I meant to do was threaten him, frighten him a little.

300

"And then it got out of hand again—another accident, when he tried to take the gun away from me. Afterwards, I told Ralph to put away all his guns, so the police wouldn't ask questions about the one that was missing. I suppose Ralph guessed. But he kept still because I was his meal ticket. I suppose he'd have blackmailed me later if it seemed a good idea."

She stopped pacing and leaned against the table. Annabella rubbed her head against Monica's arm.

"I think Saxon came to the end of his rope that day in the restaurant when he couldn't protect you against Owen. He hated being old and a coward. That must have destroyed his last shred of pride, so he was all the more determined to finish us both off with what he meant to say the night of the benefit. He told me so right there in his study."

It was hard to believe what she was telling me. "It was really *you* who shot Saxon?"

"Yes. I never meant to!" She was wailing now in despair. "But we struggled for the gun—and it went off!"

"Linda was there?"

"Yes, she saw it all, and she smuggled me out again afterwards. That's why she's been half out of her mind since it happened. One big break we had was when Owen Barclay swore that he saw Saxon alive. He lied, of course. But that kept Linda out of trouble. Oh, Carol, it was just like the other time—"

"When Saxon shot Peggy Smith?"

"He didn't shoot her! That was the awful thing. It might have been better for everyone—including me—if he had."

Monica went to the bookshelf again, and this time she pulled out a volume and handed it to me.

"Here you are! This is what you wanted to read, isn't it?"

The book was another copy of the one with the mutilated pages that I'd found in the Arlen room. Only this copy was intact.

"*I* tore those pages out," she told me. "I didn't dare let you read what was printed there and make the connection. I suppose Linda read it a long time ago, but it was a small item, so she probably made nothing of it and forgot all about it. Now you must read what it says. It's your chance to know what really happened."

I opened the book to the section that had been missing. This was the volume about old Hollywood tragedies, and at once I came upon the same early photo of Monica that I'd found separately in a file at Smoke Tree House. It had been reprinted here, and I studied it again. The large, slightly tilted eyes that had given her face such distinction even before she became famous had been evident in this youthful picture.

At first, as I began reading the missing chapter, I felt irritated by the popular exposé style of the writer, and started to skip. Then, suddenly, I realized that these paragraphs were talking about Monica only incidentally. The photograph of her as a young woman would pull the reader in, but the account took another and astonishing direction into facts I hadn't known before.

I finished the pertinent passage feeling short of breath and intensely aware of Monica watching me from across the room. I didn't need to read the rest of the chapter, but I read over again those few revealing paragraphs. Now I understood very well why those pages had been torn from the book at Smoke Tree House. All else had grown out of what had happened at El Mirador that day—and it was still happening. Yet not even Linda knew.

The memorable voice spoke to me from across the room, its tone gentler now, no longer shrill. She was almost pleading. "You know now who died at El Mirador, don't you?"

"Yes," I said. "I know who died. It was Monica Arlen."

She sighed deeply. "I'm glad it's over. I couldn't keep it up any longer. That book gives you the answer. That's *my* picture, of course. Peggy Smith's picture—not Monica's. I'd just been hired by the studio as her double and stand-in. Some reporter picked this up and ran the story in a minor magazine. We looked so much alike, that if it hadn't been for our eyes no one could have told us apart."

I looked up at the portrait that dominated the room. "Is that Monica?"

"No. I posed for that. It's my secret I'm hiding in the smile. Monica got bored sitting for portraits, and she made

302

me fill in for her sometimes. After all, I had those interesting eyes that she wanted to imitate. Alva helped her achieve that in makeup, and she did it so well that they came to be known as Monica Arlen eyes. Though they belonged to Peggy Smith! This was all before she met Saxon and their double careers made them both more famous than ever.''

''You were still her stand-in?''

''Oh no. That was for only one picture. She really didn't like the resemblance, and I knew she was going to get rid of me. So I started to make myself necessary to her. I was already a fan, and she liked my devotion—though it wasn't quite like Linda's. Linda's a much nicer person than I ever was. When I did everything I could to stop looking like her, she began to use me in other ways—as her secretary, her companion, her friend. She paid me very well *not* to look like her, and since I'd doubled for her in just that one picture, the likeness was played down and forgotten. I made it my business to seem as drab and quiet and colorless as I could. When she wore her hair in that shoulder cut, I let mine grow long, and skinned it back—which didn't flatter me. I didn't mind because there was a lot in it for me, and it gave me a chance to live in her house—this house—and be part of an exciting life that I'd otherwise never have had. She even encouraged me to do my own creative work. Or rather, Saxon encouraged me. That was another joke—the sculptured bust at the museum is a self-portrait too. Of me! She'd never sit still long enough to pose, but she loved it when we both got credit for it. Sometimes when she didn't want to go to a party or make an appearance, I doubled for her again, and no one guessed. I could *do* her so well by that time, and we both laughed about it. Of course when Saxon came along, everything changed.''

She paused, lost in her dream, her face shining white in the shadowed room. The ''Monica'' look was gone. She seemed another woman—perhaps the woman she really was.

''You fell in love with Saxon?'' I said.

''How could I not? It was Saxon who really saw my talent as a sculptor and encouraged me. It was because of Saxon that whatever talent I had began to grow. This ring!'' She tore it suddenly from her finger and threw it at me across the

303

room. "*I* created the ring. It's yours now, as it was hers. I'll never wear it again!"

I picked up the intaglio emerald from the floor and placed it absently on my finger, hearing again the rising anger in her voice.

"Did you *mean* her to die?" I asked.

"Of course I didn't! She brought her own little gun that night when I stayed at El Mirador with Saxon. Oh, he wasn't in love with me, though I pretended to myself that he was. He played around a bit, but Monica was always his real love. I think everything ended for him when she died. If I hadn't been there to take hold, I don't know what would have happened. The scandal would have rocked him out of any further chance of a career. That's the way the studios were in those days, and they could throw stars away if they became useless—unpopular.

"So I was the one who figured everything out. I was always the clever one, the strong one. We had El Mirador to ourselves that night. All those who were filming had gone to their hotels. No one heard the shot, and I saw what we could do. *I* would be Monica. I'd always believed that I could be as good as she was, if only I'd had her luck. So I told Saxon that if he would keep still, I would keep still. The Arlen-Scott pictures could go on, and there would be no murder charge. I knew her so well. I could *be* her so easily—except with a very few people."

I had never known the real Monica at all, but this was hard to grasp in an instant. I'd been living a make-believe story ever since I came, while the real story ran along underneath. When I had time to retrace it, a great deal would come clear.

"You didn't get away with it, did you?" I said. "It was all harder than you expected."

"Harder and easier. It was lucky that Monica and I were both blondes at the time—our natural color—and that recently I'd cut my hair. So all I had to do was comb my hair like hers and carry on. I was the one who put her into my clothes after she died, and cleaned off her makeup. So she'd look like me—Peggy—when she was found. No one really questioned the switch at the time."

"How *could* you?" I said. "How could you and Saxon go through with carrying her out to the desert, making it look like Peggy Smith's suicide."

"It took guts." The voice was harsh now. "*My* guts."

"Why did you hint to me one time that it might have been murder?"

"I had to hold that over Saxon. I was beginning to be afraid of what he might do. Wally was telling Linda a few things, so I knew."

"Yet in the final test you weren't an actress, after all! You failed when they had to redo those few scenes. I should think the director would have been suspicious."

"I didn't fail! I could play *her* beautifully. Only it was more difficult when she was playing someone else. I could have been as good as she was, if they'd given me a chance. But Saxon told me I couldn't act, and I didn't dare go on and risk it. The director made allowances because Saxon and I were breaking up, and Peggy had died, so I was naturally not myself. He'd never worked with me before, and he didn't know me all that well. Alva and Nicos were the only ones who guessed. Though I suppose if I hadn't gone into hiding I'd have been found out eventually."

"Why didn't *they* speak out?"

"Because of Saxon. He told them the truth and asked them to keep still. And he did a lot for them. Lately, though, I think Alva's been itching to talk, and Nicos, who feels indebted to Saxon, has kept her still. That's why she sent you to see Henry Arlen. I suppose she thought he'd tell you things that would give the truth away. But I went with you and put on a very good act. Monica had taken me to see him that time years ago, and I'd heard a lot of those old stories. I fooled him completely. He never suspected me at all."

I could understand so many things now. I remembered Saxon telling me that I looked like Monica around the eyes. He had been thinking of the real Monica—as he had later when he'd spoken of her with such affection. I knew now why he'd been shocked and angry when he'd seen Peggy looking so much like Monica in the beautiful kimono from *Mirage*. And why he'd thought Cadenza should be mine.

I could even understand why he'd put me into his will. I was his only real connection with the past, and in a sense this had been a gesture toward his lost love. Perhaps even an assuagement of his own guilt?

"How could you *want* to carry off such a masquerade? Especially after Saxon died?" I heard the break in my voice.

Her shoulders drooped. "That was the hardest part—the really awful part. When we came out of the theater I told Linda to send you and Jason to find him. I couldn't bear to think of him lying there, and no one knowing.

"In my dreams he comes back to haunt me. Sometimes I'm afraid to go to sleep at night." She straightened and stared at me scornfully. "What else could I do? You were so easy to fool. Just as Linda has always been. There was never any reason for you to suspect. And of course there was the book. I *wanted* you to write the book because I owe that to *me*. I wanted you to tell about Peggy Smith. You'd have written about the talent I threw away. You'd have given me a chance to be *me* again."

"You even sent me to college," I said. "Why—when I meant nothing to you?"

"In a way that was part of the masquerade—to do what Monica would have done. But in another way . . . sometimes I got mixed up about who I really was. Especially after you came. Sometimes I almost believed I was Monica Arlen."

I could feel a strange pity for her, in spite of everything. "What's going to happen now? Linda will be here any minute, and she'll have to be told."

"I think *you* will keep quiet." Her voice softened, as though she couldn't help the "Monica" whisper that crept into it. Only now the sound chilled me. She stood up and I knew she was closer to the door than I was. Yet I had to speak out. There could be no more pretense.

"Nothing can go on as before," I said.

"You'd better think about that. Just think about what will happen—to all of us—if you talk. No, Carol, you aren't going to say a word."

I was sure I could move more quickly than she could. I had

only to reach the door . . . Besides, she had no weapon now. There couldn't be another "accident."

She saw what was in my face, and even as I hesitated she sprang toward the door, moving like one of her own cats. With her back to the door she faced me.

"I know what you're thinking." She spoke with an unexpected sadness, a wistfulness that took me by surprise. "Don't be afraid of me, Carol. Don't ever be afraid of me. What you do is up to you. I don't care anymore. Sometimes, in the last weeks, it's seemed almost as though you really were my family. The one I never had. I told you about those gray streets—I let that slip. And about the mother I hated. But all that was in Chicago, where I grew up, not in the desert. You've been good to me, and kind. If you can't be any longer, then I deserve that too. Let's go upstairs. I'm very, very tired."

She went to the corner of the room where the white cats were huddled. "Come along, my darlings. Don't be frightened." At once the two leaped lovingly into her arms. At the table she nodded to Annabella. "You too, Annie dear. We're going to bed now."

Annabella sprang to her shoulder, and all four, human and feline, went proudly out the door together. Perhaps a tremendous burden had been shed for her tonight. Without mimicking Monica, she moved like a younger woman, walking erectly toward the stairs with the cats in her arms. This was Peggy Smith.

"I'm going to bed now," she announced. "Some of the rooms are still made up, so we can take our pick."

There was nothing to fear from her, and I followed her toward the stairs, hearing the contented purring of the cats.

When we reached the entrance hall, a sound of running feet on the floor above made us stop and look up. Jason had appeared at the head of the stairs, and he shouted down to us.

"A car's just come up the drive. Owen Barclay's out there with two of his men. I've called to the police officer to stop them."

"Keith!" I cried, and rushed toward the stairs.

Outside we heard a sound of scuffling, and then momen-

307

tary silence. It wasn't hard to guess what had happened. Our police guard hadn't lasted against Owen's men.

Peggy hurried up the stairs with me, and at the top she ran ahead to lose herself in the shadows of the upper hall. I stood frozen on the top step, with Jason beside me.

The front door was already shivering under blows as the lock tore loose. The bedrooms were far away, and it was too late to reach Keith without leading them to him.

Owen and his two thugs stood in the great pink marble room below, looking up at us. Owen was unarmed, but both men carried guns. He gestured triumphantly to the two, who started up black marble stairs ahead of him, holding their guns on Jason and me. Owen looked especially pleased at the sight of Jason.

"Good," he said. "I've got a score to even tonight."

We backed away from the head of the stairs, but the three kept coming, and Owen's voice went on almost pleasantly.

"I'm leaving the country, Carol, and Keith is coming with me. There's nothing you can do to stop me, and if you really have anything on me, you'll have to stand in line with the rest. Once I'm away, it won't matter."

He came up the stairs past his men, moving confidently, slowly, and when he reached the top he spoke again.

"You might as well tell us quickly where my son is. It will save you some roughing up. My boys are expert at that, you know. And they'll take special care of your friend Jason Trevor, as well."

Neither Jason nor I spoke, but Peggy Smith began to move in a peculiar way. She was backing toward us along the wall—and I suddenly guessed what she might do. There was no way to stop her, and I didn't think it would help. Owen might even kill her.

He watched her odd movements warily, and one of the guns was pointed at Peggy's back. Then she was close enough, and she whirled about with the three cats in her arms, and moved toward Owen.

A look of horror came into his face and he took a hasty step backwards. "Stay right there!" he shouted. "Don't come near me! Stop her!"

Before either of his men could move, she ran toward Owen, hurling all three cats into the air. They flew at their target with claws bared, the white cats spitting in terror, and Annabella's wild shriek one to curdle the blood. Owen flung up his arms and stepped backwards again—into empty air. He crashed down the stairs, and the cats flew with him, their claws slipping on marble as they landed and righted themselves. Owen lay sprawled on his back halfway down, with Annabella on his chest, all her fur standing on end.

Owen's men had watched in a state of shock, their guns useless. Now one of them ran down to bend over Owen. "Jeez!" he said. "He's dead!"

The tiger who stalked and destroyed had been brought down by three pussycats.

For an instant the two stared up at us. Then both went gingerly down past Owen's body, as though he might call them back, and rushed for the door. We heard brakes screech as they took off down the hillside.

I felt only a sense of blessed relief for my son, and I didn't know anyone who would grieve for Owen. When I looked around for Peggy, I saw that she was laughing hysterically. Leaning against the wall, she slid down until she sat on the floor, still laughing—or weeping—I couldn't tell which. I went quickly to kneel beside her and she put a hand on my arm.

"Give me credit, Carol. I've done *one* good thing. One thing that wasn't an accident. And I did it *myself*."

"You've saved us all," I told her. "If you hadn't brought the cats—"

"But of *course* I brought the cats. Annie told me Owen would come. And I remembered his face that time at Smoke Tree House, when he first saw my darlings. They were my only weapon this time."

She had left a trail of death behind her—deaths that had caused suffering to many. But about what she had just done she was triumphant and unrepentant.

"He deserved what happened to him. He earned it! Carol, you'll still write your book about Monica Arlen? I owe *her* that."

309

"Of course I'll write it. And I'll write about Peggy Smith too."

The famous eyes closed and her breath caught in sudden pain. At a sound from the hall below, I looked down through marble balusters to see Linda come through the open door.

"We're up here," Jason called to her.

Linda ran up the stairs, skirting Owen's body, all her attention focused on Monica-Peggy as she came to kneel beside her, pushing me out of the way.

"Oh, God! She's having another attack! Jason—"

Jason had already gone to phone for an ambulance and the police. For the second time that day. Then he went outside to help the officer who had been struck down.

Again we waited for screaming sirens to come up the drive. Peggy was taken in the ambulance and Linda went with her—to the same hospital where Ralph had gone earlier. And from which Ralph would leave to face a kidnapping charge when he recovered, but Peggy would never leave at all. She died quietly two days later.

The police aftermath of violent death went on again for hours that night, and I could only feel grateful for Keith's exhaustion, which let him sleep through it all. I answered questions wearily, numbly—and mostly about Owen.

When they'd finally gone, Jason and I stood on one of Cadenza's upper balconies and looked east toward a pink and gold dawn above the mountains. The three cats came with us, lost and bewildered, seeking human company.

"Shall we go home to the desert?" Jason said. "You can rest when you get to the ranch."

I understood what he was asking. All barriers were down, and by this time we knew how much we belonged together. I held on to him, nodding mutely.

When we went inside, I bent to speak to Annabella, who would be able to explain to her two friends—from the tone of my voice, at least. "You're going to live on a ranch now, Annie. I think you'll like it there with Keith."

"Monica's" death caused a tremendous stir in papers and magazines. Old photos were reprinted, old stories about her retold, and of course there was a great revival of Arlen-Scott pictures. Through all the uproar, I said nothing public about the truth.

Of course I told Jason. And after Peggy died, I told Linda. That was the hardest thing to do, because now she had to realize that years of her life had been given to a mirage—in more ways than one. It was as though Linda were awakening from a dream and hardly knew what was real and what wasn't. Wally's lively pragmatism was a good tonic. For once surprisingly sensitive, he pointed out that these years had, after all, been spent helping someone who was very much alone, and had needed desperately what Linda had to give.

Rumor—as I read it in the papers—had it that Monica Arlen's great-niece, who had married again after the tragic death of her ex-husband in a fall, was writing a book about her famous aunt. That is true enough. The book is done and will soon be published. But it is not about the masquerade. There is another, more secret journal that I've been keeping.

My desk looks out upon the desert I've come to love, and the portrait I brought from Cadenza hangs on the wall of my study. Sometimes when I search the face of the woman in the picture, I'm filled with a strange, sad feeling of loss—for exactly what or whom, I'm not always sure.

I'm glad that the painting is really of Peggy. Monica Arlen died before I was born, and I've never known her at all except through make-believe on a screen. It was Peggy who sent me to college; Peggy to whom I'd related. Between us, a precarious affection had developed that was more real than any of my fantasies.

Even the ring I wear so often had been more Peggy's than Monica's, and in a way, the emerald was the symbol that tied everything else together. Created for Saxon by Peggy, worn by the real Monica for a little while, and finally given by Peggy to me—it brought me close to all of them and made me a part of their story.

Jason's search for his daughter goes on, and now we look together, still hoping that we'll find a happy ending eventually.

All the old distrusts and prejudices are gone, and the fights we have now are just those of two people who love each other deeply.

My journal will be finished soon. I've been setting it down on paper just as it happened. To Monica, and Saxon, and Peggy. And to me. It will be ready when the right time comes to publish it.

ABOUT THE AUTHOR

Phyllis Whitney was born of American parents in Yokahama, Japan. Today, Ms. Whitney lives on Long Island. She has devoted her life to the world of books: as librarian, bookseller, reviewer, teacher of writing . . . and bestselling author. She is one of America's top writers of romance and suspense. All of her books have been best sellers.